RED GRADE

A JENN HERRINGTON WYOMING MYSTERY

JENN HERRINGTON
BOOK 3

PAMELA FAGAN HUTCHINS

SKIPJACK PUBLISHING

FREE PFH EBOOKS

BEFORE YOU BEGIN READING, you can snag a free Pamela Fagan Hutchins ebook starter library by joining her mailing list at https://subscribepage.io/pamelafaganhutchins.

PROLOGUE

Big Horn, Wyoming
  Late Spring

THE ICE CUBES in attorney Jennifer Herrington's glass clinked as she took a sip heavy on gin and lemon. She hadn't wanted the Long Island iced tea but had accepted it out of politeness. Good manners had become more important after she'd interrupted the "high tea" meeting to take a call. A crucial one. Thus, the sipping now, and the extra care not to spill any on the silk sofa.

High tea. The words sounded silly and pretentious in Wyoming. Her associate, Kid, had called this client "too bougie for Big Horn," and it was true. The old Big Horn, maybe. Not the one that was changing every day. The house was Exhibit 1 of that. A seven-thousand square foot misplaced monstrosity of contemporary architecture dwarfing the hilltop of the three acres on which it perched, heedless of the violent winds or the treachery of the steep driveway in winter months. It was all about that killer view for owners who only summered there.

Jennifer gazed out the floor-to-ceiling window on said view. She had to admit, it *was* amazing.

She and the client resumed discussion of legal matters over islands of raspberry tarts in vanilla ice cream seas. Jennifer nearly groaned with each bite. When she'd finished, she realized that she'd downed her whole cocktail. It was all she'd been offered to drink with the high tea that had not included any actual tea, unless the Long Island version counted.

"More?" her host asked, standing poised to call someone else to bring another.

Jennifer shook her head, which made her a little dizzy. "Oh, no. It would put me under."

"If you're sure."

"I am. I have lots left to do today." A wave of sleepiness lapped at her. She stood, feeling wobbly. The drink had been tall and strong. She should have passed it up. *I wish I could call Aaron to give me a ride.* Her husband would have done it in a heartbeat, if he could. *He's the best. He really is.* He'd proved it after the disaster in February, and how she'd reacted to it. It had been a long, hard couple of months. She regretted how their morning had gone and wished she could have a do-over. "Thanks for having me over for the meeting, though. Your home is lovely, and this has been a very helpful conversation." Wait— had she slurred those last two sentences?

"Please use the information I've given you with the utmost discretion."

"Of course." The room swam. Time froze, or tilted, or inverted. Something weird, anyway. Jennifer couldn't remember the last thing that was said. She decided that it must not have been critical. "Whoa." She sunk back on the couch, her legs nothing but spaghetti.

"Oh, my," her client said. "Are you all right?"

"I'm... " *not.* Jennifer regained her feet, but then she toppled, conscious of splashing into a crystal vase on her way down. "Baccarat," the client had said earlier. "A priceless heirloom."

Probably not anymore.

A Chihuahua rushed at her face, barking hysterically.

Then a terrifying thought struck Jennifer. *I can't be pregnant again, can I?*

ONE

Big Horn, Wyoming
Nine days earlier

JENNIFER PUSHED her sunglasses up her nose and tilted the brim of her hat down. The green of tall fescue and Kentucky bluegrass on the polo field was eye-popping in the summer sun. The flora was making the most of the ninety frost-free days a year in the foothills of the Bighorn Mountains. On the way to the polo grounds, Jennifer and her veterinarian husband Aaron had driven past entire fields of arrowleaf balsamroot flowers—their golden blossoms bobbing in the breeze—with purple, blue, white, and even pink lupine pushing skyward between them. The moisture from heavy snows over the winter had created ideal spring growing conditions, and the result was a historic bloom.

The temperature had been chilly the night before but had warmed to mild for the match, a far cry from their former home in Houston, where it was already topping out near one hundred. Or so said Jennifer's best friend and former colleague, Alayah. The same

Alayah, in fact, who had encouraged Jennifer to push through her resistance to Wyoming and move there with Aaron.

Which Jennifer had done.

During the once-in-a-hundred-year winter, though, she'd questioned her choice and her sanity. When all the snow had turned to slush, mud, and ice with occasional blizzards, she'd longed for Texas or the Tennessee of her youth.

But sipping mimosas and watching the polo teams warm up for the first match of the season now? Heavenly, down to the pungent odor of earth freshly turned by horses' hooves and the sweet, sweet scent of the grass. May in Big Horn was as glorious as its winters were brutal.

"Aaron, be a dear and top off my drink." Veronica Farinolo held up her crystal flute.

A five-carat wedding band sparkled on Veronica's ring finger, which was tipped with a perfectly manicured garnet nail. She rescued a strand of long brunette hair from the gloss on her plumped lips. The rest of her hair was tucked into an understated straw cowboy hat that Jennifer had seen online for over a thousand bucks. Veronica's tight skin glowed with perpetual youth, and the woman was tiny like a teenager. She was shorter and more petite than Jennifer even, in an extra small silk western shirt and size zero jeans tucked into knee high red cowboy boots. Despite her size, she radiated strength. If the rumors were true, she'd been a polo player. A good one.

Now she co-owned the Red Grade Ranch and its Strikers team with her husband Jerry. Aaron was their team vet, and he and Jennifer were here as the Farinolos' guests, front row, center seats. It was no surprise Aaron had been selected to care for the Strikers' horses. He was the star of the large animal vet practice around Sheridan these days. Because of demand, he'd hired a new vet recently—Dr. Sarah Friedman, who specialized in small animals.

Aaron excused himself from a nearby conversation with a few local ranchers. He reached into the Yeti cooler and came up holding orange juice and a bottle of Veuve Cliquot between the fingers of one hand. "Coming right up."

"Oh, I don't need the orange juice," Veronica said, giving Aaron a once-over.

Jennifer was used to the female attention her husband attracted. First off, he was a big guy and hard to miss. Blond. Muscular. Always smiling. He'd played tight end on the Detroit Lions for one short season before head injuries sent him from the National Football League back to vet school. Football still flowed in his veins, though, so he'd taken an offensive coordinator role for the Big Horn Rams high school team. He was clad now in his usual linen shirt with rolled sleeves, worn-in jeans extra wide through the thighs, and Roper low-heeled boots.

He winked at Jennifer. "You, too, Jenn?"

She put a hand over her glass. "Not yet."

He gave her a smile as he poured Veronica's champagne. The twinkle in his eye told her he had his hopes up about a baby. He put the bottles back in the cooler and returned to his conversation with the ranchers.

Jennifer had miscarried at eleven weeks earlier that spring. Losing the baby had rocked her. Absolutely rocked her. Her obstetrician couldn't give her a precise reason why it had happened, either. The trauma led to a depression, the only one in her life. She'd taken time off work. First a few days, then weeks, and finally a whole month, giving herself the space she needed to heal. She'd only recently fought her way back to a semblance of her old self, but she was still plagued with intrusive thoughts. What was wrong with her —physically or mentally—that had caused her to miscarry, and would it happen again? Was God giving her a sign that at nearly forty-one she was too old to have a baby?

She shook off her thoughts. This was supposed to be a festive atmosphere. Being truly present was a challenging part of her recovery.

Around them, the crowd was growing. She spotted a few familiar faces and exchanged waves with Leo Palmer, a deputy from nearby Kearny, who was there with another deputy, Delaney Pace, and a couple of teenagers. Leo had helped Jennifer with an IT issue on a recent case and seemed to be an all-around good guy.

She'd already said hello to a group that included her cousin Hank Sibley and his fiancée, musician Maggie Killian—with whom Jennifer had a love-hate relationship. They were seated with the Flint clan. Trish Flint, who worked with the National Forest Service, and her boyfriend Ben. Big Horn head football coach Perry Flint with his wife Bethany and their kids. Retired doctor Patrick Flint and his vivacious wife Susanne.

She looked in the other direction and saw Veronica's husband Joe Farinolo walking back from the gathering of the Strikers team on the sidelines. He took a seat beside Jennifer and flapped a hand through the air. "It's almost showtime." His excited voice sounded one hundred percent New York.

Jerry was the physical opposite of his wife. Tall and big boned with a round belly, a smooth scalp, a large mole on his cheek, and a fleshy nose, he was dressed for a day captaining a yacht. Boat shoes, pressed khaki pants, and a navy blazer over a white button-down shirt. Jennifer felt like she should salute or maybe throw him a life preserver.

A couple approached, also coming from the area where the teams were meeting. The man seemed about Jerry's age based on the gray in his hair, but he was in far better shape. Olive skin, dark hair and eyes, and a wide smile. The woman with her arm through his had also aged gracefully, but naturally. She was curvy with a narrow waist. Her dark shiny hair hung over one shoulder.

The man put his hand over the woman's. "Jerry. Veronica."

Jerry shook his head and muttered something. He didn't make eye contact or answer them.

Veronica said, "Benjy. Ginger. Have a good game."

"You, too," the woman named Ginger said. "Here's to a safe match and fair play."

As they walked away, Veronica whispered, "The Mahones. They own the Hellcats. Pretend they weren't here. It will go better that way."

Jennifer raised her eyebrows.

Two younger women flopped down on a blanket beside Veronica, giggling.

Veronica beamed at them, then leaned over to whisper in Jennifer's ear. "This is our Celeste."

At first, Jennifer wasn't sure which girl she was talking about. Neither resembled Veronica in the slightest. Both were tall, for starters. But one exuded a Wyoming vibe. Lived-in jeans and scuffed boots. On closer inspection, she had the dark hair, beautiful skin color, and cheekbones that could mean she was of Native American heritage, which was not unusual in Wyoming. The other, a platinum blonde with dark eyebrows, was belted into a swirly maxi dress over pristine boots. Scratch the uncertainty. Jennifer's money was on contestant number two.

Maxi dress immediately dug into the Yeti. "Y'all, no Dom?"

Hunch confirmed. A guest wouldn't complain about the lack of Dom Perignon in that tone. That was a daughter move.

"Sorry, my darling. We ran out. I'd like you to meet the Herringtons, though. Aaron Herrington is our vet. His wife Jennifer works as an attorney in town." The way she said *works* made it sound like a curiosity.

Celeste gave Jennifer a dead fish handshake. Her disinterest was palpable. A woman nearly twenty years older than her and her friend? No thanks, her body language screamed.

Jennifer withdrew her hand. Before her miscarriage, she'd never felt more vital, sexy, and powerful than she had at forty. Her husband's attraction to her hadn't waned that she could tell, and he told her daily she was the most amazing creature on the planet. Yet to younger people—especially younger women—she felt like she was becoming irrelevant and invisible. It was disconcerting.

Veronica said to Jennifer, "I do have a legal matter I'd like to get handled. I don't suppose you could come by my house this week and discuss it with me over coffee? We've just finished work on the house, and I'd love to give you the full tour. I worked with the most amazing interior designer."

Was Veronica wanting to talk legal work or become bosom buddies? Celeste and her un-named friend were chatting and laughing noisily, so Jennifer paused before responding, not wanting to shout over them.

"Shh, Celeste," Jerry said. "Victor's game is about to start."

"I know, Dad." Pouting, Celeste popped the cork on another bottle of the lesser-than-Dom champagne.

"I'd love to talk to you about it," Jennifer said to Veronica. As a criminal defense attorney and former prosecutor, it probably wasn't in her wheelhouse, but who knew? And even if it wasn't, something within her area of expertise might arise later, and then Veronica would remember Jennifer. Running a law practice was new to Jennifer, and generating clients was an unfortunate necessity. They each consulted the calendars on their phones and agreed on a date and time.

The teams began moving onto the edge of the field.

Jerry leaned toward Jennifer. "See the guy in the red jersey with a one on it, on the tall black horse? That's Victor Carvalho. He's Celeste's fiancé." He gave a smug nod. "He's handicapped a seven."

"Uh huh," Jennifer said.

His words and significant tone meant nothing to her, except for the description of the animal. All of the horses were trim, alert, and muscular. Beautiful. But Victor's horse stood out. A stunning creature.

Just then, Victor loped his horse to the sideline. He flashed a dimpled, bright-eyed smile at the Farinolo family. Black curls teased the bottom edge of his helmet. Under him, the horse danced in place. He was a handsome man who seemed to know it.

Celeste walked to the horse's shoulder and held up a hand, comfortable around the big, fidgety animal. "Have a great match."

"Thank you, *mi amor*. We will." Victor leaned over and pressed his lips to Celeste's fingers. "Estrella is ready for victory." He put two fingers over his heart then pointed at the sky. *"La gloria a Dios."*

Celeste stepped back and waved. Victor gave Estrella some kind of invisible signal, and the horse spun and galloped back to the Strikers team, tail high in the air like a windsock. Victor accepted a water bottle from one of the helpers. After he handed it back, he rode Estrella to midfield. The rest of the Strikers followed, and the team lined up. Four riders in Half Circle Hellcats gold jerseys on athletic looking horses faced them.

The crowd hushed. The tension in the air was palpable.

One of the mounted umpires threw a ball underhanded between the two lines of players, and cheers erupted. The match was on, and the riders began jockeying for position and swinging their mallets at the ball.

"You're the luckiest," Celeste's friend said, eyes shining.

Celeste shrugged. "Thanks."

Jennifer was about to introduce herself to the girl since no one else had, until Aaron took a seat in the folding chair beside her and put his head close to hers.

"I overheard you talking to Jerry. Do you want me to explain a few things about polo?"

Jennifer snorted softly. "It would help make this experience more meaningful."

"Okay. For starters, the frontline offensive player wears the number one and is their main scorer. He defends against the other team's main defender. That's Victor on the Strikers. And having a handicap of seven means he's a rockstar."

She nudged him with her shoulder. "Thanks. I didn't want to seem like a polo neophyte by asking."

"I've got your back."

"Why are there so many horses? Do they get hurt a lot?" She pointed at the round pens a short distance from the side of the field.

"No, but the horses do a lot of sprinting and turning. That's why focus on proactive exercises and therapy with them is so important. Preventive veterinary medicine. The reason there are so many though is because each player needs a minimum of two mounts. Some will bring as many as eight if they expect it to be a high scoring match. With four players on each team, their backups, and the umpires' mounts, that's a whole lot of horses. But don't call them horses. Call them polo ponies."

"Gotcha. I think."

The *polo ponies* were running down the field at breakneck speed. It was a terrifying melee of big bodies, thundering hooves, and red and yellow jerseys. How the horses weren't crashing into each other defied comprehension. But then Jennifer wasn't much of a rider, even though lately she'd been getting some practice on Smokey, an injured reining horse Aaron had taken in lieu of payment the previous winter. After Smokey had convalesced, Jennifer had exercised him on a longe line in the round pen. When that went well, she began riding him, until the day they'd gone into the large arena. The stallion had galloped with his neck stretched out so far she couldn't see his head from the saddle. She'd just clung to anything her hands could find to hold onto until he had burned off his excess energy. Then she'd gotten the heck off of him.

Now she and Smokey stuck to the little round pen. From what she could see on the field, she vowed never to sit astride a polo pony anywhere, anyhow.

Jerry leapt to his feet and cheered. "Atta boy, Victor."

"Our team scored a goal," Aaron told Jennifer, clapping. "Already."

She clapped, too, even though the action had moved too fast for her to really follow it. She turned to congratulate Celeste on her fiancé's success but couldn't catch the young woman's eye. Seemingly unaware Victor had scored a goal, Celeste and her friend were immersed in conversation with a couple of cowboys.

Jennifer turned to Veronica instead and said, "Go, Strikers!"

Veronica nodded. "We have a good team this year."

"Do you stay involved with them?"

"Jerry handles the business end. I select and work with the talent. The players choose their own mounts and a captain, who's basically their coach and strategist."

"Sounds fun!"

"It is. I still prefer riding. I play as much as I can but not like I did before Celeste."

Jennifer latched onto an implication behind her words. Celeste looked to be in her early twenties. The impact of a child on a woman's life choices extended well past infancy.

Jerry shouted, "Come on, Victor. Get it together!" To his wife, he said, "Something's wrong with him."

She waved him off like he was a gnat. "He just scored a goal."

"Yeah, but something has changed. He's playing sluggish now. Slower."

"He's a pro. I'm sure he'll shake it off. If not, he'll pull himself out. Or the coach will."

Jennifer raised her eyebrows at Aaron. He waggled his back at her. Veronica was a cool customer.

Play continued, and Jennifer got better at tracking the ball.

"Periods are seven-minutes long, and they're called *chukkas*," Aaron explained. "There are four chukkas in a match. The objective is to score the highest number of goals. A goal is when the ball is hit through the two poles on either end of the field."

"Chukkas? Why can't they just call them periods or quarters? But the rest makes sense," Jennifer said.

"The ball is called a bocha. The players strike it with the mallet in their right hands."

"Even if they're left-handed?" Jennifer couldn't understand how the players weren't flying out of their tiny saddles, much less clobbering each other and the horses with the long mallets.

"Yep. Other players can't cross in front of the mount of the player who has control of the bocha, but they can push the horse and rider off their line, block the striker's mallet, or steal a loose bocha."

"Got it." She eyed the bathroom line. It would only get longer during breaks in the action. Maybe she should go now.

Jerry jumped to his feet. "Victor!" he shouted.

Jennifer turned back toward the action. Estrella was charging past their group on the near side of the field, in pursuit of the bocha, or so it seemed, as other ponies crowded her from the side and back. Victor was draped over her neck, his body and arms limp. The mallet hung from one wrist, bouncing along the ground and striking the horse in the lower legs. The reins sagged on either side of her neck.

Then, Estrella tripped on the mallet and somersaulted forward. A collective gasp rose from the crowd. People surged to their feet, hands over mouths, chests, hearts. Victor went over the horse's head and—before the other riders could react—down under a crushing barrage of hooves.

It was all over in a fraction of a second.

Victor's contorted, bloodied body was motionless. His neck canted at a horrible angle. His hips and spine were badly misaligned, and his head seemed misshapen. Flattened.

People began to scream.

"No!" Jennifer pushed knuckles against her lips in horror.

Aaron was on his feet running toward the collision. The attending physician was a few steps behind him with a large black doctor's bag banging against his leg. The doctor stopped and gestured at the side of the field. An engine revved and an ambulance began making its way toward Victor.

Jennifer was dazed for a few seconds. She rebounded quickly, though. She'd honed her response to emergencies over years at gruesome crime scenes. Stabbings, shootings, beatings, vehicular homicides. She could handle this. Her eyes took in the field, trying to process what had happened, what was happening. Amazingly, only one other horse and rider had fallen, and they were clear of the scrum, the rider sitting up, the horse running toward the pens. Two riders were galloping after Estrella, who had fled at top speed, tail up. The other riders had moved their mounts in a semi-circle around

Victor and dismounted. Helpers were running onto the field to assist them.

Celeste was on her feet and sounded confused. "What happened? Is Victor okay?"

Her friend and the cowboys stood silently behind her, eyes wide, mouths slack.

Veronica put her arms around her daughter and maneuvered her face away from the scene. She whispered in her ear.

Celeste began to wail, a piercing, undulating sound. "No," she screamed. "No, no." Then, "I need to go to him. I have to go to him!"

Her mother didn't let go.

The riders caught Estrella. Aaron waved at them, and they brought the horse back to him, close enough for Jennifer to see white foam on either side of her muzzle. Aaron took the reins and began coaxing the shaking animal toward the sidelines.

The doctor was kneeling beside Victor and looked to be checking his pulse. He leaned over like he was listening for breath sounds. Jennifer wondered if he would do rescue breaths and chest compressions.

But he stood, caught Jerry's eye, and shook his head. "I'm sorry," he mouthed.

Celeste stumbled out onto the field, sobbing, with her mother right behind her.

TWO

Big Horn, Wyoming

AARON WALKED Victor's horse toward a shaded area away from the polo field. Estrella high-stepped and tossed her head beside him. The crowd's anxiety wasn't good for her. A freaked-out horse could be a danger to itself and others. Aaron was pretty shaken up himself. Everyone was. Victor Carvalho, the star of the team and the future son-in-law of the Farinolos, had just been crushed to death in front of their eyes. How could they not be?

He looked back over his shoulder at the field. The grisly event replayed in his mind, and he shuddered.

Jenn was walking quickly to catch up to him. She fell into step beside him. "Oh, my God. Oh, my God."

Even in this moment, his eyes drank in his petite wife. His sunshine. Blonde, blue-eyed, and beautiful beyond words. On her, faded Levi's and a pink silk shirt seemed like couture. It wasn't just how she looked, though. Her presence made bad things bearable and right now, that was everything. He wanted to kiss her impossibly cute nose and press his face into her bouncy hair. But that couldn't happen with nine hundred pounds of stressed horse attached to him a few feet away.

"Oh, my God is right." He motioned her back. "Estrella's rattled. Give us twenty feet for safety."

Jenn scooted away from Estrella but kept pace with Aaron and the horse. "Really, what in the world just happened?"

He looked toward her. Over her head, he saw the physician kneeling once again at Victor's side. It looked like they were getting ready to move him. The other horses and players were giving them a respectful distance. Some of them had hands over their eyes. Some were looking off into the distance. The other rider who had fallen—a player for the Hellcats—was limping to the sideline. One of the stable hands was holding his horse, who had bolted toward the round pen to be closer to the herd.

He pulled his eyes away and back to Jenn. "Hard to say. It all happened so fast. It looked like Victor passed out and lost control, then Estrella tripped and flipped them both. The rest..."

"I'll never forget the rest." Jenn hugged her arms. Her complexion was always fair, but her coloring now bordered on shocky white. Aaron wouldn't be surprised if half the crowd was in similar straits. What they'd just seen was a thing of nightmares.

"Me neither." For a second, he wondered if he'd been wrong about the cause of the accident. Could it have been an equipment issue? He eyed the saddle and pad on Estrella's back. Nothing seemed amiss there or with the bridle, although they bore careful checking. Besides, the horse hadn't bucked or acted abnormally. Estrella had been on point, playing all out, doing her part like a champ.

The problem had been with Victor.

They reached a tree-shaded area with a trough. He led Estrella to the water. It was quieter there and shielded from the turmoil on the field. The sweaty horse refused a drink, though. The whites of her eyes were still showing, and she was throwing her head around at every sound.

Aaron scanned her for injuries. She had taken a hard fall, but in her state he wouldn't risk a full physical exam without cross tying her and getting help from an assistant. Besides, adrenaline would mask minor injuries at this point. He needed to examine her in a low-pressure environment. He couldn't even send her in a circle to check her gait without a halter and lead, since she could easily snap the reins from the bit and take off. She was walking well. If she was injured, he didn't think she was hurt badly.

There was no way he was going back to ask the Farinolos to let him take away the horse when Victor was lying dead in front of them, though. That would have to wait. He would just help Estrella calm down for now.

And in the meantime, there was Jenn, who also needed his attention.

"You should splash some of that cold water on your face. And then find a seat in the shade." While not everything about being a vet translated to human medicine, his knowledge definitely qualified him to render aid in most situations. It wasn't unusual for Jenn to be on the receiving end of his people doctoring.

Often, she resisted it. Not this time. She went to the side of the trough opposite from Estrella and scooped water, dousing her face several times. "This is affecting me more than I thought it would. It's not like I'm new to seeing dead bodies."

Estrella snorted and shifted her weight away from the splashing. Aaron stroked her neck. "Shhh. Shhh." When she relaxed, he said to Jenn, "But not watching them die in unexpected and gruesome ways."

"True. Did you know Victor?" Water dripped down his wife's face. She rubbed at it with her hands, keeping her body back and dropping her head forward. *She's trying not to ruin that shirt,* he realized.

"I knew him a little." Aaron had only started working with the team a month before. "Take some slow, deep breaths for me, beautiful."

"Okay." She inhaled a long, deep breath followed by a long, slow exhale.

"Good."

After a few more repetitions, she said, "What was Victor like?"

"Talented. Cocky. The energetic center of the team. He was a rising star. The Strikers were lucky to retain him this season. It would have been his last year with them, I'm sure, if... " He trailed off into silence.

"Yeah. If." Jenn slid to a seat at the base of a tree and leaned against it, eyes closed. She started her breathing exercises again.

"I wouldn't have picked him as someone to hang out with, but he treated his horses and his teammates well. That counts for a lot. This sport is obviously hard on their bodies, but it's just as hard on them mentally and emotionally. Very risky, very competitive, very little financial reward."

Estrella's ears pricked up, and she huffed. Aaron listened for a moment. Sirens.

Jenn said, "Do you think I should go to the Farinolos? I barely know Veronica and Jerry. I don't know Celeste at all. I don't want to be insensitive one way or the other."

"It's a family thing. I think it's better to give them space."

The sirens drew closer. Aaron saw flashing lights, then two sheriff's department trucks turned from the road into the facility gate.

Jenn said, "Now we have to go play hosts at home. It's going to be hard to psyche myself up for that after this."

Aaron groaned. He'd briefly forgotten there was a couple's wedding shower for Jenn's cousin Hank and his fiancée Maggie this weekend. Maggie's bridesmaids, most of whom Aaron had never met, would be guests at the Herrington's Big Horn Lodge. Four women, plus their partners. There were three more bridesmaids, including

Jenn, Hank's sister Laura Begay, and Trish Flint, but they weren't staying with the Herringtons.

It was going to be a lot for Jenn and for him, especially after watching a guy get crushed to death. Luckily, hosting was their only duty. The maid of honor was responsible for the main event, which was being held in a private room at a restaurant in town.

Estrella snorted and shied backwards. Aaron held onto her, then turned, following the horse's wide-eyed gaze. He expected to see a deputy. Instead, Casey Hurd was jogging toward them. Casey—the daughter he'd only recently learned he had.

She was with two guys. One as tall as Aaron, broad shouldered, but with no bulk. The other flashy and muscular, maybe late twenties, and shorter than Casey, it appeared. Dark to her light coloring. He'd seen the second guy before somewhere. In town, maybe? The men stopped and watched Casey make her way over for a moment, then turned and headed toward the gate.

Aaron tamped his hand to tell her to slow down.

Casey slowed to a long-legged walk. "Aaron!" She was holding a cowboy hat down tight over her braids with one hand. Her jeans were more holes than fabric, and her pearl-snap Western shirt was tied to expose her flat midriff. She was tall, blonde, and blue-eyed, and all kinds of trouble for his relationship with his wife. In a flat voice, Casey added, "And Jenn."

"Hey, Case," he said. "And you know how I feel about you calling me Aaron."

"Casey," Jenn said stiffly.

"Who was that?"

Casey didn't answer his question. "That was intense."

"Awful. Did you know him?"

"Dr. Herrington?" another female voice called, interrupting them.

He turned his attention to the newcomer. A short brunette Sheridan County deputy was approaching. He remembered that jutting chin. He'd met her before, back when their lodge manager George Nichols had been arrested for a murder he didn't commit.

"Yes?" he said.

Estrella snorted and pawed the ground. So much for keeping her calm.

He jiggled her reins to draw her attention away from the deputy. "Shh, girl. It's okay."

"I'm Deputy Haigle. Sorry to see you again under these circumstances."

"Likewise."

"I was told you had the, uh, the horse. Of the deceased."

"Victor Carvalho. Yes, this is his horse. If you could give her a little more room, I'd appreciate it. I don't want her to accidentally hurt you. She's pretty upset."

The deputy backed up a few steps. "Can I talk to you as the team vet about what you saw?"

"Sure." He waited while she took out a small notepad and a pencil, conscious of Casey watching him intently. Jenn was still sitting, but now she was leaning forward with her hands on her knees.

"Just tell me what happened."

"Victor was just out on the field. You know, riding, playing polo. He seemed to lose control."

"What do you mean?"

"He slumped forward in the saddle."

"Like he'd been injured?"

Aaron shrugged. "It looked like he lost consciousness."

Estrella blew out a long breath. That was a good sign. He patted the animal's steamy neck.

Casey reached for the reins to take Estrella from him. Although she was working at his clinic now while she pursued a vet tech degree online at Purdue, she'd been a stable hand in the past. Aaron shook his head. Estrella was a valuable horse and his responsibility right now. Casey gave a little pout and moved away.

"And then?" the deputy prompted.

"The horse fell. Somersaulted, really. Victor was thrown under her. The other riders were in close pursuit and weren't able to avoid him."

"So, in your opinion, it appeared something was wrong with Victor before the accident?"

"Yes."

"As a medical professional, could you tell what was wrong with him?"

"I'm a vet." He half-smiled. "But, no, I couldn't. He collapsed. It could be any of a number of things."

"And what appeared to be the cause of the accident, when the horse fell?"

"Well, I don't have video replay, but from what I remember, I think it was Victor's mallet. It looked like Estrella tripped over it. She was galloping nearly full speed at the time."

"Does there appear to be anything wrong with the horse or the tack?"

"I'll have to do a more thorough examination back at the stables, but from a cursory inspection there's nothing significantly wrong with her, and her tack is all in place and undamaged. I didn't notice anything before the accident that would suggest a problem either."

"Did you see any other riders at fault?"

"No. They were playing polo. Polo is a rough game. Nothing looked out of line." He frowned. "May I ask the reason for your questions?"

"We need to determine cause of death."

He raised his brows. "I would think that's fairly obvious."

"I mean accident versus... not an accident."

Jenn stood and walked closer to Aaron. "There's reason to think it wasn't accidental?"

"You're, um—I remember you, I think."

"Jennifer Herrington. I was on George Nichols' legal team last year. You arrested him at our lodge. I was there."

The deputy's neck and cheeks flushed with color. "Right, right. Sorry."

"About the accidental versus not question..."

"We're just being extra careful."

Aaron mentally translated that to mean they expected scrutiny and pressure. It made sense. The Farinolo family was very important to the community. As was the team.

Jenn nodded, her eyes not leaving the deputy's face. Assessing.

"Anyway, Dr. Herrington, could you call me with the results of your examination?" The deputy held out a card.

Aaron took it and tucked it in his front jeans pocket. "Sure."

"And if you could drop by the station at your earliest convenience to give a full statement?"

Aaron knew the futility of citing a busy schedule. Years married to a prosecutor had taught him that. What the cops did was important. He had to respect it. "That would be fine."

The team captain, Donny Flanders, suddenly appeared, walking fast. He was large for a polo player, but small compared to Aaron. Most people were.

"There you are big girl." Without speaking to any of the humans, Donny slowed and went straight to Estrella and began stroking her neck. The horse accepted his attention without resistance. He began murmuring to her like the humans weren't around.

The deputy made her goodbyes with Aaron and Jenn. Casey crossed her arms.

When the deputy was gone, Aaron turned to Donny. "I'm so sorry, man."

Tears shone in the younger man's eyes. He nodded, not looking away from the horse.

Aaron said, "I hate to be all business, but I think you'll understand that I need to get Estrella to the ranch for an exam. For her sake, and because the police have asked for a report."

"Yeah." Donny nodded. "I get it."

"Did she belong to Victor?"

Donny wiped his eyes with the back of his arm. "Yes and no. The Farinolos bought Estrella for him. I guess that makes her theirs?"

"Okay."

"We can load her up with some of the others and take her back now. I've already talked to the deputies, so I can leave anytime."

"Great. I'll follow you." Then Aaron shook his head. "Wait. I need to drop my wife at home first. I can meet you instead."

"No problem."

Aaron handed Estrella's reins to Donny. "See you at Red Grade Ranch."

Donny clucked to Estrella and gave the reins a gentle tug. "Come on, girl. We're going home." He led the horse away.

Casey raised her hand. "I can give you a ride. You're going to need help, right?"

"I guess I do."

"And we're headed back to the same place."

It was true. Casey was living in the cottage Jenn had renovated to use as her home office and writing den. He'd set up a replacement office for her in the stables, but it wasn't the same. Jenn was being a good sport, but he knew it had been a big sacrifice for her. She'd worked hard creating a perfect sanctuary in the cottage.

"Thanks, Case." He turned to his wife. "You okay with that plan?"

An accordion of creases had formed between Jenn's eyebrows, perpendicular to the ones laddering up her forehead. "I've got to prep for the guests anyway."

That was not the same thing as being okay with the plan, and he knew it.

He closed the distance between them and swept her into his arms, holding her close and inhaling her lavender scent for a few seconds. He whispered in her ear. "Life is too short to waste any chance to do this." She relaxed into him. He kissed her nose, then released her. "See you soon."

"Yep."

"Let's *go*," Casey said.

"All right, all right." Aaron moved toward the parking area with his daughter.

When he looked back, Jenn had her hands on her hips and was staring at the ground.

THREE

Big Horn, Wyoming

LATER THAT NIGHT, twin beams shone into the living room window at the lodge. Given the length of the driveway, the first flash of headlights served as a five-minute warning. Jennifer and Aaron's two Alaskan malamutes—black-nosed Willett and Sibley, whose nose was pink and freckled—began to woo the song of their people. Joyfully, loudly, and in jangling disharmony with each other. The dogs were recent rescues from an Alabama family who had fled Wyoming when winter turned out to be a little *extra*. She and Aaron adored them.

Jennifer glanced at the clock. Their guests had come on the last flight into the little Sheridan County airport and were arriving right on time. "Guest arrival imminent." She hurried into the kitchen, took cookies out of the oven, and scooped them onto a cooling rack. The smell reminded her of home and family gatherings in Tennessee—sugar, chocolate, and love.

"That's my signal to vamoose." George Nichols yawned and

stretched one and a half arms into the air. He'd lost the other half a few months before when it had been ripped off by his own log splitter, a conical drill bit powered by a tractor engine. In his sixties with unruly white-blond hair that Jennifer thought looked like Rod Stewart after a bender, he lived in his own small cabin further up the base of the mountains. As the lodge manager, he normally checked-in guests no matter the hour, but, since these were guests for Maggie's party, George had relinquished the task to Jennifer and Aaron. Reluctantly.

Aaron started flipping on exterior lights. He'd only just gotten back from giving his statement in Sheridan.

"Quick. Before they come in, tell me about Estrella and Victor," Jennifer said.

"Yeah," George added. "Tell us." He suddenly didn't look like he was leaving.

"The short version. Okay, Estrella started limping once she cooled down and her adrenaline ebbed. I think it's just a strain from her fall. I couldn't find anything wrong with her tack. So, I didn't have much to give the police in my statement. They had a line of us in there giving them, though. I had to wait forever."

"Any idea why they aren't taking it as an accident on its face?" Jenn asked.

"They kept saying it's an unusual case that deserves an abundance of caution."

"That isn't much."

"Agree." Aaron grabbed a cookie. "After this day, I'm beat. Maybe our guests will be sleepy. They're coming from earlier time zones." But he sounded excited.

Aaron was pure extrovert. Jenn was able to function in social situations but preferred the quiet company of herself or her nearest and dearest. After hosting Maggie's friends, she'd be a drooling, brain-dead mess, glued to her favorite Hallmark romantic mysteries. Aaron would still be buoyed up for a week reliving all the fun.

Jennifer checked the living and dining rooms one last time. The overstuffed furniture. The heavy log beams in the peaked ceiling. The enormous stone fireplace. It looked good. She'd already put small welcome gifts in the four lodge guestrooms. She wanted everything to be perfect.

"Can you put the dogs out?" she asked Aaron.

The dogs were milling at the front door. Between Willett's over-friendliness and Sibley's protective, wolfy nature, neither made the best welcoming committee for strangers.

"Good idea." Aaron whistled. "Come on girls." He led them out to the dog run behind the lodge.

"I'm right behind him," George said. "Night, Jenn."

"Good night, George."

With the dogs outside, Katya—a calico cat who acted near feral half the time—and their de-stunk skunk, Jeremiah Johnson, popped out of their hiding places. Jennifer gave Jeremiah a quick cuddle. She and Aaron had socialized the dogs with the smaller animals, but she respected their good sense in staying clear of big jaws and big paws. Both littles had come with the lodge, as had an old St. Bernard named Liam who'd sadly passed over the rainbow bridge only a few months before. Skunks were Jennifer's spirit animal, and she loved Jeremiah with all her heart. So did George, and they shared custody.

Car doors slammed, one after another. Voices and laughter rang out. She set Jeremiah on the back of the couch where he perched with his tail plumed.

Jennifer's stomach tightened. She'd studied pictures online ahead of time and practiced all the names. Katie and Ava she'd met. Emily and Michele she hadn't, and she knew none of their partners.

"Our social butterflies are not happy." Aaron had returned, and he put a hand on her shoulder. "Add to that the enticing aroma of badger everywhere, and they're losing their minds." The Wyoming Game and Fish department had started bringing injured wild animals to Aaron. A badger was his latest patient from them. He barely made any money from it, but it was his favorite part of his job lately.

"Shall we go out and help them with their bags? It might be easier to do introductions out there. It'll be tight in here."

"Sure." He took her hand.

Jennifer sucked in a deep breath and together they walked out to greet the guests.

***

HALF AN HOUR LATER—AFTER enough time for everyone to freshen up—the guests began trickling back into the common rooms, two by two. They'd all insisted they weren't tired and wanted to get to know their hosts. It had been impossible for Jennifer to beg off with an excuse. Aaron was thrilled, sleep forgotten. Jennifer had given herself a pep talk and was as ready as she could be.

The first to return were Katie with her husband Nick Connell. Katie was a statuesque red head in Keds and pedal pusher jeans with a yellow plaid shirt. Nicole Kidman, but with more elasticity through the forehead. Nick was... Well, Maggie had already warned Jennifer that in what would be a group of very pretty people, Nick was the one who got all the women's pulses racing. At first glance he was manly—asymmetrical, and lanky with a prominent nose, dark eyes, brown hair, and olive skin. Not classically handsome. But within minutes, Jennifer agreed with Maggie. Nick had something different about him that made Aaron squint in recognition, one magnetic alpha to another.

"Do I hear dogs?" Katie said.

"You do." Jennifer gestured at the table. "Help yourself." Her cookies were in the center of the twelve-seater dining table along with pitchers of water, iced tea, and a bottle of spicy KO 90 liqueur.

Nick said, "We have six dogs. When she's gone, I think Katie misses her German shepherd more than our three kids or me."

"You guys travel with me most of the time. Poco Oso can't." Katie poured herself a red Solo cup of water. "But, seriously, we'd love to meet the dogs, if you don't mind."

Aaron said, "Fair warning—they're big and rambunctious."

"What are they?"

"Alaskan malamutes."

"Like sled dogs?"

"Yep."

"Oh, please, please!" She smiled winsomely.

Ava and Collin had slipped in, holding hands.

"Do any of you not like big dogs?" Jennifer said.

"Nah, I good." Ava spoke in a beautiful Caribbean accent that sounded exotic in their Wyoming lodge.

"And by 'I', she means me, too," Collin said with a smile.

"Well, I'll go get them then," Aaron said.

Ava had washed her face and changed out of body-conscious, va-va-voom clothes into sweatpants and a tank top with flip flops. Collin was also casual but light to her dark. Muscly with a blond haircut that looked post-military. He was much shorter than Nick, who was much shorter than Aaron.

The couple was eye catching, but it was Ava who Jennifer had to work not to stare at. She was the It Girl of the moment, and she radiated the electricity of a mega pop star, because she was one. Jennifer had gotten used to Maggie's fame, partly because she was local and almost family, and partly because Maggie's star had been tarnished. She'd flamed out young on drugs and alcohol then retreated from the spotlight. Only recently had Ava coaxed her out of hiding to write, record, and tour with her. The crossover appeal of Ava's pop with a hip hop vibe was amplified by her surprising collaboration with rockabilly Maggie. In their shows, Maggie opened then returned for a stripped-down set with Ava. Katie, as Ava's back-up, was the third in their doo wop session. Jennifer had gotten to see them perform in a stadium show in Denver and been blown away. It was hard to believe these people were now her—what? Lodge guests? Acquaintances? *Friends?*

Nick was pouring KO 90 into a Solo cup. "Anyone want to join me in some of this KO stuff?"

Jennifer said, "It's Maggie's favorite. She mixes the KO with iced tea and calls it a TKO."

Ava and Collin both raised their hands. Nick poured shots, added ice and tea, and handed one to each of them. The three bumped plastic cups.

"Bottoms up!" Ava slung hers back.

Aaron returned, holding a dog collar in each hand. "Let the singing begin."

And it did. With a vengeance. Aaron released the dogs, and their guests crowded around the happy, chatty malamutes.

Jennifer laughed. "I'm sorry. They don't come with volume control."

"Their fur!" Katie said, her hands deep in Willett's silky fluff.

Collin crossed his arms over his chest. "Watch out, Nick. My sister is going to want to add a seventh to her pack."

Katie is Collin's sister? The two didn't look anything alike.

Emily and Jack came down the stairs. Jennifer felt like she'd been catapulted back into Texas with Emily's drawl, her blonde hair and blue eyes, and her slightly western get-up. Jack was tall, quiet, and slouchy with startling amber eyes and a lone dimple. They shared in the dog love.

"How did you all become friends?" Aaron finally asked when the dogs had settled a little and people found seats in the great room.

Michele and Rashidi walked into the living room. Jennifer and Aaron tried to give up their chairs, but the couple refused and sat cross-legged on the floor, side-by-side. Petite and super fit Michele seemed much more introverted to Jennifer than the rest of the group. She was still wearing her travel clothes, which were sleek and serious. Upscale comfort. Rashidi in his dreadlocks and baggy jeans didn't look like an academic, but he was. A native Virgin Islander and former professor, he was a world-recognized expert in aquaponic farming. Now he worked for an agricultural extension service in Texas, according to the website bio Jennifer had found about him.

"Don't let us interrupt," Michele said.

"They were asking about our family history," Emily drawled. "I used to be Katie's legal assistant until she moved away and quit practicing law to become a private investigator with her husband. I went to work for Jack at his criminal defense practice in my hometown, and then we made it a permanent thing."

"Fellow criminal defense attorney." Jennifer raised her hand. "And former prosecutor."

Jack grunted. "Same."

"Life brought us all together and gave us no choice in the matter." Katie was petting Sibley's ears. Sibley didn't take to people quickly but seemed to be making an exception for Katie.

"It's like polarity," Michele said. "Our energies were magnetic to each other, so we all ended up together like it was meant to be. The earliest connection in the group was Baylor law school. Katie and me."

Jennifer raised her hand. "I went to Baylor for law school. Maybe I'm part of this polarity, too."

Katie did an exaggerated jaw drop. "When were you there?"

Jennifer gave the year. It turned out she'd graduated when Katie and Michele were first year students, with one year of overlap.

Michele said. "Wait. I remember you. You won the mock trial competition, didn't you?"

Jennifer was happy that for once she was remembered by a fellow student not as a University of Tennessee cheerleader or her similarity to *Legally Blonde*, but for her accomplishments. "That was me. Although my co-counsel Alayah deserves a lot of the credit. We advanced through the prelims as a team until the solo round."

"I remember her!"

"We went to the Harris County District Attorney's office together. She's still there."

"Jenn practices law here now, but she's about to be a published author. Her first legal thriller comes out in a few weeks." Aaron grinned. "Not that I'm bursting with pride or anything."

Squeals and congratulations flooded over Jennifer. "Thank you. I owe a lot to Michele. Maggie sent me her way, and Michele referred me to a great agent who got me a publishing deal."

"A two-book deal," Aaron said. "Excuse the husband brag."

"Okay, okay." Jennifer blushed, then changed the subject, explaining her connection to Hank, Maggie, Gene, and Laura.

Aaron's phone rang.

He glanced at the screen then said, "Sorry. Have to take this." He walked out to the front porch. The dogs scrambled to their feet and went with him.

"Vets are always on call," Jennifer said. Then her phone rang. She read the number. It was Ollie Singletary, the interim Sheridan County Attorney. At nearly midnight? Maybe Ollie's call was about one of the cases her firm was handling. Maybe he was working late and expected his call to go to her voice mail. "Well, looks like one I have to take, too. I'll be right back."

She went out, shut the door, and descended the steps. The midnight sky was twinkling with a million stars, dramatic against the darkness of the new moon. A chilly breeze raised the hair on her arms. Aaron was sitting on the bottom step, dogs beside him, his head tilted back and wearing a frown.

She sat on the other side of the dogs and answered her phone. "This is Jennifer."

"Ollie Singletary. Sorry to call so late. I hope I didn't wake you," Ollie said.

"It's okay. You didn't. What's up?"

"Were you at the polo match today, when that guy got trampled to death?"

"Victor Carvalho. Ye-es."

"Well, we got a tip about that earlier."

"What kind of tip?"

"That drugs caused the accident."

"Like cocaine?"

"No. Like someone drugged him."

She wrinkled her nose, trying to follow his line of thought. "Which would make his death—besides horrific and public and violent..."

"Murder. And that's why I'm going to need your help."

FOUR

Big Horn, Wyoming

AARON TOOK a deep breath of the pine-scented night air. He rubbed his eyes and asked the Strikers' team captain Donny Flanders to repeat what he'd just said over the phone.

"There's a rumor going around that Victor was drugged," Donny said.

"Who told you that?"

"My wife's best friend's cousin is a deputy."

"With what?"

"Don't know."

"Wow. That's terrible." *And seems so far-fetched on a polo team in little bitty Big Horn, Wyoming.*

Donny cleared his throat. "I just thought you'd want to know. Have you heard anything like that?"

"About Victor?"

"About drugs around the polo teams."

"Never." Aaron wasn't sure why the information warranted a call to him at midnight. He hadn't been close to Victor, nor was he tight with Donny. But he was developing a relationship with the team through his role, so he didn't question it. "Well, I'm glad you called. Listen, I'm really, really sorry about Victor."

A silence fell over the line. Just when Aaron felt like he'd have to break it, Donny said, "Uh, yeah. Well, if you hear anything about it, ring me up."

Maybe that was the reason for the call. Donny was seeking information. "I will. Good night."

Aaron turned to Jenn when his call ended. She was still on hers. What were the odds that both of them would receive midnight calls on the same night? Veterinary emergencies did happen, and Jenn used to get late night callouts to crime scenes when she was with the district attorney's office in Houston. But it hadn't happened in the one year of her defense practice.

Jenn saw him watching her. She hit speaker on her phone and motioned Aaron closer. He shooed the dogs and scooted next to her. "That doesn't make sense," she said. "Why?"

Aaron heard a man's voice that sounded familiar, but not familiar enough for him to identify the caller. "I can't say for sure, but I have my suspicions, and they point to organized crime."

"Ollie, I'm not following you."

Aha. Ollie Singletary. The county prosecutor.

"Can we make this a nonversation?"

"A what?"

"Where I tell you this, and you don't tell anyone else. Like it never happened."

She stuck out her tongue at Aaron. "Sure."

Oops, he mouthed at her.

"We don't have much organized crime in Wyoming, so I have zero experience with it."

"I can imagine."

"The word is that some of the polo team owners have mafia ties."

Aaron did a double take. His team? Its owners?

Jenn made wide eyes at Aaron. "Whoa. Interesting."

"And that there is heavy underground betting going on."

Jenn mouthed, *Had you heard this?*

Aaron shook his head. He'd been around the Strikers and several of the other teams. Surely he would have seen or heard something. Just how far underground was it? Or was this even real?

Ollie said, "Obviously, our wealthy polo patrons are important to Sheridan County."

"They make up half the population of Big Horn."

"Yeah. Not a sleepy little town anymore." Ollie cleared his throat.

"It puts a new twist on things if said *patrons* are involved in organized crime, though."

"I looked up your old cases. You know, back when we first went up against each other in court."

"Which wasn't official yet since I wasn't licensed in Wyoming at the time." She smiled at Aaron.

"You've handled organized crime cases in Houston. You've prosecuted cases involving gambling."

"Not many."

"That's several thousand percent more than me or anyone else in the state. If the rumors turn out to be true—the organized crime element or the betting, especially if either become germane to the death—I'm going to need some help."

"What do you have in mind?"

"We have open positions at our office."

Aaron's first reaction was that he hoped Jennifer would turn Ollie down. Her small practice defending criminals with her colleague Wesley "Kid" James was growing, plus her thriller novel would soon be released. He loved their life as it was, although he wouldn't mind adding a baby.

Then Jenn got a funny look on her face and avoided Aaron's eyes. He knew that look.

She had mentioned a few months ago the possibility of running against Ollie for the county attorney position. Aaron had promised to support her if she did, but deep in his heart he'd been hoping she wouldn't. Would helping Ollie give her an unquenchable thirst to return to prosecution? Or would it do the opposite? The county attorney job would be stressful and the hours long. There was a deadline to submit for the primary, though, and she might have missed it. He didn't know when it was. Since she hadn't filed, he'd assumed she'd shelved the idea.

But the look that crossed her face told Aaron otherwise. It was the look of ambition.

Jennifer stared out into the dark. "I'm sorry, but I can't go from head of homicide at one of the biggest prosecutorial offices in the nation to the assistant county attorney pool here. That just doesn't interest me. But thank you."

Aaron couldn't picture her taking that step back either.

Ollie didn't hesitate. "I understand. I could bring you on as a contract attorney for the duration of this case. Or as a special prosecutor."

She pursed her lips. After twenty years together, Aaron could hear her thoughts as clearly as if she was speaking them aloud. If she was going to prosecute in Sheridan county, she wanted Ollie's job. Nothing less.

"Ollie..."

"How about this—no one would have to know. I'd prefer it that way, too, actually. I just—I can't mess this up, Jennifer. It would be bad for Sheridan county. For all of us."

Aaron cringed. Ollie had appealed to Jenn's sense of ethics and civic duty. That was the button to push.

He watched her capitulate with a sigh. "Just a private mentoring relationship between you and me. An ongoing nonversation. Could you live with that?"

Ollie's voice was enthusiastic. "Yes. It's perfect. I'll draw up a contract."

Sure, it's perfect. Private means you don't publicly admit she's more qualified to be the county attorney than you. Aaron realized how quickly he was migrating to Team Jenn for county attorney. Conflicted, less than ecstatic, but always behind her. He envisioned a future putting yard signs up for her campaign all over the county. Ringing doorbells, shaking hands, giving interviews, and eating rubber chicken at innumerable events.

"Great. Give me a call if this moves forward, then."

"Thank you."

The call ended.

Jenn said. "Huh. That was weird. What was your call about?"

But Aaron didn't answer her. A horrible thought had struck him. If Jenn's star rose, if she ran for county attorney... Casey held a secret that could torpedo Jenn's future as a prosecutor—as a lawyer—in the palm of her hands.

FIVE

JENNIFER FLOPPED into the overstuffed armchair at Chaplain Dean Abel's office on Tuesday morning. A part-time therapist affiliated with the Veteran's Hospital, Abel had been counseling her in secret since the beginning of the year, because of her nightmares. She'd gone into it with trepidation, thinking she'd have nothing to say, but the opposite had turned out to be true. Now it seemed like her loads of baggage would never be completely unpacked.

"How are you doing?" Abel was, as usual, leaning forward in his rolling chair, his wire-rimmed glasses slipping down his off-kilter nose and his long fingers twiddling a pen. In his mid-fifties, Abel had a full head of wiry salt and pepper curls that bounced when he bobbed his head. The odor of cigar smoke always clung to him, in the few times she'd seen him in public and in this office.

Jennifer said, "Oh, my gosh, where to begin. Aaron and I were at a polo match when a player was killed."

He tsked. "I heard about that. How tragic—and how upsetting to have witnessed it."

"It will give me something new to have nightmares about."

She closed her eyes, but it wasn't the polo match that flashed into her mind. It was the images she couldn't banish from her dreams. Visiting her Aunt Vangie and Uncle Henry's ranch in the foothills with her family as a little girl. Being allowed to help pick her cousin Hank up from school and running out to meet him on the playground. A man shouting and pointing a rifle. The loud cracks of the rifle *shooting*. Shooting at them. Kids falling to the ground, screaming. Kids *dying*. Hank throwing his small body over her tiny one to protect her, even though he'd been shot. In her mind's eye, she saw a menacing tattoo of a coiled snake, and the letters D-T-O-M, an acronym she'd later learned stood for Don't Tread on Me.

She'd blocked the whole event from her conscious memory until Hank casually mentioned it to her after she'd moved to Wyoming. That's when the nightmares began.

Then she'd seen a tattoo identical to the one in those dreams on former prosecutor Pootie Carputin. She'd become convinced he was the shooter. Pootie was currently serving time in prison for a different murder. She'd been unable to get the state of Wyoming to charge him for the decades old school shooting.

Recently, she'd seen the tattoo again, on a waiter. It had shaken her. She was plagued with doubts. Was the shooter *not* Pootie? But if not him, who? She didn't feel like she could fully move on with her life until she knew. Until she helped bring the shooter to justice and herself to closure.

Abel said, "Let's hope no new nightmares. No nightmares at all would be even better."

"Agreed."

"And the rest of the weekend?"

"Hectic. We have a full house of lodge guests. They were here for my cousin's couples' wedding shower, but they're staying the rest of the week to explore the area. I like them, but... "

"You didn't have time to process witnessing that death."

She shrugged. "I process alone. I recharge alone. Which I am *anything but* until they leave. And—can we invoke therapist-patient cone of silence if I tell you something?"

"Always."

"The county attorney called and wants me to consult with him on the case."

"The case?"

"The polo player's death. It's possible he was drugged. That this was not an accident. The county is waiting on toxicology results."

"I thought you were a defense attorney?"

"I am. But Ollie—the county attorney—is afraid this case might involve organized crime and underground betting, two things I have experience with that he doesn't."

"Well, I don't know what to say except good luck. And that you'll need quality sleep."

"For sure."

"So, let's get back to your nightmares, since they're key to that. Have any of our strategies been helping?"

Honestly, Jennifer had found some relief from the nightmares until her miscarriage. "I was improving. Lately they've been more frequent again."

"Take a step back. Are you focusing on finding and embracing your joy?"

"Aaron and I are planning to go to New York for the launch of my novel soon. It'll probably cost us more than the book will ever make but—"

"But it's an enormous achievement. You should enjoy it. It's not about the money, is it?"

"You sound like Aaron." She smiled, remembering the note on the kitchen counter that morning. *I am thankful for a creative, kick ass wife who I get to celebrate.* It was the latest in a series of thousands of similar "thankful" notes over the course of their marriage, from each of them to the other. "It should be fun."

"That's wonderful. Have the two of you talked about babies lately?"

"I think I'm going to stop taking the pill." Which wasn't really the same thing as talking about it. She congratulated herself on the dodge.

"How do you feel about it?"

"Terrified. Jinxed. Like I've been given a warning I haven't heeded."

"Tell me more about that."

"Like it's hubris, you know? When we have everything in the world and now I decide I have to have a baby, too. At my age, which isn't old except in terms of ovum. Other times I still wonder if I was being punished before, with the miscarriage. What did I do to deserve it? Or what did I do wrong that I couldn't support the pregnancy? And I always worry about bringing a baby into this messed-up world."

"Okay, back to what we've worked on. Talk yourself out of this stuck state. Out of things that aren't real."

Jennifer took a deep breath, nodding. She wouldn't admit this to Abel, but she could never bring herself to do this exercise except in his presence. It was too painful. "I deserve to have a baby as much as anyone. Whether or not I become pregnant, carry a baby to term, or have a healthy baby is not about me or my past. It's about health and genetics. I didn't do anything wrong. I am not being punished." Tears sprang to her eyes, as they always did at this point.

"Keep going, Jennifer." His voice was gentle.

"My worth is not measured by whether I want to or can have a baby."

He gave her a smile of encouragement.

"I am loving and loveable with or without a child." Tears were streaming down her face now.

"Good." He offered her a box of Kleenex. She took one and mopped her eyes, sniffing. "And how does it make you feel to hear yourself say those things?"

Still terrified. But she wasn't going to say that to him. "A little bit better."

"I'm worried about you trying again when you're not in a place to be joyful about the process."

"I'm out of time."

"There are other options."

Foster. Adoption. A surrogate. "I know. But we're not there yet."

"As long as you're on this journey because you want to be."

Jennifer didn't respond. Sometimes she wondered. The pain of the miscarriage wasn't as raw as it had been, but it still hurt. "I've decided to go to a hypnotherapist to see if I can recover more of my memories. I think if I can resolve that old trauma, it would make everything less hard. That I'd feel better about children and myself." *And might help me find the shooter and see him put in prison where he belongs.*

Abel frowned. "I'm not sure that's a good idea. Memory recovery can be really traumatic. I don't know anyone I would trust with you."

Most of the time Jennifer respected Abel's opinion, but she'd do what she had to do whether he agreed with her or not. She'd had a Zoom interview with the hypnotherapist and really liked her. She'd booked her first session. If she got cold feet, she could always cancel.

She changed the subject. "There's, um, there's some pressure on me to make a decision about something entirely different. Now really is better than waiting any longer on the baby because of it."

"What kind of decision?"

"Whether to run for county attorney."

His thick eyebrows shot up, like a jumping caterpillar. "Wow. I didn't know you were considering it."

She'd been so consumed by the nightmares, the pregnancy, and then the miscarriage that she hadn't told Abel anything about her secret aspirations. "Defense work is emotionally taxing. I don't want to wake up one day and discover I'm suffering from compassion fatigue."

"Tell me what you mean by that."

"Draining myself and everyone around me emotionally because I become overinvolved in the plight of my defendants. The trauma is endless."

"Is that not a danger with prosecution?"

"It is, but it's different. At least it is in Homicide, where I worked. The victim is dead. Your client is the state. Don't get me wrong—you interact with the victim's loved ones and absorb their pain, but not on the constant basis I do in defense work, possibly because I've been lucky so far to only represent defendants I really believe are innocent."

Abel nodded. "I get it. It's a danger in my work, too."

"Of course it is." She took a deep breath. "I also left my prosecutorial career when I was on the cusp of big things, and I don't think I have the desire completely out of my system to pursue those goals. Aaron says he'll support me, but I know he remembers how hard our lives were when I was a prosecutor in Houston."

"Will it be the same this time?"

"This is a different place. I'm a different person."

"What about your defense practice and your new career as a novelist?"

She laughed. "Writing books is hardly a career. Most published authors don't make any real money at it."

"Are you going to keep writing?"

"As long as I have time for it. If I run for county attorney and, um, win, Kid will have to take over the practice. The writing would be back seat to the job. And a baby if one comes along."

He nodded, wise eyes on her. "Do you think your nightmares have anything to do with all of this other stuff—running for office, writing books, trying to be a better partner, possibly having a baby?"

She tucked hair behind her ears and looked down. It was a rhetorical question, and they both knew it. "I'm sure it does. But what if I keep having them? I don't sleep. I—I think I'm starting to see things and hear things. You know, in the middle of the night when I'm lying there scared and awake. Maybe I'm not fit to parent."

"See and hear things?"

"I've been... " She shook her head, embarrassed.

"What? It's okay. No judgment here."

"The shooter. He's been talking to me. And I don't think that's real. I don't think it really happened."

Abel blanched. "Really?! Like he walks up to you and speaks to you, up close?"

"Close-ish. I still can't see his face as clearly as I need to."

"What does he say?"

She swallowed. "He says—I can't really understand it—something like 'hey little girl' or 'hey little dolly.' It's like a term of endearment. Like... affection."

"And then what?"

"Then I wake up."

"Have you tried journaling it?"

"No. I'm always so scared. Aaron just holds me until I feel better."

"Well, you know what I think you should do."

She sighed. "Journal it, right then. Break the cycle."

He nodded. "Any other pressures making this situation worse? Like, maybe, your stepdaughter?"

Jennifer shifted in her seat. A snort came out before she could keep it in. "Aaron is so nice. Casey is so... not nice."

"So, things *aren't* better."

"No. What if we have a child who does bad things or is a bad person? It happens. I know that now."

"I don't mean to cause more trouble, but I think this needs to be said. Have you ever considered the possibility that Casey isn't Aaron's daughter?"

Jennifer nearly pumped her fist in the air. She sat upright and leaned toward Abel. "Every day, but I can't say so. I'm already public enemy number one to Casey. She would kill me." Possibly literally. Jennifer would never forget Casey holding a gun on her up on snowy Walker Prairie in the mountains. Casey had pulled the trigger. The only reason Jennifer wasn't dead was that the rifle was empty. Aaron and Casey had justified the situation, given apologies, and cited extenuating circumstances. But Jennifer remembered.

"How about getting a DNA test done?" Abel asked.

"I wouldn't dare raise the issue."

"Well, doing nothing is accepting the status quo as truth. Think about it." He looked at his phone. "Time's up. We covered a lot of ground today. Anything else or shall I just see you at our next regular appointment time?"

"I'm good, but I'll have to skip it." She didn't *have to,* but she was going to repurpose the time for her hypnotherapy appointment.

He nodded. "Remember your self-talk. Your journaling."

"I will." But she wasn't thinking about self-talk or journaling as she said goodbye and walked out.

She was wondering whether she really needed Casey and Aaron's permission to do the DNA test. If a test proved Casey was his daughter, she'd let it go. If it didn't, she could figure out how to get their permission and redo the test.

If Casey wasn't his—if she was scamming Aaron—he deserved to know.

But if she did the test without their permission, would Aaron ever forgive her if he found out what she'd done?

SIX

AARON PARKED his vintage orange Jeepster Commando—dubbed DeMarcus Ware after the linebacker who'd capped a stellar football career with the Denver Broncos— at Half Circle Ranch. He was here to treat one of the Hellcat horses, which he'd done a few times before when their regular vet wasn't available. The Hellcats were a rival of the Strikers, but it wasn't like he'd signed an exclusive contract with the Farinolos.

He jumped out in the shade cast by a Russian olive tree. This time of the year, the trees smelled heavenly, like the apricots in his grandparents' yard back in Tennessee. He made sure both malamutes were clipped in, then ruffled their ears through the open windows. With the mild temperature and breeze, they'd be good, but he didn't need them to jump out and spook any horses.

"Be quiet." He held a finger to his lips.

Willett responded with a long, multisyllabic woo.

He shook his head, smiling. The best strategy was to ignore her.

She'd continue talking as long as he engaged. He grabbed his veterinary bag.

On the other side of Demarcus Ware, Nick Connell disembarked. The other male lodge guests were golfing. Nick had asked to do a vet ride-along instead. Aaron usually took a vet tech with him on ranch visits, but the clinic was shorthanded that day, so Nick's extra pair of hands might come in handy... so to speak.

He joined Aaron now. "Nice place."

"Yeah, these polo ranches are pretty sweet. You'll see working ranches later. The upper crust versus the rest of us. The owner of the Half Circle spends big bucks on this place. Profit isn't even a consideration, whereas a working ranch doesn't have spare change for luxuries or pretty things."

As they walked toward the stable, Aaron took a long look at the pastures around him. There were several horses in each.

"What's wrong with that pasture?" Nick pointed at one that was mostly dirt.

"That's a dry lot. The grass is still high in sugar this time of year, which can make the horses founder if they eat too much of it, and founder can kill a horse. So, the owners usually turn them out to graze for only a few hours, then move them to a dry lot. It's also used when you have an easy keeper who gains weight looking at grass."

"They look healthy."

Aaron smiled. The animals were shiny, with muscles rippling under short coats. "They're athletes, and they're well taken care of."

He'd planned to stop by the ranch manager's office to announce himself, but someone he hadn't met before intercepted them as they passed by the stable door.

"Is one of you Dr. Herrington?" The man wiped his hands on the front of his worn blue jeans. From the acne on his cheeks, he couldn't be older than eighteen or nineteen.

Aaron offered his hand, and they shook. "I am. This is my buddy Nick. He's helping me out today."

"Uh, okay. Peter asked me to take you to Lucky."

Peter Galindo was the ranch manager. "And your name is... ?"

The man blushed. "Oh, sorry. I'm Jake Small. I'm one of the stable hands, and I help take care of Lucky."

"Great." Aaron shot a look at the ranch manager's office. For a moment, he wondered if he should check in with him anyway.

"Well, follow me, guys, okay?"

Aaron decided he could stop by to see Peter after he attended to Lucky, so they followed Jake into the stables. It was a nice building by Wyoming standards but older and less fancy than the Strikers's facilities. He glanced up at the loft stacked high with rectangular bales of hay. Growth had been crazy fast this year. Those were bound to be high-quality new bales, since most ranchers had just finished an early first cutting, and the hard winter meant stores from previous years had been depleted.

As they walked through the stable, Aaron imagined the stalls filled. Pregnant cattle in the spring and with sick animals in the winter. Today, though, they were mostly empty except for a few polo ponies, who had a strong preference for being outside with their herd mates. He heard one pawing the dirt floor a few stalls down. The agitated animal huffed and snorted.

"Here he is." Jake stopped at a stall with a wooden slat gate. Lucky was a handsome chestnut gelding, a little on the short side. He was standing with his head over the gate and nickered when he saw Jake.

Nick moved across the center corridor. "I'll just stay out of the way unless you need me."

"Sounds good." Aaron put his hand out, palm down, offering it for the horse to sniff. Warm breath puffed against his fingers, followed by the touch of a velvet muzzle. Lucky was friendly. "What's going on with him?"

Jake hooked his thumbs in his belt loops. "Um, well, he's just—I don't know. He seems tired. He's really short of breath in his workouts."

Aaron set his bag down. "This is a change, then? He's not just out of shape?"

Jake shrugged. "I haven't worked with him long, but I don't think so. Not from what I've been told."

"Is he off his food?"

"Not really."

"Is he drinking?"

"Yeah."

"What about his manure? Is it frequent enough? Does it look okay?"

Jake leaned over the stall and stared down at the piles. "I think so. I mean, I'm shoveling it out same as the others, seems like."

Aaron followed his gaze. The color of a recent sample looked good for early grass and was formed in nice, glossy balls. The slightly sweet scent didn't indicate any problems either. "Any cough or congestion?"

"No."

"Discharge from the eyes or nostrils?"

"No."

"Why don't you get him out and walk him around for me. Then I'll examine him."

"Okay." Jake took a halter from a hook. When he had it on Lucky, he led him into the center of the stable and walked him in a circle around Aaron.

Nick positioned himself nearer to the entrance to the building.

"Other way, please."

Jake and Lucky did a U-turn and circled in the other direction.

Aaron stroked his chin. Pain could cause anxiety and shortness of breath, but the horse was moving in nice, even strides. He didn't look stressed or tight. He wasn't limping. "Okay. Hold up. Can you cross tie him for me so I can examine him?"

Nodding, Jake moved Lucky forward until he was able to snap his halter into lead lines suspended from each side of the walkway.

Aaron let the horse sniff him again, then he stroked his shoulder.

With Aaron's height, he was eye-level with the ears, so he started by looking at them, then gently manipulating them to see past the fuzz protecting the ear canal. Aaron peered into his eyes and pulled his eyelids back revealing clear whites. When he stopped messing with the eyes, Lucky closed them and cocked one back leg lazily. Aaron slipped a thumb in one side of the horse's mouth and a finger in the other, behind its teeth. The horse obliged by opening up its mouth.

"His teeth are good. How old is he?"

"Five, I think."

Too young to have ground them down much. Next Aaron lifted and examined each hoof. They were well cared for and in perfect shape. Lucky was barefoot, which is ideal when a horse has good hooves and isn't going to work on hard surfaces. Aaron began palpating the animal, searching for hot spots, but Lucky merely swayed. *No sign of pain.* A glance under the tail revealed no discharge, as did a quick perusal of his male parts.

He put his stethoscope in his ears and checked Lucky's heart and lungs. They sounded normal. The lungs, clear. The horse hadn't shown any signs of respiratory distress in his presence. Aaron finished up by taking his temperature, which was smack in the middle of the normal range.

He cleaned his thermometer. "Hmm. Well, he seems good so far. Why don't you take him out for a run and let me see how he does?"

"Uh, it's his rest day. I'm not supposed to."

Aaron frowned. "That's unfortunate."

"Couldn't you just give him—I dunno—like something to make him breathe better?"

"Not as this point. I'd need to see him exhibit symptoms, because I haven't found any signs of distress, blockage, or congestion. Also, I'd like a blood test to know more."

Jake scuffed the ground with his boot toe. "I can't authorize a blood test. But he's a polo pony, ya know?"

"I do."

"His rider is really intent on Lucky snapping out of this."

Aaron began to feel uneasy about the conversation. Was the kid pressuring him for bronchodilators? If so, had someone put him up to this? It seemed an unfair situation to put a young and low paid ranch employee into. "Well, then I recommend you guys follow up with your normal vet. Feel free to call me in the meantime if it becomes an emergency."

Jake bit the inside of his lip and glanced at Nick. "Peter was hoping not to spend much money. It was him that suggested this."

Aaron frowned. That was even more troubling. Was Jake stonewalling because of the cost or because of what Peter thought he'd find? Either way, Aaron didn't want any part of it. Even a whiff of scandal could ruin him in the polo community.

"I'm sorry. I can't dispense medication based on this examination. I can recommend a few things. Diet changes, supplements, rest if he's been overworked, or exercise to build his wind if he's been under-worked. Getting him out of the stable in case he's bored. A stable toy or buddy if you can't. Oh, and a thorough work-over of his tack. A bad fit can make a horse anxious and huffy."

"We need something that works faster. He's got a match this weekend."

Aaron leaned over and put the thermometer back in its case, dropped the case in his bag, and snapped the bag closed. He stood and answered in a firm voice. "I wish I could help, but I can't."

He started to walk away, but Jake grabbed him by the wrist. "Please." His voice sounded strained. High pitched and tight. "I could get fired."

"Why is this so important?"

Jake opened his mouth then snapped it shut.

Aaron walked away, frowning. There was nothing about this visit that he liked.

SEVEN

Sheridan, Wyoming

JENNIFER TOOK the last sip of her iced mocha latte at the downtown Sheridan coffee shop where she'd met Maggie and the girls. Besides Nick who was with Aaron, the rest of the guys were playing golf. Jennifer would have rather been with them. Golf was her sport—she had been good enough to walk on at the University of Tennessee after turning down scholarship offers at smaller schools. She'd played there until she made the cheerleading squad. Honestly, lunches and coffees weren't normal activities for her. She was too purpose-driven most of the time. She liked these women, though, so, she'd made an exception for them.

The vibe was energetic. Everyone was still riding high on the success of the couples' shower Saturday night. It *had* been a lot of fun, with the hangovers and shared rides home to prove it. Earlier in the same day, the women held a lingerie shower and the men a honey-do party, where, literally, all the guys pitched in to help Hank on projects for Maggie. The hit of the lingerie shower was a pair of

LIGHT MY FIRE panties with arrows pointing to the kindling in question, in case that was in doubt. Maggie had run to the bathroom immediately to change into them.

Then, since Ava and Katie didn't have a show until the following week, and Emily, Michele, and Laura had taken off work, the whole group had started vacationing with a vengeance. It was first visits to Wyoming all around. The rating had been ten of ten all around so far.

Aaron and Jennifer had joined the group on a trek up Red Grade Road on Sunday. They'd passed a rock which Jennifer had always told Aaron looked like a bunny rabbit with its ears folded back against its head.

"Well, there you go. Penis rock," Collin had said.

Without missing a beat, Ava replied, "Rock hard."

The group had gone into hysterics, even Jennifer.

Today, the friends were driving up to the Medicine Wheel in the Bighorns to take in its spirituality, sans Jennifer. After the coffee, of course, and singing along to an eighties rock playlist.

Ava and Maggie were signing autographs as Journey's *Separate Ways* began blasting.

Suddenly solo, Emily belted out lyrics at the top of her lungs anyway. "Fish stick eyes... promises we made were in vain..." The woman was not a vocal talent. Nor was she singing the right words.

The others burst out laughing.

She looked hurt. "What? I don't sing that bad. Just because some of you are professionals doesn't mean the rest of us can't sing for the joy of it."

"No," Katie said, catching her breath. "It's not fish stick eyes."

"What?"

"The lyrics. You sang it as fish stick eyes."

"Because that's what he says."

Michele put a hand on Emily's. "Distant eyes. Distant."

Emily glowered for a moment, then she started laughing herself.

"She always does this," Michele explained to Jennifer. "Lyrics, expressions. If it can be scrambled, Emily has the wire whisk out and ready."

"I hear what I hear," Emily said.

"Are you sure you have to go to work, Jenn?" Maggie said. Per usual, she looked casually sultry in frayed cut off jean shorts, a tank top with a plaid shirt over it, and her hair plaited in two long braids. At forty-plus and after years of abusing her body. Sometimes Jennifer couldn't decide if she hated her or was just sick with envy. Which wasn't true. She had come to love her, so it must just be jealousy over the genetic lottery. "Can't you assign everything to your baby lawyer?"

Jennifer planned to do just that. Her work today would not be on her own cases, but she wasn't going to explain that to them. Kid James would be thrilled she passed her docket on to him, honestly. He was turning out to be a fabulous attorney, partly because he took it so seriously and worked so hard at it, and partly out of a natural talent for advocacy. Plus, he had a great mentor, if she did say so herself. He was always asking her to load him up with work. Lately, she'd made even more of an effort, trying to distract him from heartbreak. He'd fallen hard for Casey, who had kept him at her beck and call all through the spring. Recently Kid had found out she had a new guy the hard way—when he saw the two of them making out in the back of the Mint Bar. But that turned out to be just the first in a string of men. A steer wrestler for Sheridan College from Cody. A movie producer's son. A trust-fund backpacker. A wildlife photographer. God knew who else.

Yeah, that DNA test sounds better all the time.

Before Jennifer could answer, Katie said, "It would be so much fun if you could come!" She beamed. Jennifer had been surprised at how quickly she and Katie had clicked. Of all the friends, Jennifer had thought she'd bond most easily with Michele. She probably would have, except that Michele and Maggie were inseparable. Again, she felt the needle prick of jealousy. Maybe she valued Maggie's time and attention more than she'd realized.

She shook her head. "I wish I could. You guys take lots of pictures. And drive carefully. It's baby moose season."

Laura Begay said, "She isn't kidding. They're everywhere up there. Mama moose will total your car. Daddy moose will do that, too, then toss you out of it." She stood, which didn't increase her height by much. Until a few years ago, Laura had been a very successful quarter horse racing jockey. The muscle definition in her arms was crazy, as was her single digit percentile body fat. Jennifer, a vegetarian, had been doing yoga for years hoping for arms like Laura's but feared it might not be possible for her, no matter how hard she worked.

Emily cooed. "I love the springtime and all the baby animals."

Ava was frowning. "Moose an actual t'ing? They not extinct?"

This was met with laughter and teasing as they threw away their drink cups. Jennifer parted ways with the happy women on the sidewalk, then walked the five minutes to the office she shared with Kid. "Office" was a fancy term for the converted studio apartment above his mother's freestanding garage. The rent—free except for utilities—was great and the location—one block from the courthouse—unbeatable. She'd aspired to a new office that was really downtown, but that had been put on hold when she'd miscarried and spiraled downward for a few months.

She climbed the wooden exterior staircase up to the office door, breathing a sigh of a relief that the steps were secure. She'd invested in bolstering their attachment the previous week, tired of settling up with God before each use pending their imminent collapse.

"Honey, I'm home," she announced as she entered.

The office was one large room and a bathroom. Bare bones, with a drink station outside the bathroom against one wall. Today it smelled like a bakery. The good kind, filled with sugary treats. She looked to the drink counter and saw an open container of donuts, snagging one as she passed.

Kid pointed at his phone. His Airpods were in, and he was bobbing his head on his long neck, which matched his long, spare body. He was of late sporting a wispy goatee. It was all the facial hair he could muster, and it was as red as the curls on his head. Today was business casual for him—his usual three-piece suit, but without his signature jaunty bowtie.

She saluted him and went to her desk, chewing a still-warm glazed. Another of her recent investments had been the purchase of a second desk and expensively comfortable chair. Even though the practice had been Kid's originally, she'd asserted senior attorney rights when she joined him, claiming his desk and chair. He was only a year out of the University of Wyoming law school, after all. He'd been relegated to a rolling desk and a some-assembly-required chair from Walmart. Now that she'd returned his originals, she'd catch him dreamily eyeing her upgrades. She suspected he used them whenever she wasn't in.

Moving quickly, she finished her donut and used a wet wipe on her hands. Then she set up her laptop and plugged her phone in to charge. Kid's call continued, but she blocked his voice with Brandi Carlisle through her own Airpods as she navigated to the website for Wyoming's Secretary of State. There, she pulled up the Elections page. She clicked "Filing for Office" under "Candidate Information," then downloaded the form for "Major Party Application for County Offices." She took a deep breath and opened it. Printed it. Retrieved it from the printer.

She scanned the document, skipping straight to "Qualifications." If she didn't meet the quals for office, then she could quit agonizing over whether to run. She read quickly.

ALL COUNTY OFFICES INCLUDING DISTRICT ATTORNEY
- Qualified Elector
- Resident of the county in which elected during term of office

. . .

THEN SHE SKIPPED down to County Attorney.

COUNTY ATTORNEY
 • Member of the bar of Wyoming.

SHE READ on to District Attorney.

DISTRICT ATTORNEY
 • Licensed attorney for at least four years
 • Member in good standing of the Wyoming bar immediately prior to election.

SHE NODDED. So far so good, even for district attorney which wasn't the office she was considering since Sheridan had a county attorney, as long as she was a qualified elector. So, what the heck was that? She Googled it and pulled up the definition from the Wyoming statutes, mouthing the words as she read.

"QUALIFIED ELECTOR" includes every citizen of the United States who is a bona fide resident of Wyoming, has registered to vote and will be at least eighteen years of age on the day of the election at which he may offer to vote.
 Or she.
 No person is a qualified elector who is a currently adjudicated mentally incompetent person, or who has been convicted of a felony and his civil or voting rights have not been restored.

. . .

WITH THE QUALIFICATIONS HURDLE CLEARED, she had one obstacle to go. She looked up the filing deadlines for a Sheridan County office. Suddenly, she felt a flush of heat from her chest to her scalp and tips of her ears. Did she want the filing period to be open or closed? Did she *really* want to do this?

The page loaded on her laptop. She drummed her fingers. At the last second, she closed her eyes. Then she forced them open and read the words that would dictate her fate.

Filing was open through the end of May.

The closing was only days away. But it hadn't passed. There was still time.

Her mouth went dry. Now there was nothing standing in her way except paperwork... and making up her mind.

EIGHT

KID PULLED out his Airpods and snapped them into their case. "Greetings, senior attorney and sensei. How are you today?"

Jennifer felt guilty with the candidacy pages open, like she was cheating on her work husband. She opened a blank tab on her browser and flipped the filing application facedown, doing it slowly so as not to draw his attention. "Hello, Wesley. What was that about?"

"Oh, you know. Protecting our personal freedoms under the bill of rights. Keeping our democracy safe for the citizenry." He shrugged. "Different day, same story."

She raised her brows. "The unbearable weight of high minded-ness. However do you cope?"

"I have a great example to follow. How did the weekend go?"

She knew he was referring to their lodge guests and the wedding shower, but she filled him in on Victor's shocking death at the polo match. They discussed it for a few minutes, then she turned to a harder topic.

"There's something I want to tell you," she said.

"Oh?" His brows inched up at her tone.

She'd been engaged in a vigorous mental debate since Friday night about whether to share with Kid her ongoing nonversationship with the county attorney. She and Ollie had agreed to a clandestine arrangement, but she'd already taken significant unpaid time away from work that spring. Now she would be disappearing for hours at a time again. It was only right to bring Kid in on the secret.

She held up two fingers then put them across her heart. "I need your utmost discretion. One hundred percent hush hush. Absolute cone of silence."

"Is there such a word as tridundant?"

"I'm serious."

"Okay. For sure. Thanks for trusting me with something important." Kid's serious communication modus operandi. *Agree, Amplify, Appreciate.*

She closed her laptop and moved from her chair to sit on her desk, feet dangling. It was something she never could have done back in the days of form fitting skirts and heels at the Harris County District Attorney's office. "Ollie Singletary has asked me to coach him on a potential case."

Kid's already large green eyes rounded. "Whoa. I didn't see that coming."

"Nor did I. It may come to nothing. Or it may blow up. Suffice it to say that in the unlikely event the county decides that a particular death was a murder, I'll be conflicted out of the defense."

"Wha-at?"

"I can't explain why, in case you end up representing a potential defendant. I just need you to understand that you'd be solo with my blessing and that we'd need to institute a cone of silence policy around each of us. What they call a Chinese wall in the legal world."

"How would we do that?"

"I would work from home, and we wouldn't speak about our side of the cases, at all."

"What are the odds this will happen?"

She waffled her hand. "We'll know soon."

He gave her a searching look under furrowed brows. "Are you sure you want to dance with the devil again?"

Her stomach felt squirmy with guilt. "It will be okay. Ollie pitched a compelling public interest argument that I couldn't disagree with."

"Whatever you say, then."

Jennifer's phone rang with Aaron's special tone. They had an agreement to stick to texts during workdays unless something time sensitive and critical came up. "Gotta get this." She hopped off the desk.

"Okay. Back to work for me."

She walked out to the landing at the top of the steps. "Hi. What's up, my love?" The smell of honeysuckle wafted up to her. She closed her eyes and inhaled.

Aaron's breathing sounded like he was walking fast. "Just had a really weird ranch visit this morning with Nick." Woos rang out.

"Tell him hello for me. Where?" She put her hands on the railing. It felt secure.

Aaron spoke away from the mic. "Jenn says hey." Then his voice grew louder. "Half Circle Ranch." A vehicle door slammed. Then another. The woos intensified.

"What happened?"

An engine rumbled to life. Jennifer could picture her husband looking ruggedly handsome in his rough and tumble Jeepster, which smelled like dogs and whose interior was coated with slick malamute hair. Interestingly, although the dogs looked primarily black, their fur was mostly white with only black tips. It did not go unnoticed on upholstery.

"I think I was just solicited to dope a polo pony. I was asked to treat a horse for breathing problems that showed no signs of issues.

Bronchodilators are sometimes used on performance horses to improve their wind and make them run better. I suspect that is what they were trying to get me to prescribe."

"That's disturbing!"

"Peter Galindo is my usual contact. He's the one that called me out today."

"Yeah. The ranch manager."

"Well, he wasn't even there. My only interaction was with a new stable hand."

"Do you think he wanted deniability?"

"It's possible. Or to be able to chalk it up to my misunderstanding or just an overzealous new employee."

Jennifer tapped her lip with her pointer finger. "This is super fishy, especially right after we hear about possible illegal betting. Horse doping isn't a thing unless the stakes are high."

"That's what I'm worried about."

"Dang. The rumors may be true then."

"Or I may have misread the room."

"There's that." She pondered it a few more seconds. "Did anything come up about Victor or his horse?"

"No. But now I'm thinking I should suggest the county test Estrella's blood, too, if it isn't too late."

"I'll handle that. We saw Victor's collapse with our own eyes, though, and Estrella seemed fine."

Aaron sighed. "That doesn't mean she wasn't drugged. Not conclusively."

"Are you sure? Wouldn't you know if it was happening on the Strikers?"

"I want to think I would, but I can't be sure."

"What kind of drugs are you thinking she might have been given?"

"I don't really suspect anything specific. My hackles are just up."

She was pacing the small landing and shaking her head. "The weird part is that the rumor is that *Victor* was drugged. Not a horse."

"And if he was on anything, it was a sedative. A strong one and a lot of it."

"I feel like I need to tell Ollie about this. Are you okay with that?"

"Man, I don't want to get burned with Half Circle or Peter. Not to mention all the other outfits. No owners want me spilling their tea." Aaron groaned. "Fine. Can you at least keep the details and source confidential?"

"For now. But if Ollie subpoenas me... "

"Yeah. I get it."

"Thanks for telling me."

"Good luck with Ollie. See you at home, beautiful."

Jennifer ended the call and stood looking out on James's back-yard, thinking. Then she shot a quick text to Ollie. *I have something on drugging at polo ranches. I'll tell you at our meeting.* It was where she was headed soon to formalize their working relationship.

She walked back inside to her desk where her hand touched the county attorney form. She felt an electrical shock, or maybe it was her imagination. Was the shock telling her yes or no? If yes, she had time to drop it off with the county clerk on her way to Ollie's office. She waffled back and forth but decided to hold off filing for now. She still needed to talk to Aaron and tell Kid, too.

Plus, it would be professional courtesy to give Ollie a heads-up first, especially with their current working relationship. She wouldn't be able to look him in the eye without squirming only minutes after submitting her application to take his job.

NINE

SHERIDAN, Wyoming

AN HOUR LATER, Jennifer was working her way through take-out chicken Pad Thai across from the county attorney in his office. Ollie hadn't made any changes to the space since he'd been appointed to replace Pootie Carputin mid-term nearly a year earlier. Short-timer's syndrome? Or maybe he was afraid he'd jinx his chance of gaining the permanent job if he sunk in roots. The lack of personal touches made it hard to get a read on him, but she suspected that the ornate antiques and western landscape art weren't representative of the man in front of her. At least he'd taken Pootie's self-congratulatory array of celebrity handshake photographs off the walls.

Ollie wiped imaginary debris from his desk with a paper napkin even though he hadn't spilled an iota of his drunken noodles. Fastidious. It was a good word for him, including the way he practiced law and the way he dressed, favoring slim fit pants with button-down shirts. Short sleeves in the summer, long sleeves with sweaters in the fall. As a handsome black man with a premature sprinkling of white in his close-cropped beard—she'd checked his graduation dates and knew he was five years younger than her—his style looked good on him.

"I think the best way to handle our off-book visits is to hold them here in my office. It will attract attention if we meet at your office or out in public. Especially if we act sneaky or mysterious, which we won't be if we do it here. It's de rigor for defense attorneys to swing by these offices." He rolled the top of a paper bag closed and took his lunch detritus to the trash can. If he was trying to keep his office from smelling like a Thai kitchen after closing time, he was too late. "I'll just log it as one of the pending cases you and Kid are defending so it won't seem odd to Cheryl."

Jennifer was a big fan of Cheryl, his competitive and extremely likeable legal assistant. Earlier in the year, Casey had helped in Jennifer and Kid's office but that had imploded quickly. Jennifer had intended to lure Cheryl away from the county to work for her and Kid but then came her unexpected personal leave that spring. It was good timing to run lean as their income had lagged in Jennifer's absence. Who knew what the future held, though. If Jennifer ran against and beat Ollie, maybe she'd end up working with Cheryl in this very office. If not, she would revisit trying to hire her in the fall.

Jennifer wiped her eyes with her forearm. The cook had gone a little heavy on the peppers, and her sinuses were running and eyes watering. "Sounds fine to me."

Ollie pulled a document from a folder. "Look this over. It's our standard for our contract attorneys."

Jennifer pressed the lid half on her Pad Thai and began reading. While the contract was a bit one-sided in favor of the county, it was no different than she'd expected. In fact, it looked almost identical to what they'd used in Harris county. The rate was about what she would have asked for—a little less—but she wasn't doing this to get rich. The difference wasn't significant enough to quibble over. She signed and dated it and handed it back to him. He added his signature and date.

"I'll make a copy for you myself and have it for you on your next visit." Ollie steepled his fingers in front of his chin. "So, now that we're official, what did you have to tell me about Victor's death?"

That wasn't what she'd texted him. "I don't know anything about his death. I told you I have something on drugging at polo ranches."

"You have my full attention."

"I have a source that suspects one of the teams may be drugging their horses to improve performance. In this case, the team seemed to be trying to get bronchodilators."

He made a rolling motion with his hand. "And?"

"It's a drug that helps horses breathe better. It's sometimes abused with performance horses, to increase their wind."

"Okay. And how would that impact us in the death of a player? Are you saying Victor's horse was drugged?"

"There's no evidence his horse was drugged, but it might be wise to do a blood test on her, too." Ollie made a note. "It's relevant because I can't think of a compelling reason to drug a horse for performance enhancement that isn't financial. Maybe pride or sheer competitiveness, but those are far less likely than money. Money, like in betting."

"So?"

Jennifer was getting irritated. "You're the one who called me in the middle of the night because of rumors of drugs and underground betting."

"No, I mean and who was the tipster, what team, what horse?"

"The tipster has to remain anonymous because there's no proof."

"What good does it do me then?"

"It gives you a triangulating source on the betting and another reason to keep an eye on the league."

He scowled. "It doesn't feel like you're playing on my team here."

She barked a laugh. "I'm not. I'm a defense attorney who's *mentoring* you out of civic mindedness. Mentoring only. I wasn't retained to gather evidence or advocate. In fact, this arrangement with the county could cost me dearly."

"A county in which I am the head prosecutor, in case you've forgotten."

"Oh, I haven't forgotten. It's just that I owe you nothing."

"You do if you want to be paid."

"Au contraire. You're paying me for my time. At any moment I could decide to give you no more of it, and I wouldn't owe you a single minute more. And yet I just gave you something above and beyond. You're welcome."

"I can subpoena you, you know."

"Knock yourself out."

He growled softly. "I don't like it."

Her initial reticence about helping him reared its head again. She'd been right to resist this arrangement. No way was she putting herself on the line for condescension. She stood, giving him an inauthentic smile. "No skin off my nose. See you in court." She slung the strap of her handbag over her shoulder and headed for the door.

He spoke when her hand hit the doorknob. "Wait. You're right."

She held still, waiting as requested.

"I'm sorry."

She turned to him. "If you want friends to play with you, play nice, Ollie."

He rubbed the sides of his face with his hands. "We got results today."

"What results?"

"Blood test results. For Victor Carvalho."

"Why didn't you lead with this? I deserve to know whether his death was an accident, which would make my assistance no longer necessary."

"It's the reverse."

"That I don't deserve it?"

"No. That your assistance *is* necessary. Victor Carvalho was drugged. His death was murder."

TEN

Sheridan, Wyoming

AARON AND NICK finished up a ranch call east of town and drove with the windows down toward Sheridan. The breeze in Aaron's sweaty hair felt great and was cooling for the malamutes in the back. He had just called in to the clinic and confirmed no one else had called for a visit from him today. Good thing—he was beat. Large animal medicine was physically demanding even before factoring in driving a few hundred miles a day.

Nick turned to Aaron with a smile. "Not a lot of trees."

Aaron loved the stark beauty of the barren pumpkin buttes, but Nick wasn't wrong. He raised his eyebrows. "What, you don't see the state tree of Wyoming out there? We're passing one every few hundred feet."

"Huh?"

Now it was Aaron's turn to grin. "The esteemed telephone pole."

Nick laughed. "Ha!" After another few moments of silence he said, "Do you always do ranch calls for the big animals?"

"Sometimes ranchers bring their livestock in for a procedure, either to my home clinic or the main one in Sheridan. But I prefer visiting them."

"It seems like a lot of driving."

"It is. But it's better for the livestock and the rancher. A trailer ride is stressful on a sick or injured animal. The ranchers stockpile their vet issues, too. Sometimes I'm doctoring a herd. Each visit to my clinic can cost a rancher half a day or more of work. I schedule my calls by area which cuts down on wasted drive time. I charge extra for the visit, but not much. Enough to cover the gas, which they would have spent on their own travel to my clinic. I only handle the complex stuff, though. The easy cases they do themselves."

Nick chuckled. "I can't imagine treating our dogs ourselves. It's hard enough giving them pills."

"Well, vet care is pretty spendy for most of these folks. They're running businesses. They have to turn a profit to feed their families. I respect it. Most of them are pretty darn good at keeping their animals healthy."

Nick was nodding. "Makes sense."

"I've been trying to figure out ways to encourage them to call me more frequently so I can help them avoid disasters that could have been prevented. I don't charge them most times for a telephone call, and I'll even do video visits with them and the animal. I keep regular hours for it to make it easier for them to reach me."

"Is it working?"

"Change is slow, but I'm getting more calls. Which is good, because there are few things worse than an animal suffering needlessly."

"Animals and kids."

"Yes. Which is one of the reasons vets have a really high suicide rate."

"I've heard that, and honestly it surprises me. I would have thought people who become vets are working their dream jobs. Not like someone who does something soul crushing just to survive."

"Most vets do the job out of love for animals. Then they witness suffering day in and day out. Often people don't have the money for expensive treatments and surgeries to prolong their animals' lives or eliminate their suffering. Or opt out of the treatments, for whatever their reasons, and the vets have to honor that, knowing what the animals are going through."

"I hadn't thought of that."

"Vets are also called on to perform euthanasia on animals—with humans, we can't legally choose to end the lives of others even in the most extreme circumstances. And as a vet, sometimes we're asked to euthanize animals for the convenience of the owner. They got tired of pet ownership. They're moving. The pet became too expensive. They don't have the time, patience, skill, or desire to train it out of bad habits. They don't like it. So, they ask us to kill it for them."

"Jesus. Can you say no to those kinds of people?"

"Sure. Then you worry about what kind of neglect or abuse the animal will go through. Or what kind of death the owner will find for them. Hard to say which is worse."

"Shit." Nick raked his hand back through his hair, his expression horrified.

"The sheer volume of death can be overwhelming, too. Animals, especially house pets, have far shorter life spans than we do. Vets deal with a lot of sad goodbyes. Far more than the average person providing health care for humans."

"How do you handle it?"

"I'm one of the lucky ones, I guess. I've developed the ability to offer empathy without internalizing the endless grief. It's tough otherwise."

"I don't know if I could do your job. I'm liking private investigation a whole lot right now, even if sometimes the subjects do try to kill me."

They were nearing the city limits. Aaron glanced at the clock on his dash. It was only three. "Is it okay with you if we drop by the clinic in town?" There were always things to sign and questions to answer.

"Of course. I came with no expectations. Today has been fascinating."

"Great. Thanks."

They arrived five minutes later, and Aaron parked near the side door. He would be bringing Willett and Sibley into the office, which meant avoiding the reception area. Willett wanted to initiate physical play dates, and introverted Sibley played by "a good offense is the best defense" when she felt threatened by other dogs or people.

The clinic practice manager Loretta saw them as they entered. The woman looked as bleak as a Wyoming winter and as leathery as a pair of chaps. Her lips straightened from a downturn to a flat line at the sight of him. She dabbed watery eyes with a Kleenex. "Hello, Doctor H. You aren't on the schedule for today."

Willett abandoned good manners and went for a crotch sniff that Loretta quelled with a hard look. The dog dropped to her back and showed her belly. Loretta bent down and scratched it. She grunted at Sibley. Sibley glowed as if Loretta had cooed and sidled up to her for some loving.

Aaron grinned. How he'd grown to depend on and love this woman. "Is that good or bad?"

She ignored his question. "Game and Fish wants an update on the badger."

"Can you tell them I'd like to keep him a few more days?"

"Okay. Can we talk?"

"About?"

Her eyes darted up and down the hall. She slung her chin at his office, then looked pointedly at Nick.

Mysterious.

Nick caught the vibe. "Do you mind if I go back out to your Jeep—"

"Demarcus Ware."

"To Demarcus Ware to make a few phone calls?"

Aaron nodded. "It's unlocked. I shouldn't be long."

"See you in a few." Nick pushed the door and disappeared into a rectangle of golden sunlight.

Aaron and Loretta ducked into his office. The dogs flopped on their beds, and Aaron took a seat. Loretta shut the door and remained standing. Aaron couldn't help admiring how organized and clean the space looked. That was partly because he spent more time on the road or in his home clinic than here. The home clinic was Spartan, since he'd decorated this office with his special items. Diplomas and a photo tryptic of him playing high school quarterback, dancing in the end zone after a college touchdown with Jenn in the background in her cheerleading uniform and leaping high in the air to make his first catch in the NFL. Recently he'd added a picture of him celebrating the Rams state championship with the boys and Coach Flint last season. Jenn had framed it and given it to him as a Christmas present.

His foot knocked into the trash can that had somehow ended up under his desk. He pulled it out where it belonged, bringing an unpleasant odor with it. Inside were bulging fast food wrappers and two empty fountain drink cups. Not his. *Who's been eating my porridge?* he wondered. *Probably Casey.* He'd have to talk to her about that. He needed his office to be off limits to staff. All staff. And at work, she was staff, not his daughter.

"That was my friend Nick," Aaron said. "He's staying with Jenn and me, and he tagged along for my ranch calls."

Loretta stared at him without responding.

"Is something wrong?" he asked.

"We've got drugs gone missing."

He rolled his neck. That was definitely bad news. "Significant enough for concern?"

She raised her brows at him.

"Dumb question or you wouldn't be standing here. Okay. I will also assume you did the inventory yourself and triple checked it. I'll skip to what's missing, how much, is this the first time, and whether you have any idea who took it or where it went?"

She rewarded him with a nod of approval and held up one finger. "Xylazine."

He drew in a sharp breath. Xylazine was a powerful sedative. In addition to sedation, it brought on muscle relation and respiratory depression. Used correctly, it was an effective analgesic AKA pain reliever and could be used to induce vomiting in cats. Their clinic relied on it regularly, sometimes in combination with ketamine as a pre-anesthetic when they needed to intubate an animal.

Loretta lifted a second finger. "Half our stock." Third finger. "This is the first time it has happened to my knowledge." Her pinky finger rose. It was crooked, which Aaron hadn't noticed before. He wondered how she'd broken it and why it had healed badly. "Only you and I and Doctor Sarah have keys to the cabinet for the dangerous drugs. I open it each time we use it, or one of you do."

Dr. Sarah Friedman was their new small animal vet. "I log what I use."

"As do I. I'd like to put a camera on the cabinet."

He nodded. "Good idea. Should we announce it to the staff? It might act as a deterrent. In the end, what matters most is preventing it from happening again."

She narrowed her eyes. "If someone's stealing drugs, they're a thief. A criminal. I don't think it's safe for the rest of us to be working with someone like that. Plus, we have liability. We need to catch them and turn them over to the authorities."

"You're right." He sighed and felt his forehead scrunch up. "I don't get it, though. It doesn't seem like a great drug to abuse." Opioid abuse was so rampant that Aaron didn't stock any except fentanyl patches, and very few of those. If a patient needed a drug like fentanyl, he prescribed the minimum dose with no refills and made the owner pick it up at a pharmacy. He didn't need the risk, not of human abuse or break-ins by desperate addicts. He'd have to research human use of xylazine. The idea of abusing it was new to him, but it was a possibility.

"Could be for resale. Or a side hustle."

"I guess so." He hated to think one of his employees was stealing from him, whatever the reason. Even more that the new vet he needed to rely on had access and might be behind it. "Well, we have to get to the bottom of this, then. I'll talk to Sarah and let you know what next steps we need to take. If any."

But he had a very bad feeling in the pit of his stomach. This felt dangerously significant. He prayed he wouldn't find out he was right.

ELEVEN

SHERIDAN, Wyoming

"WHOA! When were you planning on telling me?" Jennifer lasered Ollie with a glare, but her mind was fixated on what he'd told her. *Murder. We all just watched the murder of Victor Carvalho right in front of us on that polo field.* It was surreal.

"I got a call from the forensic pathologist right before you came."

And she'd been in his office for half an hour. But she moved on. "Not the normal medical examiner?" The county ME was an elected official and often a mortician by trade, as they were in an ideal position to review cause of death upon receipt of a body to their funeral home. A forensic pathologist was expensive and only utilized in unusual situations, although they had one who covered several contiguous counties.

"This has the potential to be high profile. I thought it would be prudent."

Jennifer took a breath, thinking. Final, detailed toxicology tests could take weeks. There was no way that report was back. "And he said it was murder? Conclusively?"

"You know that isn't how it works. He gave me information from which I was able to conclude we have a murder on our hands."

"Back up. Back up. Start with actual information."

"You don't trust me?"

She gave one short laugh. "You're normally my opponent. Nothing about our relationship up until now has been based upon developing mutual trust. Besides, I was a prosecutor. I know how a prosecutor thinks and how they approach a set of facts. After nine months on the defense side, I've begun to see there may be a prosecutorial predisposition to view human actions through a certain lens."

"What lens is that?"

"That everything is a crime unless proven not to be."

"That's ridiculous."

"Exaggerated, but directionally sound. It's the precursor to the state's opening statement and closing argument. The prosecutor's theory is predicated on the act itself being a crime. The human who gets slotted into that worldview is thus a criminal and everything they do becomes evidence supporting the theory."

"That's... that's... bull—"

"Advocacy. Zealous advocacy. I'm not accusing you of being a bad person, just a prosecutor. And that's why I take your conclusions as opinion, and why I need to go back to the facts to be of any help in this case. My judgment must be independent of yours if I'm going to keep you from wasting taxpayer dollars and making a fool of yourself."

Ollie's eyes had narrowed to slits. She could almost see puffs of steam coming from his nostrils. Okay, that was her imagination, but if he was a bull, he would have charged. She gave him a minute. Finally, he released a shuddering sigh. "Fine. Victor Carvalho was a healthy, well-nourished, fit man with youth on his side and many healed broken bones. He had no hidden health issues. His brain showed no signs of traumatic damage, despite his occupation. He hadn't had a stroke or a heart attack. He went limp, fell off, and got stomped to death."

She cocked her head. "And?"

"And without any medical reason why he lost consciousness, we have to look at other causes."

"Like dehydration, you mean? Or sunstroke?"

He held up a hand. "I asked about those. And many others. He showed no signs of dehydration. It wasn't hot out."

"But it was sunny."

"The match had just started. He had barely been exposed to the sun."

"You know how intense the sunlight can be at 4500 feet."

Ollie stood up and put his hands behind his back, pacing the room. "I hear you. But his initial drug test came back positive for sedatives."

"Which sedative?"

"That we don't know. They have to do more tests. But the point remains he was under the influence."

"And the fact remains that he could have self-administered."

"A competitive polo player? Before a match? No way he's taking sedatives."

"An assumption."

"I grant you that it's not as clear cut as a murder with a weapon. But Victor's symptoms are one hundred percent consistent with being under the influence of a sedative in a highly dangerous situation. That makes it overwhelmingly unlikely he wouldn't have taken it himself."

"Accidental consumption remains a possibility, too."

Ollie sighed. "Jennifer, come on."

"It's true."

"Fine. But that doesn't change that we have to pursue this as a murder while evidence is fresh. If other evidence or the toxicology report rule it out later, so be it."

"I don't disagree completely, but I do think you should move with caution. Reputations and lives are hard to restore."

"You're the one who came to me today with talk about drugging."

She waffled her hand. "Of horses with bronchodilators. Not people with sedatives. What possible good would sedating a jockey do?"

"Are you kidding me? The star player of the best team loses his edge? That benefits the opponent. Or anyone who benefits from the opponent beating the Strikers. Like people who bet against them."

It wasn't *not* true. And his theory did come back upon Half Circle and the Hellcats. If they were potentially willing to use bronchodilators on their horses, they might be willing to engage in other dirty tricks. But moving from a horse to a human was a big leap. And that's if Aaron wasn't wrong about them soliciting drugs in the first place.

She raked her bottom lip with her teeth. "Okay. But what you describe would be manslaughter. Not murder."

"We'll see what the evidence shows."

Jennifer felt like the wheels on the bus were spinning too fast and they were careening toward a crash. If she was defending this case and was privy to this conversation, she'd cite it as evidence that the prosecution fixated on one theory to the exclusion of all others. If—*if*—Victor hadn't died by accident, even if there was illegal betting and drugging going on, that still ignored a host of other possibilities.

But she wasn't defending this case. She was coaching the prosecutor. And when she'd sat in Ollie's chair, hadn't she pursued theories sequentially instead of like a spray of buckshot? There had never been the manpower to do everything at once, never the governmental budget. It had been necessary to pursue the best theory until it fell apart, then chase after the next best and repeat as needed until a suspect was convicted.

Could it be handled better than how she'd done it before? How Ollie was handling doing it now? *I think so, and I believe I can.*

Her purse seemed to glow from the floor, radioactive with the application to submit for the primary election inside it. And just like that, she decided she was submitting her application for county attorney ASAP. Also, that she felt no obligation to let Ollie know first. Not with the way he'd threatened her and tried to manipulate her today. He'd shown no professional courtesy. She owed him none back.

First there was the matter of following the evidence in this case to attend to, though. "Where do you want to start?"

He wheeled to face her, eyes gleaming. "With the Half Circle Hellcats. And anyone else who benefitted if they beat the Strikers."

TWELVE

Sheridan, Wyoming

AARON HEARD a soft knock on his office door. He swallowed his black coffee, which made his answer a split second slow in coming. The stuff smelled burned. It drove him crazy when people left the burner on under the pot. He lived for good coffee on Wednesdays because of early surgeries, which made it the hardest day of his week. "Yes?"

The door creaked open. It had only been partially closed. "You want to see me?" Sarah Friedman stepped inside, all six foot one inches of her. The two of them had bonded over college athletics during her interview, although her sport had been volleyball. Jennifer liked her, too, and they'd been trying to get Sarah and her husband to go to dinner with them since she'd started, but, so far, their schedules hadn't lined up. Sarah smoothed the long black braid that hung in front of her shoulder.

"Yes, please come in."

"Do you want me to close the door?"

"That would be great. Thanks."

Sarah navigated around an empty animal carrier and two cozy malamutes on their beds to take a seat. They'd greeted her earlier that morning and didn't rouse themselves to do it again. "Is there a varmint loose in here?"

He laughed. "No. The carrier is left from releasing some prairie dogs last month. Game and Fish forgot to take it with them."

"Cool." She glanced at her smart watch. "I've got a by-request patient soon. A Chihuahua I first met in Colorado. Her owner thinks I'm her personal vet."

"Oh? Who is it?"

"Veronica Farinolo."

"Jennifer and I were with her last Friday, when her future son-in-law was killed in that polo match."

Sarah squinted and scraped her upper lip with her lower teeth. "Oh. Wow."

"Yeah. Bad stuff. Anyway, I don't think this will take long. But it needs to be kept strictly between us."

"Sounds ominous."

Aaron searched for the right words. He'd researched human use of xylazine and discovered that increasingly it was being combined with opioids for a potentially lethal combination. It made him sick that someone out there might be harming themselves or others with drugs from his clinic.

In his hesitation, she blanched. "Oh, shit. It is ominous."

He lifted his shoulders and let them drop. He hated interpersonal conflict, and that's what this felt like. "There's a discrepancy between our inventory and our drugs on hand. I wanted to see if you'd inadvertently used something without logging it. I know it's a new system to you."

She frowned. "It's not hard. I log everything. I'm used to it from my old job. What drug is missing?"

As much as he liked Sarah, she was new. An employee, not a partner in the practice. She'd passed her background check, but that didn't mean past employers hadn't withheld information. His instincts told him not to bring her into his confidence yet. "When we've finished looking into it and tracked down where it went, I'll let you know. For now, I want you to review your procedures for the last two weeks and compare what you used to what was logged. And think about whether you've seen anything that seemed off with respect to drug usage or logging."

"Okay." Her head tilted. Her eyes swept to the floor. Her lips pursed. Then she looked up and shook her head. "No one's done anything odd around me. I'm not sure if they'd talk openly in front of me, though. It seems like maybe I'm slow to grow on them."

Aaron smiled at her. "If by staff you mean Loretta, I haven't grown on her much yet either."

Sarah laughed, but it was a tight, nervous sound. "Phew. I'm glad it's not just me."

"Back to the topic at hand for a minute. Have your keys to the medicine storage area ever been out of your possession?"

"I keep them in my purse, which I keep on a peg in the office. I can't swear no one got to them." She sucked in a breath. "I'm sorry."

"It's okay. We just need to figure out how it happened so we can keep it from reoccurring."

"We had lockers in Fort Collins. That way all the staff felt safer from patients, each other, and break-ins."

"That's a good idea."

"Would you like me to look into it?"

"I'll turn it over to Loretta. If she thinks it's a good idea, I'll give you credit. If she hates it, I'll tell her it's mine."

She smiled. "Thanks."

"One more question. Have you ever gone to unlock the medicine area and found it already open?"

She shook her head. "Never."

"Okay. I'd appreciate it if you remember to keep this to yourself. If someone stole the drugs, I don't want to spook them before we can deal with it. This is serious."

"So, it's safe to say it's not diphenhydramine or Pepcid," she said, giving the medical name for Benadryl.

"Correct."

"Have you thought about asking other clinics whether they're having issues?"

"It's a good idea if we can't identify it in-house."

She stood. "I'll keep my eyes and ears open. And I'll let you know if I find anything when I review my work the last two weeks against what I've logged."

"Thanks." He half-rose and offered his hand.

They shook and she left.

His phone intercom buzzed. "Dr. Herrington."

"Aaron, it's Casey. Donny Flanders called. They have an emergency out at Red Grade Ranch. A car wrecked into their horse fence. A few of the polo ponies got out. One was hit by another vehicle. A second one is caught in the wire. It sounds bad."

He hated it when she called him Aaron, but what she'd said was too important to get into that subject again. "On may way."

"Do you need me to come with you?"

"Yes."

"See you at Demarcus Ware."

Aaron ran through a mental checklist of everything he might need. He kept the Jeepster stocked but stopped to grab more antibiotics and vet wrap and to make sure he had what he needed to put a horse down if necessary. Donny would have supplies, too. Then he ran to his vehicle, praying it wasn't poor Estrella.

THIRTEEN

Sheridan, Wyoming

JENNIFER HAD BARELY PUT her Grand Cherokee in park in the lot across from the county attorney's office when her mobile phone started ringing. She was tempted to let it go to voicemail. She'd just come from the county clerk's office, where bright and early on this Wednesday morning, she'd submitted candidacy forms for the party nomination for county attorney, along with the fee. She'd of course submitted for the prevalent party. She stood no chance of winning the general election if she ran outside that party, even for the other major party.

No one knew besides her, yet. Well, her and the clerk who'd taken her submission. Not even Aaron, which Jennifer felt horrible about, although to her it wasn't officially official yet. She'd wanted to talk to him the night before, but their guests had been chatty and rowdy, and by the time they'd gone into the bedroom, exhausted, she'd forgotten about it. That was okay, though. Submitting saved her spot, but she could still withdraw. That gave her and Aaron time to talk it over and weigh out their options, even if they didn't get around to it for a few more days. And by options she meant competing demands on her time, like their marriage, her desire to find the school shooter who lived in her nightmares, her writing, her practice, and whether they were going to try again for a baby.

And then there was Kid. She would come clean with him, just as soon as she squared things with Aaron.

The call went to her voicemail. It was a Montana number. Maybe they'd leave a message.

She jaywalked across the street, earning her a honk from a dilapidated pickup spewing noxious exhaust. She waved and trotted the rest of the way, then hurried up the steps. It had taken longer at the clerk's office than she'd expected. She hadn't planned to start her day with Ollie, but he had called and asked her to come as soon as she could for an update on law enforcement progress with the Hellcats.

Inside, Cheryl smiled at her and shook her head. "He's on the phone."

"Ollie called earlier for me to come by and meet with him."

"I know. I'll let you know soon as he's off."

Jennifer checked her phone. The Montana number had left a voicemail. She walked to the furthest corner of the reception area and put the phone to her ear. "Mrs. Herrington, this is Shaina Tyson. I'm calling to confirm our appointment Saturday. I'll text you as well. You can respond however you'd like." The hypnotherapist. Shaina's message continued. She listed a few dos and don'ts for Jennifer's preparation. Butterflies took flight in Jennifer's stomach. Was she really going to go through with this? She saw that the text had come in.

Reply YES to confirm your appointment with Shaina Tyson or NO to cancel.

She took a shuddering breath. Her thumbs flew. YES. She hit send.

Cheryl said, "Mrs. Herrington? Ollie is ready to see you now."

"Please, call me Jennifer." It wasn't the first time Jennifer had asked Cheryl to call her by her first name.

"Jennifer." It wasn't the first time Cheryl had *said* she would call Jennifer by her first name, either.

Jennifer pocketed her phone and made her way back to Ollie's office.

As she neared the door, Ollie said, "Come in."

She made a beeline for the chair.

He didn't look up as he continued typing, eyes glued to his monitor. "Don't sit. This will be short."

She felt the frown taking over her face. "Excuse me? You called me in for an update."

He lifted cold eyes to her. "Something has come up. Meeting's canceled."

"Could you not have called me to tell me that?"

"Only if I'd known earlier."

"When do you want to reschedule?"

"I don't know yet. You'll hear from Cheryl."

From *Cheryl*? Ollie always called her directly. "Is there something wrong, Ollie?"

His eyes narrowed. "Should there be?"

"No. But..." She let her words trail off. Debating his demeanor was pointless. "Never mind."

He turned his attention back to his laptop.

She stood there for a few seconds, waiting. When he didn't acknowledge her presence or say goodbye, she gave an exaggerated huff, turned, and walked briskly out. Whatever was wrong with him, he didn't have to be so dismissive. He'd asked for her help. She'd given it.

Whatever. If he thought she was going to jump next time he called, he had another think coming. And one hell of an apology to make.

FOURTEEN

Big Horn, Wyoming

JENNIFER WALKED down the lodge's back porch steps holding a casserole dish with hands encased in bandana print oven mitts. The dogs were milling around her with their noses in the air. "These pinto beans have been cooking all day. It's my mother's recipe with bacon and green onions."

She placed it on the picnic table beside the barbecue brisket George had smoked for them and the store-bought rolls, coleslaw, and potato salad she'd picked up on the way home from the office. She never claimed to be a domestic goddess, but she was proud she'd contributed something made with her own hands.

"Smells delicious," Collin said as he squeezed Ava's shoulders. Jennifer did a mental review of all she'd learned about him. *Katie's brother, Ava's man, father of their little boy, stepfather to their little girl, former cop who runs security for Ava. And a very funny guy.* Ava she needed no mental review for. The whole world knew her.

Aaron set down a tray of condiments and other sundries. Then he took the malamutes to their dog runs with two large, meaty bones George had picked up from the butcher. Jennifer poured iced tea into Solo cups, to go with the Blacktooth Brewing beer most of the guests were already drinking. When Aaron returned, he and Jennifer took seats at one end of the table.

"To our hosts!" Katie raised her cup.

The others raised theirs and toasted Jennifer and Aaron.

"We are delighted to have you all here," Aaron said.

People began serving plates, including George who made one to-go, insisting that he needed to turn in early after a hard day. Their guests were talking excitedly about their day hiking some of the lower mountain trails.

"We run into snow and have to turn back." Rashidi ladled several scoops of beans onto his plate. Jennifer would be doing the same. Vegetarians in Wyoming had limited options compared to more urban areas. Then she checked her Rashidi knowledge. *Michele's fiancé, adult step kids, aquaponics expert from the USVI living in Texas.* She gave herself a mental back pat.

Jennifer listened to the chatter with one ear and a smile on her face as she ate. Inside, though, she was rehearsing telling Aaron she'd submitted her paperwork for county attorney. She'd wanted to do it after work, but he'd been tied up with an equine emergency, arriving home only a few minutes ago. She shivered, less from the mountain crispness in the air than from nerves.

Aaron put his lips to her ear. "Earth to Jenn."

She gave herself a shake. "Sorry."

"You were a million miles away. What were you thinking about?"

She paused. "My meeting with Ollie. Working with him isn't going very well."

Aaron kept his voice low. The eating, laughter, and conversation kept flowing around them. "Why?"

"He's very dismissive and secretive. It's no fun. And I can't help him if he doesn't let me in."

"What's his problem?" Aaron took a rather large bite of his brisket. He'd served himself his share plus Jennifer's and then some.

"I don't know. He summoned me to his office to update me about progress looking into the Hellcats. You know, on doping and betting."

Aaron wiped his mouth. "Man, I hope that doesn't come back on me."

"I can't see why it would. I didn't give Ollie your name or even identify Half Circle Ranch. Anyway, when I got to his office, he canceled. Why couldn't he have just called and saved me the trip?"

"Jerk move."

"Yeah. It was."

"Maybe he has an excuse, though, if you give him a chance to explain."

She should. She might. "Unrelated, I'm having coffee with Veronica Farinolo tomorrow to talk over some potential legal work." Something she'd forgotten to tell him in the chaos following Victor's death and the onslaught of guests.

He made an O with his mouth. "Look at you, rainmaker."

"Hardly. How are the horses doing?" She finished up the last bite on her plate. The beans were amazing if she did say so herself.

"We had to put one down. We operated on the other one. I'm optimistic he'll survive, but his polo days are over. I'm just glad Estrella wasn't involved."

"What a traumatic week for the Strikers and the Farinolos."

"It really has been. The drivers took off, too. The one who hit the fence and the one who hit the horse."

"Did anyone get a plate number?"

"Not even a description of either vehicle or the drivers."

Behind them, Casey's shrill voice cut through the happy voices. "What's this?"

Aaron turned. "There are. We're doing dinner outside tonight. Grab a plate."

"It would have been nice to be invited to a party at *our* house." Casey threw Jennifer a dirty look.

He smiled at her. "It's not a party. We have a lot of guests at the lodge, and everyone has to eat. We're just enjoying the outdoors while we do it."

She looked away, toward the side of the lodge. "I have plans."

"Something fun?"

"A date."

"Anyone I know?"

She lifted one shoulder and let it drop. "Just a guy."

"Before you go, can I introduce you to our new friends?"

"Why? Will I ever see them again?" She held up her phone to read something on it.

"I'm not sure."

"No thanks. My date's here." She tossed her hair over her shoulder and sauntered away toward the front of the lodge.

Aaron looked down at his food.

Jennifer couldn't wait for the results of the DNA test. She'd collected hair from Casey's brush the night before and bagged it. Same with Aaron. All she had to do was send them off.

Jennifer nudged him now. "You didn't do anything wrong. Don't let her put a damper on your evening."

He sighed. "You're right. I should have thought of telling her about this earlier, though."

"She rarely eats with us, even though she has an open invitation. This is just dinner, not a party. It's okay."

He took a deep breath and nodded. Picking up his fork and knife, he sawed off some brisket and popped it in his mouth.

At the other end of the table, Emily said, "Jack and I saw your badger today, Aaron."

Aaron swallowed and lit up. "Isn't he a pistol? He's not my badger, though. He belongs to the state of Wyoming like all our wildlife."

"What happened to him?"

"He was injured in a trap."

For the next fifteen minutes, Aaron regaled the group with stories about his wild animal practice. Jennifer brought out dessert and turned on the twinkle lights. She found herself observing more than participating. Tiredness lapped at her. She'd enjoyed meeting all of Maggie's friends and now considered them her own, but she'd still be happy for recharge time when their week was up.

Movement caught her eye, and she turned to see three deputies approaching in a V-formation, like a flock of Canada geese. Her heart went to her throat. Her first thought was that something bad had happened to Casey. Her second thought was that Casey had done something bad. *I can't even remember what life was like before she brought her trouble into it.*

Deputy Travis Spahn was at the point of the V. He walked up and put a hand on Aaron's shoulder.

Aaron spun. He grinned and stood, not clocking that the unannounced arrival of law enforcement was never social. He and Travis were friends. "Travis. I mean, Deputy. Good to see you. What brings you out? Would you and the deputies like some barbecue? We have plenty left."

Every head at the table swiveled toward the officers.

Jennifer had a third, belated thought. They were here for Aaron. *But that makes no sense.*

Travis stared at Aaron with impassive eyes. He kept his volume low and his tone firm as he said, "Aaron Herrington, you're under arrest."

FIFTEEN

Big Horn, Wyoming

JERRY SLAMMED the door on his black Maserati. At the door to Benjy Mahone's house, he paused to smooth his shirtfront. He pressed the bell. Then did it again. And again. And again, as fast as he could. The repeating chime was loud and grating. *Good.* He ground his teeth and took a small pleasure in giving the property a once-over. He'd known Benjy since their prep school days. They'd been keeping score since the day they met. Red Grade Ranch had an airstrip. Half Circle did not. Jerry's home was bigger, newer, and more expensive than this one, with a better view. *Brick. Really?* Who built with that in Big Horn? And it was a dated brown brick at that.

A full minute later, the door opened. A curvy woman with waves of shimmering black hair opened the door. Even if his eyes had been closed, he would have known every detail of Ginger Mahones's face from her scent alone. Fruity, spicey, earthy. She still made his heart race, thirty years later.

Ginger frowned. "What is it, Jerry?"

"Where's Benjy?" he said, keeping his voice as calm as he could.

"He's out. Can I do something for you?"

Turn back time. Erase history. Choose me. "You can pass a message to him."

"You know I'm hopeless with things like that. Don't you want to leave him a voicemail or send an email?"

"No." He glared at her, steeling himself to stay righteously angry in her presence. "Today someone killed one of my horses and ruined another."

She reached for his arm. "I'm so sorry!"

He held up a hand for her to stop, and she pulled back. "This isn't the first time the Strikers have been victims of *sabotage.*"

"That's terrible. And quite frightening." She put a hand over her heart. "Are you quite sure it's sabotage?"

"Tell your husband that if I find out he's been meddling with my team, I'll make what happened to us today look like benevolence."

"Benjy's not like that. He would never. I mean, he used to hold a grudge against you, but he's over it."

"Really? Are we talking about the same guy?"

"He had reason. But that's ancient history."

"I suppose he wouldn't interfere just like he would never cheat."

"What do you mean?"

"The same thing I meant last week when I came to talk to him about the cheating."

Her jaw dropped the tiniest bit.

He didn't tell her. The thought made him happy. "I told him then that he has to stop. Looks like instead of stopping, he upped the ante."

She rose up, seeming an inch taller and ten times more emotional than she'd been since he arrived. "That's preposterous." Then her voice gentled, and her eyes grew soft. Sympathetic. "You really need to let things go. This isn't good for either of you."

Jerry clenched his fists. He didn't need her pity. "Preposterous, huh? You just keep telling yourself that about Mr. Perfect. In the meantime, ask him if he's gonna like how it feels."

"What do you mean?"

Without another word, he turned on his heel and stomped to the car. The tires squealed as he accelerated out of the driveway to go make a long overdue phone call.

SIXTEEN

Big Horn, Wyoming

JENNIFER FELT the weight of their friends' eyes upon Aaron. Their confusion mirrored hers. Her confusion and embarrassment for Aaron. She wanted to jump between him and their guests, to protect him from witnesses to this surreal humiliation. *Why is this happening? It has to be a mistake.*

Then she snapped into defense attorney mode. The next few moments were critical. Emotions were a luxury she couldn't afford. "What's this for, Travis?"

Travis held up a pair of handcuffs. "Turn around please, Mr. Herrington."

Aaron looked stunned, but he turned around without saying a word. Travis reached for one of his wrists.

Jennifer stepped so close she was nearly between the two men. She kept her voice low but diamond hard. "Uh uh. He's not resisting. No cuffs."

"Move, please, Mrs. Herrington. I'm just following procedure."

Since when are we Mr. and Mrs. Herrington to him? Her words came out as a hiss. "Can we at least do this in front of the house and not in front of lodge guests?"

"We would have, but no one answered the door when we rang the bell. Multiple times." He snapped an old-school metal handcuff closed around Aaron's large wrist.

Jennifer had never had bad blood with Travis. Neither had Aaron. Not to her knowledge, anyway, even when she'd represented people accused of crimes in the county, people he'd investigated and arrested. Whatever this was about, it had to be serious to warrant cuffs, the stiff-arm treatment, and his total disregard of making a spectacle of Aaron in front of their guests. And if it was serious, she didn't want Travis to say anything else here in the backyard. She'd wait until they were out of earshot to ask her questions.

Travis finished cuffing Aaron and took him by the arm. "Let's go."

Aaron complied, but as he turned he caught her eye. His brow was deeply furrowed. He mouthed *What's going on?*

She gave him a quick shake of her head. *I don't know.*

The two other deputies—Haigle and another man whose name she didn't know—waited for Travis and Aaron to pass, then fell in behind them.

Jennifer turned to their guests. "I'm so sorry. Whatever this is, we'll straighten it out quickly. Please excuse me."

"Can we help?" Emily asked.

Jack rose to his feet. "Sometimes when it's personal, it's good to let someone outside the situation help. Can I come with you?"

It was true, she was taking this extremely personally. *And he's a criminal defense attorney.* "Yes, thanks. But we have to hurry."

Michele swept her hand to indicate the table. "We've got everything here. The food. The dogs. Just go."

Jennifer nodded, her vision blurry with wetness for a moment. *Do not give in to tears. Not yet.* "Thank you, all."

Jack touched her elbow and the two of them started walking along the back of the lodge. "Do you want to do the talking?"

"Not exclusively. But jump in when you think it helps," she said.

As they rounded the corner, they broke into a jog. They reached the first sheriff's department truck at the same time as the law enforcement officers and Aaron did.

Travis started giving the Miranda warning to Aaron before Jennifer could speak. She didn't interrupt but stood poised to jump in with her questions as soon as he finished.

"Good evening, Jenn."

The hair rose on her arms. She looked toward the voice. It was Ollie, standing in front of a black Ford Explorer that was out of the radius of the porch lights at the front of the lodge.

She took a step toward him, hands on her hips. The smell of cigar smoke and bourbon hung in the air around him. "What are you doing here, Ollie?"

He nodded at Jack. "Who's this?"

Jack held out his hand. "Jack Holden. I'm a friend of the Herringtons and a criminal defense attorney." He left out the part about "not based in Wyoming," but it was irrelevant in the current circumstances.

Ollie shook hands with him, although it looked grudging. "Ollie Singletary. I'm the county attorney."

"What are you doing here?" Jennifer repeated, enunciating each word crisply.

"You know how it goes from your days as a prosecutor. You come in person for the big cases, to make sure they're handled correctly from the beginning."

"What big case are you talking about?"

Travis had finished the Miranda warning and Aaron said, "I understand the rights as they've been explained to me, but what am I under arrest for? Don't you have to tell me?"

"Yes," Jennifer said. "Yes, they do."

Travis was nodding, but Ollie said, "Let me do the honors." He smiled at Aaron. "You're being arrested for murder."

"What?" Aaron said.

"What?" Jennifer shrieked. "Murder of whom, Ollie? And on what grounds?"

Jennifer desperately wanted to lunge at the county attorney and strangle him. Jack put an arm in front of her. Clearly, he could read a room.

"We're not obligated to provide information about the specifics of the offense. You know that, Jennifer," Ollie said.

"Are you out of your mind? After I spent the last few days working to help you, you don't even give me the courtesy of a phone call? I could have brought Aaron in to avoid—" she waved her hand in the air, "this." She suddenly had one hundred percent clarity. She wanted to run against Ollie for county attorney. Run against him and annihilate him.

Ollie gave a derisive snort. "The county thanks you for your service."

Jack's arm went up again.

"This is crazy. Crazy! Aaron has been with us all evening. When is he supposed to have killed someone? Who? How? *Why?*"

Jack cleared his throat. "Can you please tell us who Dr. Herrington is accused of murdering?"

Travis took Aaron to the rear door of a truck. One of the deputies opened it. Travis guided Aaron into the seat and slammed the door.

Ollie said, "I'm only going to speak to the attorney representing Aaron."

"That's *me*, Ollie," Jennifer snapped.

Ollie crossed his arms over his chest. "Uh—no, you're not. You have a conflict of interest."

"That's rich. I think I can represent my own husband."

"Not in this case you can't. The State of Wyoming won't be waiving its conflict."

Jennifer's knees felt wobbly. Her vision blurred. *This can't be happening.*

"What do you mean?" Jack asked.

"She knows," Ollie said. "Ask her."

SEVENTEEN

Sheridan, Wyoming

JENNIFER PACED THE OFFICE FLOOR, gesticulating like a mental patient in the middle of a paranoid delusion. *Except this is real. They took my husband. They're locking him up.* "The only case I've discussed under retainer with Ollie is the death of Victor Carvalho. That's the one they can claim conflict of interest on."

It was only five a.m. Too early to be at the office on a Thursday morning. She'd been up all night, spending half of it at the jail trying and failing to see Aaron. The rest of the time she was raging at home. Pounding pillows and screaming into them, mindful of their house full of sleeping guests. Guests who had just witnessed Aaron being arrested for murder. Her husband. Her gentle, kind, ethical husband labeled a killer in front of them. Did they wonder if he was guilty? Had they whispered to each other in the dark, questioning whether they'd been safe sleeping in the same house as him? No wonder she was paranoid. The situation was insane.

Jack was planted in Jennifer's chair, hands steepled under his chin, eyes alert but puffy.

Kid leaned back in his chair, rubbing his eyes. "Did you know Aaron was even a suspect?"

"No. But Ollie started freezing me out yesterday. I guess I know why, now."

"What had you guys been talking about?"

Jack shook his head. "Stop right there. She can't disclose anything about those conversations to anyone, especially you. You're the first person they'd suspect her of telling."

"But I don't even represent Aaron."

Jennifer was nodding in agreement with Jack. "Remember, there has to be a Chinese wall between us with respect to my work for the county." She'd had always liked the expression, visualizing an impenetrable wall as thick and tall as the Great Wall of China around the information needing protection. She hated it now. She wanted to be able to tell whoever represented Aaron everything she knew, even if it wasn't much of anything.

Kid pushed his hair off his forehead and ran his fingers through the curls, making them taller. "Do you think Ollie did this on purpose?"

"What do you mean?"

"Contracted you to conflict you out of defending whoever was accused in this case."

"Maybe. I don't know."

"You did say he's scared of looking bad because he doesn't know squat about organized crime and underground betting. You've beaten him a couple of times, and he has the election coming up. He might have just wanted to take out the competition."

If only Ollie knew how much greater those stakes are than he realizes. If Jennifer had been able to represent the person accused of killing Victor and won, it would have been crushing to his candidacy. "If I could go back in time, I'd burn that contract instead of signing it." She felt manipulated and used. "But back to what you said about not representing Aaron. I want you on his case, Kid."

"On Aaron's case? That's...wow. Thank you. I want to help, but I'm not ready to handle a case like this without you. Especially not when the accused is your freaking husband, who I happen to love."

"That's okay. We'll find you a first chair."

"I'm licensed in Wyoming," Jack said.

Jennifer turned all her intensity on him. "Oh, my God. You're kidding?"

"I'm not a kidder."

"How did that come about? When?"

"I have an ongoing client who spends a lot of time in Jackson. He asked me to take the bar here a few years ago. Hell, I'm licensed in New Mexico, Colorado, Oklahoma, and Louisiana, too. If you need my help, I'm happy to do it."

"But you're headed back to Texas."

"There are flights to and from Amarillo."

"And there are attorneys in Wyoming."

He touched the tip of his nose with his forefinger. "True. But how many local attorneys do you want up in your business? Plus, a little humble bragging may be in order. I'm pretty damn good at what I do."

Jennifer thought about Aaron's veterinary practice, which was thriving, and his community-facing job as a high school football coach. Both would be in jeopardy from this arrest much less if he was actually charged, no matter whether he was found guilty or not. And her aspirations—would this notoriety put an end to her quest to become the county attorney? Possibly even crush her fledgling law practice? As for the lodge—people might not want to stay in a place owned and occupied by an accused killer.

So, Jack's point was very well taken. Not to be melodramatic, but if there was a way to salvage their careers—their lives—she had to keep Aaron's predicament as quiet as possible. They needed a clear victory, and they needed it fast.

She closed her eyes. When she opened them, she nodded. "Valid."

Kid held up his phone. "I Googled him. They call him the King of the Courtroom in Texas. Jeez, Jenn. People say he's 'Texas's answer to Johnnie Cochran.' You know, the lead defense attorney at O.J. Simpson's murder trial."

Jack chuckled. "That's laying it on a bit thick, but I'll take it. And even though we didn't know each other a week ago, Jenn, we're basically family now, by virtue of the unstoppable force that is Maggie. These women are a tight knit group, and they've adopted you. None of them would forgive me if I didn't help defend Aaron, who I think is a helluva guy, by the way."

Tears welled in her eyes. She tapped her lip. "You're hired. Both of you are." She took dollar bills from her purse and handed one to each man. "Okay, then. Let's get started. They arrested Aaron with a warrant. That gives them forty-eight hours to show probable cause." She shook her head, lips compressed. "I can't wrap my head around Travis doing this. There just can't be evidence. In my mind it has to come back to pressure from Ollie."

"I think they'll wait until the last possible second on probable cause while they try to dredge up evidence, because I can't imagine they have diddly now.

Kid said, "Forty-eight hours is Friday night. Our Gerstein hearing should be late Friday afternoon."

Jennifer almost smiled. Most attorneys just called Gerstein hearings "probable cause hearings," but not Kid. His bow tie was not an affectation. It was an authentic extension of his personality.

Jack said, "Which I am sure was part of their plan."

Jennifer whirled and crossed her arms. "Of course it is. Judge Ryan does arraignments at eleven on weekdays. If they meet probable cause on Friday his arraignment might not be until Monday."

"That gives us two days to convince them they don't have it—to prove to them Aaron didn't do it—and four days to keep Aaron from being charged if we fail on probable cause." Jack looked heavenward.

"I'm sure they're just going to use a written statement from law enforcement or Ollie for probable cause. But never underestimate how little evidence it actually takes to clear the path to move forward against a defendant. They'll be single minded and invested."

"I want to get Aaron out of this with as little shrapnel damage as possible. We have to beat probable cause. We just have to."

"So, let's make a plan to get the most of our resources."

"I'm supposed to meet with Veronica Farinolo this morning about a different legal matter. I could cancel it. Or I could keep it and try to get information from her."

"That's fine but otherwise let's keep you away from witnesses if you don't have a reason unrelated to Aaron's arrest to talk to them. I don't want Ollie to come after you or us on the conflict. Or on witness tampering."

"I get it, but it's a small community. I can't help but run into people. They may not respect those boundaries in what they want to talk to me about." *And I'll encourage them with every ounce of energy I can muster.*

"Shit happens." Jack winked at her. "I think my job one will be going out to Red Grade Ranch to see what I can learn. Kid, I could really use your help on researching case law and preparing for the probable cause hearing." He explained quickly what he was looking for.

Kid took notes, nodding. "I've got it."

"I'll bring in my wife Emily. She's my legal assistant." He gave Kid her contact information. "Don't hesitate to ask for her help. No task to big or too small."

Kid looked up with wide eyes. It had been months since he and Jennifer had had help. "That's amazing. Thank you."

"I'd also like to hire Katie and Nick Connell. They're private investigators. We can set them to work on creating the background information we'll need on Victor. His teammates and former employers, friends, and girlfriends. The Farinolos. Personnel with the team they were playing against."

Warmth flooded through Jennifer as the manpower available to them magically expanded. "That's a wonderful idea." The blessing of extended family a la Maggie was exponential. And since Wyoming didn't have any qualifications for private investigators, Katie and Nick could jump in without any barriers.

"I'll get them started."

The door to the office flew open and smacked against the outside wall. Kid gasped. Jack jumped to his feet and rushed toward the door. Jennifer dove for her briefcase. She didn't always carry, but she had a concealed permit, and something about the threat against her and Aaron combined with driving back to Sheridan at four a.m. had made it seem like a good idea.

A disheveled blonde bumped her way in. Casey. Jennifer put her purse down, bristling. She could smell alcohol fumes from across the room. Eyeliner and mascara was smeared under the girl's eyes and down her cheeks. Behind her was a muscular young man in Lucchese alligator boots, a pricey-looking Stetson cowboy hat, and some chunky gold bling around his neck. Trailing him was a clothes hanger of a man. Tall, thin, and hollow-eyed with wide, bony shoulders.

Jack was still blocking their entrance.

Kid said, "We know her."

Jack stood aside to let Casey pass.

She stumbled up to Jennifer and poked her in the chest. "When the hell were you going to tell me my own father was in jail?"

"Hey," Jack said. "None of that."

Jennifer stood her ground, eyes locked with her stepdaughter.

Kid said, "Jennifer is trying to get him out, Case."

Casey didn't spare him a glance. "I had to hear it from everyone else in town." She brandished her phone close to Jennifer's face. "Like, *everyone*."

Jennifer bit down hard on the inside of her lip. She had nothing constructive to say. Only damage could come from opening her mouth.

Jack said, "You're going to need to back away now." He sidled between Casey and Jennifer, pushing the girl back without touching her.

"Who the fuck are you?" Casey's voice was a snarl.

"I'm Aaron's attorney. I take it he's your dad? My name is Jack Holden. I've been staying at the lodge. I think I've seen you out there."

"She," Casey wobbled her head derisively and pointed at Jennifer, "can't even be bothered to defend him?"

"She won't be allowed to. But we're here planning strategy right now, and she's all-in on that. I promise you, he's in good hands."

Gold Necklace put his hand on Casey's shoulder. She slapped it away. He threw his hands up. "I told her not to come in. But she saw your cars. I couldn't stop her."

The other guy just watched them in silence, like a stoner watching a ping pong game at a hang.

"Who are you?" Kid said to Gold Necklace.

"Buster Kemp," the guy answered.

"No, I mean *who are you to Casey?*"

Jennifer's heart hurt for Kid. Even now when she was behaving so badly, he was lovesick.

"What's it to you, man?"

"I'm her friend."

"She hasn't mentioned you."

Something flashed in Kid's eyes. Pain. "Likewise."

Jennifer cut in. "And your other friend?"

The man shuffled his feet. He looked at Casey like he was asking for permission not to answer. Casey bobbed her head at him to get on with it. "Greg. I'm Greg."

Casey sighed dramatically and turned to Buster. "Get me out of here."

Buster gave Kid a hard look and Casey a push in the small of her back. "Like I was saying."

The three of them clambered out, and the door slammed behind them.

Kid's face was second degree-burn red.

"I'm sorry, Kid," Jennifer said.

He waved her off. "Never mind me. I'm sorry about how she's treating you. I think she's getting worse."

Jennifer didn't disagree. She thought about the hair samples in her purse. They weren't her top priority right this second, but she was going to do it. As soon as she had time, she was sending them in.

Jack cleared his throat. "That was distracting, but also informative. Word is out, and not from us. It must have come from the sheriff's office."

Jennifer said, "Just more evidence that we have to move fast."

"Not we. Kid and I."

"I may not be able to represent him or disclose anything I learned from Ollie, but I'm not prohibited from trying to find a killer. A wife can work to clear her husband's name."

Jack half-smiled. "A bit of a scofflaw, I see."

Jennifer growled softly. "I wasn't before, but after today, I'm afraid that I have to be."

EIGHTEEN

Sheridan, Wyoming

AFTER SPENDING the night in a jail cell for the first time in his life, Aaron pounded his fist on his thigh. *He'd been arrested for murder?* It made no sense, and it was driving him nuts that Travis and the county attorney wouldn't tell him *who* had been murdered. But no matter who it was, he hadn't killed anyone. Not on accident or on purpose. Maybe this was a case of mistaken identity?

He was an optimistic person by nature. He tried to look at all the things on the bright side. Like how this was going to make a great story someday. Then he hit a wall. That was the only one he could think of.

As infuriating as his situation was, he'd been careful not to show it. One of Jenn's mantras over the last fifteen years had been how important it was to cooperate with law enforcement first and fight the justice system later. *They have all the power.* He'd held his cool when they'd booked him and escorted him to the cell, when they'd put him in it with guys clearly under the influence of drugs or alcohol or both. Even though he hadn't said a word more than required—simple yeses and nos—he'd been polite. The other guys in the cell had grumbled when he didn't want to talk. He didn't care what they thought of him, though, as long as they didn't make it physical. So far, they'd kept their distance and their mouths shut, probably because they were half his size.

What he did worry about was Jenn. She had to be as dumbfounded as him. But even when she was at her worst, she lapped the competition. Any minute she'd be marching in and demanding his release, having straightened everything out. *I am thankful to be married to Jennifer Elise Herrington. Period.*

So far, though, she was a ghost.

Now, after a cold, sleepless night listening to the other guys' bodily functions, he was exhausted. His neck ached from lying on the hard bench. His stomach was alternating between growling and turning over in revulsion.

Footsteps sounded in the corridor. A guard appeared holding the elbow of a cuffed man who was wearing a rumpled business suit. After the prisoner was escorted into the cell, the door closed, and the cuffs removed, the guard said, "Breakfast in ten."

As his footsteps receded, the newcomer eyed Aaron. "I know you."

Aaron shrugged. He didn't recognize the guy.

"Well, I've seen you before, anyway. You're the vet who played pro football, right?"

Aaron nodded and looked away.

"And you don't want to talk."

Aaron laughed, one short huff. *Captain Obvious.*

The man sat down beside him. "I'm Rick Hunley." He stuck out his hand.

Aaron turned and stared into the man's eyes, ignoring the offered shake. He'd never been prone to rage, but anger started building inside him. This guy was deliberately poking the bear. Aaron's careful self-control gave way to his frayed nerves. "This isn't a networking event. Excuse me." He walked to the bars. It was a short walk.

"You don't have to be a jerk about it."

Aaron closed his eyes. *The jerk is the one who forced that interaction after I made it clear I didn't want to talk.*

"He thinks his shit don't stink like the rest of us," a second voice said.

Aaron glanced around. With the newcomer, there were now three other men in with him. They were gaining confidence. Strength in numbers.

"Aren't vets rich? Maybe he's too special to be stuck in here with us." A third voice.

Aaron lifted his gaze to the ceiling. He squeezed his fists tightly, then opened his fingers until they stretched.

Squeaking sounds in the corridor diverted everyone's attention from Aaron. A cart rolled into view, pushed by the same guard who'd been there a few minutes ago. "Come forward one at a time." He held a paper wrapped burrito-shaped object to the bars with one hand and a water bottle with the other.

Aaron was closest, so he took them. The burrito was still warm. He retreated to the bench. Holding the unopened water bottle between his thighs, he took a bite of the burrito. Egg, potatoes, and bacon in a gummy flour tortilla. If there was any salsa, he couldn't detect it. But it was food. He wolfed it down while his stomach talked to him loudly. With his size, two burritos would have been better. He'd lose weight fast in here if this was all they'd give him.

He'd no sooner finished eating than the guard said, "Herrington. You've got a visitor."

Jenn! Aaron put the water in his pocket. The guard had pushed the food cart to the far side of the corridor.

The guard held up the cuffs. "Put your wrists out." Aaron did, and the guard snapped the cuffs on, then opened the door and led him out. "Let's go."

"Bye, Mr. High and Mighty," one of the prisoners said.

The others laughed. Aaron didn't look back to see who'd called him out. All he cared about was getting to the woman waiting for him somewhere in this building.

NINETEEN

Sheridan, Wyoming

AFTER THE KICK-OFF meeting with Kid and Jack, Jennifer pulled away from the curb at loose ends. One thought kept returning to her. Travis wouldn't have done this to Aaron of his own accord. He was a careful and ethical cop. This was too rushed. There couldn't be any real evidence. Ollie had to be behind it.

Instead of heading toward home, she made a U-turn toward town. "I'll just go talk to him. Travis is a good guy. He'll see reason."

Within one block, she recognized the flaw in her logic. Whatever made Travis arrest Aaron, he wasn't going to disclose it to her. So, who could she talk to? Definitely not Ollie.

She put on her blinker to turn right toward the interstate. Then she had a lightbulb moment. She pulled over in the parking lot behind the Sheridan Inn. She knew who to call. A neutral law enforcement officer to use as a sounding board—Leo Palmer in Kearny County. She found his number in her contacts and initiated the call. It was early, but maybe she'd catch him in the office.

He answered on one ring. "Leo Palmer."

"Leo, this is Jennifer Herrington. In Sheridan."

"Hi, Jennifer. How are you?"

"I'll cut to the chase. Terrible. My husband was arrested last night."

"What for?"

"You hadn't heard about it?"

"No. What's up?"

"Deputy Spahn and the county attorney showed up at our place last night and arrested him for murder. Warrantless. They refused to give us any more information than that."

"So, you don't know the victim?"

"Actually, I do. I'd been contracted to help the county attorney prep for a potential case regarding Victor Carvalho's death. The state informed me I can't represent Aaron because they refuse to waive the conflict. Thus, it has to be Victor."

"Oh, shit. I'm so sorry."

"Aaron didn't do it. I know every defendant and their family says that. I've prosecuted, and I've defended. I hear it all the time. But he didn't. Leo, they don't even know whether Victor was murdered yet. I can't figure out whether this is a set-up, overzealous prosecution, or what."

He paused. She knew he had to be careful. "This must be so hard for you."

She took a deep breath. "It is. And I was wondering whether I could convince you to talk with me about the case. Just half an hour or so. I have some questions, and for obvious reasons, I don't have an open door in Sheridan county right now."

"Um..."

"I'd owe you. And I promise not to put you in a compromising position. If you can't answer my questions, I'll accept it."

Jennifer heard two voices in the background, muffled. Like Leo had his hand over the microphone and was talking to someone else in the vehicle with him.

Leo came back on. "Where are you right now?"

"Downtown Sheridan."

"So am I. Delaney Pace and I are in town to meet with some witnesses. We can meet, but I'd prefer it not be in public, given the temperature, if you know what I mean."

"I do. When are you free?"

"We have an hour and a half open now. We were going to grab breakfast."

"Meet me at my place. I'll cook for you while we talk." She gave him the address.

"All right. See you there."

THE KITCHEN WAS FILLED with the aroma of fresh coffee and toasted bagels by the time a knock sounded at the door. Because they housed guests, the lodge did not have a doorbell, as the sound was a disruptor of peace. This morning the guests were absent, though, for which Jennifer was grateful. Emily, Katie, and Nick had headed into town to meet with Kid and Jack. The other two couples had left a note that they were visiting the site of Custer's last stand, an hour north. She'd even sent the dogs out with George to work on fence. There would be complete privacy for this conversation, unless Katya and Jeremiah Johnson counted against that.

She opened the door and welcomed the Kearney officers inside, struck as she had been in the past by two things. First, that they both could have been cast in Yellowstone. Delaney's feline green eyes, height and taut figure, and lovely face were timeless. Leo actually looked like Luke Grimes from the cast. The second was their undeniable chemistry. She was pretty sure she'd be electrocuted if she stood between them.

Leo hugged her. Delaney shook her hand.

"Have a seat. I've toasted bagels and made coffee. I think I have orange juice. And if you want eggs—"

"Bagels are perfect," Leo said. "Do you have cream cheese?"

"I do."

"Thanks for the coffee. This has been an early morning for us." Delaney ignored the instruction to take a seat and came into the kitchen. "Let me pour."

Jennifer pointed to a cabinet. "Mugs are in there. Spoons in the drawer beneath the coffee pot." She grabbed the oat milk from the refrigerator and pulled the sugar and honey forward on the cabinet. "Will non-dairy be okay?"

"Absolutely."

As Jennifer gathered plates, bagels, and spreads, she said, "Sorry I didn't make fancy coffee for you. Aaron installed a new espresso machine, but I've been unable to master it."

Leo laughed. "We like the traditional stuff anyway." He joined Delaney in the kitchen and retrieved juice from the refrigerator. "Glasses?"

"On the shelf above the mugs."

Delaney said, "I conveniently left the cabinet open for you."

Less than five minutes after their arrival, the two officers and Jennifer were seated with breakfast. They ate in silence for a minute or two. Jennifer didn't know where to begin and found herself uncharacteristically tongue-tied.

Leo was the first to broach the subject. "How can we help you, Jenn?"

She set her bagel down. "I'm, oh, I'm all over the place. I'm not sure you can, but I'm hopeful. Here's the deal. Aaron and I are friends with Deputy Travis. He's acting sheriff while the actual sheriff is on medical leave. Now, I know our friendship should never matter if there's reasonable suspicion one of us committed a crime. But I've been working on this case. I know there's not reasonable suspicion. They have forty-eight hours to prove probable cause, but it doesn't sit right with me that Travis arrested Aaron while they go fishing for evidence. It just doesn't seem like the kind of person he is."

"I don't think so either."

"There's really no evidence, unless someone is framing Aaron, in which case any evidence isn't real. But honestly, I hadn't heard a word about any evidence when I was still on the case. If they found something, it was in a very tight time frame yesterday between when I last met with the county attorney and when they showed up last night to arrest Aaron."

"Was the county attorney present for the arrest?"

"Yes, which normally wouldn't bother me. When I was prosecuting homicides in Houston, I'd come along for an arrest sometimes, but it was rare. And I would have never done it on a case where we didn't even have proof of anything other than accidental death."

"That does seem odd." Delaney spread cream cheese on a second bagel. "More than anything, that grabs my attention. That the cause of death hasn't been classified as a homicide."

"I guess my first question is would you guys make an arrest for murder for a death in a case like that?"

The two of them shared a long look. Leo gestured for Delaney to take the question.

"I want to say no. Unless there would be extreme harm to making a potential case caused by waiting—like a flight risk defendant or someone who is an imminent threat to himself or others, which Aaron doesn't seem to be—I'd wait because the harm to a wrongly charged citizen is a real risk, too. We're in the serve and protect business. Not the blame and bully business. That being said, we're only going off what you tell us. That makes this a hypothetical. My answer might change if I knew everything Travis knows."

Jennifer pressed her hands together and lifted them to her lips. "Thank you for that answer. All of it. I respect the hypothetical nature of the discussion. What you say is where I've been landing. Even if someone is trying to frame Aaron, how can an arrest be made in absence of a crime? And why would a man like Travis make the arrest?"

Leo took a napkin from a basket in the center of the table and wiped his mouth. "Sticking with the hypothetical nature of this discussion in which we assume everything you say is gospel, I'd reiterate the reasons Delaney gave you and offer one more which you've already touched on. We can't ever ignore the possibility, however unlikely, of misconduct."

Jennifer closed her eyes. She didn't want to believe it of Travis. She hadn't thought Ollie was capable of it, as annoying as he was. But it was why she'd asked to talk to the Kearny deputies. It was a possibility that she couldn't ignore.

Delaney said, "Do either Ollie or Travis have issues with you or Aaron?"

"I hadn't thought so. Now I wonder."

Leo sighed. "Things get weird when there's an election coming up." Leo was up for election for Kearny county sheriff this year himself, as was Travis for sheriff in Sheridan county, and as was Ollie. "Occasionally, and I'm not saying it's happening here, prosecutors get a little overzealous to curry public favor, right?"

"But Travis is running unopposed in the primary. I can't see the election impacting how he acts. How likely he'd be to buckle under pressure from Ollie."

"Unless it's the prosecution itself impacting his actions."

"Which would either mean favor trading or... "

Delaney seemed to chew the inside of her lip for a moment. "Or... could it be that Ollie has something on Travis? Kind of a blackmail situation?"

Relief coursed through Jennifer. They'd arrived at exactly the place she'd had hoped they would. Now all she had to do was convince them to be the ones who figured out the answer to the question.

TWENTY

THE GUARD LED Aaron away from the holding cells and past the booking area. Down the hall was an open door. His footsteps grew lighter. His wife was waiting for him. He'd never needed to see her more. Even the final head injury that had ended his NFL career paled in comparison to this.

The guard moved aside and gave Aaron a jarring shove in the small of his back. "Here he is. Press the button to let me know when you're ready for me to come get him, or if he's a problem."

Aaron stepped into the nondescript room. It barely seemed big enough for him, let alone for the table and four chairs inside it. There were two men on the near side of the table, both facing him. Kid and Jack.

There was no Jenn. Her absence was a needle to the inflation of his optimism.

"Aaron." Kid James reached out to clasp Aaron's arm.

The guard's voice was quick and sharp. "Please keep your

distance and no touching." He backed away but stopped with his arms crossed over his chest.

Jack spoke, smooth as warm honey. "Uncuff him, please."

"I can't be responsible for your safety if I do."

"I understand."

"You know he's in here for murder, right?"

"We do."

"And, no offense, but neither of you look like you can take him. Even together."

"He's our client and a friend. We'll be fine."

The guard said, "Your funeral." He removed Aaron's cuffs. "Go around to the other side of the table. I'm not leaving until you take a seat."

Aaron did as he was told and scooted his chair in.

The guard shut the door.

Aaron said, "Where's Jenn?"

Jack held up an outward facing palm. "We'll explain. Do you need anything? I brought a Gatorade and some snacks."

Aaron couldn't care less about snacks. He'd been holding on to see his wife. But he tried to be polite. Kid and Jack couldn't help it they weren't her. "Yeah, that would be great. And I'm sorry I stink." He could smell himself. Rank from sweat and worry.

Jack placed a package of Slim Jims, a bag of cashews, and a banana on the table, then added a red Gatorade. Aaron knew he had to stay hydrated and strong, especially given that rations were insufficient for a guy of his size. He started with the Gatorade, gulping it down, then wiped his mouth with the back of his hand. "Thank you." He gestured at the empty bottle and snacks. "I'm a little stressed out. I should have started with hello and thanks for coming."

From Kid's pained expression, Aaron knew he looked and sounded like hell. "We understand. And Jenn would be here if she could. She'll visit soon, without us. But we all agreed it's important you meet with your attorneys first."

Aaron felt a glower take over his face. He didn't try to stop it. "Jenn is my attorney."

Jack shook his head. "I'm afraid that won't be possible. Not for this case."

Aaron's world tilted further off its axis. "Why can't she?"

"Because this is about Victor Carvalho. And that means she has a conflict of interest with the state of Wyoming."

"Wait—they think I killed Victor?" Aaron remembered watching the heated exchanged between Jenn and Ollie through the window of the sheriff's department truck. He hadn't been able to hear what they said, but now he had a pretty good idea. "That's insane. Why would I have done that? How would I have done it? Which I did not, by the way."

"We have no idea. Hopefully we'll learn something soon." Jack explained the process ahead of them. "We have no doubt they're going to hold you every second they can while they try to put evidence together."

"In the drunk tank?"

"We'll make sure you're moved to a private cell. Assuming you want us to represent you. Jenn asked us to, if you agree."

"Yes, of course. If that's what she thinks is best." Then Aaron hit his forehead with his palm. "Ugh. I need to talk to you about something in confidence."

"You have attorney client privilege with us so you can speak freely."

"Half Circle ranch called me out there a few days ago. I'm not their regular vet, but theirs was out of town."

"Okay."

"I got the feeling they were asking me to help them dope horses." He explained quickly what had happened. "I told them no and left. But it worried me because of the rumors about Victor being drugged. Even without the rumors it would have felt hinky to me, though."

"Why did it feel hinky?" Jack asked.

"Drugging horses endangers the riders and the horses. It's unethical. It's against the rules. A disregard of safety and ethics is a slippery slope. Who knows what else they're capable of if they'll do that?"

"You know Victor tested positive for sedatives?"

"Yeah. Jenn told me before," he waved his hand, "this happened."

"We won't have any specifics until the toxicology comes back."

"I understand. If I'm right, the Hellcats wanted performance enhancing drugs from me—bronchodilators to enhance breathing—but those would have the same impact as sedating Victor. It would give the Hellcats a competitive advantage.

Kid added, "At this point, we don't know that someone *deliberately* sedated Victor, although that's the state's theory."

Aaron said, "What I wanted you to know was that I told Jenn about all this, and she told Ollie, keeping names confidential. Mine and Half Circle's. Ollie zeroed in on Half Circle anyway because they have incentive to beat the Strikers, then he cut Jenn out of the follow-up on them. After which I was arrested. I did nothing, so there's nothing they could have found, but I wanted you to know about the timing."

Kid scribbled notes onto his yellow pad.

Jack was nodding. "Jenn has told us most of that, but I appreciative you opening up to us. That's going to be key to us getting you out of this. Open and honest communication."

Aaron put both hands on the sides of his head. "I don't get it. Why am I in here when they have so little?"

"We have to assume they think they have other evidence."

"When do we get to see that?"

"It won't be until after they charge you—if they do."

Unfortunately, this made sense to Aaron from years of talking with Jenn about her prosecutorial cases. "That's depressing."

Jack pursed his lips, thinking. "Tell me about this polo league. Why would anyone be drugging people or horses? I mean, I thought Big Horn was a town of three hundred people. And Sheridan is the only town of any size in the area and it's about twenty thousand, right?"

"You're right, but polo is still a big deal here. Big money, expensive horses, world class players."

"Prize money?"

"A bit, from sponsorships and participation fees. Less than in bigger markets. There are breeding fees to get offspring from the best horses, and bragging rights and career and team stepping stones. But it's really about the big money *spent* and the hope of a future payoff for everyone involved. Think of this as the minor league, like in baseball. The owners, the breeders, the trainers, the players, *everyone* is trying to make it into the majors by how they do here."

"Okay. That makes sense."

Aaron held up one finger. "But there's also a rumor that real money is changing hands over these matches in underground betting."

Kid looked up from his notepad. "We'd heard. And that would drive some people to unethical behavior."

Jack said, "Where there's betting there's organized crime. Bookies. Enforcers. Their bosses. My family is in quarter horse racing. I've seen it firsthand my whole life."

Kid said, "It's not just the Hellcats who had a motive to beat the Strikers. It's anyone who bet against the Strikers winning."

Aaron said, "How can we find out who did that?"

Jack's mouth bunched up on one side. "We probably can't. Not before you're charged and discovery starts, unless we get lucky and someone just coughs up the information to us. Which is unlikely."

Kid said, "Could Victor have been involved in betting? Maybe he owed money to a bookie."

"Good thinking." Jack snapped his fingers. "Or maybe he threw matches. Or refused to throw them. What do you think, Aaron? Would he have done something like that?"

Aaron shrugged his shoulders. "I didn't know him well enough to have an opinion on that."

"Tell us what you do know about him."

"He was good with his teammates and the horses. He was

engaged to the owner's daughter. He's not native to the US. He's been playing in Florida offseason, and he's a real rising star who had a chance at the majors. That's about all I know."

Jack tapped a pointer finger on the table surface. "We need to know more, Kid. His love life. The fiancée. Ex girlfriends. Women on the side. Stalkers."

Kid was scribbling fast again.

Aaron nodded, his brain now moving as quickly as Kid's pen. He still wished Jenn was here, but it was energizing to work with Jack and Kid on ending this nightmare. "Victor was about to break through to the next level. There could have been other players jealous of him. Maybe someone saw him as a threat to a spot they thought should go to them. That if they moved him out of the way that spot *would* go to them."

"Good. Good," Jack said. "We're focusing on the right motives. Lust. Love. Loot. Keep them coming."

Kid stopped writing. "Revenge. A player whose career was hurt because of him. Or maybe even physically injured."

Jack added, "A sponsor or team owner that he screwed over."

"A crazy person he cut off on the interstate," Aaron said.

"Lunacy as a motive also works. Harder to find those, but it should be noted. Any other ideas?" Kid and Aaron shook their heads. "On to you, Aaron. A good defense starts with no surprises. We need to know everything about you. Especially the things the county attorney is going to find out about."

"I'm married to the coolest woman ever. She's a defense attorney and former prosecutor." Aaron couldn't help smiling. "And a college cheerleader and a helluva golfer."

"About you." Jack smiled back.

"I played football. I coach football. I'm a veterinarian. I grew up in Tennessee. Lived in Texas. Love it here. I own a lodge with Jenn. What else is there?"

"Do you do veterinary work for any of the other polo teams besides the Hellcats?"

"Oh, man. Yeah, that's important. I'm the unofficial team vet for the Strikers. Victor's team. I'm not exclusive with them, but I only sub in for other vets with some of the other teams."

"Have you ever suspected the Strikers of drugging?"

"No."

"Have you ever provided performance drugs for animals before?"

"Never."

"Have you ever administered drugs to a performance animal?"

"Not performance drugs. But normal drugs to manage their health, yes."

"Have you ever administered or given veterinary drugs to people?"

"Well, sure. Some of them are the same drugs people use. On occasion, Jenn or I have taken some of my veterinary drugs when I know what our problem is and don't want to take the time for an emergency room or urgent care visit. Like on weekends or vacations."

Jack waved the answer away. "Besides you and Jenn."

"Then, no."

"Have you ever bet on a polo match?"

"I haven't."

"Have you placed other bets?"

"Yes."

"On what?"

"Horse racing. I grew up just across the border from Kentucky in Tennessee. Horse racing country."

"Any others?"

He hesitated for a beat. "Does fantasy football or March madness basketball count?"

Jack clicked his pen. "I don't think so. But what about all the other sports betting that's advertised everywhere now?"

"Nah."

"What about your finances? Any debts or problems?"

Aaron exhaled. "No. We're pretty comfortable."

"Are we going to find anything ugly in a background check?"

Aaron took his time to think about the question and how to answer it. "No. Nothing."

"Have you ever been unfaithful to Jenn?"

"Absolutely not."

"Has she to you?"

"Never."

Jack turned to Kid. "Do you have any more questions?"

Kid licked his lips. "No. I don't."

Jack put his palms on the table. "Okay. I think that covers it, until we learn more. I'm sure you know the drill from your wife, but I need to say these things anyway. Don't talk to anyone, don't trust anyone, don't make friends. Assume the walls have ears. Whatever you say can and will be twisted, manipulated, and used against you by a snitch."

"Got it."

"We'll get to work trying to get you out of here and get this off of you. We're very mindful of the detriment it could cause you in many facets of your life."

"And Jenn. She and Kid have been building a practice. This could hurt them."

Kid closed his notebook. "We'll weather the storm."

Aaron closed his eyes. "Her book launch! We were going to go to New York for it next weekend."

Jack said, "Maybe you still will."

Aaron put his head in his hands. "What if she loses her publishing contract because of this?

And now that she's considering running for county attorney, it could derail her completely."

Kid made a funny, strangled sound. He worked his jaw like he was going to say something, but no words came out.

Aaron saw the color bleed out of Kid's face, leaving it whiter and the freckles more pronounced. Too late, he realized Kid hadn't known. Of course he hadn't. *Foot in mouth. Shit.* "Someday, Kid. She wants to get back into it someday. Right now, she's very happy working with you."

Kid nodded, his lips pressed tightly together in a grim line. "I understand."

He sure doesn't look like it. Jenn's going to be pissed at me.

Jack cleared his throat. "All right then, I'll let the guard know you're ready." He rose and knocked on the door.

Aaron said, "When will Jenn come?"

"Very soon."

Aaron's eyes felt dry, hot. He managed to give a quick nod without tears falling.

"Do you need anything?"

Aaron's voice cracked. "Underwear. Socks."

The door opened.

"Ready?" the guard asked, jangling the handcuffs.

Aaron stood and put his hands in front of him. The guard came over and refastened them.

"Take care of yourself, Aaron," Jack said. "We'll talk to you soon."

Kid still looked pale. "Yeah. Be safe."

"Thank you both."

"Come on." The guard gave Aaron's cuffs a rough jerk.

The walk back to the cell was a quiet one. Something was nagging at Aaron, at least one thing, but he couldn't put his finger on it. The guard locked him back in the holding cell with the unfriendly occupants, who eyed him now like he was contagious with some dread disease he'd picked up in the half hour he'd been gone. He'd have to be sharp and focused until he was moved to a private cell. Any deep pondering would have to come later.

Whatever it was tickling around the edges of his conscious brain, he just hoped it wasn't something that would make his bad situation any worse.

TWENTY-ONE

Big Horn, Wyoming

JENNIFER APPLIED a pale lipstick using the mirror on the sun visor of her Grand Cherokee after she parked in the Farinolos's driveway. She looked like she felt—battered. This was the last place she wanted to be right now. She owed it to Aaron to keep the appointment, though. Her meeting with Veronica was an opportunity to learn something germane about Victor. What her husband was going through was far worse.

Honestly, about the only thing that had lifted Jennifer's spirits enough to get her here had been that Delaney and Leo had agreed to very gently poke around behind the scenes regarding Aaron's case, to try to determine whether there was any prosecutorial or law enforcement misconduct. She knew better than to get her hopes up too far, but they were up a little.

She capped her lipstick and put it in her handbag. Actually, she'd expected Veronica to call and cancel. Aaron had been arrested for the murder of her daughter's fiancé. Word had gotten out about his arrest. So far, though, Jennifer hadn't heard of anyone who knew *who* Aaron allegedly murdered.

Far from protecting him from gossip, the mystery had only fanned the flames of speculation. Jennifer's phone had been blowing up about it all morning. Veronica, however, might be outside the growing fire.

Jennifer stepped into the bright sunshine, which seemed to spotlight the magnificence of the house. *Here live the chosen ones.* Lately, the multi-millionaires who were being driven out of Jackson Hole by the billionaires had their sights set on Big Horn as the place to ruin next. The Farinolos's house faced Little Goose Canyon and the Bighorn Mountains, with rolling green pastures descending from the yard. Longhorns grazed on one side of the driveway and mares and foals on the other.

She studied her reflection as she walked up to the house, since the entire front of it was a prism of picture windows framing the view. Good thing she'd already put on her lipstick. Touch-ups would not escape the notice of anyone watching.

Before she could ring the bell, the door flew open.

Celeste Farinolo nearly ran her over. "Oh. I was just leaving. Are you here for my mother?"

Jennifer stepped out of her way. "I am. Nice to see you, Celeste."

Celeste stared at her blankly, clearly not recognizing her. Jennifer had hoped she'd open the door and call for Veronica, but she didn't.

"I'm very sorry about Victor's death. You have my deepest condolences."

The younger woman drew in a sharp breath. "Yes. Thank you. But you should probably save that sentiment for one of his girlfriends."

"Oh. My apologies. I thought the two of you were..."

"Engaged?" Celeste snorted. "Me, too. But apparently that didn't stop him from fucking half the women in Sheridan county. Anyway, I have to go."

A woman scorned and pissed off enough to air her dirty laundry with a near stranger. Jennifer made a mental note to let Kid and Jack know about the interaction ASAP.

Jennifer frowned sympathetically. "Do you think I should call your mother or ring the doorbell after you leave?"

Celeste sniffed. "Her phone's on silent most of the time. Best to ring the bell. But give her a minute. She's all the way upstairs on the far side of the house. And she's two cocktails in by now."

"All right then. Have a good day."

Celeste shot her one more look then clicked the remote to a Porsche Cayenne, which was parked beside a Land Rover. The girl was probably an emotional wreck, so Jennifer cut her slack for the bad manners.

Jennifer rang the bell and waited. And waited and waited and waited. She rang it again and texted Veronica. *I'm out front for our 10 am appt. Is now still good?* She backed up until she could see the entire front façade of the house. A vertical blind shifted on the second floor. Veronica. No dots or reply on the phone, though. Jennifer waited some more.

Five minutes later, the door opened. Veronica was holding a Chihuahua with a pink spiked collar. One of them smelled like a bottle of Listerine, probably not the dog. "Mrs. Herrington. Something has come up. I'm—"

Two days in a row Jennifer had been met with that tired excuse at meetings she hadn't asked for. Was it them or was it her? "Shall we get right to it then? You have a legal matter you asked to discuss."

"Well, I—okay, just for a minute."

Jennifer stepped in quickly, before Veronica changed her mind.

The dog started barking. Tiny, sharp yips.

"Shh, Angel. Mommy's here," Veronica whispered in the dog's ear. To Jennifer, she said, "Let's sit at the dining room table."

No coffee, then. No parade of homes tour. No braiding daisy chains and trading friendship bracelets. This was better. She wasn't sure she could have handled the other. "Great."

The two women took seats across from each other at an enormous table polished so brightly it reflected Jennifer's face. The dog finally stopped its racket.

Jennifer gave an encouraging smile. "Tell me how I can help you."

Veronica splayed the talon-like fingers of one hand and pressed them into the tabletop, Angel still nestled in the crook of her other arm and staring at Jennifer with outright hostility. "I don't know how to say this politely, so I'll just say it. Your husband murdered my future son-in-law. I—"

Jennifer held up both hands. "I'll need to stop you there. As a former prosecutor, let me assure you that being arrested does not equate to guilt. Aaron absolutely did not kill Victor. We'll have this straightened out in a few days. However, I am very, very empathetic about the emotional distress this situation has caused you. Has caused all of us. Aaron thought the world of Victor, and he thinks the world of you and Jerry."

"Be that as it may, it doesn't seem the appropriate time to enter a business relationship."

"I couldn't agree more. But if you give me a hint of your issue, I might be able to refer you to another attorney."

Veronica's left cheek twitched. After a long pause, she licked her lips. "It's regarding protection from some unscrupulous and aggressive creditors of a person… outside our family. They're trying to hold Jerry and me responsible for this individual's debts."

It wasn't Jennifer's specialty, but she had spent time prosecuting white collar crimes at the Harris county DA. Between her and Kid—who was a research whiz—she was sure they could handle it, once Aaron's situation was resolved. "I'll definitely ask around for the best Wyoming attorneys to handle that. Would you consider pursuing criminal charges against these individuals or entities if warranted?"

Veronica shook her head vehemently. "Nothing public."

"Understood."

Veronica pushed back from the table.

Jennifer rushed her next words. Her time was running out.

"Celeste seemed quite upset when I spoke to her. She mentioned that Victor was cheating on her."

Veronica bit down hard on her lower lip. "My daughter can be quite dramatic." Her voice had a closed-door tone of finality.

Angel growled to further the point.

"As I'm sure you can imagine, part of proving Aaron's innocence so that he can come home and put this misunderstanding behind him will involve his team speaking to people who knew Victor."

"About what?"

"Anything he was involved in that would make someone want to hurt him. And who those someones might be."

"Why would anyone want to hurt him?"

"Indeed. Certainly, Aaron didn't. But do you know anything that would fit in that category?"

Veronica stared at the table for several seconds. Finally, she lifted her eyes. "I'll ask my husband whether he thinks the two of us should talk about Victor. I'll let you know."

Jennifer suspected this was Veronica's way of shifting the blame for saying no to the conversation. *Expect to be ghosted.* Celeste would know the names of Victor's other woman or women that she'd alluded to. *Kid*, she thought. Kid could approach Celeste. They were about the same age. Celeste was far more likely to talk to him than her.

She smiled at Veronica. "Thank you. That was very helpful." *In no way whatsoever.* "I'll get back to you about an attorney for your legal work."

Veronica jumped to her feet and hurried to the door. She held it open. Angel barked at Jennifer to move her tush. "Mrs. Herrington?"

Jennifer stopped on the stoop. "Yes?"

"I think you need to look in your own hen house."

"What?" Jennifer was legitimately puzzled.

"You heard me." Veronica shut the door in her face.

TWENTY-TWO

Big Horn, Wyoming

JACK CLEARED his throat and knocked on the door frame of the Red Grade Ranch manager's office. He was there for a surprise visit. Jenn had given him the guy's name and told him where to find him. As the only member of Aaron's team unknown to the locals, Jack held the element of surprise, and he intended to play it up to the hilt. "Excuse me. Are you Cliff Reidlinger?"

A burly man looked up from a stack of paperwork on the desk in front of him. "You got him."

"I'm Jack Holden. Can I have a minute of your time? I raise some nice horses that I have questions about, and I'm told you're the man to talk to."

"Save me from reviewing these invoices and you can have an hour." Cliff stood and popped his neck. "I'd offer you a seat, but I don't have one. Let's take a walk outside. I need a break anyway."

Jack preferred that. He loved horses, but that didn't mean he always wanted to smell them, and this office was smell adjacent. "Lead the way."

Outside, Cliff headed toward a cluster of cottonwood trees near a ditch with water flowing through it. They stopped in a shady spot looking out over a pasture full of lean, muscled thoroughbreds. Beyond the pasture a flat rectangular field appeared carved out of an otherwise rugged landscape. A few horses and riders were galloping around the edge of it, the riders swinging mallets.

Cliff said, "Okay, Mr. Holden—what can I do you for?"

Jack gestured at the horses. "First off, this place, these animals. Magnificent."

"Why, thank you. We're pretty proud of what we've got here." His voice thickened, and he pinched the bridge of his nose. "Excuse me. I'm feeling a little emotional. We lost a horse yesterday to a hit and run driver after another vehicle plowed through our fence. A second horse was seriously injured."

"I'm very sorry. Any lead on the drivers?"

"Absolutely none. But if I ever find out who they are, they'll rue the day they were born."

"I get it. I grew up on our ranch in New Mexico where we raise quarter horses for racing."

Cliff's expression brightened. "I got my start in that world. Any horses I'd know?"

"We had one place second in the All-American Futurity a few years back."

"The biggest purse in the field! What's the name?"

"We call him Jarhead. And he's still the king of the ranch."

"I remember him, not only because of his win but because a female jockey from around here rode him, if I recall correctly."

"You do. Laura Sibley."

"Quite a family. Her brother won bull riding at Cheyenne a decade or more back."

"He sure did. In fact, I'm in town for Hank's pre-wedding festivities."

"You're practically local, then."

Jack smiled. "I guess so. That's how I learned about your operation."

"That's good of him."

Jack let this misunderstanding slide. Better for this guy to believe Hank sent him than Jenn. "Pardon my ignorance, but what do you do here in the winter when polo season is over?"

"Well, my job gets a lot easier, that's for sure. But there's still a lot to do between seasons just taking care of this place and preparing for next year. The owners expect me to run a pretty tight ship."

"I'd imagine." Jack turned away from the view of the horses to face Cliff. "Let me get to the reason for my visit. We're always looking for options for our horses that don't pan out on the track. We've got some quick, strong animals."

"I'll bet."

"I had this idea that even though they're not thoroughbreds, some of our horses might be well-suited for polo, if for nothing else than breeding stock. Do you think that would be possible?"

Clint shrugged. "I don't see why not. Thoroughbred-quarter horse crosses definitely are finding success in the sport. I could talk to our owner. I can't promise anything, but I can have him get in touch with you if he's interested. Jarhead's bloodline is intriguing."

"That would be great." Jack gave Cliff his contact information, which Cliff saved in his phone.

"I'll warn you, though. Last week we lost a player. Our best player. Then yesterday, we had the tragedy with the horses. The owners are preoccupied with that. Don't expect a fast response, if any."

Jack kept his face impassive. "Holy smokes. You've had a helluva week. How did your player die, if you don't mind me asking?" He was interested in hearing how people in the Strikers organization looked at the circumstances of Victor's death.

"It was gruesome. He fell off his horse and was trampled to

death." Clint lowered his voice. "The cops are saying he was drugged. That it was murder."

Jack made a shocked face, raising his eyebrows as high as they would stretch. "Drugged?"

"So, they say. It's crazy. I'm not naïve—horses get drugged occasionally. Not ours, of course. We've made it clear we won't tolerate that."

Jack shook his head. "Drugging happens in the world of horse racing, for sure. Do you know who's doing it locally?"

"I won't slander a rival, but I've heard things about a team that would do anything to win. Even endanger their horses. We played them last week. If the game hadn't been called off because of what happened to Victor, we would have beat them, too. But I'm talking horses, not people. For the drugging, you know."

Jack knew exactly which team that was. The Hellcats. "Drugging a player before a match seems like a pretty uncertain way to kill a fella, unless he would have died anyway of an overdose. But to put him in danger like that? Someone must have really had it in for the guy."

"Right? That's what I've been saying." Cliff started walking back toward the buildings. "Victor was a rising star, but he was a magnet for trouble. Girls. Money and money people. And he had a major beef with Joaquim Ramirez."

Jack walked alongside the ranch manager, deliberately trying to slow him down by his own pace. "Hmm. Haven't heard of him."

"He's an up-and-coming rider for that other team I was telling you about. It's his first summer here but I think he and Victor have been up against each other in other leagues."

"What's up with their beef?"

"Honestly? I think they manufacture it for drama. The stars are kind of prima donnas. The real issue between all the players is the limited spots at the next level. They need playing time, exposure, and resources to make it. The right backers. Victor and Joaquim both have

—had—their sights set on the big time. But I wouldn't think that would be motive for murder."

"Murder wouldn't surprise me in our world. We have a serious problem with the criminal element infiltrating racing. There's big money in the betting. Above and below board. I think that's the reason for the drugging. And the reason for jockeys throwing races, sometimes because they're instructed to by an owner, sometimes because someone else pays them to do it."

Clint looked around, then lowered his voice. "It's starting to be a problem here, too."

"There's betting on your matches? The legal kind or the under the table kind?"

Clint drew his fingers across his lips in a zipping motion. They'd reached the stable and now stood outside the door.

"I won't tell anyone. But I'm interested if they're some of the same people we're having issues with. Any names?"

Clint frowned, his forehead bunching up like a bulldog's. Then he pulled out his phone. He opened his texts and typed in a message without sending it. He held it out for Jack to read. *People are placing bets through a bookie called Lou out of Newark, New Jersey.*

Jack said, "Yep. I know who he is." Which he didn't. But he would soon enough.

Clint deleted the text.

Jack typed into his own phone. *Any particular people or organizations involved in placing the bets?*

Clint read the message and backed away, averting his eyes. "If there's nothing else, I need to get my ass back to work."

"No problem." Jack heard the subtext loud and clear. Clint was scared of something or someone, and it related to the bets being placed on the local polo matches.

TWENTY-THREE

BIG HORN, Wyoming

"WHEN WE BOOKED a trip to Wyoming for Maggie's party, never in my wildest dreams did I think we'd end up working a murder case." I kept my eyes on my screen as I talked, even though the bay window at the dining room table—where I was sitting with my husband Nick, playing dueling laptops—looked out on mountains so close, they didn't seem real. Growing up in Dallas, I'd loved visiting New Mexico and Colorado, but Wyoming was a first for me. Different than the Caribbean, but in some ways the same. Rugged beauty. Low population density. In other ways it was a different world. Wildlife everywhere. No ocean, of course. And then there was the whole winter thing, which I was glad to miss.

Nick hadn't so much as twitched, so I added. "Yet here we are."

We had just returned from a team meeting in town where Jack had made assignments for those of us working on Aaron's defense. Nick and I owned and operated Stingray Investigations, so getting sucked into friends' problems was not an unusual occurrence for us. Honestly, it was a privilege.

In the continuing absence of a response from Nick, I went on. "I just feel so terrible for Jenn and Aaron."

"Mm hm." Nick was becoming more like his taciturn Mainer father every year. Luckily for me I loved them and was good at carrying both sides of a conversation.

I deepened my voice to mimic my husband. "Yes, Katie. Me, too, Katie."

He finally shot me a quick grin. "Yes, my beautiful wife, love of my life. Although I have no idea how you can work and talk at the same time."

"Multi-tasking is an inherently female quality."

"Shh." He buried his face in his screen. "Let us poor single taskers concentrate."

I needed a break, mentally and to avoid repetitive motion issues. I walked over to pet Jeremiah Johnson, Jennifer's little skunk. We'd introduced him to our kids when on Facetime earlier. He'd been a huge hit, until their nanny, Ms. Ruthie, announced lunchtime. She was staying with the kids, so they barely missed us, what with six dogs, each other, and her. Not to mention the entirety of our big rainforest house, the pool—only to be used when their swim instructor came for lessons—and one hundred acres of mango trees and bush for Ms. Ruthie to chase them through. Thank goodness for her, because it was nice to get away with just Nick, even if we were now working. It was *rare* to get away with just him.

Jeremiah chirped.

"Are you hungry?" I tried to remember if I'd seen food in his bowl that morning. I wouldn't have been surprised if Jenn had forgotten. Her emotional plate was quite full, and I felt sure her mind was fully occupied with all the things she could do to help Aaron.

I had a lot on my plate, too, since Jack had set us up with enough work for an army of Stingray investigators, and we were obligated to a short timeline. Like, yesterday short. He wasn't being unreasonable, it was just how things went after an arrest.

It was our first time to team up with Jack, and so far, it was great. He was clear, smart, and organized. Direct. A waster of very few words. So few, in fact, that after our meeting with him, Emily took us aside to translate and explain more about what he'd be looking for. Then we'd headed home, and she'd stayed in town. She'd be working in the law office with Jenn's associate Kid and Jack. Meanwhile, the rest of our friends were riding off road vehicles at Hank and Maggie's ranch. It had been hard for them to accept that it was okay to have fun when Aaron was in a jam, but there really was nothing they could do at present. Maggie, especially, was torn up about it.

"You'll call if that changes?" Maggie had said to me over the phone.

"Of course."

"I mean it. I'll have my cell phone on me. We won't go out of range for more than a few hours at a time."

"I promise. You'll be my first call."

That had mollified her. A little bit. She was going to ruin her reputation as a prickly hardass if she wasn't careful.

Jeremiah chirped again to remind me that a hungry skunk is a loud skunk. I had seen Jenn and Aaron feeding him over the last few days, so I knew where everything was. I retrieved Jeremiah's food from the pantry and filled his little bowl, which I returned to an alcove in the kitchen. Not where I would have chosen, because *hygiene,* but it wasn't my house.

I returned to my laptop and reviewed the information I'd compiled so far on the former life of Victor Carvalho. Some people think compiling a work-up on a person is as easy as entering a name in Google and pressing enter. *Au contraire.* Not if it's done correctly. Each name variation of a subject has to be chased down. Every address, every job, every school and degree followed up on. Credit, prison, and public records pulled. News databases and socials scoured. And, then the kicker: criminal history searches in every state a subject has lived in. Often, character witnesses, too—say, within the last ten or so years.

Ten minutes later, I said, "Babe, are you ready to reconnoiter and see if we have any crossover links yet?"

Nick grunted, which I knew meant *Absolutely* and *What a great idea. You really are brilliant.* He'd been researching the two polo teams involved in the fateful match. He made a series of high flourish keystrokes then threw his hands in the air. "Ladies first."

I blew him a kiss. After reading off Victor's somewhat boring vital statistics, I delved into the meaty stuff. "Victor is not good with money. Was not, I mean. Looks like several credit card companies are going to be writing off some bad debt. His credit score is circling around the lower region of the toilet bowl, and he already has several things in collections. Rent on a house he moved out of. Loan payments on a car that got repo'ed."

"Sounds like he was counting on a big pay day in his future. Or living like he was."

I noticed some crusted food on the table and went to the kitchen for the cleaner and a rag. "Yeah, in the form of a rich fiancée." I sprayed the table and gave it a vigorous rubdown.

"Do any of the creditors seem like they'd track him down and kill him in this unusual and yet strangely uncertain way?"

I laughed. "Hardly. I can't help thinking this is a dead end. That the kind of people who'd slip him downers before a dangerous polo match wanted to see him humiliated, maybe injured, and definitely out of the game. They couldn't have counted on him dying. Plus, creditors only get paid if the debtor lives. What I've found so far really just paints a picture of how he treated life and the people in his." I looked at the kitchen. I might as well give the countertops a once over while I had the cleaning supplies out. The skunk and cat did walk across them after all. I sprayed and wiped, sprayed and wiped.

"Agreed. Administering poison is a close-in method, too. They'd need to have a current connection with him or with someone near him. Creditors already on the wrong side of the ledger wouldn't spend more money coming out here. Not these kinds, I wouldn't think. The knee-breaking kind, maybe, but still unlikely. What else?"

I went back to my machine and read his professional history from the Google Sheet. Cities. Team names. Former teammates. "One former team, the Storm in Miami, filed a lawsuit against him for breach of contract.

"I found that in my research because the suit was amended to name the Strikers and its owners. It's pending a summary judgment motion. Any other litigation?"

I'd saved the best for last. "A claim for past due child support."

"Whoa. Did we know he had a kid and an ex-wife?"

"Kids. Twin boys. And an angry baby mama who never had a ring put on it."

"I'm not liking this guy."

I went back to disinfecting the kitchen. "Join the club. But here's the thing. By every account he is a charming guy who everybody— except us, his creditors, the baby mama, and his former team—loves."

"With a history of reneging on responsibilities."

"And running from problems." I looked around for something else to clean. The house was tidy, but it still left me many opportunities.

Nick smiled at me. "Katie, enough with the OCD. That kitchen is spotless."

He wasn't wrong, at least about the kitchen. I put the supplies back under the sink, except for the rag which was going straight into the wash. "I made some notes and sent them to Jack to see whether he wants us to follow up with anyone I've identified. I also pulled together the contact information for the various parties of course. Now, what do you have?"

The door burst open, interrupting us and causing the cat to yowl and the skunk to chirp and skitter out of sight.

A woman with a helmet of straight gray hair stalked in, hands on hips, looking for all the world like a fire hydrant "Why are the police pulled up out front? What's this bull crap I hear about Aaron being in the pokey?" Then she seemed to register our unfamiliar faces. "And who the hell are the two of you?"

TWENTY-FOUR

SHERIDAN, Wyoming

JENNIFER PACED the waiting area at the jail like a racetrack. Her stomach growled, reminding her that she hadn't eaten anything today. She didn't care about food, though. She only cared about Aaron. She'd finally been granted a visit with him. She'd be able to see him. Talk to him. Reassure him. The only thing she could not do was the thing she wanted to do most—touch him.

"Are you ready?" a man asked. A deputy who would take her to Aaron.

"Yes." She all but leapt at him.

He gave her a startled look, then escorted her to a small, white-walled room with a chair in front of a countertop and plexiglass. It smelled like fresh paint. Aaron was on the other side, waiting for her. She rushed into the seat and scooted it forward, drinking in the sight of her husband despite his bloodshot and puffy eyes. The man normally slept like a baby but looked like he hadn't gotten a wink in a month.

She put her hand to the barrier. He touched it on the other side. It wasn't good enough. Tears sprang into her eyes.

"Hello, beautiful. You're a sight for sore eyes," he said.

She spoke into the vent holes in the barrier. "As are you, my love. Are you okay?"

He sighed. "As much as possible given the circumstances."

"I'm so sorry."

"Me, too." For a second, she wondered why he would apologize. Did he know something about Victor's death? God forbid, had he had some involvement? But that was crazy thinking. Of course, he was just expressing agreement about the horror of the situation they were in.

"I brought you underwear and socks. I was promised they'd be given to you."

"Thanks."

"Are you in a private cell yet?"

"No."

"I'll get Jack to follow-up on that. They were supposed to move you."

"My cell mates are doing everything they can to provoke me. They think I'm some kind of prima donna."

"Don't let them get to you."

"I won't. I've got this."

"Jack and Kid told me about their visit, what they could anyway. Attorney-client privilege."

"Doesn't that extend to spouses?"

"No. I have spousal immunity. That prevents me from being forced to testify against you. We're all being really careful to keep a wall around things you tell them and advice they give you. If there are things you need to tell only them, do it. But do know that I won't ever have to testify against you for anything you say to me."

"That won't be a problem. I have nothing to hide."

"I know."

"I wish you could represent me. I know you're the best."

"Not for you, I'm not. But I'm here. I'm with you. And I'm helping in any way I can."

"What are you doing?"

"Best we don't talk specifics out here. Just trust me. I've got you." Jennifer wished she could tell him about her conversation with Leo and Delaney and the potential of prosecutorial or law enforcement misconduct, but that was the last thing she'd mention in the jail.

"I do trust you." He bit his lip. His eyes glazed. "You can't imagine how seeing you lifts my spirits. My world is gray. Then you show up. A walking rainbow in a sky full of sunshine."

"I miss you terribly. The dogs miss you." Her voice broke, and she changed the subject so she wouldn't cry in front of him. Rain clouds were the opposite of the sunshine he needed. "There's a whole team working on getting you out of here as fast as possible. Jack is talking to people. Nick and Katie are investigating. Kid's working on the legal end. Emily is helping everyone. Full court press."

"Wow. I didn't know the others had pitched in. I'm so grateful."

"You are loved."

He put his hand up, and she touched it again. Or almost did.

"Still no word on what the prosecution thinks they have against me?"

"No. And we won't hear anything until they try to show cause for the judge to charge you."

"That sucks."

"It's a tremendous prosecutorial advantage."

"I'm beginning to have a lot of empathy for defendants."

"Yeah. This last year working for defendants has changed me, too."

"Do you think you really want to change sides again?"

She examined her hands. She'd hoped this wouldn't come up. It wasn't the time to put any other heavy burdens on Aaron's mental and emotional state, and her submitting county attorney paperwork was definitely one of those. "I don't know. We'll talk when you're out."

"Sounds good."

Behind her the guard said, "Time to go, Mrs. Herrington."

She held up one finger without looking at the man. "Is there anything else I can do for you?"

"Just love me forever."

"How am I doing so far?"

"A plus plus."

"I love you, Aaron."

"I love you, too."

Getting up and walking away from him, leaving him in there—was one of the hardest things she'd ever done. Hiding the sobs that were fighting to escape her lips was the next hardest. As soon as the exterior door closed behind her, she ran a few steps away and let it out. All of it. The fear, the grief, the exhaustion. She didn't care who saw or heard her. She opened her anguished heart to the sky and howled.

Until her mobile rang. Then she wiped her tears and checked her phone. The clock was ticking, and she had to remain available in case this was *the* call with *the* information that proved Aaron hadn't hurt Victor.

It was Aaron's clinic. *His clinic. I didn't call and tell them about Aaron's arrest!* Probably everyone had already heard what happened anyway. But Aaron would want her to take the call and reassure them.

"Hello? This is Jenn Herrington." She walked briskly to her Grand Cherokee.

"This is Loretta. Something happened." Loretta's crusty voice had an edge to it. An edge of... panic?

"I know, and I am so sorry I hadn't called yet. I just got done visiting Aaron. He's in jail—I'll bet you've already heard—but he absolutely didn't do anything wrong. It's just a horrible misunderstanding that we'll get straightened out quickly." She climbed into the car and started it, then turned the fan up on the air conditioner.

"We did hear. But that's not why I'm calling."

"Um, okay. Is it Casey?" She knew that Casey had about worn out her welcome with the clinic practice manager.

"No. It's, uh—the county attorney was here. He and a bunch of deputies. They had a search warrant and—"

A search. Of course. It had to be expected. By now they might have already searched the lodge and grounds, too. Although wouldn't she have heard from George, if so?

She broke in. "I'm sorry. Did they make an awful mess?"

"MRS. HERRINGTON. You're not understanding me. I have to tell you about what happened."

Jennifer's heart felt like it was blocking air from getting to her lungs. "Okay. I'm sorry. What is it?"

"They took our drug inventory and our usage log. And they asked me about it. I didn't know what to say. I had to tell them the truth."

Jennifer grabbed the steering wheel with her free hand and braced herself as if she was about to crash the vehicle, which hadn't moved from its parking space. "What's the truth?"

"That we're missing a lot of xylazine. It's a really dangerous sedative."

A sedative? Ollie was going to have a field day with this information. Her hands began to shake. "How did it go missing?"

"I don't know. But I told Doctor H. about it a few days ago. He said he was going to get to the bottom of it."

Jennifer's mouth went dry as dirt. She didn't prompt Loretta. She just sat in silence, waiting. Waiting for her to tell the rest of it.

"But he didn't. And the only people who had access to it were me and him and Doctor Sarah. They asked her. She said she didn't take it. And I told them I didn't."

"Oh. Oh, my."

"I didn't know what else to do. I had to tell them the truth."

"Of course you did. Thank you for letting me know. Someone will be in touch with you from Aaron's team about next steps. Thanks again." She ended the call. The rasp of her breathing sounded abnormally loud in her ears, a heavy metal riff of an electric guitar against the bass drum of her pounding heartbeat.

Aaron had known xylazine was missing from his clinic. Now Ollie knew. And her husband hadn't told her. *Why hasn't he told me?* There wasn't a single good reason she could come up with.

Aaron had just handed the prosecution probable cause on a silver platter.

TWENTY-FIVE

Big Horn, Wyoming

I STARED with an open mouth at the squat woman standing three feet away from Nick and me. I recovered and answered her last question about who we were. "We're lodge guests and friends of Jenn and Aaron. I'm Katie. This is my husband Nick. And you are?"

"Sorry. I should have figured you was guests. I'm Black Bear Betty," she said.

Somehow I kept a straight face as she said her name. I waited, thinking she'd give us her real one, but she didn't.

"I expect they'd tell you I fill in around here for George from time to time and handle contracting work for them. Put in their septic tank, in fact. I'm the only female septic tank installer in Wyoming, you know." She hitched up her pants, which were sagging dangerously. "But I call 'em friends. They're good people. And they need to know there's a sheriff's posse at the end of their driveway, looking ready to ride in."

I went into lawyer mode, and I could almost hear the squeaking and clanging of gears and feel the rust scraping off as they went into motion. In Jenn's absence, I was the best they had for this situation. "Jenn's not here. Neither is Aaron."

"Of course, Aaron's not. Those yayhoos went and threw him in the pokey. Dumbest thing they've done since they tried to pin a murder on me."

That's illuminating.

Nick stood and held out his hand. "Let's start over. Nick Connell. Private investigator. I'm actually working on Aaron's case. So is my wife. He's got two attorneys and a legal assistant in town on his team, too. We're going to get to the bottom of this."

Betty shook it. "Pleased to meet you. Glad to hear it."

Belatedly, I offered mine and endured a vise grip of a shake. "I'm an attorney, too.

Betty put her hands on her hips, creating a diamond shape out of her short body. "Another attorney? We got Kid and Jennifer and you?"

"And Jack, another friend, who's working with Kid." I decided to leave out Michele so as not to derail the conversation. Plus, Michele didn't do much criminal work. It was highly unlikely she'd end up on the case.

Betty shook her head, growling. "I don't know. I don't know how much I like that. Attorneys is one of the things wrong with the world today. Except for Jenn, just barely."

By now I realized there was little chance Betty was joking. "I hear you, Betty. I'll just—"

"It ain't Betty. It's Black Bear Betty."

I rolled my lips inward. "Sorry. Black Bear Betty. And I am a *recovering* attorney. Trying to wean myself out of the profession to make the world a better place."

She nodded. "Apology accepted. I think maybe you're the ones who need to hear what I have to say, though. You can pass it along since you're helping Aaron."

"What's that?"

"I been doing work at Half Circle ranch. You know, home of the Hellcats team."

"Okay... "

"I was out there last Thursday before their match with the Strikers. The owner—Benjy Mahones—took a call on speaker and started yapping like I was a fence post."

"That doesn't sound very sharp of him."

"Darn tootin'. He was talking to somebody about putting money on the Hellcats winning. The other guy said, 'That's a lotta dough unless it's a sure thing.' And Benjy laughed like a durn guinea hen in full mating call mode and said, 'Oh, it's a sure thing all right.'"

Nick said, "Whoa. Thanks for telling us. That's going to be helpful."

I added, "We'll make sure Aaron's whole team knows. Now, I hear vehicles out front. I'm going to talk to them."

A knock sounded at the door before I made it outside. I walked briskly over to it and yanked it open to reveal the posse Betty—Black Bear Betty—had warned us about. At the front was a tall officer in a cowboy hat. He looked like the guy who'd arrested Aaron.

"Yes? May I help you?" I said.

The tall officer said, "I'm Deputy Travis Spahn. These are my deputies behind me. We're here to execute a search warrant on these premises."

I held out my hand. "May I see it, please?"

He shuffled his feet. "Well, I don't know who you are, so I can't answer that question."

"My name is Katie Connell. I'm part of Aaron Herrington's legal team." My law license wasn't current, and it certainly hadn't entitled me to practice law in Wyoming when it was, but I made a highly overqualified paralegal. And I hadn't falsely claimed to be his attorney.

A slim black man—believe me, his race stood out around here—who was not in uniform and who would have looked more at home in a downtown Dallas skyscraper stepped forward. "You may see the warrant, but you may not prevent the search, Mrs. Connell. Please move aside to let the officers do their job."

My eyebrows shot skyward before I could tell the little devils to stay put. "As soon as you put the warrant in my hand, I'll be happy to, as I need to confirm its existence before I willy nilly grant entry to an army of law enforcement. From there, I'll ensure that the search remains within the boundaries indicated on the warrant. Actively." I held out my hand.

Deputy Travis Whats-his-face waved a second deputy forward, a woman with a very strong chin. She presented me with the paperwork. I read it quickly. Physically, it covered the house, the onsite clinic, and the on-road vehicles. Good luck on those, though. Jenn and Jack had each taken one today. Specifically, it seemed that medications, veterinary drugs and paraphernalia, and electronic and other communications were within the scope.

"Satisfied?" the un-uniformed man asked.

"I'm satisfied the warrant exists and that there are limitations as to the type of items it covers and the locations that can be searched. I won't stand in your way."

The deputies filed into the house.

"Can someone show us the vet clinic?" Deputy Travis asked.

Nick had come to stand behind me. "I can."

Deputy Travis indicated with his head that the chinny deputy should follow Nick. My husband led her out the back.

"And we'll need access to the vehicles," Deputy Travis said.

I put the warrant on the flat surface of the rolltop desk by the front door. "I haven't seen them since they left this morning."

"They were both taken?"

"Yes."

"By whom?"

I tilted my head. "What does that matter?"

"Dr. Herrington is in jail."

"I'm well aware of that."

"So?"

"There are other licensed drivers besides him in the state of Wyoming."

"Do you know who took them?"

"I do. But the real question is where are they, and the answer is I have no idea."

"They're subject to a valid search warrant and hiding them would be obstruction of justice and possibly spoliation of evidence."

"No hiding. They're just in use for the day, and I wasn't given a by-the-minute itinerary. I suggest you coordinate with Mrs. Herrington."

He gave a snorty sigh and turned to the un-uniformed man, who was the only person who'd stayed behind with him. "Anything else, Ollie?"

Mental note made. Find out who Ollie is. Best guess: a prosecutor.

Ollie shrugged. "Not at this time."

I moved aside to let them in, and Black Bear Betty pounced. I hadn't sicced her on them purposefully, but I didn't hate it.

"You proud a'yourselves? Railroading another upstanding citizen of the county that votes for ya?" she said. "Or *against* ya."

Ollie jumped back as if she were a rattlesnake.

Deputy Travis looked nonplussed. "Black Bear Betty. How are you doing?"

"Less good than I should be, thanks to the two of you."

"We were just doing our jobs," Ollie said, his tone snippy and defensive. I winced.

"Not very damn well, then. Do better. Do *better!*" Black Bear Betty wagged her finger in front of his nose. Then she turned to me. "Nice to meet you and your husband." She stalked out, shouting, "Nobody better've blocked me in, or I'm ramming my way outta here!"

Nick returned from his guide duties and crooked a finger at me. I glanced at the table. Both our laptops were there. And our phones. I scooped them up.

"Electronics are subject to the warrant!" Ollie snapped.

"We are guests of this lodge from the US Virgin Islands. We arrived here Friday night on the late flight. These belong to my husband and me. The Fourth Amendment protects the right to privacy of individuals and requires you to show probable cause. If you have a problem with this, arrest me. Call a judge. I don't care. You're just not taking them."

Ollie turned to the Deputy Travis. "Do something."

Deputy Travis said, "Would you mind showing me something on each of them that proves they belong to you and not the Herringtons?"

It was a reasonable request. I showed him the screensaver pictures of us and our children. For good measure, I retrieved the e-tickets for our flight into Sheridan. "Not that it matters, but we'd never met nor spoken to Aaron Herrington before we arrived. Will this suffice?"

Ollie harrumphed. "I don't like that they can dump evidence now."

Was he referring to Nick and me? My cheeks burned. "Excuse me? Dump evidence? For starters, if you have technology resources and personnel worth their salt, you'd be able to retrieve anything currently on them, even if we deleted it. But more importantly, what kind of jerk are you? A simple request or at most an instruction not to interfere in any way with digital files that might be germane to your investigation would be the normal and frankly non-asshole thing to do."

Nick grinned. "I recommend y'all let this drop. She's just getting warmed up. I speak from experience."

The big deputy tamped his palm down. "Ollie, we're good. Mrs. Connell, we're good."

I fumed, waiting for Ollie to flap his jaws, but he got smart. "Fine. If we deem it necessary, we can obtain an additional warrant."

"Whatever." I handed Nick his devices and took mine. "We'll be on the front porch until you all are ready to leave."

Once I'd slammed the door and we were out on the porch, Nick said, "You held it together longer than I expected you would, Red."

I gave my husband a beatific smile. "With age comes dignity and restraint."

We settled ourselves in two Adirondack chairs. A yellow biplane flew low across the foothills.

"Oh, man, that's a beauty." My husband was an avid pilot who'd owned a plane until it was sabotaged and crashed into the ocean with him in it. Not to be foiled, he'd immediately bought another, after I'd rescued him from a desert island. We do not lead a boring life.

"Uh huh."

"I wonder who owns it and whether they'd let me fly it?"

"Babe, you having time for that is slightly less likely than us dying in a tsunami this week. Can we table that for now and get back to work?"

"Sorry. Time to update Jack?" Nick asked.

"One hundred percent. But I don't want him on speaker. Want to use one of my Airpods?"

"Good idea. And let's take it for a walk. I remember everything I need to tell him."

"Me, too." I divvied up the Airpods and pressed the number for Jack in my contacts. Then I slipped my arm through Nick's, and we walked down the driveway, well out of range of any potential eaves-droppers.

The call was picked up. "Jack here."

Nick nodded at me.

"Katie and Nick with a whole lot of updates. Is now a good time?"

"It's perfect. I'm just heading back to the lodge."

"Don't. The sheriff's department is executing a search warrant that includes the Herrington's vehicles. You and Jenn don't need to make this any easier for that little jerk that's with them."

"The county attorney?"

"If his name is Ollie."

"It is. Why don't we patch Jenn and Kid in? You can tell her about the search, plus we can do this update all at once."

"Good idea. Hold on."

One by one, I added Jenn and Kid. When I had everyone on the phone, I started with the execution of the warrant. Then I began filling the group in on everything I'd found so far. Jenn told us about Ollie's search at the clinic and the missing xylazine—an obvious black eye for Aaron and us that we'd have to deal with soon—and Jack added his progress.

Kid said, "Emily and I have been scouring the very thin Wyoming case law on a variety of theories I've had. We're starting to make progress. I'll have something for you guys tomorrow."

I motioned for Nick to chime in.

He said, "We just had an interesting visit from a woman named Black Bear Betty."

Kid and Jenn exclaimed over her, professing their undying love. I could see why. She'd grown on me fast.

Nick continued his story. "She overheard Benjy Mahones placing a bet on the Hellcats and telling the bookie it was a sure thing."

"Benjy Mahones being... " Jack said.

"Owner of Half Circle Ranch and the Hellcats."

"And this was when?"

"Last Thursday. A day before Victor died."

"That's gold," he said. "Solid gold."

Now Nick's face split from the expanse of his smile. "It gets better."

I gave him a questioning look. That was all Black Bear Betty had told us.

"I spent the afternoon putting background together on the team owners and players. And it turns out that one of them is related to the biggest crime boss in New Jersey. Want to guess which one it is?"

And I crowed with delight. "Benjy Mahones," I shouted.

"Yes, ma'am. Mr. Mahones. Nephew to Yuri Mahones. And brother of Lou Mahones, a notorious bookie from Brick City."

"Newark," I translated for the group. Only because Nick had already used that line on me once long ago.

Nick laughed, and I gave him a swat on the posterior. No fact was safe when this man of mine was on the hunt. "He's married to a woman named Ginger. She went to the same fancy private school in Suffield, Connecticut that Benjy was kicked out of."

Jenn said, "Kicked out for what?"

"Drugs. Had an industrial size baggie of coke in his jacket pocket, just hanging in his dorm room closet. They charged him with intent to distribute."

"Did he plead guilty?"

"Refused to. Said the drugs were planted. Tried to blame it on a roommate. Fast forward a few years. He goes to a community college, gets into one of the family businesses. Waste removal. Marries Ginger. They go on to live a happy and privileged life, in New Jersey and other locations, including Big Horn, Wyoming."

"Waste removal. I had an organized crime case once where the family was laundering money through a sanitation company."

Jack said, "We have the owner of the Hellcats—a guy with a drugs record who's from a suspected crime family—betting on them to win? There's our candidate for 'another guy did it.' Now let's go get the evidence to prove it."

TWENTY-SIX

SHERIDAN, Wyoming

THAT EVENING, Kid James smoothed his hair at the door to the Mint Bar. It was already clown red, and when it kinked, he looked like Ronald McDonald. He thought he had some green flags—great career potential, loved his mom, loyal to his friends. But the hair? A literal red flag. Casey had laughed at it the first time she'd slept over. He shook his head and pushed his way inside the bar. Not a great memory.

Then a worse thought hit him, and he froze.

Someone ran into him from behind. "Seriously?" a woman said, her voice querulous.

"Sorry," he said. His mind was on Casey.

Had she been laughing at his hair or was it *other* aspects of the night? *Dear God, please don't let it be my bedroom game.* He tried hard, and he focused on her needs first, like he was supposed to. Hopefully that made up for his relative lack of experience.

Great. Now here he was, racked with self-doubt, not the coolest guy, and definitely the one with the least cool hair, yet he'd been sent to initiate a conversation with Celeste Farinolo. *Sure, that makes perfect sense.* He'd rather be arguing losing motions on the minutiae of tax law in court than this.

Groaning, he walked up to the bartender, who was engaged in deep conversation with a guy who was guzzling a Ranier Beer, one elbow on the bartop near a puddle that not surprisingly smelled very beery. As in Raniery.

"Excuse me," Kid said.

Crickets.

"Excuse me. I'd like a club soda and lime, please."

The bartender rolled her eyes, the whites dramatic against thick black lines drawn to a point from her eyelids, like a Halloween cat. "You wanna open a tab?" She wiped up the spilled beer.

"No, thanks."

After she pushed his drink to him and he slid her some cash, she turned away. He worked his way through the crowd and spotted Celeste Farinolo almost instantly in the back near the pool table. She was recognizable from the (many) pictures she posted on Instagram. Almost every photo, she seemed to be dressed straight from central casting. Vacationing girl on a beach in Tahiti. Studious girl on campus at Smith College. Tonight, she was Urban Cowgirl in the old west with literal rhinestones on the breast pocket of her shirt.

The girl with her was someone he'd gone to high school with. Sandi Long. Even though Sandi had been more popular than him, they'd had some advanced placement classes together and been friendly. She had a horsey laugh that was infectious and hair curlier than his, only it was a nice streaky brown.

He went up to her. "Sandi Long! I haven't seen you in a while."

She squealed and threw her arms around him, enveloping him in tequila fumes and the softness of girl parts. "Kid! Oh, my God! You look like a lawyer!"

Celeste leveled an appraising gaze on him.

He grinned. "I do. And then some. Thanks, if that's how you mean it."

"I do! How's it going?"

"Great. I love the law life. What about you—what are you up to?" He noticed something had changed about her. She still had great curves and a pretty face. The change was a large scar on her arm that she wasn't trying to cover.

"Oh, you know. Teaching school, so I'm off for the summer."

He could feel the weight of Celeste's continued inspection, but for now he focused on Sandi. "That's great. Are you dating anyone?"

"Teddy and I—you remember Teddy?—broke up. After the wreck."

A wreck—the source of the scar? "I'm sorry to hear that. That's tough. My girlfriend just broke up with me, too."

"Oh? Who were you dating? Do I know her? Because I can talk some sense into her. You're the best thing to come out of our graduating class at Sheridan High."

He snorted and almost spilled his drink. "Thanks. You can be my wingman any time then."

"And her name??"

"Casey Hurd."

Celeste spoke, and her tone was acid. "That slut slept with my fiancé."

Her words were a slap. "Seriously? When?"

Celeste sucked a sip of her pink drink through a tiny red straw. "A few weeks ago. I just found out."

"We were still together then." Which wasn't true, to his relief. But he could connect with Celeste over shared pain. "She cheated on me. Wow. This sucks."

"Yeah. Big time."

Kid stuck out his hand. "Founding member of the getting screwed over club. Kid James. "

She put limp fingers in his hand. "Celeste Farinolo."

He kissed her fingers, bowing his head slightly. "Pleased to meet you, fair lady."

A slow smile spread over her face, and Sandi giggled. He released her hand.

Celeste sucked down the rest of her drink. "She wasn't the only girl he hooked up with while we were together."

"Good Lord, what kind of fool was this guy?"

Now she smiled big enough to show off a mouthful of perfect, whitened teeth. "The worst! I mean—I'm not too hard on the eyes, am I?"

"Not too hard on the eyes? You're gorgeous!"

She air smooched in his direction. "Smooth talker."

"Who were the others? I want to know who to stay away from."

"Buy me another drink and I'll tell you all about it."

Sandi held up her empty glass. "Me, too, successful lawyer."

Kid took out his wallet. "But of course." A few drinks was a small price to pay for getting everything he'd come for.

TWENTY-SEVEN

BIG HORN, Wyoming

JENNIFER BATTED HER TIRED, dry eyes, staring at the ceiling. It was twilight at nine p.m. on one of the longest days of the year, and the curtains on the bedroom window were open. A mistake, since she was trying to crash out early, but getting up to close them felt like too much effort. If she didn't fall asleep soon, she'd take some of the Tylenol P.M. she kept in a drawer in her nightstand.

For once, it wasn't her nightmares keeping her awake. In fact, she hadn't thought about the school shooter at all since Aaron's arrest—possibly because she hadn't fallen asleep since then. The butterfly effect in action. The arrest had distracted her from the nightmares but might ruin Aaron's career and reputation, scare off her clients, and derail her candidacy for county attorney.

A horrible thought struck her, and her hand flew to her mouth. It might prevent them from having a baby. Tears welled up in her eyes. She might be uncertain about whether she wanted to bear a child, but she didn't want the choice taken out of her hands.

None of those things mattered, though, compared to Aaron's freedom.

So, really—how could she sleep? She was reeling from... everything. How Aaron was doing. The bed without him in it. Him not telling her about the xylazine. Ollie finding out about it before her. Her sideline role in his defense.

She knew there could only be one lead attorney, and she might be blind to negative interpretations. Jack had to take the lead, and part of that was keeping his defendant's wife from hurting the defense. He'd extracted reluctant promises from her, like not to talk to Aaron at the jail about the missing drugs, where they could be overheard. To stay away from witnesses, for fear of attracting the wrong kind of attention from Ollie. Not to confront Casey about her hook-up with Victor, which Jennifer had learned of earlier from Kid.

It wasn't that she disagreed with Jack, it was just hard. And because she had a strong hunch he wouldn't approve of her going to Leo and Delaney, she'd kept that to herself. Talk about attracting the wrong kind of attention from Ollie. She had faith the legal team would investigate the issue themselves when it became a priority. She just wanted to know for herself from people she trusted. If they learned something, she would turn it over to Jack and Kid, that very second.

She growled and switched on her bedside lamp. From a dog bed on the floor beside her, Willett lifted her head and whined an anxious question. Beside her, Sibley opened one eye, then closed it, seeming to be satisfied nothing required the emergency services of a she-wolf. They did make the bedroom smell doggy, but they made up for it in protection and companionship. Jennifer patted the mattress. Willett jumped onto the bed and snuggled into her thigh.

As Jennifer massaged the dog's ears, she reached a decision. Sometimes checking things off her to do list, even minor things, helped her relax. She rolled over and lifted her laptop off the nightstand, much to Willett's chagrin. Once she had it open, she pulled up the final draft of her second novel. Her agent Joe had been asking for it, but she'd been too terrified to send it to him. Everything had gone so magically with her first book. *What if this one isn't any good and the publisher rejects it?* It would be devastating, because she really loved it. It was the story of defending Black Bear Betty against a murder charge, and how she and Aaron had uncovered the real killer, who'd tried to kill them, too, until Sibley had intervened. Thank God for their slightly grouchy, introverted, and very protective dog.

She attached the manuscript to an email, took a deep breath, and clicked Send.

It felt liberating.

She set the laptop on Aaron's side of the bed and spent another minute loving on Willett, feeling more tired by the second. Maybe she was ready try to sleep again. Then her phone danced across the nightstand, vibrating. Her heart leapt into her throat. Had something happened to Aaron? But, no—it was a text. She'd get a call if there was a problem.

She grabbed her phone and used her face to unlock it.

It was Joe. Already about her email? She frowned. It was two hours later on the east coast than in Wyoming, making it eleven o'clock.

W/publshg frds 2nite & evry1 buzzing abt yr bk! Can't w8 4 u & A 2 celebr8 w/me!!!

His texts were next to impossible to read, but once she'd figured it out, she groaned. Would Aaron even be out of jail by next weekend? If he wasn't, she wasn't going. No way she'd leave him in the Sheridan jail while she was wined and dined in New York City.

She turned her phone over. She couldn't respond now given all the uncertainty. Hopefully receiving her manuscript tomorrow would placate him. Immediately, her phone vibrated again. She almost didn't pick it up. How much more could she take?

But she checked anyway—she had to.

The message was from Veronica. *Jerry and I don't feel it's appropriate to discuss Victor with you. Please don't contact us again.*

She put her arms around Willett, who grunted in protest, but she didn't let go. No way was she going to fall asleep now.

TWENTY-EIGHT

Big Horn, Wyoming

FRIDAY MORNING BRIGHT AND EARLY, Jack smiled into his phone camera as his daughter Betsy chattered away. He was taking the call from Aaron's enormous orange Jeepster. The one the sheriff's department had the hots to search. Jack would be happy to let them do it, whenever they caught up with him. He was under no obligation to make it easy for them, though.

"Sissy said I'm invited to her birthday party!" Betsy beamed.

"That's great, sweetie pie!" he said.

Emily's mother appeared in the background. Agatha Phelps. He'd had a soft spot for the woman since before he fell in love with her daughter. Emily described Agatha as "trailer park meets the Southern church lady" because of her teased blonde hair and propensity for tight Walmart clothing. It was true, but it was part of her charm.

"I think your daddy has to get to work, honey," Agatha said.

Jack frowned. "I do. I'm sorry."

"Tell daddy we miss him," Agatha said.

"Miss you, Daddy!" Betsy trilled. "Snowflake, too!" Snowflake was their tiny old Pomeranian.

"I miss you all, too."

"When will you and Mommy be home?"

"Tuesday, I think." To Agatha he added, "Arraignment is Monday. It's full court press until then."

"We understand. Us girls are having a great time. Aren't we, my precious?"

"We are! Grammy painted my nails." Betsy shoved bright red nails too close to the camera.

Jack smiled. "Beautiful."

Betsy blew him kisses.

He blew one back. "I love you."

"Love you more," Betsy shouted.

He ended the call and pursed his lips, still holding his phone. Years before, he'd lost his first wife and their two children in a car bomb meant for him, back when he was working as a prosecutor in New Mexico. In fact, Snowflake had belonged to his first daughter. She'd loved her like Betsy did now.

His family's deaths had nearly been the end of him. He would have sworn back then that he would never be able to love anyone again. Not just because he missed them so much, but also because he was numb. Numb and scared of opening himself up to more pain. Then along came Emily, years later, and with her, Betsy. His love for them was different but just as big as it had been for his lost family.

Every time he was away from his girls, though, he fought the fear that he'd seen them for the last time. *Lightning doesn't strike the same place twice.* Or at least not often enough to worry about it.

A knock on the window startled him. It was Casey, who'd agreed to coffee before she went to work, since talking at the lodge would have been awkward. The coffee she wanted was in a food truck. He'd already purchased a Colombian coffee for himself. It was darn good.

He opened the door and stepped outside. "Good to see you, Casey. Thanks for meeting me."

She shrugged. "At least you're trying to help my dad."

Jack didn't acknowledge the implication that her stepmother was not. "What can I get for you?"

"I'll do the ordering. It's complicated."

He handed her a ten-dollar bill, which she snatched without saying boo. She was nearly as unlikeable as her father was the opposite. He hoped he and Emily could raise Betsy to act nicer than this.

He leaned against the dented front quarter panel while he waited on her. They were parked in Big Horn in front of the post office. Besides two bars and two restaurants, that was about all there was to the little downtown, but it was quite tranquil, between the burbling of Little Goose Creek and the notes of bird song floating out from the branches of the graceful cottonwoods.

When Casey returned with her coffee, he said, "How about we grab those rockers?" He gestured with his own coffee cup at the front porch of a restaurant across the street.

She pulled out her phone, checking the time. "Okay. But I only have fifteen minutes."

"Then we'd better get moving." He didn't mention that they would have had thirty minutes if she hadn't been late.

Jack settled into his chair, and Casey perched on the edge of hers, leaning forward. *She's nervous.* "I guess the best way to do this is to dive right in. I'm wanting to know about you and Victor Carvalho. His fiancée is saying the two of you had an affair."

"Affair?" She guffawed. "This isn't the 1980s. Puh-leeze. We hooked up a few times. No big deal."

Lord give me the strength to keep my thoughts to myself. "Potayto, potahto. How'd you meet him?"

"At the bar down the street." She pointed, chomping something. *Gum? With coffee?*

"What ended things between you?"

"He's too small for me. I like bigger guys. I mean, he was fit, but—

yeah. I like *older* guys, too." There was the hint of a come-on to her smile.

Now she puts on the Lolita act. He wasn't touching anything near her comment with a ten-foot pole. "How'd he take it?"

"I think he just moved on to the next woman who walked in. He's a slut."

"Any names?"

"Nope."

"You don't happen to know anyone he owed money to, do you?"

"It was just sex, Jack." She blew a bubble with her gum.

Criminal defense attorneys are professionally unshockable, Jack more so than others, but that didn't mean he enjoyed her attempts. "Do you know if he was taking any bribes?"

"Nope. But he did throw a lot of money around. I just assumed it was from Celeste. I do know he made bets. Lots of bets."

"On what?"

"On everything. He was like addicted to it or something."

"Did he have a problem with any other players?"

She stretched her arms high over her head, exposing her midriff. "Yeah. He and the number one guy on the Hellcats. They were always bumping chests. The whole teams were like that with each other, but especially them."

"Joaquim?"

"Yeah. That's his name."

"Anyone else?"

"Not that I know of."

"Do you hang out with anybody else on the Strikers or who works out at Red Grade Ranch? I'm looking for contact information."

"Anyone in particular?"

Jack thought about how things worked at his own ranch. The stable hands knew everything, because people talked in front of them. It was roughly equivalent to how people spoke in front of cleaning staff. "I really want to talk to stable hands. The ones who work closest to the horses. Preferably with Victor and Estrella."

She scoffed. "Um, I don't hook up with stable hands."

"But do you know how to contact any of them?"

She pulled out her phone. "Sometimes Victor would use this guy's phone to contact me. You know, so Celeste wouldn't see the messages. I'll send you a contact card. What's your number?"

Jack gave it to her, and she texted it to him. "Manny Smithfield?"

"As it says."

"Did you ever hear Victor say who he bet with?"

"Uh uh."

"Or did he talk about mafia or organized crime?"

"What the heck are you talking about?"

Jack tried again. "Did he mention that anyone in Big Horn was part of a crime family?"

She laughed. "Sounds a little far-fetched. But no." She slugged the rest of her coffee, spit her gum in the cup, and wedged the cup between her thighs. "So, how is this going to go for my dad?"

Jack cleared his throat. "The county attorney seems to be under pressure to label Victor's death as a murder and charge someone for it. He's got his sights set on your dad. If we can't prove he didn't do it, they'll probably charge him Monday."

"And Jenn is working for the other side." Her tone was bitter.

"No. Jenn had been helping the county attorney, but she's not anymore. But because she helped him before, she can't represent Aaron now. It wouldn't have been the right thing for her to do it anyway."

"Yeah. He deserves better."

"No. She's great." He knew many Texas attorneys who'd faced her in Harris county. They spoke of her very respectfully. "It wouldn't have been the right thing because Aaron is her husband. The jurors wouldn't have believed her as an advocate."

"Are you going to get him off?"

"I'm going to do my best."

She rolled her eyes. "Spoken like a lawyer."

"I don't have a crystal ball, Casey."

She chewed her lip for a few seconds then turned to face him. "Jenn is not who you think she is."

Jack didn't respond.

Casey put her hand on the arm of his rocker. "She's done some unethical shit. Stuff I know all about."

Jack stood. "I don't like where this conversation is headed. But I'll leave you with this thought. What hurts Jenn hurts Aaron."

"Maybe. Or maybe it could be what sets him free." She sprang from her rocker and trotted to her old truck.

Jack watched her go. He had no idea what dirt she thought she had on Jenn, but Casey's bad side seemed like a pretty dangerous place to be.

SINCE HE WAS ALREADY in Big Horn, Jack drove over to Red Grade Ranch to find Manny Smithfield, the stable hand who had covered up Victor's affair—or "just sex"—with Casey. He parked by a row of horse trailers and walked to the door of the stable, hoping not to run into Cliff, the ranch manager. His office looked empty, which saved him from making up a story. From where Jack was standing, he could see three people inside tending to horses. Two guys and a young woman. He texted the number Casey had given him for Manny.

Casey gave me your number. I've been hired to find out what happened to Victor. I need to talk to you about Victor and Estrella.

He congratulated himself on the careful wording. Truthful but not overly so. One of the guys didn't react. The other took out his phone, read the screen, and stuffed it back in his pocket. *That's him.*

Jack waited until he'd led his horse into a stall and latched the door. "Manny?"

Manny's head swiveled around. Dust-colored hair, shifty eyes, and a wispy moustache. "Yeah? Who are you?"

"The guy who just texted you."

Manny shot a glance at the stable door. "I'm working right now, man. Later." He scooped sweet feed from a barrel. The molasses smell made Jack homesick.

"It can't be later. I've been hired to find out what happened to Victor. It's very time sensitive."

The other two stable hands paused in what they were doing, all ears.

"Everyone knows what happened to him." Manny dropped his voice and turned his back on his fellow stable hands. "He fell off and got stomped. Now our vet is in jail for poisoning him."

"All of that is accurate but omits key facts. Like that the vet is not the one who did the poisoning and that no one knows who that was or how they did it. You were seen helping Victor and Estrella right up until the match started. I need to know everything you saw and heard."

His horse stuck its head over the stall door and let out a vibrato whinny. Outside, another horse answered. Call and response. Manny returned to the stall and poured the feed into the horse's feed bowl. It began gobbling it up. Sweet feed was like crack to horses.

"Are you going to give me a job if I get fired for talking to you?"

"You could get fired for talking to *me*?"

"To anyone. Because I'm not working."

Jack pulled out his wallet. "I have a quarter horse racing ranch in New Mexico. If you get fired, I could give you bus fare and a job down there." He handed Manny a card.

Manny slipped it into his shirt pocket. "Not in here. Outside with the horses. I can do my rounds out there while you talk."

"All right by me."

Jack followed Manny to the nearest pasture.

Manny let them in and shut the gate. "Please make this fast."

Jack hooked his thumbs in his jeans pockets. He could do fast. "On Friday before the match, did you see Victor take any medications?"

"No."

"Did you see anyone give him anything or interact with him oddly?"

"What do you mean?"

"Some drugs can be administered by injection or by breathing it in. Could someone have stuck him with a needle or tricked him into inhaling something?"

Manny frowned. The horses had gathered around the two men. Manny held out his hand for the closest animal to sniff, then he rolled the hand over and opened his fingers. There was a treat in his palm. The horse lipped it up and chomped contentedly. "No."

"Did you see him eat or drink anything?"

Manny made a circuit around the horse, running his hands under its belly, lifting its tail. "Sure. I keep his water bottle for him in a little cooler. He drinks some before the match and on every break."

"So, you saw him drink before the match?"

"Yeah. I handed him the bottle myself."

"How long before?"

Manny approached the next horse. "Maybe five minutes?"

"Did you prepare the water bottle yourself?"

"I did. It's not just water, though. He likes me to add packets of electrolytes and some other stuff that he mixes himself and puts in these little baggies. I used one of his packets."

"He gave you the packets?"

Manny frowned. "Uh, they were just there, with his stuff. Where he said they'd be."

"Did anyone see you making the water bottle?"

He shrugged. "How would I know? Maybe."

"Was the baggie or the water bottle ever out of your sight before Victor drank?"

Manny froze. "Well, yeah. Of course."

"Was anyone else around then?"

"Yeah."

"Good. Let's make a list."

"It was lots of people."

Jack smiled. "Luckily, I've got lots of time."

ARMED WITH A LIST from Manny that included players, stable hands, owners, friends and family, and vet staff for both teams, Jack made the short drive to Half Circle Ranch. He parked the Jeepster on the end of the stable farthest from the manager's office, not ready to meet him yet. Then he Googled *Half Circle Hellcats polo team Wyoming* and clicked on an image of the team from a press piece a few weeks before. In it, the players were sitting astride their mounts. Even when he blew the photo up, it was hard to see their faces on his phone screen, but the caption identified one of them as Joaquim Ramirez. He re-ran his search, adding Joaquim's full name. This time it yielded a close-up of Joaquim. Jack cocked his head, studying it. The man had a rat-like face with squinty eyes.

Jack pulled a Big Horn Rams ball cap out of the glove box. He jammed it down low and added sunglasses he found in there, too. *That'll do.* Before he shut the glove box, he noticed a small pair of binoculars. He palmed them, then scanned the area in search of his witness. It was a sprawling facility, with the stable, a barn, multiple pastures and pens, and a polo field in the distance. Most of the riders on it looked to be exercising their horses, but two were practicing one-on-one. There were no other riders in the areas he could see.

He looked around for signs that he'd been noticed. *All clear.* He pointed the binocs at the field and took a few seconds to focus them. He honed in on one rider at a time. Joaquim wasn't in the exercise group. It was harder to get a fix on the practicing riders since their horses were running and quickly changing directions. The riders, too, were moving around in their saddles. Up, down, twisting, leaning. He practiced patience and was ready when they slowed to give the horses a breather.

Bingo. Even with the helmet strapped tightly under his chain, Joaquim was easy to pick out. Jack settled in to wait for Joaquim to return to the stable. It wasn't long before he began riding toward Jack. He passed through a gate, then turned to follow the fence.

Jack waited on the fence line to intercept him.

The horse nickered as they neared Jack. Joaquim rocked back in the saddle. The horse stopped, huffing.

Jack waved. "Joaquim Ramirez?"

"Who are you?" His face pinched in on itself, and his voice sounded as suspicious.

"I'm Jack Holden. I've been hired to find out how Victor Carvalho died."

"Hired by who?"

"Dr. Aaron Herrington."

Joaquim winced. "He's a good guy. Did he do it? Did he kill Victor?"

"No."

"I hope not. I like him, man."

"I've heard you're a guy who may have important information."

"You mean you heard we were rivals." Joaquim shifted forward and the horse walked around Jack. "I had *nada* to do with him dying."

Jack had long legs and could walk fast when called for. Thoroughbreds had longer legs and could walk faster. He half walked-half trotted to keep up with the horse. "I didn't think you did. But I'd guess you knew him better than most people did."

"This is my first year here."

"You've been on the circuit together for a while."

"We never played together."

"You're deliberately missing my point, I think."

Joaquim stopped the horse again. "Okay, fine. Our rivalry. It's all about the show. I've known him a few years. We're *amigos*."

"You know about his past. Could someone from it have killed him?"

"Victor had troubles. Money. Women. His old team." Joaquim leapt to the ground, nimble as an elf and not much taller, and led the horse. Jack appreciated the slower pace. "But he had a way of shaking mud off, you know."

"Sure seems that way. What about his baby mama?"

"No way was Kaylee here."

"Kaylee's her name?"

"Kaylee Wynter. And she's broke. She needs Victor to play so he can keep up with child support. That's how it was with him, man. He got away with all this shiz because everybody needed him playing. Earning that *dinero* and feeding some to them. Ain't nobody from his past showing up and taking him out over money."

"Maybe one of them just wanted to hurt him. To scare him."

"Aren't you listening? They needed him in the saddle."

"Even bookies?"

He gave Jack a wary look. "Yeah, man. Same story. And his team owner most of all. The Strikers are nothing without Victor."

"By owner do you mean Jerry or Veronica?"

"Jerry, man. The same *jefe* who showed up here last week calling Mr. Mahones a dirty cheat."

This was news to Jack, and it felt significant. "Is Mahones a cheat?"

He made a zipping motion over his lips. "You'd have to ask him."

"Okay, then. How about Victor? Is he a cheat?"

He chuckled. "Are you asking about Celeste?"

Jack made a rolling motion with his hand. She was as good a place to start as any on the subject of cheating.

"Well, now, that girl was different. She didn't need nothing from him."

"Except for him to be faithful to her."

Joaquim threw his fingers in a snap. "Why you asking me if you already have the deets, man?"

"I'd like to hear it from you."

"She didn't know what he was getting on the side, if that's what you're asking, or he wouldn't be dead—he'd still be in the hospital having his *pene* reattached."

Jack hadn't met Celeste. He'd pictured her as a spoiled rich girl. Joaquim made her sound feisty and vindictive. Feisty and vindictive enough to punish her fiancée by poisoning him? "You knew about his other women?"

"Sure. Victor always had a side chick, never any one for very long."

"Were any of them angry at him, especially lately?"

"I don't know about angry. Hurt, I'd say. But they all knew the score before they dropped their panties."

"Pissed off boyfriends or husbands, then?"

"If there were *problemos* there, I never heard about them."

"What about Casey Hurd? Was Victor upset when she dumped him?"

Joaquim laughed so hard that he spooked his horse. "Whoa, boy. Sorry." Then he said, "Who told you that? He ghosted her for his new piece, just like he did the one before her." He laughed again. "Dumped him. That's funny."

"Did you know the others?"

They had reached the ranch buildings. Joaquim headed toward the stable door. "I already told you everything you need to know."

Jack stopped. "I beg to differ."

Joaquim looked over his shoulder, grinning. "You don't gotta beg. You just gotta let me be. I like myself employed, *vivo*, and in one piece."

Jack held out his card, and the rider took it. "Think about it and call me."

Joaquim waved the card in the air as he walked away, shaking his head.

TWENTY-NINE

SHERIDAN, Wyoming

JENNIFER TURNED TO FACE EMILY. They were in her Grand Cherokee, parked in front of Aaron's Sheridan clinic. She was anxious to go in and get started, but she'd made the team hold off. The clinic's opening hour was hectic, and Loretta wouldn't be able to help them. But there was also no time to waste. Ollie and his staff sure wouldn't be sitting on their thumbs.

Beside them, Kid pulled up in a white Denali. It was a vehicle he shared with his mother. Jennifer knew he'd been combing through ads for used vehicles before she'd taken leave that spring, and that he'd had to hold off buying one when their income dipped.

"I really appreciate you handling this," Jennifer said. She understood that she couldn't lead the investigation into the missing xylazine, but it was really hard to put something so important to Aaron in anyone else's hands.

Emily touched Jennifer's shoulder with light fingertips. "You're welcome. I promise I'll get this figured out."

Swallowing down a lump, Jennifer nodded then got out of the SUV. "Hey, Kid."

"Good morning, boss." Kid had gone grunge for the clinic in pressed jeans and tasseled loafers. Sometimes it was hard to believe he'd grown up in Wyoming.

Jennifer led Kid and Emily inside, where they were met with an antiseptic smell that didn't quite mask eau de pets and farm animals. The small lobby was cluttered but clean and had an old-timey feel that Aaron worked hard to preserve. While the clinic carried modern veterinary products, the artwork and furniture were vintage bordering on past-their-shelf-life.

A pale, freckled young woman stared at them, mouth an O in her round face, eyes magnified behind thick lenses. "Mrs., uh, Mrs. Doctor H. I mean Mrs. Herrington. I... "

Jennifer smiled. Not a happy smile, but a reassuring one meant to ease the girl's discomfort. "It's been a day already, Wendy. Is Loretta in?"

Wendy nodded like a bobblehead. "She's in her office. Should I get her?"

"We'd like to go back to her office and see her. Maybe just ask her if that's okay?"

Wendy punched something into a handset phone. She lifted the receiver and mumbled into it, nodded, said thanks, then hung up. "She said go on back."

The bell on the front door jangled.

"What are *you* doing here?" a female voice asked.

Jennifer braced herself. She wheeled to face her stepdaughter with a tight smile. "Good morning, Casey. Kid and Emily are working to get your dad home. I'm facilitating." She nodded at her colleagues and headed for a door behind reception.

"Hey, Casey." Kid sounded a little less lovestruck than usual. Internally, Jennifer cheered him on.

Casey rolled her eyes and didn't answer him.

Jennifer motioned Kid and Emily through the door and into a hallway. "Loretta is in the third door on the right."

The two of them walked ahead and waited for her outside Loretta's office. Jennifer knocked on the closed door.

"Come in." Loretta's voice sounded as dry as the plains and raspy as an emery board.

The team crowded into the small space in front of Loretta's desk.

"Good morning. Thanks for making time for this." Jennifer had a sudden urge to hug her, which she didn't indulge. She almost smiled as an image of herself hugging a porcupine flitted through her mind.

"I'm sorry I don't have chairs for everyone."

"Don't worry about us." Jennifer waved a hand in the air in front of her, like she was brushing away Loretta's concern. "This is Kid and Emily."

Kid tried to shake Loretta's hand, and Jennifer almost smiled when Loretta stared at it like he was offering her used toilet paper. Jennifer should have warned them that Loretta saw no need for touching of any kind. "I'm, uh, I work with Jenn, and I'm representing Aaron, along with Jack Holden."

"Nice to meet you, ma'am. I'm on the team, too. I'm a legal assistant." Emily's Texas accent underscored her perfect manners. She did not try to shake Loretta's hand.

Loretta nodded. "You know I'm Loretta. "

Kid said, "I understand you're the practice manager." They'd agreed in advance that Kid would take the lead. Jennifer suspected he was uncomfortable with her there, but it was good for his development.

"Yes."

"Aaron was arrested before he could get to the bottom of the missing medication."

"I know." Her voice was sharp, cutting him off before he could continue.

Kid looked disconcerted. "Have you looked into it yourself since then?"

"No. Doctor H. said to let him handle it."

Kid's chest enlarged with a giant breath. "Getting to the bottom of it is critical to getting him out of jail. My co-counsel spoke to him last night, and Aaron asked us to work with you to finish in his absence."

Loretta directed her reply to Jennifer. "Whatever Doctor H. wants."

Kid added, "We think it will appear more neutral with us involved, too."

"Can't be too neutral if you're his lawyers." Her face was expressionless.

Jennifer smiled. "It would seem that way, but attorneys have an ethical obligation to be truthful. Not that you wouldn't be, but that brings up the other advantage. You'll be assisting in the investigation under Kid's direction as Aaron's attorney. The clinic's attorney. That relationship might keep you from being questioned on it at trial, if it comes to that."

That teased a non-frown from her. "Good." She crossed her arms. "Where do we start?"

Kid licked his lips. "Let's talk about process. What would you do if you were looking into this without us?"

"I'd look at the logs then pin down the dates when the xylazine went missing."

"The logs?"

"Anybody who takes medication from inventory is supposed to log it. What it is, how much, what it was used for, and who took it out of inventory."

"Got it."

"But I already did that."

"Excellent. And then what?"

"Only ones that have keys to where we keep the meds are him, me, and the other vet, so I'd talk to Doctor H. about it. Like I did."

"Okay."

"And Doctor Sarah, which she says he did."

"Doctor Sarah?"

"Dr. Sarah Friedman. The other vet."

"Got it."

"Then I'd compare everything to the schedules. Who was working, who was on vacation. I'd review the notes from treatments and procedures in that time frame. You know, to see if there was something that would have required xylazine in the quantity that's missing."

"So that's the point in the process we're at?"

"Yes."

"Emily will be the one working with you. There are some things she can't do."

"I'll access the schedule. Doctor Sarah can analyze the treatments and procedures."

"And you're comfortable Doctor Sarah didn't take it herself?"

Loretta shrugged. "I haven't the foggiest. But she says she didn't."

Kid nodded. "Anything else?"

She closed her eyes and leaned back. When she opened them, she said, "I'd look at our security video for off hours. During a workday, it'd be hard for someone to access the meds without getting caught."

"That's great you have video. Any other steps?"

"If I still didn't know who'd done it after all of that, I'd interview the employees."

"Yeah, we'll definitely want that to be a last resort. People aren't always truthful. Plus, they talk." He rubbed his hands together. "I think we have a plan. Jenn and I will leave you and Emily to it, then. Emily can call me if she has questions. Sound okay to you?"

Loretta lolled her head to one side then the other, like she was stretching before a strenuous activity. "Anything for Doctor H. Cause any fool knows he wouldn't do this."

Jennifer felt a knot of tension ease in her stomach. Kid had done well. Loretta was supportive and cooperative, as much or more than she ever was. They'd get to the bottom of this.

Outside the office, something crashed to the floor.

Everyone in the office sat stock still for a second. Then Jennifer ducked out into the hall. Broken glass was all over the floor, but whoever had dropped it—and been eavesdropping on them?—was nowhere to be seen.

THIRTY

Sheridan, Wyoming

I WIPED my mouth as I admired the pictures in Aaron's office, where I'd been set up to work. There were some sweet shots of him and Jenn. Jack's office was filled with pictures of Betsy and me and his two children who died years earlier, and one of their mom. Why didn't Jenn and Aaron have kids? Based on the college photo, I'd bet they'd been married fifteen years or more. Maybe, like me, Jenn couldn't have kids of her own. Maybe I'd drop the fact that Betsy was adopted into conversation with her somehow and see what came of it.

I folded my paper plate in half with my napkin inside and threw it in the trash. Lunch had been pizza delivery to the clinic. Pepperoni and mushroom. It smelled nice and yeasty, but in truth it had tasted like cardboard. That didn't matter. I was hungry enough to line up at a pig trough for a meal of slop by the time it came.

It had been an intense morning after Jenn and Kid left. First, Loretta and I had a confab. Then I reviewed the inventory and logging system with her. When I had a handle on it, I pored over it alone in Aaron's office, even though Loretta had already done this part of the work once. For the investigation to truly be under the direction of the attorneys, I had to review this part of it myself before moving on to the next steps. Luckily, I was able to verify that the time frame had been short between when the xylazine had been entered into inventory and when Loretta had discovered the shortage. Praise the Lord and pass the biscuits—only three days.

Using the payroll system—one I was familiar with from my days as a legal assistant in Dallas, and which Loretta logged me into—I set up an employee spreadsheet. Who validly should have been at the clinic and when, and who should not have been there. The shortage didn't occur over a payday, luckily, or everyone would have had reason to show up, according to Loretta.

Loretta knocked. "You finished eating?"

"I am." I brushed the last few crumbs off the desktop into my hand and dumped them in the trash.

Loretta entered with a sheaf of papers. She set them on the desk and patted the stack. "This is a copy of the printouts of all our treatment notes. I didn't like the records going digital. It took us months to get it right, and the employees moaned like laboring cows every step of the way. But Aaron was determined. I guess now I'm glad we did it. This would have taken days before we made it electronic. Going over the schedule, pulling patient files, making Xerox copies. Now I did it in five minutes."

"I get it. Jack won't let me modernize his practice. Maybe after I tell him about your experience he'll soften up." It was only a mild exaggeration. Jack's practice was small enough that we brought our dog Snowflake to the office, and that we still got by with only minimal technological intervention and innovations. But truthfully, I'd brought it up to try to connect with Loretta. Earlier, I'd found common ground with her over our shared past in rodeo, in the short windows of time when we talked about anything other than the missing xylazine. We weren't exactly besties, yet, but we were working together just fine.

"Doctor Sarah is going to review these now. I gave her a set of the copies. She'll be able to do it fast."

"Could I be of any help to her?"

Loretta shrugged. "I don't think so. Suit yourself, but I think we're better off reviewing the video."

I knew Loretta had to watch the video with me, since I wouldn't know the faces of the staff members from Adam. "Let's do the video."

I scooched aside, and Loretta logged into the security system on Aaron's desktop computer. She typed with stiff fingers but no mistakes.

"What's your security setup like?" I asked. "Besides the video monitoring, I mean."

"An alarm if someone comes in a door after hours without turning off the system by entering the code and motion sensors at the windows."

"But there's no monitoring or alarms if someone breaks into the med storage area, is there?"

Loretta shook her head, her mouth a straight line. "But we'd see signs of tampering with the locks, or they'd be broken or gone."

Since the locks had been pristine, I couldn't see how forced entry to the meds storage was probable. Still and all, one never really knew. "And there haven't been any motion or door alarms?"

"No."

"Would you know if there was one?"

"Yes. The security company would call me."

"Would there be notifications in the app, too?"

The logo for the security system came onscreen, and Loretta entered a username and password. "I've never gotten a call, so I don't know."

I kept mum about the weaknesses in their system and its installation, even as I itched to fix all their problems for them. Loretta, I intuited, would not take kindly to my unsolicited opinions. "Okay. We're going to start with after-hours video, right?"

"Yep. And the system's s'posed to issue notifications of clips with animals, people, or vehicles that come into the camera range. No calls unless they trip the door alarm or sensors." Loretta clicked a bell icon to access the notifications. "We should only have to watch those. I hope."

"Do you look at notifications regularly?"

Loretta snorted. "I stopped after a week. Too damn many. Rabbits. Stray cats. Deer. Raccoon. A possum once. A few fox. Even a coyote. No reason to worry unless we get a call. Or so I thought."

I nodded. The clinic bordered on prairie. It wasn't like mine and Jack's upper floor office in downtown Amarillo. There, a notification after hours on the door camera for someone other than cleaning staff would be quite concerning. With the violent criminals Jack represented, we were careful. On the other hand, Jack was known to let clients work off their legal fees in the office, at our home, and on the New Mexico ranch. His great big heart was one of the things I—and his clients—loved about him most.

Loretta scrolled through notifications. I saw what she meant about the volume. Animals. Animals. Animals. "I'm hoping it's a stranger. I hate to think it was one of us."

"How would a stranger have gotten in, given that there were no alarm calls about a break in?"

"If they'd gotten access to the security code and med storage key somehow. It's not likely. It's just what I hope."

"Who all has the security code?"

"All the employees. We take turns opening and closing." Loretta frowned, pausing her scroll. "Here's some notifications worth looking at. Two for a vehicle and two for a person. Both on the same night, ranging over about ten minutes, starting at twelve fifteen." She clicked on the first vehicle notification and played the video clip. Bright headlights shone into the camera, obscuring the license plate. The second one showed the same video backing away, again with the blinding lights.

"It looks like something big. A truck or SUV," I said. Despite spending half my life around horses—which meant trucks and trailers for hauling—I gravitated toward sports cars myself.

"It's a late model Ford F-150. Probably a 2020 because it looks like mine."

I bit my lip to contain a grin. Such certainty and specificity. Loretta was a hoot. "How can you tell?"

"The shape. I've driven them all my life. I have the same model but mine's red."

A color I wouldn't have matched with Loretta's personality. Color me in-cor-rect. "Do you recognize it?"

"I don't. Let's go look at the people clips." She accessed one of the notifications and hit play on the video. I saw the backs of two heads walking to the truck. Loretta grunted. "A man and a woman. He's holding a cloth bag."

"I'd say she's tall, blonde, thin, and young based on the way she moves. The man is about her height, maybe a little less. Muscular. Fit. Dark-haired. Do they look familiar to you?"

"I'm not sure. Anyway, 'pears I clicked the second one, from when they were leaving. Maybe we'll get their faces when they're coming in."

The video started to play. The truck's headlights were off. The man was walking toward the clinic door.

Loretta cackled, but not with a laugh. Frankly, the sound was a little terrifying. She paused the video and enlarged the picture. It pixelated some, but the face that filled the screen was still fairly clear. I'd never seen him before, no surprise, but I'd recognize him if I saw him again and he was wearing that whopper of a gold chain around his neck.

Loretta was shaking her head. "I don't know what the hell he's doing here. We fired him back before Doctor H. ever bought the clinic."

"Who is he?"

"The world's laziest vet tech. At least he was when he worked for us. Buster Kemp ain't got no business being up here anytime, let alone in the middle of the night." After returning the image to its normal size, she clicked to continue playing the video.

The blonde woman trotted up behind the man, her face angled down, like she was avoiding the camera. He wheeled around, grabbed her by the back of the head, and kissed her.

"That's some impressive tongue wrestling," I said, fanning my face with my hand.

When they were done making out, the camera briefly caught her face before she ducked her head again. I felt a frisson of recognition but couldn't place her. She punched something into the keypad and opened the door. The two slipped inside.

Loretta was shaking her head. "Well, now I know why no alarms went off."

"The woman?"

"Don't you know who it is? She's our only staff member with hair and a figure like that. And she knows it's against the rules to bring in someone after hours who isn't an employee, too."

And then it dawned on me. "Spit in a well bucket. Was that Aaron's daughter?" I braced myself for a question about the expression, but it didn't come.

Loretta leaned back and crossed her arms. "Yes. That was Casey Hurd."

THIRTY-ONE

BIG HORN, Wyoming

INSIDE HER LITTLE office in Aaron's home clinic, aka the stables, Jennifer booted up her laptop. She didn't mind the smell of animals—feed, straw, and the rest that came with them—although it would be incorrect to say that she was used to it. She and Aaron had never had any pets until they moved to Wyoming. She'd spent nearly twenty years working in downtown Houston, too, where the only animals were the cockroaches that no amount of pest control services could control and the grackles that swarmed customers in the grocery store parking lots.

She ran her hand across the antique desk she'd found at a shop in nearby Buffalo. This office wasn't bad. It was nice, really. If she hadn't spent the first six months of her time in Wyoming loving the old cottage into a new life as her writing retreat and home office, she would be happier with this one now. She did appreciate the effort Aaron had put into it, creating a miniature replica of the cottage, down to coordinating the décor with her pink and black leopard print rug and surprising her with a comfortable love seat. Good thing, too, because Casey had, without permission, immediately repainted and redecorated the cottage. It would never again be the same sanctuary of quirky femininity she'd created.

But in this office, she had a direct view of the mountains out the window, and she'd never had that in the writing cottage. It had even been worth it to turn her desk around and her back to the office door to take advantage of the frame around mother nature's masterpiece.

She pulled her email up, hoping there'd be something from Leo or Delaney, since she hadn't heard from them by phone or text and felt the magnitude of seconds, minutes, and hours ticking by in their ongoing silence. Her inbox was at critical mass, and as she scanned the senders and subjects, she saw that most of them were about Aaron, but none were from the Kearny officers. The last thing she wanted to do was open any of the emails. What she wanted to do was drop by the jail. She'd almost headed there straight from the meeting with Loretta, Kid, and Emily. His hearing was in a few hours. She wanted to talk to him before then. But Jack had made her swear on her life she wouldn't do it until she was completely in control of her emotions.

"It won't hurt Aaron to think about how his lack of communication is damaging to everyone and everything right now. He needs to get motivated for his defense. I think he believes he'll get out of this because right beats might. What he needs to get clear on is that is a myth, and this is a *fight*. He needs to be smart, tactically and strategically," Jack had said. "This little 'oops' will really hurt him and you, too. Don't rescue him yet. See him tomorrow. You love him, and I know it will be hard, but do it for the case."

She'd had to make similar speeches to clients and their families over the years. Jack's job was to get Aaron out of jail, not to make them feel good.

At the last second, she'd swung her Grand Cherokee away from the jail and west toward the mountains and home. It was the right thing to do, for Aaron, for her. Besides, she and George were caring

for the badger boarding in the stable in Aaron's absence. He needed
to be checked on several times a day.

So, she'd gone to see him as soon as she arrived home, leaving the
dogs in their run so they wouldn't harass the pugnacious little fellow.
They'd been in to see him once before, and the badger wasn't cowed
by them at all, but there was no reason to stress him out. Seeing the
badger had raised her spirits the tiniest bit. Then she'd taken the dogs
on a long walk around the property before returning them to their
run for naps while she worked.

Now, her eyelids were fluttering closed, and she had to force
them open repeatedly. There was plenty she could do from here
before it was time to leave for Aaron's hearing, if she could just stay
awake. *Why can't I be tired like this at night?* When she'd finally
fallen asleep in the wee hours of the morning, her nightmares had
returned with a vengeance. The dreams were focusing now on things
she was sure had never happened. The shooter talking to her. Acting
like a father figure. Calling her his dolly. Telling her that everything
would be okay. He'd even very clearly said that she needed to protect
herself. Remembering it made her feel icky and dirty. This man was
Svengali'ing her in her sleep! It was not only disturbing and robbing
her of precious rest, but it was unproductive and didn't move her any
closer to identifying the shooter.

She slapped her cheeks just hard enough to sting. "Wake up and
do something!"

Casey's face floated into her mind. Emily had texted her a few
minutes ago, telling her about the girl's after-hours visit to the clinic
with some former vet tech. If she was behind the theft of the xylazine
that was endangering Aaron, Jennifer didn't think she could ever
forgive her. It was time to send in the DNA sample now.

Jennifer opened a browser tab and researched the best labs for
paternity tests, then selected one with great reviews and a stellar
Better Business Bureau rating. Their process looked logical and
simple enough, so she downloaded their form, reviewed it, filled it
out, printed it, and signed it. She pulled the samples out of her hand-

bag, put them in a padded envelope, and added the form, then sealed the envelope and addressed it. *That felt great.*

She would FedEx it from Kid's office in the morning.

In the meantime, she'd waited as long as she could for an update from Leo and Delaney. She sent them a quick group text. *Anything?*

Something shut in the front of the building. Not a loud noise. It sounded like the sliding door to the clinic, actually. She hadn't looked at the schedule when she came in. Was Aaron's vet tech Tron in today? He hadn't been there when she walked through earlier.

"Tron?" she called.

Silence.

A patient's owner then, she decided, early for an appointment. They probably felt odd with no one to check them in. She decided to greet them and see if she could do anything to help them. She'd go from there for a late lunch and some coffee in the house with Jeremiah Johnson. He'd cheer her up even more than the badger had. After that, it would be time to leave for the hearing. To face her husband and whatever the judge decided on probable cause.

She leaned over and grabbed her handbag.

A tremendous blow to the back of her head blanked out all thought except a recognition of the blinding pain. She felt herself falling forward, toward the floor, then nothing else.

THIRTY-TWO

Sheridan, Wyoming

KID PUSHED coffee in a Java Moon cup across the table to Aaron.

Aaron put his hands around the cup and slumped over it. It was still warm, and it smelled great. He was too agitated to drink it, though. He was grateful Jack and Kid were there, but they weren't who he'd been hoping to see. "Where's Jenn? She hasn't been in today."

Jack pulled at his collar. "I asked her not to come."

Aaron's rare temper flared, and he shot up in his chair, nearly spilling the coffee. "Why the hell would you do that?"

"Keep it cool or the guard is going to cuff you."

Aaron took a few deep breaths. He knew his anger could be terrifying to people. Not to Jenn, who knew he was a normal guy—a nice guy— in a big body. Other people just saw the big body. "I'm fine," he said through gritted teeth. "But *why?*"

"She's upset. Her judgement is compromised, and the jail is not a place to have heated discussions with you that can be overheard and impact your case."

Aaron was even more confused. "What are you talking about?"

Jack looked at him like he was dense. "You didn't tell her about the drugs in the clinic."

Aaron struggled to wrap his head around Jack's words. "I already told you—it slipped my mind. I had an emergency call-out and was arrested when I got home. It wasn't intentional. You told her that, didn't you?"

"I did. She'll come around. Just give her time. When she's calm, she'll be here."

Aaron sunk back in his chair, all of the energy sapped from his body. He'd counted on a dose of Jenn. Things were darker than ever after this xylazine debacle. He'd slept less than his first night here, even though he'd been moved into a private cell. His mind just wouldn't rest. It was desperately trying to figure out the hows and whys. "Do you think someone stole the xylazine to frame me?"

"Anything's possible at this point." Jack held his hand out toward Kid.

Kid cleared his throat. "Emily is with Loretta now. They're going to get to the bottom of it."

"What do they know?"

"I had an update from Emily right before we came in. They'd made a lot of progress. Last I heard, Dr. Friedman is reviewing the notes of treatment on the days it could have gone missing, and Emily and Loretta are reviewing security video."

Aaron felt more caged than he had back in his cell. If only he was at the clinic. He could kick himself for not having kept the investigation going. He'd known then it was a big deal, but things had come up. Gotten in its way. Put it on the back burner. Now, in light of his arrest, it was a huge deal. "Maybe you'll hear from her soon."

"Well, there is one significant development, and we need you to know about it before your hearing."

His hearing. He'd be leaving for it soon. They all would. Why hadn't Kid just told him about the significant development in the first place instead of dragging this out? Emotion flashed off inside him again. He concentrated on keeping it off his face and out of his body language this time. "Tell me."

"I don't get any pleasure from this."

He clenched and unclenched his jaw. "Just tell me. Please."

"During the time frame when the xylazine went missing, Casey brought Buster Kemp into the clinic after hours."

Aaron felt a sensation like falling off a high dive. Casey. *Not trouble with her, again.* "Who's Buster?"

Kid's voice held a trace of bitterness. "Someone she's hanging out with, apparently, since she made out with him in front of the camera."

Aaron stared at him. He felt bad for Kid, but right now, he felt worse for himself. "*Who* is Buster?"

"Sorry. A former vet tech who Loretta fired from the clinic."

"I don't know him."

"She said he predated you."

Jack said, "He showed up at the office with Casey on the morning after you were arrested. He's dark-headed, thick like a gym rat, and average height."

Kid added, "And he wears a pretty ridiculous gold chain around his neck."

Aaron closed his eyes. One of the guys with Casey at the polo fields matched that description. "I think I've seen her with him."

"Have they been dating long?" Kid said.

"I don't know that they are, but, if I'm right, they were together at the polo match. After it, anyway."

Jack rubbed his chin. He had a little stubble, but nothing like the bristle growing on Aaron's face after a few days without a razor. "*The* match? The one where Victor died?"

"Yes."

"Interesting."

"Have you seen the video?"

"Not yet." Jack pursed his lips to the side. "So, would Casey have the keys?"

"To the drug storage? No. But she would have the security code to get in the building."

"Okay. Well, Kid is going to find out everything there is to know on Buster Kemp, starting as soon as we leave here today."

Aaron nodded. "You should talk to Casey."

Kid sighed. "She won't really speak to me."

"She will if she wants her dad out of jail." Jack leaned his chair back on two legs. "I talked to her this morning." He sat forward with a thump. "As a result, I also talked to Joaquim Ramirez, Victor's rival. It sounds like they were actually friends. He said that Victor dumped Casey recently, for another woman."

Aaron felt like a punching bag. "Wait—Casey was with Victor?"

"I'm sorry. Things are moving so fast, I didn't realize you didn't know that. Yes, she was."

"Victor goes through women faster than Casey does men," Kid said.

Aaron shot him a look. He didn't like to hear other people talk bad about Casey, however justified.

Kid had seen the look, and his cheeks reddened. "I'm sorry, Aaron."

Aaron took a deep breath and shrugged. Kid was helping him. He had to let it go. "Don't worry about it."

Jack said, "You'll need to find out who Victor's new sidepiece was, Kid."

Kid nodded. "Maybe Celeste will know. She and I are buds now."

Aaron raked his hair back with both hands. "I just can't believe Casey would steal the drugs. I really need someone to come back and tell me when you figure out who did it."

Jack gathered his papers and squared them against the tabletop. "We can either work on your case or make trips to the jail to keep you up to date on things you can neither change nor act upon. Before you state your preference, remember your hearing is in an hour, and we have a hard deadline of Monday to figure out how to keep you from being charged."

Aaron closed his eyes. *I need my wife.* When he opened them, he spoke as gently as he could. "I understand. Do whatever gets me out of here. And please send Jenn. Please."

Jack and Kid exchanged a look that spoke volumes of something he really, really didn't like.

THIRTY-THREE

Sheridan, Wyoming

FROM HER BENCH at the front of the courtroom, Judge Peters peered down at the defense table where Aaron sat between Jack and Kid. The judge had long, curly gray hair and an air of energetic intensity. If Jack wasn't mistaken, though, she wasn't taking pleasure in her job. "The court finds that the prosecution had probable cause for the arrest of Mr. Herrington."

"Thank you, Your Honor," Ollie said, beaming from behind the table for the prosecution.

The gallery behind them in the courtroom buzzed with excitement. Jack couldn't believe how many people had come out on a beautiful Friday afternoon for a hearing like this, and in a fairly small town. It seemed that people who didn't even know Aaron were rooting for his downfall. *It's not good to be famous in a small town.* Aaron would have a hard time coming back from the damage to his reputation.

"Quiet, everyone." Judge Peters frowned at the gallery. "If I hear another sound while the court is in session, the bailiff will start escorting you out."

Jack stood. "Your Honor, the defense asks for a continuance on arraignment."

Judge Peters pushed her hair behind her ears on both sides of her head. "That's unusual."

Jack held his ground without speaking.

"Do you have a response, Attorney Singletary?" she said.

Ollie jumped up. "Um..." He remained silent for a few more seconds.

"Ollie?" the judge said, with just a hint of annoyance.

"We object, Your Honor. There's no reason not to proceed with an arraignment and get Mr. Herrington on his way to a speedy trial."

"Dr. Herrington," Jack said.

"Oh, of course. *Dr.* Herrington."

The judge screwed her face up. Finally, she dipped her head and said, "If Dr. Herrington isn't in a hurry, there's no need for us to rush him. Arraignment will be Monday at eleven a.m. See you then."

"Thank you, Your Honor," Jack said.

"Thank you, Your Honor," Ollie parroted. *Sycophant.*

Judge Peters banged her gavel. "That's all for today. Court is adjourned. Bailiff, remand Dr. Herrington to custody."

Immediately, the courtroom erupted in sound. People began to talk about the hearing as they gathered their belongings and headed for the door.

Jack turned to Aaron, who was wearing an orange jumpsuit too short in the legs and too tight in the thighs and shoulders. His client's dour face said it all. Even though they'd coached him to expect this result, it was a disappointment made worse by the fact that Jenn had not shown up for the hearing. Jack felt terrible for him.

Jack gripped him by the shoulder. "We'll see you soon. We've only just begun to fight. Keep the faith."

Aaron nodded, his eyes far away. "Thank you."

The bailiff approached. "This way, sir."

Aaron kept his head up as the bailiff led him away. Jack gathered his files and stuffed them in the briefcase he'd borrowed from Kid.

"Kid, a word," Judge Peters said.

Jack looked up in surprise. He'd assumed the judge had exited the courtroom.

Ollie bristled. "Don't you need me too, Your Honor?"

Judge Peters snapped, "If I did, I would have summoned you."

Kid hurried to the bench. Jack watched as the judge held a muffled conversation with him, her hand over the microphone to be sure it didn't pick up anything they said. When she'd finished, she got up and swept out of the courtroom in swirling black robe, and Kid returned to the defense table.

"What was that about?" Jack whispered, aware of Ollie's close proximity and the way he was leaning toward them.

"She's worried about Big City." Kid's low tone matched Jack's.

"Big City?"

"It's what she calls Jenn." Kid's eyes were bright. "I am, too. Why isn't she here?"

"I wish I knew." *Whatever her reason, it had better be good.* Her absence had sent the wrong message to the judge and the community, not to mention to her husband.

"I'm sorry," Kid said. "I wish I'd found something that would have helped."

"It wasn't your fault. If the prosecution hadn't come up with the missing xylazine at Aaron's clinic, we would have won. Judge Peters seemed sympathetic to our arguments that Victor's death hadn't been ruled a homicide yet, and that Aaron was arrested *before* the county knew about the missing drugs, but, at the end of the day, the prosecution cleared the legal hurdle. Just barely."

Jack's phone rang. The caller ID said Jennifer Herrington.

A voice behind him said, "Where's Mrs. Herrington?"

Jack pivoted to make eye contact with his adversary. "None of your business," he said with a smile.

"Rats and a sinking ship." Ollie walked through the batwing doors into the gallery, whistling.

Jack pressed Accept to take the call.

THIRTY-FOUR

Big Horn, Wyoming

ONE HOUR earlier

JENNIFER AWOKE to the sensation of something wet on her cheek. Her pillow was really hard, and her head... what was wrong with her head? It was on fire with pain, especially the back of it, and when she opened her eyes—big mistake—strobing lights hit her retinas like accelerants. Odors assaulted her senses. Dirt. Mildew, maybe? And something coppery. Nausea roiled inside her, and she closed her eyes very tightly until it passed. What had happened to her? Her mind was a cavern. Dark, empty, echoing and eerie. There were no answers to be found in there.

Her breaths had become shallow and panicky. She took a moment to slow down, then she eased her lids halfway open and gently probed her cheek. It was sticky and pressed into something that was not a pillow. She patted it. Prickly. Wooly. A rug. Whatever had made her cheek sticky was all over it, too. She tried to focus on the rug, to see the pattern. It was a kaleidoscope of colors and shapes. The movement in her visual field was overwhelming, and she eased her eyes shut once more. Somehow, the chaos settled in her brain. Pink. Black. She recognized the rug. Her own rug, in her own office.

Then the memories crashed landed in her brain. The noise in the clinic. Something hitting the back of her head, so hard, so, so hard. Falling. And then... Then, nothing. Nothing until she'd woken up on the floor.

So, this is where she'd landed after she'd been hit, which meant someone had been in here with her. In the stable, the clinic, her office. She'd been attacked.

Whoever it was might still be in here.

She pushed herself partway up. Everything went blurry for a few seconds. Focus came slowly. She reached out and touched the leg of her desk. Her chair was tumped over beside her. Her beautiful leopard print rug was ruined with her own blood. She touched it. Cold and thick although not dry. She'd been out for a while.

What time had it been before *this* happened? She reconstructed her day. She'd been at the Sheridan clinic that morning then she'd come home. She'd checked on the badger then walked for a good hour or more with the dogs before coming to the office. It must have been about one or one-thirty by then. Maybe half an hour later, she'd heard a noise she'd thought was an animal owner visiting the clinic.

An owner? Boy, had she ever been wrong.

Slowly, she turned side to side, looking for her phone, but she didn't find it. She wanted to cry at the thought of getting up to go for help. Biting her lip, she reached for her desktop and fell short. She tried again. Managed to grasp hold, gasped with pain.

You have to do this.

She scooted her body closer to the desk. The effort amped up the pain at the back of her skull until it was a blazing, roaring fire again. When she was nearly under the desk, she rose to her knees, rested, then, using the desk as a brace, she stepped onto one foot. The room swam, and she held still until it came back to equilibrium. *One to go.* Swallowing back bile, she used all her strength to lift herself to her other foot. If she hadn't had a death grip on the desk she would have toppled back to the ground. She closed her eyes for a few seconds of stillness as the fire in her head raged.

The first thing she saw when she reopened them was her phone. She'd left it on the desk. *Thank God.* She grabbed it, thinking she'd call Aaron, until she remembered that wasn't an option. A wave of hopelessness washed over her. Her anger at him earlier felt insubstantial. Fluff off a dandelion in a spring breeze. She just wanted him home, where she could have shouted for him, and he would have come running. Or maybe this wouldn't have happened if he was here.

But he wasn't, and there was no use thinking about it. She began to dial.

THIRTY-FIVE

Big Horn, Wyoming

"TAKE LITTLE SIPS." George held a cup of water in front of her. He'd made it from the lodge to the stables in less than a minute after she'd called him. He was still on the phone with 911 when he'd arrived. After he'd propped her up against him and moved her to the love seat, he'd made an ice pack for her head and gently cleaned her up.

"I'm afraid I'll throw up." *Again.* Jennifer lowered her cheek onto the arm of the little sofa.

"I brought you a trash can. It's right on the floor beside you."

"You're an angel. Do I hear sirens?"

"You do. I need to meet them and bring them in here. I'll be back as fast as I can. Will you be okay?"

It hurt to smile, but she did. "Yes, thank you." She let her eyes shut out the light again.

She must have drifted off then, because it felt like no time had passed before she heard his voice in the hallway, coming closer to her, plus the voice of another person. A woman.

"I'm back, Jenn. I have help with me," George said.

"Thank you." Jennifer kept her eyes closed.

A woman said, "Mrs. Herrington, how are you?"

A familiar voice. She squinted her eyes open and saw the aggressively chinned Deputy Haigle. It was the third time she'd seen her that week, and all three she could have done without. Speaking softly, Jennifer said, "I have a really bad headache."

"An ambulance is on its way."

Jennifer groaned. "Okay." She didn't want an ambulance, but she knew there was a risk of internal bleeding and swelling in her head. She'd been out a long time. Based on her time estimate of when she'd been attacked, she'd been unconscious for two hours. She could foresee an overnight in the hospital on her horizon.

"Can you tell me what happened?"

Jennifer wished it could wait until her head felt better. Tomorrow. If it even felt better by then. Right now, she would have guessed it wouldn't for years. She let her eyes waft closed again. It felt much better that way. "I got hit in the back of the head."

"What time did this happen?"

"Maybe two and a half hours ago, I think."

"Did you see who did it?"

"No. I was at my desk. My back was to the door."

"They completely took you by surprise?"

"I heard the stable door open and close. I thought it was Aaron's vet tech or the owner of a patient. Then when there were no other noises, I decided to check on whoever it was. Then boom, out went the lights before I could do it."

"The door was unlocked?"

"Yes. Because I was out here."

"What about video?"

"We have cameras that face the doors on the house. Aaron was going to install them here at the clinic, too. I'm not sure if he did it yet, though. Maybe those will show who it was."

"Anything pointed toward vehicles?"

"No."

Haigle said, "Mr. Nichols, did you see any vehicles or people here?"

"No, but I left early this morning. Had some doctor's visits." He waved his stump by way of explanation. "I'd been back here about half an hour when Jenn called me for help."

Jennifer had a thought and opened her eyes. "The dogs."

"I left 'em in the run."

"I wish I'd brought them in here with me."

"Yeah. Nobody woulda messed with you with Sibley around." He pursed his lips and shook his head. "I should have brought 'em out here when I came to help you. I didn't think. I just ran. You sounded pretty bad."

Haigle said, "You mentioned a vet tech."

"Tron. Yes. I don't know his schedule, and I haven't seen him today. His contact information is in my phone." She talked George through texting the contact to Haigle. He did as she asked then returned it to her.

Haigle walked to the desk. She brushed her fingers across the clean surface, empty except for Jennifer's laptop. "Is anything missing?"

Jennifer held up her phone. "I have no idea, really. I haven't been able to search the clinic, obviously. They didn't take my phone or laptop, though."

"Is there someone who could tell us?"

"Aaron." She managed a pointed glance at Haigle, who didn't blink. "Or Tron. Call him."

Haigle shut her notebook, nodding. "I hear the ambulance out front. I guess that's all I need for now."

Jennifer held out her hand. "Wait. This was scary. I was attacked. Don't you have any thoughts?"

Haigle shrugged. "It's kind of hard to know without a suspect. Robbery gone wrong? Vandals afraid of getting caught? Someone out here retaliating for your husband's part in a murder? We won't know without more evidence."

Jennifer ground her teeth. "What murder? And what part exactly did my husband play?"

Haigle held her gaze for a moment, then shook her head.

"What evidence are you going to collect, then?"

"We'll send someone out to take fingerprints and look at your video. Take care, Mrs. Herrington." And she walked out.

If Jennifer hadn't been sure she'd fall the second she stood up, she would have run after the deputy. Someone had attacked her. She could have died. And unless she was mistaken, law enforcement didn't seem to care.

THIRTY-SIX

Sheridan, Wyoming
Two hours later

KID POPPED the tab on a Blacktooth Brewing Copper Mule while waiting for Casey at the clinic. The ginger lime cream ale went down smooth and easy, although he felt a twinge of guilt enjoying a beer with Jenn in the hospital. He hadn't even had a chance to go see her yet. Maybe after Casey.

The clinic had just closed, so he expected Casey to walk out at any second. Emily had left hours before, when Loretta had to handle an emergency involving the multiple participants in a dog fight. Emily planned to finish the investigation the next day. Loretta had promised the investigation was hush hush. Kid was watching and listening as the employees walked to their cars. He hadn't seen any signs things had gotten out about it, which was good. Kid could talk to Casey about the video without her defenses up about it ahead of time.

Casey appeared in the door in low-slung jeans and a top she was in the act of adjusting to try to expose her belly. Then, as if she knew she had an audience, she sashayed out like a Victoria's Secret model on a catwalk. His heart did a belly flop. Why was he attracted to this woman? Everyone thought she was a beast. He'd thought they just didn't know her like he did. When it had just been the two of them, she'd been different. But now he was figuring out what everyone else already knew. For Pete's sake, she hadn't even cared enough to show up at her dad's hearing that afternoon. He deserved better, and he needed to move on. To that end, he'd signed up for a dating service a few weeks ago. He hadn't opened it since he posted his profile.

Apparently, it only worked if you used it.

He got out of the Denali where he'd been waiting with the windows rolled down, clutching his can of beer like a life preserver. "Casey."

She tossed her ponytail. "What are you doing here?" *Yeah. A beast.*

"We need to talk."

She'd made it to the door to her old truck, and her hand grasped the handle.

"It's about your dad."

She opened the door, paused, then slammed it shut. She turned to face him, fists on her hips. "What about him?"

"For one, he really wants you to come see him."

"He said that?"

"Yes." And Kid didn't feel an iota of guilt for lying. She'd lied to him enough to deserve a small taste of what she'd been serving. "He's being held through the weekend until his arraignment."

"Okay. What's the other thing?"

"What do you mean?"

"You said 'for one.'"

"Oh. Let's talk about it over a beer."

She cocked a hip. "I'm not going out with you, Kid. Good try, but it's over."

He wasn't made of Teflon. Her words pierced his defenses. He hadn't been asking her out, had he? "I brought a six-pack." He lifted his can. "Copper Mule."

She looked wary, but she walked over. He opened the back door and pulled two cans out of the webbing. His empty went in a garbage bag hanging off the back seat. His mom did not appreciate a mess in her Denali. God, how he wanted his own car.

"I'm not getting in your car."

"That's fine. I'm good out here." It was a nice night, and it was probably for the best that he wasn't near her in close quarters where he'd get sucked in by the heady lilac smell of her. He didn't know what it was, but it had to be illegal. It literally made him feel high. He handed her the beer. Waited for her to slug some down. "Your dad is concerned about this guy you're dating."

"My dad or you?"

"Your dad. Is he the guy you brought to the office?"

"Yeah. Why is he concerned?"

Kid had to think fast. "Loretta."

"Loretta?" Casey's scowl was bulldog worthy. "What did that nosy bitch say about him?"

"Apparently she fired him from here awhile back."

"They didn't fire him. He quit."

"Huh. Where's he working now?"

"At a solo practice. Dr. Wyles's clinic. He's a vet tech."

"So, you guys have a lot in common."

"As a matter of fact, we do."

"Does he live in Sheridan?"

"Why the third degree?"

"Literally, I'm your dad's proxy here. He asked me to ask you."

"Well, I don't like it."

"Does that mean he lives here?"

"No. He lives in Ranchester, if you must know."

Buster and half the young people in Sheridan lately. The price of living and cost of housing had been skyrocketing. It was nothing compared to the east and west coasts, but, for Wyoming, it had gotten pretty spendy. Hence Kid still occupying the same bedroom he had his whole life. "I'll pass it on."

"You do that."

"I heard you talked to Jack this morning. He said it was really helpful."

"If you're just going to yatter, I need another beer."

She'd basically shotgunned the first one. He retrieved one and tossed it to her. She threw her empty in the back of her truck. "Jack has already done some follow-up interviews from the leads you gave him."

"I didn't think I was that helpful."

"Well, he talked to that stable hand you told him about."

"Manny."

"Yeah. And Joaquim."

She seemed to stiffen, but her face didn't change. She chugged several long gulps. If she asked for a third beer, he'd tell her no. She was drinking too fast. He wasn't going to be responsible for putting her behind the wheel buzzed. Buzzed driving is drunk driving, as the billboards around town had been saying.

When she didn't comment, he added, "Joaquim said Victor had a new girlfriend before he died."

"Like I told Jack."

"Who is it?"

"I have no idea."

"No one has talked about it?"

"Not to me."

"If you had to guess?"

"If I had to guess, I'd say that girl who hangs out with Celeste has been pretty hot for him."

"What's her name?"

"Shiva or something. She's a Crow chick. I don't really know her."

Kid knew a Shiva in high school, although not well. A really good-looking Crow girl. It had to be the same person. "Is she why he dumped you?"

She dropped her empty can to the ground and crushed it with her boot. "What did you say?"

"Joaquim said Victor dumped you when he found someone new. Like he dumped his old girlfriend when he hooked up with you."

"You're an asshole, Kid. Before I just thought you were a wimp, but I've changed my mind."

Thank you for making it easier for me to dislike you. A surge of anger emboldened him. "I'm not the one who slept with Victor when he was cheating on the girlfriend he was cheating on his fiancée with. Still, that must have been tough. I know Shiva. She's really hot. Was it because she's better looking than you, or did he just get tired of you being such a bitch?" He'd never talked like this to anyone in his life, and he was torn between feeling horrified and vindicated.

She flipped him off and fumbled with the door to her truck. She got in and slammed it behind her. The engine roared to life, and she backed up so fast he was glad no one was behind her. Then she slammed on the brakes. Her window came down. Her face had changed. It was red and splotchy and something else. Something softer. "I don't know why he dumped me, all right. I just know he didn't want me anymore. He treated me like garbage. There. Are you happy, now?"

She sprayed gravel as she accelerated away from him.

Kid knew he'd scored a moral victory, getting information on Buster from her and forcing her to tell him about Shiva. It was his job. Jack had asked him to do this. Aaron needed him to. But guilt replaced his vindication. Casey was right. He'd been an asshole.

That didn't mean he felt sorry for her, though. At least not much.

THIRTY-SEVEN

Sheridan, Wyoming

AARON HELD out his hands for his cuffs to be removed. Jack sat across the table, and Aaron didn't like the look on his face. It spelled bad news. Or more bad news, to be precise.

He had a moment of disembodiment. What day was it? Losing a sense of his place in time was like floating in space without oxygen or a space suit. He pieced it together. Yesterday had been the hearing, which was Friday afternoon. Then he'd slept. Without clocks or natural sunlight from windows, his only way to gauge time was by meals. He'd just finished another gummy breakfast burrito and could still smell his own coffee breath, so it was morning. Saturday morning. Two days until Judge Peters would decide whether the county could charge him with murder. One day after his wife had failed to visit him or show up for his hearing.

The guard shut the door, and Aaron skipped hello and good morning. "Where's Jenn?"

Jack put his palm in the middle of the table. "I have news. The important thing to take from it is that everything is okay."

Sweat immediately broke out on Aaron's forehead. "Just tell me."

Jack licked his lips. "Jenn was working in her home office. There was an intruder. She was hit on the head, and she spent the night at the hospital, but the doctors have said she's fine."

Aaron jumped to his feet, blood pounding in his ears, his face, his chest. "She was attacked and spent the night in the hospital? She could have been killed!"

He felt impotent. He wanted to tear the walls down to get to his wife. It was wrong that he was in here and she was out there, without him. That someone had hurt her, when he considered it a sacred honor to protect her. But something he'd done had led to him being here—damned if he could figure out what it was or how this had happened—and she was alone.

The door burst open. "Sit down or I'm cuffing you!" the guard yelled.

Jack held up his hand. "We're fine, officer. His wife was attacked and injured, and he's worried about her. He's sitting back down. Aren't you, Aaron?"

Aaron sank back into his chair, barely registering the guard's entry or the words of either man.

"Stay seated. Having guests is a privilege, not a right. Follow the rules." The guard glared at Aaron and left.

"I promise, Aaron, her condition is great. They're releasing her soon. They ruled out a brain bleed and monitored her for swelling all night. She definitely has a concussion and a headache, but that's it. Of course, that is why she missed the hearing."

"She was unconscious?"

"Yes. But she called George when she woke up. He took good care of her and got emergency services right out there."

"How long was she out?"

Jack squirmed a little in his seat. "About two hours."

Aaron lowered his head into his hands. "That's practically a coma."

"Not quite. But the doctors have definitely advised her to rest her brain for the next few weeks."

"Does she have traumatic brain injury?" Aaron had taken far too many hits to the head in his football days. Like most players, his brain had suffered, and he worried about TBI and chronic traumatic encephalopathy. Jenn's cousin Hank, a former bull rider, was battling TBI himself.

"There's no reason to believe that at this point."

Aaron's adrenaline ebbed. His fingers tingled. Tears built up in the corners of his eyes. "Shit."

"Yeah. I'm really sorry."

"Who did this?"

"No idea. Jenn was the only person on the property. No witnesses. And the cameras were in their packages in your office."

"I hadn't gotten around to installing them." He felt like the worst husband in the world.

"After the xylazine was stolen at your other clinic, I'd make that a priority."

Too little, too late. "Do you think this is related to my situation and Victor's death?"

"It would help your case if it was."

"Was anything missing?"

"No one knows. The deputies have been trying to get in touch with your vet tech to see if he can do an inventory."

Aaron shook his head, over and over. "He can't. Tron is on vacation. A float plane fishing trip in Alaska. He's not reachable and won't be back for another week."

"Unfortunately, then, Aaron, even if this was related, we'll know too late for us to avoid charges."

Aaron closed his eyes. That was bad news, but far less important than how much worse this could have gone for Jenn, with him stuck in this god-awful place.

He had to get out of here. He just had to.

THIRTY-EIGHT

Big Horn, Wyoming

I HOBBLED around the kitchen as I made a second round of double espressos for Nick and me with Aaron's fancy new machine. The hobbling was from horseback riding the day before at Hank and Maggie's ranch. We'd driven Ava, Collin, Michele, and Rashidi out there to stay for a few days. That's when the ride opportunity had come up. We'd checked in with Jack first since Aaron's case was the priority, but Jack had just thanked us and told us to go have fun—promising to ruin our weekend instead.

It had been a blast. So much fun that it went on well into the night, with everyone but me drinking too much KO 90. I haven't touched a drop of alcohol in years and don't intend ever to do so again. Booze and Katie are not a good match. But even lack of sleep does a number on me these days. I'm officially too old to stay up past my kids' bedtime. At least my husband had a safe ride home with me, and I was entertained by him singing AC/DC at the top of his lungs out the car window.

Jack had waited up for us and met us at the door with the news that Jenn had been attacked and was in the hospital. God, did we ever feel guilty. Maybe she wouldn't have been assaulted if we'd been here. True to his word, Jack said he'd emailed us a work list earlier in the afternoon for Saturday. We'd gone to bed, but I'd stared at the ceiling for much of the night, worrying about Jenn.

So, here we were on a Saturday morning, booting up laptops and pumping caffeine. Jenn wasn't home yet, but she'd called to assure us she was okay.

"I wish we'd been here," I said for the millionth time as I stirred honey and oat milk into our espressos.

"It might not have made a difference." My husband has a very male way of using logic when discussing emotional subjects. I haven't killed him for it yet, but it's not out of the question.

"Maybe not, but maybe it would have. And it doesn't change me wishing it." I brought the espressos to the table. "What's on the list for today?"

Nick turned my laptop to face me. I opened the email from Jack.

Here's Saturday's wish list. Thanks!

The list was long, but there was nothing too difficult on it. Most of it was continued research into the backgrounds of various players—or suspected players—including some new ones since Thursday.

But I couldn't start until the kitchen was clean. I returned to deal with the espresso mess. Willett got up from where she'd been sleeping by Nick's foot, pausing for a downward dog, and followed me. Sibley snoozed on, laying on her side in a patch of sun near the table. I put away the oat milk and honey, dropped spoons in the dishwasher basket, rinsed the portafilters and put them in the drying rack, and wiped down the counter.

Nick looked up from reading the list on his own laptop. "I'm supposed to place a bet on the Hellcats for this weekend, using that mobbed-up place."

"Suspected mobbed-up place."

He grinned. "Lou's."

"Are they open on a Saturday morning, I wonder?"

"My bet—did you catch my pun?—my bet is yes."

I moaned and rolled my eyes, rejoining him and taking my seat at the table. Willett flopped to the floor beside me this time.

"Weekends are for sports. That's prime time for placing bets." He pulled up an excel spreadsheet. "I already logged their info. No time like the present."

I leaned back, all ears. I'd never placed a bet before. Never talked to a bookie. "Could you put it on speaker?"

Nodding, Nick dialed the number and activated the speaker. The phone rang only once before someone picked up.

A man spoke in a gruff New Jersey accent. "Yo, this is Lou's. What are you having—we're offering a dynamite deal on a parlay."

"I want to place a polo bet."

"What's the magic word?"

"Uh, please?"

The man's tone changed, just shy of menacing. "Who is this?"

"My name is Nick Connell."

"Don't ever call here again, Mr. Connell." The line went dead.

I paused with my cup halfway to my mouth. "He just hung up on you."

Nick looked at me with incredulity. "What the hell are we supposed to take from that?"

I snorted. "Some great PI once taught me that the person with the most to say is the least willing to say it."

He winked at me. "Was he handsome, too?"

"What makes you think it was a guy?" Then I thumped my cup down. "Now we have to figure out how to get Mr. Strong and Silent back on the phone."

THIRTY-NINE

Sheridan, Wyoming

JENNIFER ROTATED her head gingerly on her favorite pillow, glad to at least be in her own bed. Even with painkillers, the back of her head hurt. While she hadn't seen it with a mirror, she'd been told that they'd shaved a small patch to stitch and bandage her up, but that it didn't show once her other hair fell over it. It was going to itch like crazy. The hospital staff hadn't let her sleep all night, checking on her every few minutes and shuttling her back and forth for imaging and tests. *Hospitals are the absolute worst place for healing.* That made three nights in a row with little or no sleep. The exhaustion was almost worse than the headache from the assault. Or maybe they'd merged together. Misery was misery at this point.

The absence of Aaron during the experience had been razor sharp. Coming home without him on Saturday morning, imagining the note that wasn't there—*I'm thankful you're alive and with me*—was excruciating. At the lodge, she'd submitted to the caring questions of George, Katie, and Nick until she couldn't keep her eyes from closing any longer. The dogs had followed her into the bedroom where they'd all settled in to finally, finally sleep.

The closed-eye thing had only lasted until she'd put her head on the pillow.

After fifteen minutes of dark intrusive thoughts, she accepted her fate. She'd be a zombie for another day. Oh well—she would have had to be up soon to make her first hypnotherapist appointment, anyway. She'd gone back and forth for the last few days on whether to keep her appointment or postpone it until next month, but there was nothing she could do for Aaron right now, and the hypnotherapy might help her handle the current stress. Hopefully her concussion wouldn't impact her receptiveness to hypnosis.

She swung her legs out of bed and slipped her feet into her warm weather slippers. Criss cross straps and open toes, but still fuzzy and pink. Four ears perked and two heads rose. "Come with me, girls."

She padded out and across the grassy expanse to the stables with the two malamutes bouncing happily alongside her. A recurring culprit in the thought parade that had kept her awake was the DNA test. She'd suddenly realized that she hadn't sent in the test packet yesterday. The envelope was in her office. She'd just grab it and then, on her way to town, she could stop to ship it.

The door rolled quietly open. Aaron could have installed a normal door for his clinic, but he had kept the stable slider. She loved it, and she was glad for the sound it made when she shut it, announcing her presence. Returning to the stables less than twenty-four hours after her attack was a little frightening. If anyone else was in there, she wanted to warn them off. Her dogs would let her know if she wasn't alone, though.

"Hello?" she said.

There was no answer.

The two malamutes raced into the small reception area of the clinic, sniffing frenetically. Hair rose on their backs. Whatever they smelled, they didn't like, but they gave no indication of another presence. Jennifer walked around the room, trailing one hand over the reception desk, the back of one of the waiting room chairs, the top of a coffee trolley. There didn't seem to be any fingerprint dust. It was disappointing.

She passed her office and went to the stalls, closing the door to block the dogs. Loretta had left her a voicemail that Game & Fish were coming for the badger tomorrow. She'd really grown to love him. He chirped at her as she prepared his meal, refilled his water bottle, and slid his dish into the extra-large dog crate he was staying in.

"Rest and heal, little guy. You've only got one more day with us."

She went back into the main building and was met by the malamutes.

"Inside." She pointed for the dogs to enter her office ahead of her.

They bounded in. She wasn't always sure whether they were acting upon the words themselves or her body language. Either way, the girls were incredibly intuitive companions. Sibley ran straight to the bloody spot where Jennifer had been unconscious. The dog turned to Jennifer and wooed her displeasure. Willett whirled, frantic, bombarded by signals that upset her. Woos turned to growls.

"It's okay. I'm fine now."

Sibley nosed Jennifer's hand. She rubbed the dog's ears. They were pretty good at communicating by body language themselves.

"Okay. On to the DNA test."

But the only thing she saw on her desk was her laptop. She lifted it. No envelope. She opened the drawers, thinking maybe one of the law enforcement officers had stuck it in one of them. When she didn't find it in a drawer, she looked on her bookshelves, then on a filing cabinet, and in the filing cabinet drawers. Next she checked the trashcan, which was empty. She turned in a slow circle. There was nowhere else to look. Unless someone had stuck it into a filing folder or the pages of one of her books, it was not there. And no one would have had reason to do that.

The envelope was gone.

She took her phone from her pocket and texted George. *Did you mail an envelope that was in my office yesterday?* It was at least a possibility. Certainly, no cops would have done that for her.

Three dots appeared. George was quick to reply, but a slow one-handed typist. She snapped her fingers to get the dogs' attention and pointed in an arc—out of the office and toward the clinic door. They bounded out, tails up, and she followed with her laptop under one arm. By the time she was back to the house, George's reply had landed.

Nope. Didn't see any envelope.

She opened the door for the dogs, frowning. So, something was missing. Her envelope with the DNA request form and samples. But who would have wanted that?

For a second, Jennifer contemplated asking Deputy Haigle about it. But to do that would be to alert the woman of its existence. The information would be recorded and end up in the public record. That couldn't happen, so she didn't call her.

She turned on the shower and waited for it to heat up, still pondering the mystery. She couldn't think of any reason a person breaking into Aaron's clinic would have wanted her envelope.

It had to have been removed by mistake. Didn't it?

FORTY

Sheridan, Wyoming

"I WISH I could say I found that we used the xylazine—legitimately used it—and just forgot to log it, Emily, but I can't." Doctor Sarah scrolled slowly down a spreadsheet. "Here's everything we did for three days. Every patient. Every treatment. Every procedure. We did use xylazine once, but in that instance it was logged." She waggled the cursor under a line of text. Surgery on a horse. "In fact, I was the one to log it."

I rolled my lips inward and rubbed them together. *All information is good information.* It didn't tell us where the drugs had gone, but it told us where they hadn't. One avenue of inquiry closed off. "Can you email this to me, please, along with a summary of what you just told me?"

"Of course. I'm just sorry I didn't crack the case."

"That's okay. Your work shows that our discovery yesterday is critical."

"Oh? What did you find out?"

"We saw something on video that shouldn't have been there. People entering the clinic."

Doctor Sarah's eyebrows peaked. "What was it?"

"Um... " Was it okay to tell Dr. Friedman? What if we were wrong? But Doctor Sarah was Aaron's partner, and he'd vouched for her. "If I tell you, you absolutely have to keep this under wraps. And remember, the investigation is ongoing. This isn't conclusory."

"Of course."

"One of the employees and her boyfriend, after hours."

Dr. Friedman gasped. "Which one?"

In for a penny... "Casey."

"Aaron's daughter?!"

"Yes. But we have a lot of footage left to review. There's a chance they were here completely innocently."

Doctor Sarah made a zipping motion over her lips. "Got it. Good luck. I hope this helps Aaron."

"Thanks again." I returned to Aaron's office and called Loretta. "Ready to look at video when you are." I booted up his desktop.

"On my way."

Loretta was true to her word and had replaced me in the chair behind the desk within one minute. "How is Mrs. Doctor H. doing?"

"Ugh. It's just awful what happened. She's going to be okay, though."

"Did the police catch her attacker?"

"No."

Loretta opened the security app and queued up the notifications for the clinic hours on the first day. "Are you ready?"

"As I'll ever be."

Loretta began scrolling. "Oh—what did Doctor Sarah have to say?"

I shook my head. "She had nothing. It's up to us."

Loretta gave a sharp nod. "Doctor H. can count on me."

***

Four hours later, my eyes were bloodshot and bleary. There had been no other access outside normal business hours except for emergencies, so we'd switched to daytime hours. Even watching videos at double speed and skipping between appearances of animals or vehicles, viewing every person who had entered or exited the clinic had been tedious. And, ultimately, non-revelatory. Loretta had identified every person as an employee, patient, or known guest, including drug reps and the UPS guy. I checked the employees against the schedules. No one showed up on the wrong days or at the wrong times. No one acted weird or appeared to be carrying anything unexpected out of the clinic.

Our best suspects remained Casey and Buster, and if it wasn't them, it was going to mean employee interviews, which wouldn't necessarily yield an answer.

We broke away for an hour for lunch. Me, offsite at Micky D's, where I saw mothers with young children. It made me miss my Betsy. Loretta, at her desk over leftovers and critical tasks to keep the clinic's practice flowing.

When I returned, I knocked on Loretta's door jamb, holding up a USB memory stick and catching a whiff of hamburger and fries. *Oops, that's me.* I'd have to wash my hands soon. "I'm back. Do you have a few minutes for me to copy those video files?"

Loretta waved me in. "We'll just do it here. You only want the four after hours videos, right?" She took the memory stick from me and inserted it into her USB drive.

"Yes. Casey and Buster and their truck."

Loretta typed and clicked. Then her forehead folded into deep, dry furrows.

"What's the matter?"

"I'm having trouble finding them. I'll just log in and out again."

"Okey dokey." I moved around behind her to watch.

A minute later, Loretta shook her head. "Still nothing."

I felt a flicker of concern, but on/off solved a lot of technology issues, so I didn't panic. "Reboot?"

Loretta nodded and initiated a restart, then tapped her foot. "This makes no sense."

"I'm sure it's just a glitch." I *hoped* it was just a glitch.

The desktop came to life. Loretta punched at keys like she was stabbing them with a fork. Her face lost color, and it wasn't exactly colorful to begin with.

"What is it?"

"All of the footage from those days is missing."

"What do you mean?"

"Everything we reviewed in our target time period. It's all gone."

"But we were just looking at it an hour ago!"

Loretta put her face in her hands. "This can't be happening."

"Who has access to the security files?"

Loretta opened and closed her mouth. "Me. Doctor Sarah. Doctor H."

I felt sick. *This is my fault.* "Oh, no! I told Doctor Sarah about the video of Casey."

"You don't think... "

"I don't know. Maybe. But why would she delete it?"

"No reason that's good."

"I mean—what if it was even her. Maybe someone hacked in. Can we tell who did it? And from what machine?"

Loretta sighed. "I'm sure someone could. Someone better than me. Old dog. Not many new tricks."

"Okay. Okay." If I were back home in Amarillo and had a problem like this, I'd call the guy who handled our IT. "Let's contact the IT person. They can find out who deleted the files and retrieve them."

Loretta took a shuddering breath. "I am our IT person. We've been meaning to hire an outside consultant for the tough issues, but we hadn't gotten around to it. When I can't figure it out, I just call whatever company made the hardware or created the software or application. That's worked so far."

I tapped my lips with my pointer finger. "All right. We can figure this out. It's not rocket surgery."

"What?"

"Rocket... science. Or brain surgery." I hated it when I derailed conversations with malapropisms. It was very embarrassing, so I rushed on. "I mean the answer is easy. We find an expert and pay whatever we have to and get them out here as fast we can."

Loretta nodded. "I can find somebody." Then she looked at me with more emotion than I'd seen from her in our time together. "But what if it's too late to keep Doctor H from being charged?"

I knew well what it would mean, but I wasn't about to make her feel any worse than she already did. I already felt bad enough for both of us.

FORTY-ONE

Sheridan, Wyoming

KID'S FINGERS were flying over his laptop keys. In absence of finding evidence that would clear Aaron from suspicion of wrongdoing, he was concentrating on case law relating to what he would contend was malicious prosecution. He would put on a full court legal press that charging before the county attorney could conclusively label Victor's death a homicide was blatant overreach, prosecutorial abuse of discretion, and damaging precedent. His problem was a dearth of truly on point case law. How did you prove something no one thought it necessary to prove? That was how ridiculous the county attorney was acting. Earlier in the day, Kid had given up and switched his focus to gathering more general cases on abuse of prosecutorial discretion and breach of public trust. It would help a lot if the tooth fairy left evidence of misconduct by Ollie or someone in law enforcement under his pillow tonight.

The office phone rang. It had been a blessing to have Emily's help the last few days. She was sharp as a whip, took time consuming tasks off his hands, and did an excellent job on everything she touched. And she was one more person to answer the phone, when she was there. Unfortunately, she was still working on the investigation into the missing drugs at Aaron's clinic.

He snatched up the handset after saving his document. Fourth ring. It had almost made it into voicemail before he could get to it. "Law office." He sounded breathless, like he'd run up the stairs. Stress was a killer.

"Wesley James, please," a man's voice said.

"Speaking."

"This is County Attorney Ollie Singletary." Ollie sounded like he had a stick up his backside. In other words, normal. "I guess your office staff isn't in on Saturdays."

"I guess not." Had Kid somehow summoned the county attorney by his research topic? As if even the specter of professional embarrassment had reverberated through the air and smacked Ollie right upside his head?

"Huh."

Kid waited for Ollie to say something. The silence on the line was like a fly buzzing around Kid's head. Wait—was there a fly buzzing around? He had left that banana peel in the trash for two days. "What do you need, Ollie? I'm actually pretty busy."

"I'll bet. And you're about to get busier."

"What's that supposed to mean?"

"Jennifer isn't going to be much help on your caseload once she's campaigning. And if she's elected—well, how are you even going to keep your practice alive?"

Kid felt like he'd been dunked in an ice bath. "What are you talking about?"

"Hmm?"

"I said *what are you talking about?*" Too late, he reeled his emotions back. He was playing into Ollie's hands. The oldest strategy in the book—divide and conquer. He should have been nonchalant. Acted like he already knew. Because, while it may have taken him a second, he'd figured out what Ollie meant. Jenn was running for county attorney. *Of course she is. Dammit.*

Instead, he was about as chalant as an elk on the opening day of hunting season. Embarrassingly chalant.

"She filed her papers to run for county attorney last week. I assumed she would have told you."

Kid tried to recapture some cool "Oh. I knew about that. I thought from what you were saying that she was disbanding the practice without telling me or something."

Ollie laughed. "Tell yourself whatever helps you sleep at night, Kid."

And then he hung up. *The bastard hung up!* Kid had just thought he was out of breath before. He didn't know who he was madder at. Ollie for telling him, or Jennifer for not.

FORTY-TWO

Sheridan, Wyoming

JENNIFER SHOOK the hem of her shirt. She was sweating and it was sticking to her. She'd just come out of hypnosis, but she felt like she had back when she'd run steps at the Rice University stadium in the Houston heat and humidity. "Am I really back?"

"You really are," the hypnotherapist said with a smile.

"Thanks for returning me safely, Shelley." Which the hypnotherapist had insisted on being called, citing a need for them to be respectful but comfortable with each other.

Shelley added a patchouli incense stick to a terra cotta holder where the old one had burned up. She wasn't old enough to be a hippie, so Jennifer guessed the description of her would be Bohemian. With long, gray-streaked brunette hair, swirly skirts, and jangly bracelets, she was Bohemian bordering on hippie, whereas Maggie was modern western Bohemian. And until that moment Jennifer had never considered that there might be multiple classifications of Bohemian. The room they were in was sterile in comparison to Shelley. Industrial carpet and off-white walls. No art. Two armchairs and a coffee table upon which rested the incense holder.

"You're very welcome. How do you feel?"

Dazed. Refreshed. "Pleased and surprised. With my head injury and my penchant for control, my hopes were low." Her head was hurting less, too, the opposite of what she'd expected.

"I'm very pleased, too. Unfortunately, we ran long—you were resistant at first—and I have another patient coming. I made a lot of notes. Could we debrief over a Zoom call Monday?" She named a time.

"That would be great."

"Here's the short version. While you were under, you said you were talking to a man. That you were his dolly. Then you told me you needed to leave with him. That's when I woke you up."

"Oh, my God."

"Does that mean something to you?"

"Yes. I've been having nightmares about this guy. Lately, they've gotten weird. It's one of the reasons I came to you."

Shelley looked pleased. "It's a great sign that you opened up to me about it in your first session. I'll talk to you soon, and, in the meantime, I appreciate your flexibility. Same time in four weeks?"

"Perfect."

"Now, go home and rest. Hypnotherapy is exhausting for your brain."

As if. Jennifer was glad she hadn't told Shelley about her concussion. She had a suspicion the hypnotherapist would have canceled this long-awaited session.

The two women shook hands, and Jennifer exited the office. Shelley had hung a cute sign on the door. SHELLEY PROCTOR, LICENSED HYNOTHERAPIST with a little hedgehog on it. The sign gave Jennifer a sense of comfort. This had been good. It was a safe space, even if she didn't like the sound of her telling the therapist she needed to *leave* with the man in her nightmares.

She looked up and met the eyes of a guy not much taller than her who looked like he needed a bath and a good meal. Shelley's next patient? She nodded at him, turned, and walked the long hallway, the only sound the soft thumps of her tennis shoes.

She descended a flight of stairs, holding on tight to the railing. Her depth perception was off. *I should have taken the elevator.* She made it to the bottom upright and heaved a sigh of relief, then pushed the door. Wind worked against her, and she had to throw her weight into it, which didn't feel great at that moment. A blast of warm air buffeted her once she was outside. Sheridan was two thousand feet lower in elevation than the lodge. Temperatures here were often ten degrees warmer in the summer and ten degrees colder in the winter. The phenomena had defied logic to Jennifer at first. She'd thought the weather would be cooler at their elevation, when actually the mountains acted as a chimney up which heat would rise, at least up to a certain elevation and between storms. Once serious weather hit, all bets were off.

She started walking along the sidewalk toward the hockey rink, peeking into storefronts that had until recently been empty and were filling up with stores, bars, and restaurants. This area of town was developing quickly into something surprisingly chic, at least by north central Wyoming standards. She was dying to see if she'd heard back from Leo and Delaney, so, she stopped and checked her phone. She'd group texted them before her session, under the theory that they might not have seen her last text, or that it had gotten buried in an avalanche of new texts. But neither had answered her. It was disappointing. Maybe she'd follow-up one more time, but after that, she'd take the ghosting at face value.

Now, where had she parked? She scanned the area for her Grand Cherokee, drawing a blank. Then it came to her. Much closer to the hockey rink but in a lot to her left.

As she set off in that direction, she had the sensation of someone watching her. She looked up, then around. A man was standing ten feet behind her holding up a cell phone. Late twenties looking, scruffy, skinny, short. She frowned. It was the guy from the hallway outside Shelley's office. *He's following me.*

"What are you doing?" she said.

He didn't answer her, nor did he lower his phone.

"Are you filming me?"

No answer.

"What's your name?"

By now, his silence was no surprise, but it was disturbing. Frightening even. Could this be the man who'd attacked her? She doubted it, only because surely he wouldn't approach her in daylight. Besides, who the heck wanted pictures of her? And here?

Here.

The location sounded an alarm bell in her brain. She was exiting a hypnotherapist's office. A place where she'd gone for a controversial treatment often associated with mental health issues. She'd kept her therapy with Chaplain Abel private, and she wanted the same for the hypnotherapy. She didn't ever want it to become an issue raised in court about her.

Or in an election for county attorney.

She knew she had lowered expectations of privacy on a public street, but even in public first amendment rights weren't infinite. Stalking and harassment limited photographic rights. Filming done in a way that was threatening or frightening could have legal repercussions. And she was frightened. She decided to lean in on those concepts.

"Whoever you are, you are following me and scaring me. I do not consent to you videoing or taking photographs of me. I demand that you stop and delete them from your phone."

The phone stayed up, but this time the guy smiled, met her eye, and winked. "You've made yourself into a public figure. Or at least into someone aspiring to be a public figure. That comes with greater attention, and now you're getting it, Mrs. Herrington. Anything to say to that?"

"Who sent you?"

"Why should someone have to send me?"

"Media?"

His grin grew wider. His teeth were discolored.

And then she knew. Knew with as much certainty as a good guess could give her. This was dirty politics. He'd been sent by an opponent to gather dirt on her. But who knew she'd filed? Her name hadn't been in the news yet.

"Never mind," she said. "I don't care why you're here."

"But I'd hazard a guess voters would care about why you're visiting a hypnotherapist. Isn't that something like a witch doctor?"

Jennifer turned and started walking quickly to her car. Anything she said now would look defensive, which would only make things worse.

"Awfully new age if you ask me. What other types of treatment are you getting?"

She sped up.

"That's okay," he called after her. "You don't have to tell me now. I'll be around. And I'll be watching you. So will everyone else."

FORTY-THREE

Big Horn, Wyoming

I PACED the kitchen floor like my red hair was on fire. Jeremiah paced me on the countertops, chittering as if he was asking me what the heck was wrong. For a de-stunk skunk, it was my opinion that he still smelled a little skunky. Anyway, I was pacing because I'd called Lou's to make a bet on the Hellcats. The guy who answered asked me for the magic word, like he had with Nick. I'd said, "Go Rutgers." He hung up on me before I could even say my name was Katie Connell.

Now I said to my husband, "We both used our U.S. Virgin Islands cell phone numbers. One after another. Maybe the unfamiliar 340 area code made him suspicious?" Just thinking about home made me miss the kids. The twins were at an adorable age. And Taylor— well, he was a Tasmanian devil-level energetic, but the most loveable Tasmanian devil ever.

"Could be. Or maybe you have to pre-register to place bets. Like they have to recognize your number." Nick was leaning back on two legs of a kitchen table chair. I wanted to tell him not to break other people's furniture—like he'd done to one of ours by the way—but it didn't seem like the time. Besides, he looked kinda cute when he did it. He could fix it if he had to. Replace it if he couldn't.

"Or could be you have to know a code word." I leaned on my hands on the butcher block island. "Maybe we can get someone who's bet with them before to place the bet or give us the code word."

"Except that we don't know who could do that."

"And we don't want to burn through any more chances. It could be 'after four tries with the wrong password this checking account will self-destruct' kind-of-thing."

He rubbed a hand through his thick, dark hair, something he did when he was in thinking mode. As it fell back into place, I noticed a few strands of silver and felt a big, big love. "Let's call Jack before that happens."

"He'd probably appreciate that."

Nick had his phone to his ear in seconds. "Holden, yo. We've run into a roadblock. I'm putting you on speaker." He set the phone on the table. "Katie's with me."

"Hey, Katie."

"Hi, Jack."

"What's the roadblock?"

Nick said, "We've both tried to place that bet with Lou's that you asked us to make on the Hellcats. We've both been denied." He filled Jack in on the details.

I put my hand on Nick's shoulder. "Our Virgin Islands numbers might be a red flag. Also, they seemed to be asking for a code. We hate to really get their hackles up by continuing to make weird call-ins for the Hellcats. We're thinking we need help from someone who's already placing bets with them."

"The question is who? It would need to be someone who isn't a suspect, and at this point, almost everybody still is. The two I feel least wary of are the Strikers captain and the Hellcats number one. Donny and Joaquim. Hmm." He paused. "Let's go with Donny. We can call him together. I'll make the intro and turn it over to you."

"Sweet, man." Nick held his knuckles up for me to bump.

I did it, feeling like a sports bro. It was one of the hazards of being the only person around for him to celebrate with. He'd taught the move to Taylor, who did it all the time now. I was growing so accustomed to it that I was afraid I might use it with Emily or Ava, who would wonder who'd body-snatched me.

Jack said, "Hold on. I'll be back with Donny, I hope."

The line went silent. I hummed the Jeopardy music.

Jack returned. "Katie and Nick, I have Donny Flanders on with me. He's the captain of the Red Grade Strikers. Donny, these are my friends Katie and Nick. They're private investigators, and they're helping me figure out what happened to Victor."

"You mean whether Herrington killed him or not."

I winced. "Hi, Donny."

"Hey back. Now, what's the deal?"

Jack said, "We're hoping you can do us a favor."

Donny made the raspberry sound. "I don't like the sound of that."

"We'd like you to place a bet on the Hellcats match this weekend."

I must have held my breath while Donny thought about it, because all of a sudden I could hear the faucet dripping in the hall bathroom.

"What makes you think I'd want to? Or that I even can?"

Because of that last thing you said about whether you even can…

"Listen," Nick said. "We know Victor was betting with Lou's."

"Yeah, but that was him, not me."

"So, he was."

"Wait. You didn't know?"

"Not for sure."

"You tricked me! Jack, what is this?"

Jack said, "We were confirming a hunch. What else have you left out?"

"About Victor betting? I know his summer bets were on us. The

Strikers. He lost a lot of money last summer. I don't think he'd been able to pay it off, either."

How would Victor pay off a bookie without any money? Service in kind?

Jack was thinking similar thoughts. "If he was so broke, how did he get all that cash he was flashing around?"

"I assumed it was Celeste."

I said, "Was he still able to bet?"

"No. Not directly, anyway. Lou's had cut him off."

"How was he betting indirectly?"

Donny sighed. "I did it for him. But it was only one match. Our last one."

"Now we're getting somewhere," Nick said. "Could you make one for us on the Hellcats this weekend?"

At this point, he didn't even ask why. "No, way. It would look bad for me if I bet on another team."

I said, "Not when yours isn't the team they're playing."

"Maybe... "

"Or—if there's a code word or something, we could place it ourselves."

There was a long pause. "That might work."

This time I was the one who held up my knuckles to bump Nick's.

FORTY-FOUR

JENNIFER SLAMMED ON HER BRAKES. She was ten miles an hour over the speed limit in a thirty mile per hour zone. Just what she needed on top of someone following her around filming her mental health crises—a ticket for speeding near an elementary school.

Five minutes later, she parked in front of Kid's office. Hers and Kid's office. She trudged up the wooden stairs to the office, completely devoid of energy. As she shut the door, she said, "Honey, I'm home, and I've had a really long day."

Kid didn't look up from his laptop. "Hey."

She threw her handbag on her desk. "How are you, Jennifer? Was the assault scary? Was the hospital a drag?" She lowered her voice. "I'm mezzo mezzo, thanks for asking. Fighting off panic with my husband in jail. Surviving even though the hospital nearly killed me. A little scared of someone coming back and finishing the job. Nursing a whopper of a headache. How are you?" She stopped in front of his desk, fisting her hands on her hips.

Kid raised his eyes to hers, slowly. "I'm shit, Jenn, thanks for asking."

"Not that it's a contest, but I bet I win."

"Oh? Did you just get a call from the county attorney asking how you're going to handle your case load while your partner campaigns for his job and then whether you're closing your law firm if she wins?"

Ollie has known I'm running. But since when? And how? "Wait. Did he tell you how he knew?"

Kid jumped to his feet. "That's your response to me?" His voice cracked. "You don't care at all how I feel?"

If a hole could have opened up and swallowed her whole, she would have welcomed it. "Oh, Kid. I'm sorry. I was going to tell you, then—"

"Going to tell me? Don't you mean discuss it with me? Listen to how I felt about it and what it would do to my life?"

"Yes, that's what I meant, I—"

"Bullshit."

"What?"

He looked disgusted. Worse, disappointed. "Bullshit. You've already filed. It's a done deal."

"I honestly haven't made up my mind whether I'm running. The deadline came, and I submitted to keep my options open."

Kid shook his head.

"I promise. I hadn't even gotten a chance to talk to Aaron about it yet. My plan was to talk to you as soon as he and I made up our minds."

He guffawed. "Wait—you filed without telling Aaron?"

"I mean, we've talked about it, of course."

"But he doesn't know you've *filed*?"

"I did it the day he was arrested. There was no time."

Kid laughed, but it wasn't a mirthful sound. "Do you hear yourself? At least I'm in good company."

Anger warred with hurt and humiliation inside her. She couldn't come up with a response. And then a thought nearly brought her to her knees. Kid was a once in a lifetime law partner. The way he was standing up for himself. The man he was becoming just in the year they'd worked together. Her emotions swung all the way over to guilt and regret. She was trying to find a way to express some of this or all of it when her phone rang.

She ignored it. After four rings, it stopped, but then it restarted again. She pulled it out of her back pocket. She read the caller ID. Ollie Singletary. She denied the call.

"Kid... "

It started ringing again immediately.

She opened her mouth. Shut it. "I'd better... it could be about... "

"Whatever."

"It's Ollie."

"Maybe he's calling to concede. Better take it."

"It will be about Aaron, Kid. Be professional. You're his attorney."

"Which is why he would be calling *me* if it's about Aaron. Because you're *not* his attorney. This is all bullshit. Bullshit, bullshit, bullshit."

Jennifer had never seen Kid so upset about anything except Casey before. How she wished she didn't have to take this call right now. She skipped her normal professional greeting and gave a breathless, "Hello?"

"Jenn Herrington."

For a second she wondered if Ollie was calling because she'd been attacked. If the assault had been about Victor, it did cast doubt on their entire misguided investigation into Aaron. She paused, giving him time, but he didn't ask about her condition.

The misplaced rage she'd nearly taken out on Kid spewed out of her. "Thanks for your phone call to Kid. The way you treat the defense community is duly noted."

"Oh, that's only half of what I have to say to him today."

"Great. How else do you plan to harass him?"

"I wouldn't have to if your team had just told us. It would have looked so much better if you had."

Was this about the missing drugs? "I have no idea what you're talking about."

"I highly doubt that. Maybe Jack and Kid don't know, but you're his wife. There's no way you don't know."

"Know *what*, Ollie?"

"His record for bookmaking?"

Jennifer forced a laugh. "Funny."

"Do I sound like I'm joking?"

Kid had moved closer, sitting in front of her on his desk. His angry face was morphing into one of concern. He mouthed *What is going on?*

She turned away from him, putting one hand over her ear. It felt hot. She felt hot. "I don't believe you."

"I have all the records right in front of me. He plead guilty in a bookmaking scheme, paid some fines, did community service. Got off easy because he was a football star. I'm seeing a pattern here."

She bit her lip so hard she tasted blood. "This was in college?"

Now it was Ollie who laughed. "Oh, my God. You really didn't know. And I thought the two of you were the perfect couple. Guess not. I'll be sending the records over to Aaron's counsel shortly."

Jennifer was regaining her composure. "This has nothing to do with Victor Carvalho."

"It's goes to motive, *Jennifer*. A pattern that leads us straight to it."

"You're out in left field now."

"A man with a lifelong connection to the betting world who skirts the law? Then you're blind. We're going to find the bet he placed on the Hellcats. It will go nicely with the drugs he took from his clinic. Means, motive, and—oh yeah, the easy one in this case—opportunity, which you are well aware of since you were with him at the polo fields. And when we find that bet, it's going to be game, set, match."

FORTY-FIVE

Sheridan, Wyoming

JACK STORMED into the jail's interview room. He'd been working in Aaron's big Jeepster in the parking lot behind Java Moon. Seat pushed all the way back. Laptop open. Phone in his hand. Easy access to coffee just twenty feet away. It was a great mobile office even if it did smell like two malamutes.

Then Kid had called and told him about Aaron's record. Jack had been pissed off at many clients in his career, and it always seemed to be for the same thing. Lying and withholding. He just hadn't expected it this time from this client.

Jack had raced back to the jail, making a handsfree call to Ollie on the way. Been forced to endure the prosecutor's lip in order to pry a few details out of him. Had to learn from him that Jenn had filed to run for county attorney and not told them. *Withholding seems to be a core family value.*

Now, he drummed a pen on the desktop.

The door opened and the guard nudged Aaron through the door and to his chair.

"You can leave the cuffs on him this time. I won't be long," Jack told the guard.

"Is Jenn okay?" Aaron said. He didn't comment on the cuffs, and his face was haggard.

Jack kept drumming the pen. He didn't trust himself to speak in front of the guard.

Aaron sat and the guard left.

Aaron said, "What's the matter? Please, if it's about Jenn, if she's worse, just tell me."

Jack spoke in a clipped tone. "Is it true?"

"Is what true?"

"I can't help you if you're not open with me. With us. The team of people working on your behalf, night and day."

Aaron raised his cuffed hands. "I've been open."

"I told you to disclose anything to me that might be relevant to this case. Any skeletons in your closet. Was I not clear?"

"You were. I did."

Jack scoffed. "I'm this close to heading back to Texas. Emily and I miss our daughter. I have clients there that also need my help. I took your case because Maggie vouched for you and Jenn."

"I know. And I appreciate it more than I can say."

"You know what's funny? Jenn didn't even know about this."

"Jenn didn't know about what? What did you tell her?" Aaron scooted his chair back. He looked angry. *Join the club, buddy.*

"I'm giving you one more chance to tell me."

"This is insane. I have no clue what you're talking about."

Jack stood. "You can ruin your career and your wife's chance at county attorney on your own time."

"She hasn't even made up her mind about whether to run for county attorney yet."

"Really? Not according to Ollie Singletary. I just got off the phone with him, and he said the county clerk called and told him five minutes after Jenn filed her paperwork. *Last week.*"

Aaron gaped at him. What little color was left in his face drained out.

Jack almost felt sorry for him, except that he was getting what he deserved. Live by the sword, die by the sword. "So, you can see why I said that you withholding your bookmaking conviction isn't going to do her a lot of good."

Aaron's face went completely slack. "Can you elaborate on that, please?"

Jack noted the lack of denial, and it made him want to scream at Aaron. Instead, he spoke in little more than a hiss. "The county attorney has court records from when you plead guilty in an illegal bookmaking scheme. Ollie knows everything. The size of the fine you paid. The dates and times of your community service. I have copies now myself in my email inbox."

Aaron licked his lips.

"Well—do you have anything to say for yourself?"

Aaron's Adam's apple bulged. "I thought those records were sealed."

FORTY-SIX

SHERIDAN, Wyoming

KID TEXTED Celeste and asked her to grab a coffee with him. Not because he wanted to, but because Jack had told him Donny Flanders confirmed Victor owed a great deal of money to Lou's for gambling losses. Kid was going to ask the one person who might know where Victor's cash came from, even if he had to spend too much money on a shot of espresso and milk foam to do it. And would be up all night on a caffeine buzz from drinking coffee midafternoon.

Celeste had thrown him a curve ball by calling him instead of texting back. "Let's go to Smith Alley for a burger. I love their craft beers."

His mouth went September-in-Wyoming dry.

"Kid?"

"Uh, yeah, sorry. My partner was asking me a question."

"So... is it a date?" She giggled.

He couldn't date a witness. Only, she didn't know she was a

witness. *This is going to go bad for me. Somehow, someway.* It always did. "Sounds great. It's a, um, a date."

And that was how he came to be sitting on a bar stool half an hour later with Celeste Farinolo. He felt like everyone was looking at them, but who was he kidding? They were looking at *her*. Today, Celeste was dressed for a *Dukes of Hazzard* remake. Her jean shorts were *really* short, her tank top was *really* form-fitting, and her fringed boots were *really* high heeled and rose almost to her knees. Cats-eye makeup and bright red lips, long, straight hair, and a cowboy hat. If there had been a camera following her into the restaurant, he wouldn't have been surprised.

It made him feel extra in all the wrong ways. Extra red haired. Extra gawky. Extra geeky.

She leaned into him, soft and sweet smelling. "What are you ordering?"

"The barbecue burger."

"No, silly. Which beer?"

"Stacy's Mom." It was a random choice from a menu of random—but funny—names.

"I'm a Johnny Ringo girl myself. Yum."

A waitress took their order, including a Reuben and tater tots for Celeste and his burger and fries.

Celeste bumped his knee with hers. Kid's mouth felt parched, and he slurped down half his giant water through a straw. He tried to remember what he'd come here to ask her about, but his brain was blue screen.

"What are you doing this weekend?" she said.

"Oh, no big plans." Did his voice squeak or was it in his head?

She winked. "Me, neither. I was thinking you might want to take me somewhere authentic. I've been hanging around the polo crowd for way too long."

"Authentic?"

"You know, like Parkman Grill." A place Kid had never been to. "Or the Wyarno Bar and Grill." A second place he'd never been.

"That sounds... fun."

She gazed up at him through downcast lashes. "Oh, it will be."

I'm in so much trouble.

"How has your recovery been going?"

"Recovery?"

"You know. From that slut Casey." She smiled sweetly.

"I backslid a little. I had a beer with her."

She punched his arm. "You can't do that. I'm going to have to make you forget all about her." Then she pouted. "I guess I'm not one to talk, though."

"What do you mean?"

"I suspected Victor was cheating, and I didn't do anything about it."

"Who did you think he was with? Casey?"

"I had no idea about her. But my girlfriend Shiva had a thing for him. She was waaaaay too interested in him. Like *slobbery* every time he came around."

The waiter delivered their beers. Kid tried his. Light and crisp. And something fruity. Raspberry, maybe? What was the thing lately with fruity beers everywhere? He should have read the description.

Celeste took a long sip of hers. She set her glass down, and Kid's eyes were drawn to the little bit of foam on her lip.

She said, "I found out later I was right. He was with her. I won't have anything to do with her anymore. I just wish I'd known while he was alive so I could have made him regret the day he was born. But I guess God knew what he was doing."

"What do you mean?"

"He was saving me for you," she cooed. "If I'd dumped Victor earlier, I might have met someone else. You know, before you saw me at the Mint Bar."

Kid gulped down half his beer. *Oh God, did she have it in her head he'd been hitting on her at the Mint Bar?* He smiled like he was embarrassed, which was easy. He was embarrassed. This seemed like a good opening for what he was supposed to talk to her about. "Victor didn't seem good enough for you. I mean, I don't picture him as a guy with enough money to give you the things you deserved."

She rolled her eyes. "Worse than that. He was up to his eyeballs in debt."

"How come?"

"Well, he has child support."

"Oh, wow."

"Yeah. I would have been a stepmom. To two boys." She shuddered. "And he made some bad investments last year."

"What kind of investments?"

"I don't know. Boring stuff. I barely listened."

So, was it investments or bets? "Did he gamble?"

"All the damn time. That's where most of his money went."

"Were bookies after him?"

"What? No!" She put her hand on his arm. "It's the 2020s in Wyoming, Kid. Not the 1920s in Chicago."

His face burned. "I didn't know him, obviously, but I heard he was a big spender. Where does a polo player even get that kind of cash?"

She shook her head. "It wasn't from me. Believe it or not, my parents are so tight with me. All my money is in a trust fund until I'm twenty-five, so I have to live on the income from it." She pouted. "Except for clothes and stuff. My mom likes me to dress nice, so I have a credit card for shopping. And going out. Restaurants. Travel. But other than that, yeah, I'm as poor as anybody."

"That makes sense." In an alternate universe. *I could never afford to date this girl, even if I wanted to. Which I do not with a capital NO.* She was sexy, but she was Casey all over again, only spoiled and entitled.

She rolled her eyes. "You know, I think the only reason he was with me was like... as an insurance policy. You know. Because of the money I'll have in a few years."

"That sucks."

She lowered her voice conspiratorially. "Believe it or not, he was making money outside playing polo. He'd asked my dad for a raise, and dad turned him down. So, his new gig was a big F-you to my parents, which I thought was metal as hell." She sipped her beer, batting her lashes.

He grinned and leaned down. "What were the two of you up to?"

"It was just him. I wasn't even supposed to know, but I heard him talking about it on the phone." She shimmied her shoulders. "Are you sure you want me to tell you?"

"One hundred percent."

"He was being paid by the Hellcats." She giggled and clapped her hand over her mouth.

"The rival team? What for?"

"I have no idea. But I can guess."

Unfortunately, Kid could, too. And it was the kind of things that could get a guy killed.

FORTY-SEVEN

Big Horn, Wyoming

FROM A CHAIR IN HER BEDROOM, Jennifer balanced her laptop on her thighs and clicked to join a video call with the defense team. According to Zoom, the host wasn't on yet. Jack had arranged the meeting. She'd told him she'd come into town for it, but he'd told her not to.

"Kid needs to focus, and he'll have trouble if you're in the room," Jack had said. "Plus, I don't want your car out front. Things are heating up, and Ollie is treating this case personally. Let's not give him fuel."

It had been fine with her. She didn't want to face them, partly because of the situation with Kid, but also because she was humiliated. Aaron had a record and had never told her. They'd had their ups and downs and even been on the brink of splitting up when they first moved to Wyoming. In the last year they'd rebounded. They were stronger than ever now. Or she'd thought they were, only to learn that once again Aaron hadn't been open with her, about something important.

Last winter when she'd learned about Casey, he'd explained that he had simply buried a bad memory. He'd thought his high school girlfriend had an abortion, even though he'd begged her to keep the baby. He'd never known about his daughter's birth. Jennifer had taken his explanation at face value. She'd asked him then if there was anything else he wasn't telling her, and he'd told her there wasn't. He'd sworn there was nothing.

A conviction for bookmaking was not nothing. Not to her or to the prosecution. In a strange twist of fate, Aaron could be charged and convicted because of the same issue that might end their marriage. Honestly, she wasn't sure which thought was more devastating. Aaron in prison or the two of them divorced. Because here was the irony—she couldn't bear the thought of life without him, no matter the reason. A sob threatened to bubble up, and she pressed her lips together hard to stop it.

Jack still wasn't on. She muted her video. She'd been dry-eyed the whole way home from the office. When she arrived at the lodge, Game & Fish were just arriving to pick up the badger. She'd gone out back to help them. For some reason, seeing them heft it, crate and all, into the back of their truck had been what finally set her off. And boy, had it ever. Her face was tear ravaged and haggard now.

She went to the bathroom and grabbed cotton balls and makeup remover, then wiped away the mascara and eyeliner ringing her eyes. Sibley's nose nudged her knee.

"I'm okay," Jennifer told her.

The dog didn't look like she believed it. Both of the malamutes were as. . . well, *hangdog* as she was. Canine empathy. The purity of their love was powerful and somehow devastating at a moment like this. She squatted and pulled Sibley into her arms. Willett squeezed in, and for a few seconds, she let her heart float on a cloud of fluffy sweetness. Why had she resisted dogs for fifteen years?

From the counter, her phone pinged with a text. She stood back up and read the notification. It was from Delaney Pace, and she snatched the phone up.

We haven't forgotten about you. Making progress but it's slow due to a search for a missing hiker. I'll have something for you Sunday night.

Jennifer sent a very heartfelt *Thanks* with several emojis that she immediately wished she could take back.

From the bedroom, she heard the sound of Jack calling her name. A last mirror check was disheartening. Removing the black had only revealed the red.

She grabbed her laptop and flopped on the bed. Willett landed on it at the same time she did. "I'm here."

"Good. I'm with Kid and Emily. Katie and Nick are connected, too," Jack said.

"Where are they?" Jennifer hadn't seen or heard them at the lodge.

Katie's voice piped in. "We're outside the Big Horn Mercantile. We're about to grab some pizza. We'll have plenty if you want some."

"Thanks, but I'm not hungry."

"Is your video not working?"

"I have it off. I'm a mess."

"You're allowed to be. You're in the thick of it. I think it would help all of us to see you, though. We're worried about you."

Jennifer closed her eyes and tried to swallow. Her throat felt dry and lumpy, but she managed. She put the laptop on her bedside table and turned on the video. The screen reflected an image of her and the somber dog. Two squares showed the others. One from the office, the other of Nick and Katie.

Jack said, "All right. Let's get started. We have less than forty-eight hours until the arraignment. I've called this meeting to make sure we focus on the right things with the time we have left. First, I want to give you all an update. I met with Aaron. Aaron confirmed that he does have a record for bookmaking from when he was in college. He'd been told the records were sealed. Because of that, he said he eventually forgot about it."

There was mumbling from Katie and Nick. Jennifer realized they probably hadn't even heard about this yet.

Jack held up a hand. "While I wish he'd told us, the situation is what it is. His story is that he was a broke college student and got pressured into the scheme by some football team boosters who threatened his scholarship. He said he hadn't even known it was illegal until he was arrested. His role was quite minor."

"Sounds plausible," Nick said.

He's probably only saying that to make me feel better. It didn't work.

Jack said, "He authorized us to review his financial records to prove he doesn't currently gamble, with Jenn's permission."

It was hard for Jennifer to force any words out, but everyone seemed to be waiting for her to reply. "I'll download the files and email them."

"Emily, why don't you take that one."

Emily winked. "Got it, hot boss."

Jack gave her an affectionate eye roll. "Kid, kick us off."

Emily held up a dry erase marker. "I'll make a to-do list on the white board."

Kid cleared his throat and told them about his meeting with Celeste. "I wonder who knew the Hellcats were paying Victor. And *who* was paying him."

Jack nodded. "I'll take a run at talking to Joaquim again. And the Half Circle Ranch manager."

Jennifer opened her eyes wide. "The manager is Pete Galindo. He's not going to like it."

Jack shrugged. "Can't be helped. Kid, why don't you track Shiva down and talk to her, please."

"Got it." Kid tapped into his tablet. "By the way, I'm drowning in case law that doesn't help us much to prove malicious prosecution, short of evidence of actual misconduct. I mean, our argument makes perfect sense—how can you arrest someone for murder if there's no real evidence of murder yet, but we all know that didn't fly in the probable cause hearing."

Jennifer squeezed her eyes shut. The hearing she'd missed because she'd been unconscious on the floor of her office. When she opened her eyes, she said, "Hold that thought. I may have something for you soon."

Jack's head shot up. "What?"

"I've, um, heard from someone that may have information on misconduct. I'm supposed to get something definitive, one way or the other, by Sunday night."

"Can you give us any more than that?"

"Not yet. You're going to have to trust me."

Jack stared at her for three long seconds. Too late, she thought about how Kid felt that she hadn't talked to him before she filed to run for county attorney. Jack, too, probably. Heat rose in her neck and face. "Okay. I'll look forward to that update. Let's move on. Nick and Katie, were you able to place a bet with Donny Flanders on the Hellcats?"

Katie smiled. "Yes. We have screenshots of the money transferred and audio of the phone call."

"Good. Now we can show betting on the local polo games was real, and we have the familial relationship between the bookie that took them and Benjy Mahones, the Hellcats owner."

Jennifer wasn't sure what any of this proved yet, but in her experience evidence often took a long time to take shape. They needed more facts. They were getting them, one laborious extraction at a time, but it was too slow.

Katie said, "Here's an idea, given that familial relationship, could Victor have been paying off his gambling debt with Lou's in kind by working for the Hellcats?"

"Good idea." Jack flipped his pen. "I'll explore that when I'm back out at Half Circle."

"Also, we can't forget that Black Bear Betty heard Mahones placed a 'sure thing' bet on the Hellcats. I know we haven't tracked down any other bettors, but we do have him."

"As the owner of Hellcats who were supposedly paying Victor, that's big."

"Should someone talk to him?"

Jack tipped his head from side to side. "Eventually, for sure. I definitely want to put his name in front of the prosecution as someone they overlooked. I can't imagine him admitting to anything, and if he thinks we're circling around him, he might make our jobs a lot harder. For now, I think it's more important to gather evidence around him. If I can find a way to approach him casually, I will."

Jennifer said, "I agree. What would his motive be for giving Victor sedatives, though? He already has plenty of money."

"Most rich people think you can never have too much. Plus, there's pride and winning. I'd guess that in his world—coming from a crime family—playing dirty is normal operating procedure." Jack smiled at his wife. "Emily, your turn. Tell us about that missing xylazine."

Emily put her marker down and told them about the deleted video. "We found an IT person who'll come in tomorrow to restore the clips and figure out who did it."

"What does your gut tell you?" Jack asked.

"Doctor Sarah had means and opportunity. Casey and Buster had opportunity, but did they have the means?"

Jennifer said, "You mean the key to the drug supply room?"

"Yes."

"I know Aaron didn't give her any keys, but she lived here. They rode to and from work together. I wouldn't assume she didn't find a way to use his keys."

"Or copy them," Emily said.

"What would be the motive to steal the xylazine, for either of them?" Kid asked.

Jack said, "I would think financial. Resale of vet drugs is lucrative.

Dr. Friedman has a lot to lose if she's caught though. Her job, her family, her freedom. We need to know her background and financial situation. Maybe she's got problems that make the risk worth it." Emily added it to the board. "I'd think there's more motive than financial for Buster. He might want to punish the clinic for firing him."

Kid said, "Same for Casey. She has a beef with everyone."

Jennifer said, "One thing that's important to keep in mind is that we don't know whether xylazine was what was in Victor's system. Even if it was, we won't ever know where it came from. The person who stole the xylazine from Aaron's clinic may have nothing to do with Victor's death. But proving Aaron isn't the one who took it, obviously, will help a whole lot."

Jack nodded. "Excellent point. That brings us to your attack, Jennifer. Any word from law enforcement?"

"No. I don't think they're really trying."

"Whoever did it was brazen. Coming on your property in broad daylight where anyone could have seen them. Would that mean it was someone who had an excuse for being there, or that they didn't care, or that they managed to access the property without being seen?"

"You could definitely walk from the neighbor's property and approach us from the backside of our buildings. They're in Maine for the month, too."

"I wish we knew if drugs had been stolen."

"We won't know anything until Tron returns. Except for one thing." Jennifer hated telling her secret, especially when everyone knew Aaron had kept his bookmaking record from her. This was going to make their marriage look even more shaky, but she'd decided it couldn't be helped.

"What's that?"

"This is top secret, so I'm begging you all to keep this to yourselves. It's very personal."

There were nods and agreements all around.

"I was sending in hair samples for DNA analysis. From Casey and Aaron." She took a deep breath. "The envelope was on my desk. It's gone now."

Kid cocked his head. "Sending them in? For what?"

"A paternity test." Jennifer averted her eyes. The others were silent. "I don't know for a fact that the person who broke in took it, but no one else has seen it. And, even if they did take it, it might mean nothing. I know that."

Nick was the first to say it. "Or it might mean Casey did it."

Emily shook her head. "This was Friday afternoon, right? Casey was at the clinic. I was there. That would have taken—what? An hour minimum, roundtrip? She couldn't have done it."

"Okay. Then someone who did it for Casey."

Jennifer frowned. "But Casey didn't know about the paternity test."

"Ohhhh," Emily said. "Okay, then."

There was murmuring that quieted quickly. Jennifer wanted to crawl under her covers and hide.

Kid said, "Well, Casey lived out there. Could she have gotten wind of it somehow?"

Nick said, "Or could the person who attacked you have called her and said, 'hey there's a letter on your stepmom's desk going to some DNA lab place.' If they opened it, it would have been clear what it was."

Kid nodded. "And then Casey could have told them to remove it or destroy it. One hundred percent."

"Oh, my God." They were on to something. Jennifer could feel it.

"One person who might have done that for Casey is also one of our suspects from the clinic," Emily added.

"Buster," Jennifer breathed. "And Casey would know how to get onsite without being seen. She could have told him about it."

As the others discussed the theory, Jennifer's mind was a million miles away, on Casey. Had her stepdaughter been behind another attempt on her life? She looked out the window at the little cottage. The lights were on. Casey was home. Jennifer excused herself and went and locked all the doors. She'd be keeping the malamutes close tonight.

FORTY-EIGHT

Sheridan, Wyoming

LATE SUNDAY MORNING, Jennifer sat across the glass from Aaron at the jail. She would have been there earlier, but she was getting over a Chardonnay headache from another long night. Worry about Aaron and fear of Casey and Buster had kept her up. Then, when she'd finally closed her eyes, her nightmare visitor appeared— the school shooter, rifle slung over his shoulder, kids around her on the ground bleeding and screaming.

What he said made no sense and all the sense in the world. "Dolly, he shouldn't treat you like that." Had she somehow created a savior out of this killer in her mind? Someone who was now her confidante about her problems with Aaron?

She'd woken and poured herself more chardonnay, then worked through the night on the financials for Emily. By morning, the bottle was empty, and she had cotton mouth and breath like a vulture, but the documents were ready. The dogs had been as tired and grumpy as she was. Her lack of sleep was theirs. She'd left them in their dog run with a promise to do better that night.

Now that she was here at the jail, she wished she'd skipped the Chardonnay. Her head still hurt from the assault even before she drank the wine, and it was infinity times worse after. She was tired, too, of course, but most of all, she was upset with her husband. The coffee she'd drunk on the way had scalded her tongue but done nothing to make her sharper. She had wanted to be at her best for this discussion, and she was far from it.

Aaron's gaunt face and hollow eyes told her he hadn't fared much better. The guard removed Aaron's cuffs and left the room, shutting the door behind him.

Aaron's voice through the holes in the plexiglass was flat and cold. "Nice of you to show up."

"I came as soon as I could," she said.

"Really? You couldn't come at all on Friday or Saturday?"

"You know why I wasn't here Friday. And Saturday I was in the hospital."

"Which I was very sorry to hear. I worried about you. I needed to see that you were okay, after you got out. Which was in the morning, according to Jack."

Damn Jack for giving too much information. "I had a hypnotherapy appointment."

"Which you could have postponed, if you'd wanted to."

She didn't argue with that. It was true. "Jack didn't think it was a good idea for me to come."

His blue eyes flashed like light off a steel blade. "Jack makes your decisions for you?"

"I agreed with him."

"Because?"

"He doesn't want us talking about things that can be overheard. Or that might show I am more involved in your situation than some people would like, given my conflict."

"And that's the only other reason?"

He was pushing her. He wanted this. So, she gave it to him. "No, as a matter of fact. There's also that I hate the things you somehow don't tell me." She lowered her voice until she was nearly just mouthing the words. "The missing drugs, your... record."

Aaron's face dropped all expression. It was chilling. It was surprising. He didn't look defensive. He looked angry. "Isn't there something you somehow didn't tell me?"

Her first thought was the DNA test. "I—"

"That you filed to run for county attorney?"

For a moment, she was relieved it wasn't the DNA. But from his cold expression, this was bad enough. "How do you know that?"

"How doesn't matter. What matters is you decided without including me and deliberately chose not to tell me after you did it."

"We had talked about it. Many times."

"Theoretically. Never once did you say, 'Aaron, I think I'm going to file next week. Or tomorrow. Or in five minutes.' Hell, you didn't say 'five minutes ago or five hours ago or five *days* ago.'"

"That's not fair. You'd been arrested, and—"

"I thought we were on the same team."

"Running for county attorney is a positive. Unlike your criminal past. Did you never think that would affect me?"

"Affect *you*?"

"A husband with a criminal record when I'm running for public office."

"Which I didn't know."

"I meant to tell you! Then all this happened. I was only waiting. It wasn't like I was deliberately not telling you. You *deliberately* never told me about the record. I asked you after Casey whether there was anything else and you said no. You told me *no*."

"Because I had forgotten about it."

"Is it that, or is it that you thought the records were sealed?"

"One being true doesn't negate the other." He snorted. "I don't guess it occurs to you that this also affects me."

She threw up her hands. "Of course it does. It affects you most of all. I can hate that at the same time as I hate that you didn't tell me." She took a deep breath and spoke in a calmer tone. "Let's do this one more time. What else don't I know about, Aaron?"

Instead of answering her question he said, "Same question for you."

"I've been open and honest with you."

His eyes narrowed to slits. "Then when were you going to tell me about the paternity test you were running on Casey and me?"

FORTY-NINE

Big Horn, Wyoming

LATE SUNDAY MORNING at Half Circle Ranch, Jack and Emily made their way across the dirt packed parking area toward the stables. She stumbled, and he took her elbow.

"This place is gorgeous. But not as pretty as yours, of course." Emily pointed at three sorrel polo ponies grazing in an adjacent pasture. "For one thing, the horses are too skinny."

"For another thing, that ranch of which you speak is *ours*," he corrected. He pointed at two horses on the private polo field in the distance, their riders tiny on their backs. The horses might be thin compared to quarter horses, but they certainly weren't short. "See the riders out there?"

"I'd noticed them. I wonder if one of the riders is Joaquim?"

"My guess is probably so."

As they neared the stable, a man was hurrying out. A tall man with a sprinkling of gray in his dark hair. His spiffy attire—pressed jeans, dressy Boots, and a collared short sleeved shirt— said he wasn't there to muck stalls or exercise horses. This could be their guy.

Jack removed his hand from Emily's arm. "Excuse me. Are you Peter Galindo?"

The man slowed, turned, and started walking backwards as he passed them, stopping five yards away with his hands halfway up. "I am. I'm on my way out, though."

"That's a shame. We were hoping to grab a minute of your time."

"And you are?"

Jack cocked his head. Peter looked more than hurried. He looked *harried*. "I'm Jack Holden and this is Emily Bernal. We're representing Aaron Herrington. I need to ask you some questions."

Peter shook his head and took another step away. "That won't be possible."

"Why?"

"My boss has made it clear that everyone who works here is to stay out of that mess."

"By mess, you mean Victor's death?"

"By mess, I mean you need to leave, please."

Jack smiled. "I'm meeting someone. That would make me an invited guest."

"You'll have to hold that meeting somewhere else. The only one who can make an exception to the edict is Mr. Mahones himself, and he isn't here."

"Where is he?"

"Out of town." Peter lowered his voice. "Where I wish I was."

"How about you give me his number. I'll just give him a call."

"No can do."

"Has your boss told you not to do that as well?"

Peter made a finger gun and shot it at him.

Just then, Joaquim came riding across the yard on a different horse than the last time Jack had seen him. He looked away from Jack, like he didn't know him.

Emily spoke for the first time. "Excuse me, Mr. Galindo. We've driven a long way to get here, and I've had too much coffee. May I *please* visit your little girls' room before our drive back?"

Atta girl. She didn't mention where they'd come from, and he wasn't sure she could have named a city outside Sheridan County in Wyoming if Peter had pushed back on her, but he didn't. Most men didn't. Couldn't. When Emily wanted something, she was like funnel cake at a county fair. Even when you knew you shouldn't, you gave in to the temptation.

Peter gestured toward the stable entrance. "There's one inside on the right. By the office. But hurry, and then the two of you need to go."

"Thank you so much!" She twinkled at him.

"Absolutely. Sorry to bother you," Jack said.

Peter smiled involuntarily at Emily. Then he frowned like he couldn't make up his mind whether to wait and be sure they left or not, but whatever had him fired up to skedaddle won out. He waved over his shoulder as he got into a red pickup truck.

"I'm afraid I may find myself dawdling in the bathroom," Emily drawled as they entered the stables.

Jack laughed. "You are as amazing as you are smart and beautiful."

She winked. "I really do have to go, though."

"I'll just mosey around while you're indisposed. See what I can see. Strike up a few conversations."

Emily paused with her hand on the doorknob. A picture of a dog squatting to defecate was pasted to the door. She grimaced. "Wish me luck."

Jack paused to admire the view as she disappeared inside. From down the corridor, he heard raised voices.

A man shouted, "You're not going to take me down with you."

BANG. BANG. BANG.

Jack dropped to the floor. The sound was unmistakable. A handgun firing. For a moment, he held still, trying to get a fix on exactly where it had come from. He wondered if it had been something innocent. A stable hand shooting at bottles or maybe scaring off an animal. He didn't think so. That shot was the end to the argument he'd just overheard.

The bathroom door opened, and Emily's face peeked out. She whispered, "Was that gunfire?"

"It was. Too close. I'm going to check it out. Call 911. And stay inside with the door locked. Please."

She nodded and shut the door. He waited to hear the lock turn before he took off at a sprint. The voices and shots had sounded like they came from a stall at the far end of the stable. He looked right and left as he flew past each stall, seeing nothing but horses surprised by the nutjob who was running through the stable. The sliding door was open at the last stall on the left. As he started to turn to go through it, his boot landed in the one pile of manure in the hallway, and he slid, nearly falling before he caught himself on the stall door.

He had just enough time to catch a glimpse of the scene inside—a young man crumpled on the ground, blood pooling in the straw, open, fixed eyes facing the door. A stream of red trickled from his gaping mouth.

Then something out of his peripheral vision barreled into Jack. He clung to the door, barely keeping his feet. The something was a man. Jack was just able to get a foot out and trip him. He crashed to the ground.

"What the f—" the guy rolled over. It was the blinged out gym rat who'd come to the office with Casey. Buster.

As Buster started to rise, Jack planted a foot on his chest, knocking him onto his back. Then he dropped to his knees on the younger man's diaphragm. Buster let out an explosive breath and groaned.

Jack barked, "Drop your weapon, Buster."

"I don't have one, man."

Jack didn't believe him. Not for a second. He started patting him down.

Buster bucked and struggled against him. "Who the fuck are you?"

Jack ignored him and kept looking for the gun he'd heard. It wasn't easy when the subject was writhing like an anaconda. Still, he was able to find something. A cell phone. He ignored it and kept searching. "Why are you running?"

Buster stilled and looked away, then back at Jack. "For help. I was running for help for Jake."

"That's Jake?" Jack chinned at the man on the stable floor.

"Yeah. Jake Small. He's one of the stable hands."

"Is he okay?" Jack knew he was not. He had a clear view of him. The kid was dead. He kept his hands moving on Buster, looking for that damn handgun. *Behind his back, maybe? I need to flip him.*

"Um, I dunno."

"Did you call 911?"

Just as Jack was becoming suspicious about how compliant Buster was acting, Buster exploded off the ground, throwing Jack aside and back into the horse mess. Jack's head bumped hard on the concrete floor. It hurt like hell. Before Jack could get up, Buster was sprinting out of the stable. Jack slipped and slid and started after him. *Damn, forty-two feels old.* He heard an engine roar to life and the ping of gravel hitting metal. He ran outside anyway in time to see the rooster tail of dust with a vehicle somewhere on the other side of it.

Buster was gone. Jack thought about driving after him, but it made no sense. He wasn't a cop. He walked back into the stable, aware that he smelled like the back end of a horse. What he needed was a towel. No, a hose. Soon, but not now. First, he needed to talk to law enforcement.

Emily emerged from the bathroom holding up the phone. "It's on speaker. This is 911."

He stepped over to her and spoke into the mic. "There's been a shooting at Half Circle Ranch. A man is dead. And Buster Kemp just fled the scene."

FIFTY

Sheridan, Wyoming

KID RUBBED HIS EYES. His fifth coffee was ready, so he walked over and stirred maple syrup into it. Sundays were usually his lazy days. *There's not enough caffeine in the world.* He threw his apple core in the trash and washed and dried his hands. His next order of business was Shiva. He needed contact information for her, but he couldn't remember her last name. He'd gotten Sandi Long's number at the Mint Bar the other night, so, he decided to call her.

He sat back down at his desk, rolled his neck, and faced his laptop screen. The background photo stopped his heart. It was Casey on an early morning with no makeup, when she was most beautiful. He jiggled his mouse to banish the image then flipped to his settings and changed it to one of the standard backgrounds. It left a dull ache in his chest.

He dialed Sandi, and, as the phone rang, he moved to Jenn's fancy chair and put his feet up on the desk, coffee in hand. He sipped it. The burning in his stomach seemed to indicate he was overdoing the brew. He kept drinking anyway.

Sandi skipped hello. "My caller ID says this is Kid James. Is it lying to me?"

Kid smiled. He liked her sense of humor. "Your phone is a truthteller. How are you?"

"Barely functioning. Do you have any idea what time it is?"

"Time for the good people of northern Wyoming to be in church."

"Don't tell my parents."

"Listen, I have a reason for dragging you out of bed at this, in your case, ungodly hour."

"Ha ha."

"I am trying to track down someone we went to high school with. Shiva, I think she's called. All I have is her first name."

"Oh, sure. You're calling me about other women instead of asking me out. I get it."

Was Sandi interested in him? It seemed impossible. For starters, she was normal. But also, the women of Sheridan had never found him this magnetic before. But if she was, he felt bad. "No, I mean, uh—"

She laughed. "Gotcha. What do you want with Shiva?"

He closed his eyes. *You're no Casanova.* "It's about a case I've started working on."

"Oh? Which one?"

"A good attorney never tells."

"Don't let Celeste know you're calling her." She laughed. "Yes, Celeste told me you guys went out. And another date this weekend."

"It's super casual."

"She doesn't know the meaning of that word. Anyway, they're on the outs. Apparently Shiva hooked up with Victor. But don't say you heard that from me."

"Really? Wow. Yeah, I won't even mention I'm talking to Shiva."

278 PAMELA FAGAN HUTCHINS

He gave it a beat. "So, tell me about her. I didn't really know her in school."

"She was a year ahead of us. A cheerleader. I think she played volleyball, too. She's from a family with a big ranch southeast of town."

"Do you like her?"

"Truthfully? Not really. She's always been a user. And vindictive as hell."

Kid sat up and put his feet down. "What do you mean?"

"Don't you remember our freshman year when she was dating Eli—"

"The star of the football team."

"Yeah, well, he dumped her. Word is she spiked his drink with something at an after-game party. He crashed his car on the way home."

Kid's pulse sped up. He got to his feet. The story was only slightly familiar to him. He'd been consumed with debate and taking extra classes so he could graduate early. But this was good stuff. "Wow. Was he okay?"

"He broke his leg and was out of athletics the rest of the year. I think it cost him a chance at a scholarship."

"Did she get in trouble?"

"No. I don't think they could prove it. But everyone knew she did it."

"Poor guy. Do you have her phone number? I'd really like to talk to her."

And Sandi gave it to him. Just like that—the dirt on Shiva and her number. He thanked her and they agreed to grab a drink some time to catch up.

He walked around the office, thinking. He'd never considered keeping in touch with his old schoolmates something that impacted his job, but it wasn't hurting on this case. Honestly, though, he was feeling a little pigeon-holed by Jack. It was like, "that's a Gen Z interview, give it to Kid." That and the legal research, which, again, felt like it was because of his age. The youngest attorneys always get stuck in the proverbial library—even if research was all online these days—searching for obscure cases that never get used.

He wanted to *contribute* on this case. He and Jenn had defended people they cared about before, but never like this. This was *Aaron*. Why couldn't Jack see Kid's value as well as his commitment?

Then again, maybe he wasn't being fair. Working with Jack was going fine. He was nice, smart as hell, organized, and knowledgeable. Kid would have considered him the perfect boss, if he'd never worked for Jenn. Of course, technically, he and Jenn were colleagues, but he'd never kid himself. *I hate it when I'm punny.* She was calling the shots, and he was darn lucky. He was learning from her and developing in leaps and bounds from her.

Or he was lucky for now. Until she left to be the county prosecutor.

He made himself a record sixth cup at the Keurig. Even the smell of it was unappealing at this stage. As he stood at the coffee maker, he probed at the scab from his call with Ollie the day before. He was less angry at Jenn today and deeper in the pain of it. She hadn't betrayed him exactly. He'd just thought they were closer than she did. He would have told her. But she hadn't trusted him enough to confide in him. Or maybe it was that she hadn't cared enough about his feelings to tell him before he found out from someone else.

You're rabbitholing. And, again, possibly not being fair. Jenn's life had imploded this week.

Sighing, he dialed Shiva's number and went to the window. He parted the slats of the blinds with his fingers and looked out into the backyard. His mother was hanging laundry, which she loved to do in the summer. It made the towels too scratchy, but he liked the smell of outdoors, and he loved that she loved it. He thought back to his freshman year when all the guys his age had been into football. She'd driven him to and from debate practices and tournaments after long days at work. She'd lobbied for him at school when he was bullied. She'd let him fight his own battles when he was ready, but she was always there, mama tiger in the background. He put his fingers to the glass.

The call went to voicemail. A woman's voice said, "I'm not here, ya know what to do, so do it." Beeeeeep.

"Hello, Shiva. My name is Kid James. We went to high school together. I got your number from Sandi Long." He recited his number for her. "Could you call me back?" He didn't tell her what the call was about, deliberately so. There was no way she would call him if she thought she was in the hot seat about Victor.

The door flung open. Emily burst in with Jack close behind her.

"Oh, my goodness!" Emily collapsed into Jenn's chair, panting. "We were just out at Half Circle Ranch, and somebody *shot* Jake Small!"

Kid looked to Jack who was rubbing his face. "That stable hand who tried to get Aaron to drug one of Hellcat horses?"

Jack nodded. "He's dead. We've been out there giving statements."

"Holy guacamole, Batman. Do they know who did it?"

Jack took a seat in Kid's chair, leaving Kid the loser in musical chairs. "Buster Kemp was at the scene. Literally in the stall with Jake's body. Then he fled."

"Jack tackled him and questioned him." Emily gave a proud smile.

"Sort of. Not that it did any good. He still got away. The cops are looking for him now, though."

"Did he do it?" Kid asked. "Or was he just scared?"

Jack cocked his head. "Why would he be scared? Does he have a record?"

"No, I mean because Wyles is their vet. I would assume Buster was out there for the horses. And since Jake asked Aaron to drug a horse when Wyles was out of town, well—I'm assuming again—maybe Wyles and his *employees* are helping with drugging. Buster being an employee..."

Emily said, "Whoa, Nellie! You're making my head hurt. You think Buster was involved with the horse drugging?"

"Yes. And if Jake was shot because he knew about the drugging—"

"A big if," Jack said.

"Yes. But if he was—"

"Then Buster could be the next target, not the killer." Emily pumped her fist.

"Exactly." But Kid was damned if he could figure out whether that was good or bad for Aaron's case.

FIFTY-ONE

Big Horn, Wyoming

JENNIFER PULLED her Grand Cherokee into the first space in one of the snowmobile parking lots on her way home from her disastrous visit with Aaron. She barely made it out of the car before she tossed up coffee and Chardonnay. The acid burned her throat. She stumbled around to the other side of the car, away from the road where every off-road vehicle driver heading up or down the mountain could watch her hurl.

She wished she could jettison the morning's images from her mind as easily. The conversation couldn't have gone much worse. After Aaron had confronted her about the DNA test, he'd told her that Casey had visited him the night before and told him about it.

All Jennifer could do was admit it.

Aaron had been as angry as she'd ever seen him. "You hate Casey so much that you'd try to take fatherhood away from me? That doesn't feel like love. Not the kind I thought you and I had." He'd slammed the phone down before she could respond.

What would she have said if she had gotten the chance? She was sorry he found out from Casey. She wasn't sorry that she wondered if Casey could be his or that she felt the need to protect him from her. Honestly, the thing that she'd wanted to do was ask him how Casey knew.

The memories only upset her stomach worse, so she pushed the rest of them away.

She stepped back and put her forehead on the front hood of the car. She forced herself to concentrate on nothing more than breathing. One breath. Another breath. Another. And another. Until a breath morphed into a sob that became an endless stream of them, sweeping her into a current of deep, unstoppable grief, pure and separate from conscious thought. It just was, and she felt herself sink below the surface where she hoped there'd be no need to breathe anymore.

How long it was before the river spit her out on the rocks, she didn't know. When she became aware of her breaths again, sweat was rolling down her sides and back. The wind had dried her salty cheeks. She was still facing downward, and she began to notice the world. The round disks of cracked brown rock on the ground, like flying saucers crash landed at her feet. Crashed, like her. Although wrecked would be closer to the truth. Complete with rubberneckers, if the sounds of traffic slowing as it passed was any indication. She must be a spectacle.

She didn't want anyone to see her like this. People might recognize her car. Her.

She opened her passenger door and pulled wet wipes from the glove compartment. Living rurally, they were useful in a variety of situations. They'd also come in handy when she was pregnant. She mopped her face and hands, checked her shoes—clean, luckily—and threw the used wipes in her trash bag, then popped breath mints.

She straightened, which was a mistake. Her face was visible to drivers on the road. A truck immediately slowed. The window rolled down.

A woman called, "Are you okay, ma'am? Do you need some help?"

Jennifer forced something she hoped looked like a smile and waved. "Just enjoying the view. Thanks. Have a nice day." As if to prove it, she turned and gazed out over the valley. She focused on a distant butte, a desert island in a slate blue sea of shade from the clouds overhead. It was lovely, actually, but she had no interest in it.

The woman waved back and drove on.

I have to get out of here. She wanted to clap her hands twice and be at home in bed. But not home as it was right now. Home as it was a week ago, before Victor had died, Aaron had been arrested, and she'd learned about his criminal record. The magnitude of her own actions hit her. Her knees buckled, and she caught herself on her car door. *Before I did the things I did.*

She opened the door and got into the car. She'd left it running, and air conditioner blasted her face. She wanted to talk to someone. Needed to. Whenever she felt this way, the someone was mostly Aaron and sometimes Kid. Neither of them were a possibility now. Her twin brother or her mom were options but admitting what was going on and her part in it all, as well as breaking her own rule of never badmouthing her marriage to her family, made them a no go. Maybe she could call Alayah, her best friend back in Texas. Or Trish Flint, her good friend here in Wyoming. She thought of Maggie. Or Maggie's friends—Katie, Emily, Michele, Ava—her new friends. Pastor Abel. Shelley the hypnotherapist.

Who was she kidding? The *only* person she wanted to talk to was Aaron, for him to forgive her, and she wanted to move past this, somehow. His mistake had happened twenty years ago. It meant nothing compared to what they'd built together. But she was really afraid the damage she'd done this time might be irreparable. *How self-absorbed I've been. How utterly, irredeemably selfish.*

Her phone rang. Knowing it wouldn't be Aaron, she almost didn't check caller ID. It wouldn't be good news. There was no good news. But, after three rings, she pulled it out of her cup holder.

Her eyes widened. It was Veronica Farinolo. On a Sunday morning?

She answered quickly before the call went to voicemail. "This is Jennifer Herrington." Did her voice sound as quavery as it felt?

"Hello, Jennifer. This is Veronica Farinolo. I'm calling with an olive branch. I was emotional last time I saw you. I overreacted. It was so soon after Victor's death and your husband's arrest." Her voice was smooth and sweet. Warm honey from a wooden spoon.

"How nice, Veronica. There's no need for an olive branch, though. You've had a horrible week."

"But so have you. I can't imagine what you're going through. If Jerry were in Aaron's shoes, it would be devastating to me."

Maybe Jerry should be in Aaron's shoes. While Mahones stood to gain the most by drugging Victor, and Buster the most by stealing the drugs, in her heart she harbored a deep suspicion about Jerry. He'd been cheated by his rider, which could have cost him dearly in terms of pride and pocketbook. He might have even known Victor had cheated on his daughter. "Okay."

"I think it's important for you to know that whatever Aaron did, I don't blame you. I understand that you have to defend your husband, even if I can't talk about my family with you."

Jennifer's fist balled in her lap. As olive branches went, this one was pretty limp and lifeless. How would she feel in Veronica's shoes, though? Law enforcement was saying by their actions that they thought Aaron had killed Victor, Veronica's former future son-in-law. The star player of the polo team owned by her and her husband. Could she really take it on blind faith that Aaron hadn't done it? Jennifer would have required proof, as she suspected Veronica would. "Well, it's very nice of you to reach out. You have a great day."

"Wait. There's another reason I called."

Jennifer transferred the call to her sound system and set the phone down. "Oh?" She turned on her blinker and put the car in drive.

"That legal work we discussed. I do want to talk to you about it, and the situation unfortunately has really heated up. I can get past the thing with Victor... and Aaron. When I looked around for another attorney, everyone just pointed me back to you. People say you're the best, and we need the best." She paused, then added, "Only if you don't mind, I'd appreciate it if you didn't tell anyone about this, since everyone in town knows you're an attorney. This thing is very embarrassing for me and my family."

There's no way I'm promising her secrecy. Jennifer neared the far side of the road and saw a short, scruffy guy pointing a phone at her. She felt sick. The photographer who'd caught her coming out of the hypnotherapist's office. He'd still been following her and caught her at her worst.

But she cast him out of her thoughts. This call was big. *An opening for me to talk to the Farinolos?* Jennifer accelerated onto the road heading west. Dust rose behind her as pavement gave way to gravel.

"Jennifer, did I lose you?"

"Sorry. I'm here. When did you have in mind?"

"Actually, the matter is pretty urgent. Could you come now?"

"Now? On Sunday morning?" Jennifer put on her blinker.

"If you possibly could."

Jennifer stopped at the turn into her long driveway. She was torn. She still wanted to go home and fall apart. Phone a friend. Hug a dog. Brush her teeth. But how could she pass up the chance to learn something useful for Aaron? "Will it just be the two of us?"

"Jerry and Celeste are out."

That settled it. Jennifer could try to work in questions about whether Veronica and Jerry knew Victor was cheating on their daughter *and* on their team. If it cost her the legal work, who cared? The first step to winning back Aaron's trust was finding his killer and securing his release.

She wheeled her car around. "I'm on my way."

FIFTY-TWO

EMILY TORE the crust off a ham sandwich. Mayo plopped onto the desk as she popped it in her mouth. "I'm making good progress on the Herrington's financial records, and our IT expert is in the clinic today working on file recovery. I hope to hear from her soon."

Jack handed her a napkin. They'd come down off the high of the possible connection between Buster, the horse drugging, and at least Jake's if not Victor's murder, and they were getting themselves organized for the final push before arraignment the next day. "Katie and Nick are working up Sarah Friedman next and then going deeper on the Farinolos after that. Since Peter Galindo told me Mahones had forbidden anyone to have anything to do with the mess around Victor's death, I wasn't able to talk to him or Joaquim about what Victor was doing for the Hellcats."

Kid was drinking coffee. The way he was hunched over suggested it wasn't agreeing with him. "I got some background on Shiva, the last known girlfriend of Victor's. According to a friend of mine, she is a

288 PAMELA FAGAN HUTCHINS

vengeful woman with a history of harming others. I'm still trying to reach her directly."

Emily went to her white board from the previous evening and added notes. "I've been thinking. If we believe Buster was drugging the Hellcat horses, does that mean Wyles is the supplier?"

"Buster could be acting alone," Jack said. "Without Wyles's knowledge."

"If this turns out to be true, Aaron might be a target for violence as well," Kid added. "He didn't drug the horses, but he knew enough to believe somebody was."

"It elevates the importance of talking to Wyles, for sure." Jack crossed his arms. "I think it's time to call Ollie. We've got another polo murder in a small community, and Aaron couldn't have done it."

"Do you want me to call him on my phone?" Jack nodded, so Kid pressed the number in his contacts, put the call on speaker, and set it on his desk.

Ollie picked up on the first ring. "You better have a damn good reason for bothering me on a Sunday morning, *Wesley*."

"We do," Jack said.

"Who is this?"

"Jack Holden on Kid's phone. I'm calling about the murder out at Half Circle Ranch."

"What about it?"

"Jake Small. He works for the Hellcats. He was drugging horses."

"So?"

"Aaron is in jail. It wasn't him."

"Obviously."

"And it shows Aaron didn't kill Victor."

"How?"

"It's another drugging-related death in the polo community involving one of the teams that was playing when Victor died."

"Again, so?"

"Victor was on the Hellcats's payroll."

"I don't know anything about that."

"Ask around. Then you'll find out just like we did."

"No need to. We don't see any reason Victor's and Jake's deaths were related."

"I just gave you the reasons."

"None that hold water with me."

"Then you're blind *and* incompetent." Jack stabbed a finger to end the call then slammed a palm on the desk. "Jesus, Mary, and Joseph. Is it just me or is he on a personal vendetta?"

Kid gave him a sympathetic look. "He makes Jenn crazy like that, too."

FIFTY-THREE

Sheridan, Wyoming

EMILY SPUN BACK and forth in Jennifer's office chair—the most comfortable one she'd ever worked in—and dialed the number for the Wyles clinic.

A pleasant female voice answered. "Dr. Wyles' Veterinary Clinic. How may I serve you?"

Emily stopped the motion of the chair. She pitched her voice high and tried to sound emotional. "My cat is hurt. She got stepped on by a horse. She needs a vet."

"We're open from ten to six today. You can bring it on in. Do you know where we are?"

"I do. Thank you! We're on our way soon." She hung up, smirking. "They're open and ready for you."

Jack glanced at his wrist. She loved that he still wore a real watch. Not a smart watch. A battered Seiko that had belonged to his father. "Okay. I think I can head over there in about half an hour."

Kid said, "I'm feeling optimistic."

"It would help if we knew whether Buster was involved in stealing the xylazine. He could have taken it from his own clinic much more easily."

"But he'd risk getting fired if Wyles caught him. Or who knows—maybe he had been stealing it from there, too."

Emily lofted her Fanta Orange can into the trash underhanded. A few drops landed on her as it left her hand. Nice. Now her shorts had an orange stain and the essence of fizzy pop. "Go in like you're sure, babe. It's bound to be him."

"You're right," Jack said.

Emily tossed her hair. "Like I'm ever not." Her phone rang. She held it up. "It's the IT lady." She accepted the call. "This is Emily. May I put you on speaker with our team?"

"Sure," a scratchy female voice said.

Emily activated the speaker. "Thanks for coming in on a weekend. What do you have for us?"

"You're welcome. First, let's talk about the login for the file deletion. As you know, the clinic only uses one login for the security app."

"Right."

"But the computers in the clinic are set up to track usage."

"What does that mean?"

"System administrators have the ability to see what users have been up to on their machines. Like what apps they access, when, and for how long."

"That's pretty slick."

"It is. I was able to check all the computers in the clinic. I found two logged into the security app during the time in question."

"Two? Oh, no! I was hoping for certainty."

"Oh, it's not as bad as it sounds. One of them had been logged in for days. Loretta's computer. She's basically always logged into it."

"And I don't think it was Loretta."

"The other computer hasn't been logged into the security system since initial training. Someone logged in on it smack in the middle of the time range in question, too, and logged out ten minutes later."

Emily threw her head back and arms up. "Hallelujah! That's it. That has to be it. Who is it?"

"Well, I hope this isn't a bad surprise." The woman paused. *Just get on with it, lady!* "The computer that the login came from belongs to Dr. Sarah Friedman."

Emily's jaw dropped. That had *not* been the answer she was expecting.

FIFTY-FOUR

Big Horn, Wyoming

I RUBBED MY BLEARY EYES, yawning, then used a microfiber rag on my screen. Nick and I had been glued to our laptops all morning. That wouldn't change until after Aaron's arraignment, assuming we didn't find something that would keep it from happening. We'd rescheduled our flights so we could stay through it, although the rest of our friends besides Jack and Emily had flown home.

This kind of work was a little like panning for gold. Hard with very little pay off. Sarah Friedman was making our job significantly more challenging, too, although probably not intentionally. The woman had gone by a lot of different last names. A birth name. The one of a stepfather who adopted her. A fresh, new name when he'd stolen all her mother's money and run off in the dead of night. Three married names, the number of which at her relatively young age probably shouldn't have been a surprise given her upbringing.

Things had gotten messy in her last hitch. Marriage, job, and town.

"Boom!" I said, throwing my hands in the air. "Bankruptcy filing a year ago."

"Do you know how hot you look to me right now?" Nick went for the fist bump, but I pretended I didn't see it.

I blew on my fingertips instead then started typing and reading at the same time. "Strap in for the details. It appears husband number three—Greg Friedman—started a cannabis shop in Fort Collins, Colorado."

"Oh, no. Did it go up in smoke?"

"No. Greg did. Multiple driving under the influence charges with the last one resulting in a trip to rehab. The business went under while he was there and took the household finances with it."

"I thought vets make a lot of money."

"She grew up poor. Went to college on a volleyball scholarship and worked her way through vet school, maxed out on student loan debt. She's solely responsible for her two kids from previous marriages *and* paying her exes' support. I actually feel sorry for her. These losers are bleeding her dry."

I continued compiling legal filings, property records, and financial records about the fiasco in Fort Collins, including the associated public drama. Nick had moved on to criminal records and prison records.

I was thigh high in the weeds when Nick snapped his fingers. "I just don't buy it that a determined, successful woman like Sarah would keep marrying the type of guys she does unless she has some problems herself."

"What do you mean?"

"These guys aren't rule followers. I poked around on the backgrounds of all three of them. They all have criminal records."

"Maybe she has an 'I can fix him' complex?"

"Or maybe she isn't a rule follower either."

"Does she have a criminal record?"

"Not that I've been able to find. But if she was ever going to be desperate enough to play outside the rules, my bet is that it would have been when her husband was in rehab and they were about to lose everything. What a pressure cooker for her."

"Right... but you haven't found anything."

"Nothing that made it into the legal system. That doesn't mean nothing *happened*. I'm going to call the Fort Collins Police Department and see what they have to say."

I snagged a cookie out of the bag on the table. Oreos. Processed junk, but who has time to cook during a high stakes case for a friend? "They're not going to talk to you."

He shot me a look. "Want to wager on it?"

"You always lose our bets."

"I'll bet you an hour-long massage."

"Including feet?"

"Absolutely."

Nick is a sexy guy, but his feet have to be the ugliest in the history of the world. Of the universe. As much as I love the rest of him, I try to avoid touching them. "I'll take forty-five minutes with no feet, please."

He gave me a cheerfully rude gesture, then dialed and put his phone on speaker. "Watch and learn."

I gave him the rude gesture back.

"Fort Collins PD." The guy answering the phone sounded sleepy and bored.

"Hello, my name is Nick Connell. I'm a private investigator in Wyoming looking for background on a case I'm working involving a veterinarian recently of Fort Collins, suspected of stealing drugs from the clinic she's working for here. I know this a long shot, but I'm hoping it's a slow Sunday and that there might be someone I can chat with about it?"

There was dead silence on the other end. It stretched out for five very long seconds. I pondered whether I preferred lavender or vanilla scented massage oil.

"Hello?"

"Yeah, I'm here. I'm filling in at the front desk, so I'm not at my normal machine, and I was trying to look something up. I had a similar case last year—well, I've had a couple in the last few where people broke into vet clinics and stole all their opioids. But there was one that involved a vet. Give me a second and I'll get you the name."

Nick waggled his head at me. "Man, I got lucky you were the one on phone duty."

"Yeah, here it is. No arrests because we couldn't make a case, but we all believed one of the vets at the clinic did it. Her husband was a loser with a record for assault, burglary, and drugs. A real lowlife. They were going through a lot of financial shit, too."

"That's great!" Nick surfed his upper body in a chair dance. I put my hand on his shoulder where I could choke him if he didn't stop gloating.

"I can't remember her name. I'm looking."

"But it's a she?"

"Yep. Cara or Taryn. Or... Sarah. Yep."

"Sarah Friedman?"

"That's her."

Nick pointed at his shoulders with both hands, and I gladly obliged. It was worth it. He'd just unearthed pure gold.

FIFTY-FIVE

Big Horn, Wyoming

VERONICA STOOD outside the Farinolo house waving as Jennifer pulled into the driveway. *So much for time to check in with Jack and Kid.* Jennifer had been planning to let them know where she was and what her intentions were about questioning Veronica. Plus, she needed to tell them what she'd learned from Aaron—that Casey had visited him the night before and told him about the paternity test. Jennifer didn't know for *sure* how Casey had found out. She suspected it was Buster, though.

The information transfer would have to wait. She climbed out of her car.

"Thank you so much for coming!" Veronica embraced Jennifer, then held her at arm's length and scrutinized her. *She smells like she bathed in angel wings and baby kisses, and me...* "Oh, my. I don't have to ask how you are."

Jennifer saw herself through Veronica's lens. The dark circles under her eyes. The hair in a messy bun. A University of Tennessee vintage sweatshirt and yesterday's jeans. And, most of all, her splotchy, tear-tracked face. "I came as soon as you called. I'm sorry about my appearance. You, on the other hand, look amazing."

Veronica adjusted her collar. A silk pantsuit in a blue that popped. Heels. *Heels.* In Big Horn, at home. Make-up and hair, perfection. Any trace of the anxious, emotional woman from earlier in the week was gone. She exuded strength and confidence. "Jerry and I went to brunch at the Brinton straight from church. Come on in."

The little yapper met them at the door. *Angel.*

Veronica scooped up the dog and cuddled her against her cheek and neck. Angel's barks softened to whimpers then stopped altogether. "This way."

She ushered Jennifer into a formal living room across from the dining room where they'd met earlier in the week. The other rooms in the central section of the house flowed together—a high-ceilinged great room, a kitchen, and a breakfast area. Jennifer compared the footprint to her impression of the house from the outside. There had to be wings on both sides of the ground floor, where she pictured offices, guest rooms, and an industrial-size laundry room. And the grand staircase off the great room must lead to the family quarters. *But where does she stash the help?* Because who could run a house of this size alone?

"Would you mind if I visited your bathroom before we start?" Jennifer said. Splashing cold water on her face would help.

"Of course. Exit the great room to your left before you get to the kitchen. Take a left. First door on the right."

It was a lot of directions, but Jennifer managed to make her way to the half bath. Opulence meets the old West. Solid brass fixtures. Antiqued wallpaper with a late 1800s vibe. A painting of a cattle drive so realistic that Jennifer shied away from the horses galloping at her from the canvas. She washed her face and dried it on an ultra-plush hand towel.

Back in the empty living room—or was it a parlor?—Jennifer settled in an armchair and set up for the meeting. Luckily, she'd brought her briefcase with her that morning in the event she ended up at Kid's office. In it were her laptop and an old school yellow pad, which is what she retrieved, along with a pen.

She sensed a presence and looked up. Veronica was standing in the doorway with a woman in a black and white service uniform. The modest kind, not the bunny kind.

Veronica gave an imperial smile, chin and nose high. Angel stood by her heels, similarly posed. "I thought high tea would be in order." *If she wasn't born into money, she sure adapted well.*

Her helper placed a tray on the side table near Jennifer. Raspberry tarts, tall iced teas, and a dish of lemons. "I'll be back with the ice cream, ma'am."

"Thank you, Yolanda."

The helper left the room without being introduced. Veronica sat adjacent to Jennifer in a matching armchair. Angel trotted to a fluffy pink bed and settled herself in it with a harrumph.

Jennifer swept her hand at the tray. "This is lovely and much appreciated. I missed lunch."

"We can't have you starve."

"And this room. That vase." Jennifer nodded at a crystal vase that looked like it cost more than the Big Horn Lodge.

"Baccarat," Veronica said. "A priceless heirloom. Now, please, have a drink, and we can talk about legal matters while Yolanda fetches the ice cream."

The word fetches set Jennifer's teeth on edge. She hadn't spent enough time with Veronica at the polo match to get the full measure of her personality, which was not particularly appealing. Jennifer lifted an iced tea. Her crying and stomach emptying had left her thirsty. She took a big sip. The bite of hard liquor seared her throat and nasal passages. She fought to keep her face straight and not choke.

"Long Island iced tea. I made them myself. They're a Sunday afternoon ritual for me."

"Mm." Jennifer pretended to take another sip then set the drink down and lifted her pen. "Now, how can I help you?"

"It's Victor's creditors, I'm afraid. They've been threatening us. I think I alluded to this at our last meeting. It's been going on for some time."

Jennifer's bad day suddenly began improving. This was about Victor! And she thought of another positive. In just a few hours, Delaney Pace would be contacting her about whether she and Leo had been able to find any evidence of misconduct by Travis or Ollie. Her last text had sounded promising. *Focus on Veronica.*

She nodded at her host. "Tell me why Victor's creditors are chasing you guys. Did you sign anything legally obligating you to cover his debts, like a guarantee? Co-signing on a note? Or did you co-own some sort of business together?"

"Not exactly. But it is related to the team."

"In what way?"

"Well, it seems he represented himself to be an agent of the team when he committed to fund some investments."

"What type of investments?"

"Some sort of club that buys and sells cryptocurrency."

Interesting. Celeste had mentioned Victor lost money in investments the year before. Jennifer wondered if they were with this crypto group. It sounded a lot like gambling, which they already knew Victor was into. "I'd love to take a look at any documentation you have and hear all about it." Her phone rang. With only twenty-four hours to go until the arraignment, she had to see who was calling.

"My apologies." Jennifer fished her phone out of her purse and stared at it. A Facetime call from Ollie. *Facetime is weird. Maybe it's a butt dial.* Or maybe not. She stood. "Is there a place where I can take this? It's about my husband and very time sensitive."

"There's an office just down the hall from the bathroom."

"Thank you."

Jennifer pressed Accept as she walked away. She practically had PTSD from Ollie's last call. Her entire body tensed with dread over what she was about to hear.

FIFTY-SIX

Big Horn, Wyoming

JACK PARKED the Jeepster in front of a house that looked to be very recent construction. Gray Hardie board with black and white trim, sitting on an acre with a hanging swing on the front porch. The neighborhood was near Big Horn. New and clean with no vegetation aside from grass so recently planted the sod lines were still visible. It was the home of Sarah Friedman and her family. When the IT expert had revealed the video was deleted on Sarah's machine, the criticality of her interview had increased exponentially. Jack and Kid had swapped interview subjects. Kid was on his way to the Wyles clinic while Jack was here with Emily, who occupied the shotgun seat.

Her fingers were flying on her laptop, dropping numbers into a spreadsheet. The Herrington financials.

"We're here. I'll be back," he said.

She didn't look up. "Uh huh." When she needed to focus, she could block out the world.

Jack walked up to the front door and knocked. It was opened by a girl of about the age his older daughter would have been, if she had survived the car bomb. All arms and legs with braces on her teeth and a smattering of acne. "Is Dr. Sarah Friedman here?"

"Mom's running errands. You want Greg?" the girl asked.

Jack handed her a card. "No, but thank you. Could you give this to your mom and ask her to call me as soon as she can?"

A man's voice bellowed, "Who is it, Charity?"

Charity said, "Yes, sir," to Jack. Then she hollered back. "Someone leaving a card for mom."

"Thanks again." Jack gave her a salute and hurried back to Aaron's orange behemoth. As he climbed into his seat, he saw a square-shouldered man whose head was high enough to bump the door frame. The guy was sporting two shiners. For a moment Jack thought he recognized him, but he couldn't be sure, and he didn't want to look back. Instead, he pretended he didn't see him and moved the vehicle away before Greg could come out and ask him questions.

"Sarah isn't home," he told Emily.

Emily glanced at the doorway and the man standing in it. "You ducking Dad?"

"Or some sort of possible father figure. What do you think about working from home? We can finish up at the office tonight if we need to. I'd like face-to-face time with Katie and Nick."

"Fine by me. I can do this wherever I land."

They drove in silence, Emily working, and Jack's brain chasing theories around in circles like a drunken cattle dog. Sarah deleting the video had thrown a spanner in the works. He'd been sure it would be Casey. Did it call into doubt the analysis Sarah had done about use of xylazine at the clinic? Possibly. But if she were to falsify that, wouldn't it have been to clear herself? By the time they reached the lodge ten minutes later, he hadn't resolved anything. He hoped Kid was having better luck than him.

Bad news was waiting for them outside the lodge. Deputy Travis

Spahn was leaning against his truck, arms crossed. Deputy Haigle stood beside him with a piece of paper in her hand.

Jack greeted them as he got out of Demarcus Ware. "Good afternoon, Deputies. Can I help you?"

"We have a search warrant for that vehicle." Travis pointed at the Jeepster. His brows were dark clouds over his eyes.

"Warrant," Haigle added, thrusting it in front of Jack.

He barely scanned it. Katie had read the warrant and had no problem with it. "Be my guest."

Emily walked with him up the steps to the lodge. "They're a cheerful duo."

He shook his head. "What does it cost to live on the bright side?"

The dogs mobbed them as they entered the house. Katie and Nick were working two laptops at the kitchen table. The little skunk was dozing on it in the sun.

Emily said, "Hey, y'all." Then she frowned. "Where's Jenn?"

"Haven't seen her," Katie said. "Should we have?"

"I'm not sure. Do you know what she was up to today?"

"She went to visit Aaron hours ago. You haven't heard anything from her?"

"Not a peep."

Jack found the exchange a little disquieting. He'd expected Jenn to hunker down at home and try to help on Aaron's case in ways she shouldn't. The visit with him was bound to have been tense, but it couldn't have lasted this long. He shot her a quick text. *Where are you? What's up?* Then he put his phone away. "What have you two found on Sarah so far?"

Nick laced his fingers and inverted his hands, stretching. "A lot."

Katie turned her laptop to face Jack. On it was a bankruptcy filing. "She and her husband Greg filed for bankruptcy last year in Fort Collins, Colorado."

"Greg. I was just at their house and think I saw him."

"If he looked like a stoner, that was probably him. He had a cannabis business that went belly up, then he went into rehab after he was pulled over for driving under the influence. His third time in six weeks."

Jack raised his eyebrows. "Interesting. Does Sarah have a criminal record?"

"No, but I called the police department there. I talked to an officer who said he was called out to the clinic where she used to work. The issue was... wait for it..." Nick drum rolled on the table, "drug theft. He said she was definitely a suspect, partly due to the financial crisis their family was in. They couldn't prove anything, so there were no arrests. But he didn't like the husband either. Greg has a record. Assault and burglary. Drugs."

A door opened and closed at the back of the house.

Jack felt a frisson of excitement. This was breakthrough info. "Assault, huh? He was sporting two black eyes less than an hour ago. My guess is he's living the same lifestyle here. Great work."

Katie shrugged. "Thanks. We're close to done on her and switching to the Farinolos next. Jerry is up first."

"What about Dr. Friedman?" It was Casey's voice.

Jack turned and saw her standing in the hallway. The look on her face was odd. Was it chagrin? Sympathy? Guilt? Clearly she'd over-heard them, which wasn't good, but how much? "We're just gathering information."

"Why?"

"I'm afraid that isn't something I can talk to you about."

She cocked a hip and put a hand on it. "It's my dad in jail."

"But you aren't one of his attorneys or his wife. Those are the only people I can talk to about details of the case."

She wheeled and marched out. Jack thought about that inexplicable expression on her face.

He chased after her and caught up to her on the back porch. "It's time for you to come clean, Casey."

"What are you talking about?" She didn't face him. Her voice was high pitched. The anger was gone. In its place was... fear?

"You know very well what I mean. This isn't a game. Where's

Buster?" He hoped the police had found him. If not, it wasn't a long-shot to think he might be hiding out with Casey.

The question drew her eyes to him. "Buster? How would I know? And why is that any of your business?" She looked legitimately confused.

"Did you hear Jake Small was shot today?"

Her mouth made an O. "Jake, the guy who works for the Hellcats?"

If she didn't know about Jake, then she hadn't talked to Buster. Or she was a good actor. "Yes."

"Is he okay?"

"He's dead, Casey. He was drugging horses, and now he's dead. There's a good chance anyone else involved with it is in danger, too."

She took a step back.

He didn't let up. "Victor was drugged with sedatives. The cops think it was the xylazine stolen from your dad's clinic. That looks really, really bad for him."

She pressed a fist into her stomach.

"I was in the Half Circle Ranch stable when Jake was shot. He was arguing with someone, then I heard the shots. When I got to him, guess who was there, right there in the stall with him? And then ran away from the scene?"

"I—"

"Buster."

Her eyes darted to her cottage, to Jack, to Aaron's clinic, then back to Jack.

"Anyone with any relation to what's going on, and I mean anyone, could be next."

She straightened, a look of defiance returning to her eyes. "Talk to Dr. Friedman then."

"Why would we do that?"

"Because she deleted those videos."

Jack knew for sure they hadn't said a word back in the house about the videos being deleted from Dr. Friedman's machine. There was no way Casey would know that was the machine used *unless she was the one who did it.* The slow smile he gave her was feral. *Gotcha.* Confusion mixed with elation, though. If Casey deleted the videos, then how was Dr. Friedman involved? Had she given Casey the keys to the drug storage? Was she getting a cut of the proceeds from selling the xylazine? There were so many unanswered questions. Too many.

He smiled at Casey. "And how in the world would you know that?"

The color drained out of her face.

It was time for a bluff. "We had an IT consultant work on this for us. We know it was you on Dr. Friedman's computer who deleted the videos of yourself and Buster entering the clinic after hours. What we don't know is why'd you do it?"

"Because I didn't want to get fired, and I didn't want my dad to be disappointed in me."

"Because you stole the xylazine."

"No! For taking Buster in there with me when the clinic was closed. It's against the rules."

"Why did you take him in there then?"

"I had to go back. I forgot something."

"What did you forget?"

She hesitated a beat too long, so he rushed his next question, applying more pressure. "We have you on the video as you left. We saw the bag. You guys came in without it and left with it."

Her voice grew shrill. "I didn't do it. I don't even have a key."

"Casey." He softened his tone. "The only way this is going to go well for you is if you talk to me. I can help you."

She bit her lip. *Is she considering it?*

He gentled his tone. "This is serious. I know you guys took the xylazine. And if it was used on Victor... well, he died, Casey."

"You think I don't know he died?" she snapped. "It wasn't me!"

"Talk to me."

"Why? You don't believe me."

He went with his best guess. "Maybe I don't believe you because

Buster walked into your dad's home clinic, attacked Jenn, and took the DNA kit she was about to mail in for a paternity test."

"Again, not me!"

It wasn't an admission, but close to it. "But you knew about it because he told you." Another guess.

She crossed her arms and spoke to her feet. "I need collateral."

"What do you mean?"

"I need, like, insurance. A promise that I'm not the one who's going to get in trouble if I talk to you. Because I didn't do anything."

"I can't make promises, but if you tell me everything, I will do my very best to help you."

She threw up her hands. "You're just like her."

"Like who?"

"Last winter, Jenn said if I confessed to something, she'd keep me out of jail. And you know what? I didn't confess, but she didn't say boo about it to anyone."

"You've lost me–boo about what?"

She sneered. "You really don't know who you're working with do you?"

"Stop the games and just tell me."

Casey bobbled her head sarcastically. "Hypothetically, someone like me may have been involved in something where someone else committed a murder. Hypothetically, conspiracy murder, according to *her*. Hypothetically, someone also pulled a trigger at her fugly face, which she said was attempted murder. And hypothetically she only kept quiet because someone's dad asked her to. I'm not stupid. I worked in a law firm. She could get disbarred for burying it."

Jack felt sick. Casey had it in for Jenn, and she had the goods to bury her. Jack thought about his daughter Betsy. His two children who had died. He didn't love it that Aaron had put Jenn in this situation, but what parent wouldn't help a child? Now Jack was in on Jenn and Casey's awful secret, too, but luckily, the girl hadn't given him details. He didn't want to know anything he might have to disclose.

The key point was that Jenn was at risk. Casey had exposed her to him. She would tell other people.

Jack narrowed his eyes. "If you want my help, don't say another word about any of this. Not to me or to anyone else."

"Are you threatening me?"

"No. I'm establishing the guardrails for our relationship. Are you in or out?"

Casey stared at him. Her face was blank but in her eyes he could see her brain working overtime. *If I handle this just right, she'll talk.*

"Let's get back to the issue that has your dad in jail. This is your chance to show him how much you care about him." Jack waited for her to speak, sure that she would.

But Casey just shook her head.

FIFTY-SEVEN

Sʜᴇʀɪᴅᴀɴ, Wyoming

KID KNOCKED on the locked door to the Wyles clinic and peered through the glass.

Inside, a grandmotherly woman stood up behind a desk. She moved like a penguin to the door and opened it for him. "How may I be of service, young man?"

"I need to talk to Dr. Wyles," he said.

"Where's the patient?"

"What—uh, no patient."

"May I ask what this is about?"

"No offense, but I really need to talk to Dr. Wyles or a practice manager. If that's you, then I can divulge a little more, but this is about sensitive information involving a murder."

"A murder?" Her hand flew to her mouth.

"One of the stable hands at Half Circle Ranch was shot out there."

"Oh, my goodness. But—"

"Please? Can I talk to Dr. Wyles?"

"Let me go ask him. And your name is... ?"

Kid handed her a card. "Kid James."

She frowned. "You're an attorney? And the card says Wesley."

He wished he'd used his given name. He usually did. "Just a nickname."

"I'll be right back."

She locked him outside. He guessed he should take it as a compliment that she thought he looked rugged enough to be some kind of threat, but maybe she didn't trust his card after the name discrepancy. Or she might just not like attorneys. He rocked back and forth onto his heels while he waited. In less than a minute, she returned with a man in a green smock. His bald head shone like a polished nickel.

He opened the door and came outside. "An attorney?"

"A vet keeping office hours on a Sunday?"

He sighed. "The town is growing and there's not enough vets. We have hours seven days a week. If you hear of anyone in the field looking for a job, send them my way." He put out a hand. "Dr. Larry Wyles."

"Kid James." He stuck to the nickname for consistency.

"Minnie told me about the murder out at Half Circle. I'm sorry to hear it, but I don't understand what that has to do with me. Or with you for that matter." He led Kid outside to a picnic table under a cottonwood tree.

They sat across from each other. Kid's phone notified him of a text. He checked it quickly. It was from Jack. *Casey admitted deleting video & that Buster assaulted Jenn. Denied she stole drugs. Didn't confirm Buster did. Refused to talk anymore.* Kid's heart sank. He'd really, really hoped Casey wasn't involved. He closed his eyes briefly. That raised the stakes for this little chat, then.

"Are we going to talk or do you need to be on your phone? I've got patients."

"Sorry." Kid put it away. "My co-counsel Jack Holden was out at Half Circle during the shooting."

The vet's brow formed a V. "What's your stake in this?"

"Last week, a polo player died during a match."

"He got trampled to death, I heard."

"The county attorney thinks it was murder. Victor had sedatives in his system. Our client is currently in jail. He was arrested on suspicion of murder."

"Your client is Aaron Herrington?" He frowned.

Kid gave a selective response. "Yes. Has Buster been in today?"

"He was supposed to be, but he called off sick."

Kid took a deep, slow breath. He made steady eye contact with Dr. Wyles. "Were you or was he on your behalf involved in any way with drugging horses at Half Circle?"

"What the hell did you just say?" Dr. Wyles stood.

"Are you really going to pretend you haven't been involved?"

"You've lost your mind. I think you should go."

Kid kept speaking, raising his voice. "Dr. Wyles, did you have Buster steal xylazine from Dr. Aaron Herrington's clinic?"

"I'm about to call the cops."

"I suppose you don't know Jake Small?"

"Forget the cops. I should kick your skinny butt. If you repeat any of that anywhere to anyone in any form, I'm going to sue you for slander!"

Kid finally stood, but he didn't walk away. "In case you're wondering, he's the Hellcat stable hand who was murdered, and he was facilitating the horse drugging."

"I know who he is, but that has nothing to do with me. Get the hell out of here!"

"So, you don't know why Buster was caught fleeing from the scene?"

The vet looked like he'd been slapped across the face. "Buster was there?"

"He knocked my co-counsel over as he ran from Jake's body.

Speaking of cops, I'm surprised they haven't been out here looking for him. Either they've found him, or they'll be visiting you soon, because we haven't been able to find him and his girlfriend doesn't know where he is."

Dr. Wyles sighed. "Start over at the beginning, please. And call me Larry."

FIFTY-EIGHT

Big Horn, Wyoming

MY BUTT WAS way past the point of going numb. Armchair sleuthing isn't my favorite part of investigative work. Nick and I had divvied up the work on the Farinolos, and we had started our hunting with Jerry. Very quickly I sketched out his early background as the eldest son in a disgustingly wealthy WASP family in Westchester county. Off to boarding school he went in elementary school. By high school he was in Connecticut at Suffield Academy.

Bor-ing.

Yet there comes a point in most cases where after a long slog, directional signs appear and compound, roads converge, and you accelerate unabated toward the unknown destination taking shape before your very eyes.

My brain clicked. Suffield. The name was familiar.

I'm getting there now! I can feel it!

I clicked through tabs, opening the one for Benjy Mahones in my Excel witness file.

Suddenly, my seat was a Formula 1 race car, and I had whiplash from mashing the pedal to the floor. I jumped to my feet. "Nick, Jerry Farinolo and Benjy Mahones went to high school together!"

He tipped his head back. A grin spread all the way to his gorgeous cheekbones, activating the laugh lines that somehow made him look younger. "Oh man. Is it just me or are you about to break this case open?"

I sat back down, excited to continue now. "It doesn't feel insignificant, that's for sure."

"It's not the only thing they have in common. They both went to work in their family's businesses. Although in Jerry's case, that was steel manufacturing. And by 'work' I mean they put his name on the letterhead. His real passion is, and has always been, polo."

"Must be nice."

"Here's an article about his wedding to Veronica." Nick held up a finger. "'Veronica Rabinski, who plays polo for the team owned by her groom and his family, hails from Dover, Delaware.' Funny, the picture of them isn't from a church wedding. I think they got hitched at city hall. Wait, let me just... yep. Celeste was born four months later." He continued shouting out facts as they struck his interest. "Homes in Rye, New York; Big Horn, Wyoming; and Boulder, Colorado. It doesn't seem like enough to me. What do they do when they're in the south? Or on the west coast?"

I was only halfway listening, because I'd found another juicy nugget. An article in the school paper—handily digitized back to the Stone Age for my researching ease and pleasure—about Jerry's junior prom. But it wasn't the article that had my attention. It was the photo and caption accompanying it. "Oh, Ni-ick."

"Hmm?"

"I'm staring at a picture of Jerry in his junior year. Want to guess who's in the same photo?"

"I think you gave it away already. My guess is Benjy Mahones."

"Yes, but it gets better."

Nick frowned. "I give up then. Tell me the better part."

"Ginger Nederland."

"I don't know her."

"You met her at the polo match. Ginger Nederland *Mahones*... she married Benjy."

"Oh, yeah. That's right. I remember from our research on the Mahones that they went to high school together."

I laughed aloud. "Yes, they did. But, according to the caption, she was not Benjy's date. And I quote, 'Roommates enjoying the junior prom, Jerry Farinolo with his *girlfriend* Ginger Nederland, and Benjy Mahones, with his date Sharon Cleveland.'"

"She dated Jerry before she married Benjy? Nice work. I wonder if there's some bad blood there."

"If so, the wound's had a long time to fester."

Nick tapped his head. "That's not all the two of them might be scrappy about."

Unfortunately, I didn't have the Mahones research committed to memory. I shook my head. Nothing was rattling anything loose.

"Benjy has a criminal record for drug possession with intent to distribute."

"I remember."

"He claimed the drugs belonged to his roommate. Benjy said he was set up by the roommate, who put them in his pocket. And I believe you just told me that Jerry Farinolo was Benjy's roommate."

I drew an imaginary equation on a chalk board. "Seven times three, note the one, carry the two, and that equals..."

Nick grinned. "Two men that hate each other's guts."

FIFTY-NINE

JENNIFER ANSWERED her phone as she walked quickly away from the Farinolo's living room and toward the office, keeping her voice down. She prayed Veronica couldn't hear her. "Facetime and on a Sunday? Really?"

The look on Ollie's face could only be described as gloating. Jennifer had really hated his predecessor, Pootie Carputin. Originally, she'd thought Ollie was an upgrade. How wrong she'd been.

He said, "I wanted you to be the first to know about the drug testing results."

Her stomach did a cannonball off a high dive. *How could he have them this quickly?* He had to have paid a fortune to a private lab. His vendetta against her must not have a price limit. She wouldn't give him the satisfaction of a reaction, though. "You should be talking to his attorneys. But I think I've told you that recently. Oh, yeah. Yesterday."

She entered the dark hallway. Sunlight streamed out an open

door, so she hurried to it and poked her head in. Definitely the office. Floor-to-ceiling shelves of ornate, pristine books. A large, ornate desk. She walked around it. From the boudoir photos on its surface of Veronica working a polo mallet like a stripper pole, it seemed to be Jerry's.

Ollie was barreling onward. "Victor died of a lethal dose of xylazine and opioids. That deadly concoction makes this first-degree murder, and the xylazine is from your husband's clinic. "

But not the opioids. Or at least she hoped not. Would a more thorough scrutiny of their inventory show some of it missing, too? She sank against the credenza behind the desk, swallowed, and licked her dry lips. "Oh? I didn't know drug testing identified who administers a drug or where it comes from."

"Very funny. It doesn't, but I will."

Her mouth was parched. "Best of luck to you." Did her voice sound tinny? *Don't cry. Don't cry.*

She pressed her trembling lips together and let her eyes wander to the vanity wall. Pictures of Jerry with a succession of men, horses, and trophies, with an occasional appearance by Veronica, clad appropriately in all of them.

"That's not all."

She braced herself. *Keep it flippant. Don't show weakness.* "Is there another body I don't know about?"

"We had the residue in Victor's water bottle tested. The one he drank from before his match."

"Good for you."

"Xylazine and opioids in his water bottle. And your husband was there, with the team, with access to that bottle."

Her stress was so high now that her vision was spotty, but her perch on the credenza kept her steady. To make herself appear unconcerned, she picked up a business card off Jerry's desktop. CARL BECKETT, SPECIAL AGENT, FEDERAL BUREAU OF INVESTIGATION. It barely registered with her. "So were a lot of other people."

"But only one of them stole xylazine from his own clinic."

She snapped the card down on the desk. "Oh, good grief. Aaron is a very intelligent man. If he was going to take something from his own clinic, he would have and could have covered it up. You can't make charges stick by leaping to fanciful conclusions. You need actual evidence." And if Ollie had some—like fingerprints on the water bottle—he would be crowing about it. Crowing to her, who he shouldn't have been calling. The man had lost his mind and his restraint. His anger about her running for county attorney was overcoming his common sense. If she'd been him, she would never have revealed these things to the wife of a defendant, especially at this point in the proceedings.

"You keep telling yourself that."

"Anything else before I resume my Sunday?"

Ollie frowned. "Where are you?"

"Please make sure you call Jack and Kid next, the two of you should have called in the first place." She ended the call.

After waiting a few seconds to be sure the line had disconnected, she leaned over with her head in her hands, gasping for air. The holes in Ollie's logic were so big a polo pony could have galloped through them. But he had the authority and power to pursue her husband. To ruin him. The Wyoming public believed in the blue line, law, and order. They trusted their officers and prosecutors, so, they believed the stories they wove.

The drug test results were nothing you didn't expect. They don't change anything. They don't prove anything.

But why did she feel so awful?

When she had regained her composure, she straightened and took a few deep breaths. She started pacing the office. Her thoughts whirled like a tornado as she tried to snatch relevant facts out of the wind cone. "The people closest to Victor's water bottle were the Strikers. The Hellcats were further down the sideline in a different area. Jerry was there. I saw him myself. Opportunity. If he knew what Victor was doing... motive. He could afford to get xylazine—and opioids—illegally. We just have to prove his connection to the thief for the means."

In the hall, a sound interrupted her. Clicks and thumps. Very soft. Footsteps, possibly? The footsteps of a woman in heels tiptoeing?

Then, complete silence. Jennifer's words seemed to echo around the room in it. She put her hand over her mouth. She'd spoken her thoughts out loud. *Oh, my God, so stupid.*

She hurried to the doorway and checked the hall. The demon Chihuahua stood there, legs splayed. She growled at Jennifer then emitted an ear-splitting bark.

Jennifer heaved a huge sigh of relief. It was just the dog. "Go away, Angel. Go back to your mommy."

Angel spun and sprinted away, toenails clicking.

She was losing it. The stress was killing her, and she had to pull it together. Put her big girl pants on. She nodded and exhaled with all her might. *Okay, then. Time to get what I came for.*

A thought stopped her. This was her chance to update the team. She whispered into her phone to voice record them a group text.

I'm at the Farinolos. Veronica asked me over to talk about her legal matter, which is that Victor committed to a crypto investment group then didn't fund it. They're coming after her and Jerry. Also, Casey visited Aaron last night and told him about the DNA test. This makes me CERTAIN it was Buster who attacked me. Lastly, Ollie just called me about a positive test for xylazine and opioids in Victor and his water bottle. I'm going to try to find out from V if J knew Victor was cheating on his team and his daughter.

She paused, remembering Veronica had asked her to keep the meeting a secret. *As if.* She hit send and returned to the living room to get some answers.

SIXTY

Big Horn, Wyoming

JACK WALKED BACK into the lodge in a daze and stopped in between the kitchen and dining room. His eyes found his wife's. He stopped, saying nothing, doing nothing.

Emily had added her laptop to the crowded kitchen table. She tilted her head, concern written across her face. "Jack? What's the matter?"

He snapped out of his fugue. "Casey. She deleted the video using Sarah's computer. She didn't deny Buster assaulted Jenn. But she's adamant that she didn't steal the drugs and that she had no idea Jake Small is dead."

Katie and Nick's heads popped up.

"Oh, my gosh! That's a lot!"

"I told her I'd help her with the legal end of things if she'd come clean, but she clammed up and took off." *And dumped an earful on me about Jenn.*

"Are you going to call the sheriff's department?"

He rubbed his face vigorously. "I'm not sure it's time yet. She didn't admit to breaking any laws, just breaking a clinic rule about bringing a non-employee in after hours. I'm sure the clinic will take a dim view on her deleting security videos, too. I kind of believe she didn't have anything to do with drugging Victor. And I'm not convinced she was involved in stealing the xylazine, as crazy as that sounds."

"But she might have information that will lead to who did!"

"Yes, and she's scared."

"For herself?"

"Maybe. But I suspect it's more for Buster."

Katie said, "Does she know where he is?"

"She says she doesn't."

Nick was shaking his head. "Where does Doctor Sarah fit in?"

"I have absolutely no idea. Less now than ever."

Emily hugged herself. "Jack, what if she's playing you? She could have Buster out in that cottage right now. If he killed that stable hand and he's on the run, then he's dangerous."

Jack's phone rang. He held up a finger. "It's Kid." He answered on speaker. "You're on with Nick, Katie, Emily, and me."

"And you're on with Dr. Larry Wyles. Buster Kemp works for him."

"Hello, Dr. Wyles. I'm Jack Holden. I represent your fellow vet, Dr. Aaron Herrington."

"Hello, Mr. Holden."

"Just call me Jack, please. Kid, do you have something for us?"

"We do. Larry didn't know Buster would be out at Half Circle today. His clinic isn't missing any xylazine, but they are missing bronchodilators and opioids. Albuterol mainly and some morphine. Wasn't bronchodilators what Jake Small was trying to get from Aaron?"

"I think it was."

Dr. Wyles said, "Minnie and I did inventory yesterday. We'd been so busy that we'd fallen behind a few months on it. Turns out, we're missing quite a bit of it. I'm about to try to find out where it went."

Jack exchanged a glance with Emily, whose eyebrows were halfway to her hairline. "I feel pretty sure we know who your culprit is."

Kid said, "Full disclosure, Larry was quite upset with me at first. I all but accused him of being involved with drugging horses and Jake's murder, but I'm satisfied he knew nothing about any of it. Buster may have been working alone on the drugging."

Dr. Wyles said, "If it was him. I don't discount what you're saying, and he sure had access to my meds here, but I don't jump to conclusions."

Jack was fast nodding. "We understand. I really appreciate you talking to Kid. This is sensitive stuff. Dangerous stuff. I highly recommend you report your missing drugs to the police. Obviously, it will help Aaron Herrington if you do it as soon as possible."

"If we determine it isn't an error, I definitely will. We'll work on it today."

"That's all we can ask. Kid, will you stay on with us and take the rest of this call at your car?"

"Will do." Kid's voice was muffled as he bid Dr. Wyles goodbye and thanked him. Then a door opened and closed. "Okay, guys. I'm outside by myself now."

Jack filled him in quickly about Casey then said, "While we have no proof Buster stole the xylazine, he was inside the clinic, and he had means and opportunity to steal from Dr. Wyles, too, which would make this a pattern. Plus, he would have blended in with the teams perfectly before the match."

Emily yanked at her bangs. "I can buy that he would steal meds and drug horses. But it's a big difference to drug a person. Did he have it in for Victor for some reason we don't know about?"

Kid said, "Victor's involvement with Casey?"

Jack shrugged one shoulder. "Maybe he didn't have anything

against him at all. Maybe he was very well paid, either to supply or administer."

Kid's car door slammed. The background noises went away.

Katie said, "Nick and I have some information that may help. We've been working up the Farinolos and discovered that Jerry and Benjy Mahones have hated each other for decades. Jerry was the roommate in high school who Mahones accused of planting drugs in his coat. Remember, Mahones was charged and convicted of a felony in that case."

Nick added, "But the bad energy might flow both ways. Mahones married Jerry's high school girlfriend, Ginger."

The sound of a car engine could be heard over the phone. Kid said, "So Mahones had a personal reason to hurt Jerry through his team as well as a financial motive as a bettor?"

"Exactly."

Emily gasped. "Oh, my God. You guys! I have something. Jack, you know how your email downloads to my outlook so I can handle it for you?"

He smiled. "Because I have the best legal assistant in the world. And the best looking."

She ignored his teasing. "You just got an email from Joaquim with the Hellcats. There's no text. Just a picture. But it's definitely worth a thousand words." She turned the laptop around so the others could see it.

"What is it?" Kid asked.

"Shee-yut," Jack said. "It's a picture of Veronica Farinolo wearing nothing but her polo boots, up against a stable wall, engaged in... an intimate act. With Victor."

"It's Jerry!" Kid shouted.

Nick added, "Victor was cheating on the team with Jerry's worst enemy, cheating on his daughter, and sleeping with his wife."

Jack felt a spark ignite inside him. Jerry was a man with a whole lot to be pissed off about. Maybe there was a little hope for Aaron after all?

SIXTY-ONE

Big Horn, Wyoming

THE ICE CUBES in Jennifer's glass clinked as she took a sip heavy on gin and lemon. She hadn't wanted to drink the Long Island iced tea but had accepted it out of politeness. Good manners had elevated in importance after she'd interrupted the "high tea" meeting to take Ollie's call and since she'd solidified her plan to question Veronica about Jerry and Victor. Thus, the sipping now, and the extra care not to spill on the silk sofa.

High tea. The words sounded silly and pretentious outside London or the east coast. It reminded her of what her colleague Kid James had said about this client. "Too bougie for Big Horn." The old Big Horn, maybe. Not the one that was changing every day.

She and Veronica resumed their discussion over islands of raspberry tarts in vanilla ice cream seas. Jennifer nearly groaned with each bite. Still, she made notes of names, dates, and amounts. Veronica promised to email all the documentation plus the notes she'd made of the calls from the crypto group. When they'd finished,

Jennifer realized that she'd downed her whole cocktail, too, which if anything had tasted stronger when she came back from her call. It was all she'd been offered to drink, after all, with the high tea that had not included any actual tea unless the Long Island version counted.

"More?" Veronica asked, standing poised to call someone else to make another.

Jennifer shook her head, which made her a little dizzy. "Oh, no. It would put me under."

"If you're sure."

"I am. I have lots left to do today." A wave of sleepiness lapped at her. She hadn't asked Veronica the questions she wanted to about Jerry yet. She couldn't even remember what the questions were. Decided that they'd have to wait. She'd call Veronica later. "I may have to take a nap as it is." She stood, feeling wobbly. The drink had been too much. She should have passed it up. *I wish I could call Aaron to give me a ride.* She regretted how their morning had gone and wished she could have a do-over. *I love him. I don't deserve him.* "Thanks for having me over for the meeting, though. Your home is lovely, and this has been a very helpful conversation." Wait—had she slurred those last two sentences?

"Please use the information I've given you with the utmost discretion."

"Of course." The room swam. Time froze, or tilted, or inverted. Something weird, anyway. Jennifer couldn't remember the last thing that was said. She decided that it must not have been critical. "Whoa." She sunk back on the couch, her legs nothing but spaghetti.

"Oh, my," Veronica said. "Are you all right?"

"I'm... " *not.* Jenn regained her feet, but then she toppled, conscious of splashing into a crystal vase on her way down. "Baccarat," Veronica had said earlier. "A priceless heirloom."

Probably not anymore.

Angel rushed at her face, barking hysterically.

Then a terrifying thought struck Jennifer. *I can't be pregnant again, can I?*

SIXTY-TWO

Big Horn, Wyoming

JACK HELD his hand up for silence, for all the good it did. The dogs were running in circles. The skunk was chittering. Everyone was hyped up. That picture of Veronica and Victor. Combined with everything else they'd discovered, they had a landslide of information to take to the county attorney. But would it convince him to agree to hold off charging Aaron? Probably not. They needed something definitive. A slam dunk. Maybe the misconduct information Jenn had teased about providing them that night? But they couldn't count on that coming to fruition.

He had to figure something out himself. The complete whodunnit. That meant he couldn't fixate completely on Jerry without a smoking gun. Mahones also had solid motives. Either man could have done it, acting solo or with help.

He shouted over the din. "Okay, here's what we're going to do."

Katie jumped to her feet, holding up her phone. "You guys, we have a group text from Jenn. She's at the Farinolos's."

"Read it out loud," Jack said.

"I'm at the Farinolos. Veronica asked me over to talk about her legal matter, which is that Victor committed to a crypto investment group then didn't fund it. They're coming after her and Jerry."

Jack interrupted. "Damn. Even more motive for Jerry. Sorry for interrupting, Katie." He waved her on.

"Also, Casey visited Aaron last night and told him about the DNA test. This makes me CERTAIN it was Buster who attacked me."

"Yes!" Jack pumped his fist. Again, he waved for Katie to continue.

"Lastly, Ollie just called about a positive drug test for xylazine and opioids in Victor and his water bottle. I'm going to try to find out from V if J knew Victor was cheating on his team and his daughter."

Nick pushed his hand through his hair and left it standing nearly straight up. "This guy just straight up did this. And he bought the drugs from Buster. The xylazine and the opioids."

Jack's phone showed an incoming call. "It's Ollie."

Kid growled. "I'll bet we know what he's calling to say."

Katie was still clutching her phone. "Do you think Jenn's going to *confront* Jerry?"

Jack pushed Decline. He grabbed his keys off the kitchen counter. "She shouldn't be there and certainly not alone. I'm on my way." Then he stopped. "Dammit! The sheriff's department is still searching my vehicle!"

Kid said, "I'm pulling in the driveway at the lodge now. Meet me outside. We're going together."

SIXTY-THREE

Big Horn, Wyoming

DROOL RAN down Jennifer's chin. She was awake. She had to be awake, but she felt like she was spinning. Floating. Something had happened to her. It had knocked her on her butt, literally. But she had no idea what it was. She just needed a moment to breathe and rest, and then she'd get back up, apologize, and go home. Stress. She was under so much stress, plus the possibility, however remote, of a baby. Last time hadn't been identical to this, but she'd had dizzy spells. Before... before... before she'd lost the baby. Before the anguish and grief and depression and feelings of loss and failure. God, how she didn't ever want to go through that again. *But if I am pregnant, maybe it's a good sign that this time my symptoms are much stronger. A stronger pregnancy.*

"Are you okay, Jennifer?" Veronica sounded calm and very, very far away.

"Uh huh," Jennifer mumbled, eying the little dog who had stationed herself a foot away, like she was preventing Jennifer from escaping. Angel the Guard Chihuahua. She would have laughed if she could.

"You don't sound all right to me." There was a lilt to Veronica's voice. Like something was funny to her.

That was odd. If someone had been splayed out on Jennifer's living room floor, she would have been down there with them, comforting them, checking on them as she called for help. Mopping up the drool, for goodness sakes.

Someone was knocking, but it sounded like it was coming from the back of the house. Heels clicked near Jennifer's head then receded.

From a few rooms away, a man said, "Where is she?"

"In here." Veronica's heels made their way back to Jennifer, accompanied by the thuds of softer soled footwear.

"How much did you give her?"

"I had some left. Whatever amount that was. Do you think it's enough?"

The gears in Jennifer's brain locked like they had run out of lubricant. Gave *who*—her? Veronica *gave* her something? What was it? *I'm not pregnant.* Her brain confirmed it with a memory. The nurse at the hospital had told her she wasn't after they'd run the standard pregnancy test on Jennifer Friday. And who was this new person? It wasn't Jerry. His New York accent was distinctive. This guy sounded more middle America. Nonspecific. Generic.

"With that information to go on, how would I know? Jesus, I don't get it. Things were going so good. Why the *fuck* did you do this?"

"Because I heard her on the phone. She was telling someone that if Jerry knew, he was the one who drugged Victor."

"So? He doesn't know, and he didn't do it."

Jennifer's mouth twitched. It hadn't just been the dog. Veronica had been in the hall. She'd heard everything Jennifer stupidly said. But this guy was saying Jerry *didn't* drug Victor. She begged her sluggish brain to replay her own earlier words, but it refused.

"Yes, but she was going to talk to him. Which meant she would tell him. Don't you get it? Then he would know."

"Don't you get it? If she was on the phone, then she isn't the only one who knows. Who was she talking to?"

"I'm not sure. I don't even know how she knows. No one knew about Victor and me. I was so careful." Veronica nudged Jennifer with the toe of her shoe, so rough it was just short of kicking her.

Jennifer was too busy working out what Veronica had just said to care. Veronica and Victor had been involved? And Victor had dumped her for Casey?

"Great," the man said. "This is a complete and total cluster."

"You've got to help me."

The man's voice grew menacing. "I'm going to clean up your mess, Veronica, because it's my ass on the line, too, but after that, I'm done. I don't care who she was talking to. This is it. I don't want you to speak to me if you see me. I don't ever want to talk to you again. I don't want you to talk to Sarah, either, or see her."

"She's Angel's vet!"

"Get a new fucking vet. God, how I wish I'd never met you."

"I've been loyal to her since the minute she first subbed for our vet in Boulder. She's the first vet Angel has ever trusted, and the only one who ever helped with her skin condition and anxiety. Sarah knows how I feel about her. She'll be suspicious if I just switch to a different vet."

"She won't be suspicious. I made a copy of her key when she was at a parent teacher conference at the school, and she has no idea."

Sarah the vet? This man copied her key? *Oh, my God.* He stole the xylazine.

"But won't she find out you took the stuff? There are security cameras everywhere these days."

He laughed, sounding full of himself. "You think I'm an idiot? I didn't do it myself. I had a buddy do it for me."

"Someone I know?"

"Of course not. A guy who was already stealing drugs from his own clinic and doping polo horses for your competition. The perfect fall guy."

Buster! This man had stolen the xylazine through Buster! Casey had gotten Buster into the clinic after hours, and this man had given Buster the key. Which meant... the drugs leftover... the ones Veronica had given to Jennifer... it had to be xylazine. And what else had Ollie told her was in Victor's system? Opioids. He'd called xylazine and opioids a deadly combination.

She was going to die without medical help, soon, or maybe even with it. *I'll never see Aaron again. I won't be able to tell him how much I love him and how sorry I am.* She had to get out of here. She tried to rock back and forth. All that moved was her head, barely. She tried again and was able to inch her hand forward.

That was it.

Veronica was still whining on. "So, the drugs can't be traced to me?"

"They cannot. And with what I have planned for my so-called buddy, soon no one will be able to trace them back to me through him, either. The little fucker beat the shit out of me when he found out how the drugs were used." He mimicked a dumb jock accent. "Yo, there's a big difference between helping horses and killing people, and it's a line I don't cross." He cackled. "Thinks he's hot, but he's about to figure out he ain't shit. I already dealt with the dumbass stable hand who knew Buster was stealing vet drugs. So, he won't be able to tie it together either. And that is why you should chill your tits and let Aaron Herrington take the fall for this. No one will be able to prove a goddamn thing."

Jennifer wished she could crawl across the broken crystal and out the door. This man was a sociopath who was planning to kill Buster, had killed Jake Small, and had helped Veronica kill Victor. He was here to clean up Veronica's newest mess—Jennifer—and conspiring to see Aaron spend his life in prison.

Veronica huffed out a giant breath. She moved close to Jennifer's head again. Close enough to bite if Jennifer had been able. "Okay. That's good. Very good."

"Only no more Dr. Sarah for Angel, understand?"

"I understand." A feminine hand scooped Angel from her guard perch and out of Jennifer's sight line.

"Are you sure?"

"I said I understand, Greg. I get it. I appreciate everything, and this is the last time you're helping me." She paused. In a tremulous voice, she said, "So, how *are* you going to help me?"

Jennifer tried to rouse herself, but all she could muster was a few spastic leg movements, like she was pedaling a bicycle in her sleep. Greg. Greg who had copied Sarah's key while she was at a PTA meeting. He had to be Greg *Friedman*. The husband Sarah had never introduced her or Aaron to. The drug source for Victor's murderer, whose motive was the oldest in the book. Revenge for love scorned.

Greg Friedman had helped Veronica Farinolo kill Victor, and Jennifer was next.

SIXTY-FOUR

Big Horn, Wyoming

"VERONICA, what in God's name is going on?" The male voice with its full-on New York accent thundered right above Jennifer.

Jerry Farinolo.

She batted her eyes, forcing them to open. She saw hairy calves, blue cargo shorts, tattooed hands. Fingers holding a syringe, moving behind thighs, hiding.

"Jerry! I, um... You're home!" Veronica's voice was twittery.

Angel yapped like Jerry had come to steal her fancy collar.

Jerry can help me. He was innocent in all of this. She tried again to move while all of Greg and Veronica's attention was on Jerry. This time she managed to shift her arms and legs. The effort was monumental. Black spots danced across her vision. Her throat closed. Her heart stuttered.

"Who are you?" Jerry demanded. When Greg didn't answer, Jerry's voice changed. "Good God. Is that Jennifer Herrington on the floor?"

Help me! Jennifer's mouth formed the words. The breathy sounds she made weren't audible.

Veronica said, "It's Jennifer. Yes."

"What is she even doing here?"

"She dropped by to give me a referral to an attorney for our situation with Victor's investment scheme."

"That doesn't tell who this guy is."

"He's an EMT, honey. I called for help when Jennifer, uh, fainted."

"There's no ambulance out front."

"He was the closest person they had, and he came even though he's off duty. Isn't that nice?"

"No. I recognize him." Jerry's voice was a sneer. "You're not an EMT. You're a bus boy at the Brinton."

Greg finally spoke, his voice tight. "I'm kitchen staff."

Jerry cackled, but it didn't sound like he found anything funny. "Am I going to be sent dirty pictures of you with him, too, Veronica?"

Veronica gasped, long and dramatic. "What in the world are you talking about?!"

"You know, *honey*. Like the ones someone sent me of you and our daughter's fiancé?"

"What kind of pictures? I'm sure there are many of us all together."

"The special kind of the two of you having sex in the stable. The photographer definitely got your good side. If I didn't know better, I would have guessed you were in your thirties."

"You... you knew?"

Jerry barked a laugh. "About your affair with Victor? Of course I did. Almost from the moment you dropped your panties and kept your boots on. Utterly ridiculous. I'm sure you gave my private investigator quite a thrill, though."

"You hired a PI to follow me? That's... that's..."

"Apparently necessary with a wife like you. Victor was appropriately terrified when I took him his courtesy copy. But we had a nice chat. In the end, I paid him handsomely for a few favors. More than you'd been giving him. He seemed quite happy with the arrangement."

Veronica's reply was an octave higher. "Did you pay him to break up with me?"

"No. I paid him to stop working for Benjy."

"What do you mean?"

Jennifer moved her arms again. Each effort was harder than the last. None of them seemed like enough to get her out of this situation. But maybe she didn't need to get Jerry's attention. He knew she was here. He didn't trust Veronica or Greg. He would help her. He had to. She just hoped it was before the drugs killed her.

"Just what I said. Benjy paid Victor to do things to hurt me. It was payback from our high school days."

Her tone was haughty. "Are you suggesting Victor slept with me for money?"

"I'm not suggesting it. I'm telling you. Victor was paid to sleep with you. I gave him a larger sum to flip the tables on Benjy. He had no reason to continue the nonsense with you, so he stopped. Luckily, that was before Celeste found out about it. You would have broken her heart, you know."

"I don't believe you!"

"I don't care, Veronica. Victor and I got what we wanted from the transaction. He delivered everything I needed to turn that shark over to the feds for money laundering. Happiest phone call I ever made." Jennifer could hear a smile in his voice. Her brain recalled an image. The business card of an FBI agent on his desk. "But now I have to deal with you. Let's start with what you've done to Jennifer?"

The doorbell rang.

Jennifer cried, "Help. Help." Her voice worked, but it was only a croak.

"Looks like your victim is coming around, Veronica."

"She's not my *victim*."

"Spare me. Aren't you going to answer the door?"

The doorbell rang again, then fists pounded on the door. A strong voice rang out. "This is Jack Holden. I'm here for Jennifer Herrington." After a long pause, he banged the door again, even harder. "Jennifer's car is out front. She texted me that she is here. Open the door. I need to speak with her."

Greg said, "This is your bullshit Veronica. I'm out of here."

Jerry said, "I don't think so, kitchen boy."

Greg and his cargo shorts moved two giant steps toward the sound of Jerry's voice. With all the strength Jennifer had, she turned her head and lifted her shoulders. It was enough. She caught her weight on her elbow just in time to see Greg reach Jerry. She saw the hand hanging down by his thigh. The hand with the syringe. Jennifer was sure it contained the lethal mixture he'd brought to deal with her.

"Jerry," Jennifer croaked. "Watch out!"

Greg brought the syringe up and jammed it in Jerry's upper arm as he grabbed the older man by the elbow. Jerry tried to jerk away, but Greg held him fast.

Jerry shouted, "Ouch! What is—let go of me!"

Greg depressed the plunger. Behind them, Veronica squeezed Angel against her chest. The dog yelped.

"What is—what did you just do?" Jerry broke free and stumbled away from Greg, needle still in his arm, syringe bouncing. Jerry grabbed it and threw it across the room. "What did you just put in me?"

Knocking started on a door in the back of the house.

Jerry grimaced. "Veronica, call 911."

She stared at him, unmoving. She bit her lip. Then she slowly shook her head.

The pounding on the front door intensified. "This is Jack Holden. If you don't open the door, I'll have to call the police!"

"Fine. But you should know, the front door isn't locked." Jerry turned toward the foyer and shouted, "Come in, Mr. Holden!"

Greg ducked behind the wall on one side of the entrance to the living room, only a foot away from Jennifer. He drew a gun from the back waistband of his jeans. *The gun that killed Jake Small?* Greg didn't look down at her. He didn't seem to notice she'd risen to her elbow.

Veronica whimpered. "You have to help me, Jerry. I'm your wife. I love you."

Jerry threw his hands up. "There's no need for guns. Put that away."

"Please, Jerry," she said.

The front door flew open. Jack burst in.

Jennifer screamed, "It's a trap!" Or she tried to. What came out was on the low end of conversational volume, and Jack didn't act like he'd heard her.

Jerry stepped toward Greg, pointing. "He has a—"

Greg brought his gun down on Jerry's head. The sound was sickening. A dull thump. Jerry crumpled to the floor as Jack stepped into the living room. Veronica shrunk against the window with her wriggling, barking dog.

"Jennifer!" Jack's eyes were locked on her.

"Jack, no!" she said.

He kept coming, his eyes locked on her. Greg lunged, wrapping an arm around Jack's neck and jamming the barrel of the gun into his temple.

Out of nowhere, a man darted past her in a blur. Tall. Thin. Red haired.

It was Kid.

He launched himself at Greg. Greg who was holding a gun.

Faster than she could have believed she had in her, Jennifer swept her free hand across the floor, groping for she didn't know what. Her fingers landed on something sharp. A piece of crystal. *The vase. The broken Baccarat vase.* It bit into her flesh as she closed her fingers around it.

She braced herself for the sound of Greg's gun. He was going to shoot Kid. She knew he was.

But he didn't. As he'd done with Jerry, Greg lifted the gun and bashed Kid's head. Kid staggered and went down near Jerry, who was motionless. Unconscious. Jack tried to jerk away from Greg.

In dealing with Jerry, Jack, and Kid, Greg had moved closer to Jennifer. Greg pointed the gun down at her. "Stop or I shoot her."

"Okay, okay. I'll stop." Jack stilled.

Kid's mouth was opening and closing like a fish. He blinked. *At least he's alive!*

"He broke in and tried to kill us!" Veronica said.

Greg jerked around to face Veronica. He aimed the gun at her. "You bitch!"

Jack said, "Easy, now. The police will be here any minute. Don't do something that will get you in more trouble."

The gun returned to Jack's temple. "I'll be long gone by then." Greg flicked the safety off.

Jennifer had to act, and she had to do it now. She threw her body forward—not much, six inches maybe—but it was enough. She stabbed the jagged edge of the broken crystal into Greg's exposed calf. Her vision tunneled. Why was it so hard to breathe?

He screamed as she stabbed him again. He jerked back, and his gun clattered to the floor at his feet. Right in front of her. She dropped the bloody crystal and grabbed the gun with both hands. The safety was already off. She raised it toward his leg and pulled the trigger.

The kick knocked her onto her back. She wheezed and fought for breath. Around her, chaos broke loose. She was dimly aware of bumps, thumps, and grunts. Objects crashing to the ground. Shouting, screaming, and cursing. The shrill barking of that damn dog.

Inside her, everything slowed down. She took a shallow breath. It didn't matter whether she had enough air anymore. Her vision narrowed until all she could see was what was right in front of her eyes. Part of the ceiling. A nice white ceiling with a yellow light. She'd done what she had to. They had the evidence to get Aaron out of jail. The thought felt floaty and wispy. It made her happy. Aaron.

Then Kid's face blocked out the ceiling. "Jennifer, what did they do to you?"

She had a lot of important things to say. She managed a thready, slow whisper. "Xylazine. Fentanyl. Jerry, too."

"Help is on the way." Kid lifted her head and shoulders. He scooted under her and cradled her head in his lap. "You're going to be fine."

"Gooooood," she hissed. Spots replaced Kid's face. *So hard to breath.* Her eyes closed.

"Jack, she's barely breathing. What do I do?"

Jack shouted, "Keep her awake. She needs Narcan. Dammit, why aren't they here yet?"

Kid shook her. "Don't you give up on me, Jenn Herrington. You can't rob me of the chance to vote for you, just to leave me." The panic in his voice pulled her back. She forced her eyes open and stared up into his. "There you are. You've gotta stay with me, you hear me?"

She smiled. Kid was a good egg.

And then she slipped away.

SIXTY-FIVE

Sheridan, Wyoming
The next day

"DOLLY, dolly. Please don't be mad, my little dolly." It was him again. The man with the long gun and the scary tattoo. The one who'd hurt all those kids.

Jennifer moaned and struggled into consciousness. She wanted the man to go away. To stay out of her confusing dream. Why did he act like he was her best friend? Why did he say things she knew had never happened back then? And what in the world was he talking about?

She rolled her dry lips. She didn't want to be awake, even if she didn't want to be asleep either. Her throat hurt. Her stomach hurt. Her hand hurt. The bed was uncomfortable. The room was cold. She felt empty, like her brain had been cleaned out with steel wool, and she heard nothing but static.

She batted her eyes open, intent on dealing with the myriads of issues, starting with another blanket or turning up the heater. She frowned. There were machines and an IV pole and two strangers.

She wasn't in her bedroom.

"Easy, it's okay." That voice she knew. Aaron. His big hand took hers. Warm. Reassuring.

She lifted her shoulders and turned toward his voice. "Where are we?" She laid back—*so tired*—and touched her throat. She sounded like a sandhill crane. A drunk one.

He put his other hand on her cheek. "The hospital."

That made no sense. Did it? She dug around in her empty mind, trying to grasp a memory, any memory. Found nothing. "Why?"

He looked away, toward one of the strangers. A woman in a white coat.

She said, "It's okay to tell her."

Aaron stroked her hand with his thumb. "You drank something that made you sick."

Alarm bells clanged. Again, she tried to sit up. *Mistake.* She tried again and pushed up on her hands. One of them hurt. She ignored it. "I don't remember."

The woman came closer. She was carrying an electronic notepad. "Everything is going to be okay, Mrs. Herrington. Things will come back to you, but you've got to stay calm. Can you try to relax?"

Jennifer nodded, then regretted it. She laid back again and cradled her hand. "What about my hand?"

"You have stitches."

"Why?"

The woman nodded at Aaron. "I'll let your husband fill you in on the details." She gestured to a person who was adjusting a bag of fluid on the IV pole. "Let's give them some privacy."

The two of them walked out.

Aaron smiled at her. "First of all, you're a badass. Do you remember I've been in jail?"

She frowned, then a picture came to her. Aaron behind plexi-glass, wearing prison orange. "Ye-es."

"You were trying to figure out who did the things I was accused of."

The volume of the static decreased. The empty feeling in her brain receded. Memories took shape. "Killing... killing that polo player. Victor."

"Yes. You were at the Farinolo's house—"

"The Strikers."

"Yes, the owners of the Strikers. Veronica put drugs in your drink because she thought that you had figured it out. That she'd killed Victor."

"I..." She didn't remember figuring anything out, much less visiting the Farinolos.

"You saved Jack's life. Kid's life. Jerry's life. Your own."

Jack who? The Jack who had been staying with them at the lodge? And Jerry had to be Jerry Farinolo, the owner of the Strikers. But she couldn't come up with a memory that involved saving the life of anyone. "I don't know what you mean."

He squeezed her hand. "That's okay. The important thing is that an ambulance came for you. They shot you full of naloxone and pumped your stomach. You've had a tube in your throat, and they've mostly kept you asleep since yesterday."

None of it made sense, except why her throat hurt. But it was Aaron telling her. He wouldn't lie to her.

"Jack went straight to the county attorney and presented him with all the evidence you guys put together. So, instead of charging me today, they released me."

The evidence? "That's... good." She was having trouble keeping her eyes open.

"Go to sleep. We can talk more later."

"You'll be here?"

"Always."

WATER BURBLED through a rocky creek bed. "Wake up, little dolly. There's no baby, and it's time for you to wake up."

For a few moments, she kept her eyes closed against the light. *Dear God, is this what death feels like?* A jerky slide show played in her head, images in rapid succession. It started with a phone call from Ollie at the Farinolo's house and ended with her head in Kid's lap as he begged her to stay with him.

Then nothing. Nothing until Aaron was holding her hand in her hospital room.

She opened her eyes. "He called me dolly. There's no baby."

The burbling stopped, replaced by voices. Friendly, concerned faces gathered around her bed. Familiar ones. Jack and Emily. Katie and Nick. Kid. Aaron. *The burbling was their voices*, she realized. The man from her dreams receded. More memories solidified. She'd been working with Kid and their new friends to gather evidence to keep Aaron from being charged with Victor Carvalho's murder. The details were still fuzzy.

"There you are," Aaron said.

Her heart seized. She loved him. Her breath caught. She was mad at him about something. She wasn't sure what. And she felt ... guilty... very guilty. But he was here. That was good.

"I remembered."

Jack put his hands on the bed rail. "You remember what happened at the Farinolos?"

"Yes. Thank you," she said. "All of you, for helping us. And Jack and Kid for coming for me."

"Thank you for dealing with Greg and thank God we'd called 911 before we came in," Kid said. "Otherwise, I don't know what would have happened to you and Jerry."

"Is he okay?"

"Yes. About the same as you."

She winced. "I shouldn't have shot that gun. I could have killed one of you."

Jack said, "You didn't hit anyone. It went into the ceiling. But it was enough of a distraction for just long enough. I took the gun from you and got Greg. Kid caught Veronica when she tried to make a run for it."

"I'm just glad you're okay," Kid said.

"Me, too." She looked at her other guests.

"This is goodbye. We're flying out tomorrow morning," Katie said.

"Our nanny is waving the white flag. She needs a break," Nick said.

"Plus, I think you need some space to recover without having to entertain us," Emily said.

One by one they kissed Jennifer goodbye. Her throat felt tight. She'd dreaded hosting these strangers. She hated seeing these friends go now.

Jack turned to the others. "I need a moment. I'll catch up with you guys in the hall."

Emily looked perplexed, but she followed Nick and Katie out.

"Do you need me to go, too?" Aaron asked.

"If you don't mind. For just a minute."

Aaron frowned but he nodded and disappeared into the hall.

"What is it?" Jennifer asked. Her throat was raw, and her voice was wearing out.

"It's about Casey. She told me about what you had to do to protect her and said she could get you disbarred. I stopped her before she could get specific. I don't *know* anything, but she has it in for you."

Jennifer felt like a chasm had opened in the hospital floor. She was scared to look down. "Thank you."

"I'd be careful about provoking her."

"Everything I do provokes her. She'll be holding this over my head my whole life."

"I may have bought some favor with her. The cops caught up with Buster on the run between Douglas and Wheatland. I helped him cut a deal for stealing the drugs at both clinics and for assaulting you. Casey swore she knew nothing about him stealing the drugs, and he backed her up on it. I'm not one hundred percent sure on that one, but he's the only witness. She seems to be quite smitten with him."

"Thank you. You've been amazing. I can't tell you how much I appreciate everything you and Emily have done. Aaron and I will never forget this. We owe you, big time."

"You're welcome."

Tears welled in Jennifer's eyes. Jack hugged her. His eyes looked wet, too.

After he was gone, Aaron came back in and sat in the chair beside her bed. "I don't suppose you'll tell me what that was about?"

Something about how he said those words brought it all back. The things she'd withheld from Aaron. His decades old secret. The fight they'd had the last time she'd seen him. An intense wave of regret pinned her head back to her pillow. More tears slipped out of her eyes. A flood of them.

He took her bandaged hand gently. "What is it?"

"Oh, Aaron. I love you. I was wrong, and I was horrible and selfish. I'm sorry. Will you forgive me?"

"Of course I will." His face was tender as he leaned in to kiss her nose. "I'm thankful for a wife who says she's sorry. Will you forgive me?"

"I already did."

"Scoot over." He lowered the siderail and slipped half his body onto the bed beside her.

She put her head on his warm, solid shoulder. "Casey told Jack about the dirt she has on me."

Aaron tensed. "Oh, my God. I'm so sorry, Jenn. More than you'll ever know."

"So am I. About everything."

"You already said that. It's okay."

"It isn't. I want to be the partner you deserve."

"You are. And I am going to be that partner for you." He kissed her nose again. "I promise you have my full support to run for county attorney, too. I want that bastard Ollie out of the job."

"God, me, too. What he did to you! How he tricked me. Our county deserves better. Just imagine—he could be doing this to any defendant. People who don't have an attorney spouse and friends who are hot shot criminal defense lawyers, legal assistants, and private detectives."

"Tell me about it. I'll get the posters and yard signs printed and put them all up myself."

She laughed, even though it hurt. Then she grew serious. "Someday I do want the whole bookmaking story."

"You can have it now if you want it."

"The short version." She felt a lot better, but already she was exhausted again. If she closed her eyes, she'd be asleep in seconds. *And if I sleep, that man will come.*

"I'd lost my spot as quarterback. I was young and insecure. Some team boosters convinced me to work with them getting college kids to do offline sports betting. They made me feel like they could pull my scholarship if I didn't cooperate. I had big dreams, and I was afraid of losing everything. I know now it was ridiculous, but at the time, it felt real, and I was scared. It turned out that Tennessee had very strict gambling laws, although I didn't even think about it being illegal. When we got busted, law enforcement threw the book at us. All of us. I think they overcharged me to put pressure on me to testify against the others, and it worked. They promised my records would be sealed and expunged when I was twenty-one. I never heard a word about it again until this week. The reason I didn't tell you about it then was because it was humiliating. Then, as years went by, I forgot about it." He held up two fingers. "Scout's honor. I'm very, very sorry, Jennifer. There was no reason not to tell you. I trust you with my life."

Jennifer smiled at him. "It's okay. I actually feel sorry for that kid with the big dreams."

"I promise, you didn't marry a hardened criminal."

She laughed but it was weak. She was weak. "I'm really tired, but I'm afraid of going to sleep."

"Close your eyes then, beautiful."

"No, I mean I'm afraid to go to sleep because the nightmares are back. I hate it. They're different now."

"Different how?"

"The shooter. After he finishes firing and I'm lying in the playground, he comes over to me. He reaches out his hand and calls me his dolly, which never happened."

"That's creepy."

"It is. The way he says it is very familiar. Very affectionate. He's starting to appear in my dreams out of context, too. Like, *in the present*. Earlier, he's the one who told me to wake up, when all you guys were in the room."

Aaron was shaking his head. "I hate this for you."

"Do you remember that while you were in jail, I had that hypnotherapist appointment?" She remembered the guy filming her when she came out of the building and then the next day when she was crying on the side of the road. She wanted Aaron to know about it. She'd tell him as soon as she had the strength.

"I remember. We didn't really talk about it, though. How'd it go?"

"She did a test session with me, just to make sure I was a good candidate. You know—whether I'm capable of being hypnotized. About a quarter of the population isn't."

"Let me guess, my beloved control freak. You aren't."

"Believe it or not, I am. I'm going to keep going with it."

"Well, I'm shocked. Congratulations. Man do I ever hope it helps."

Jennifer nodded. "Me, too. Anyway, the reason I brought it up is that she said I relived it in front of her, but that I wasn't scared of him. I asked the man why I was his dolly. Then I told the therapist I would need to leave with him. That's when she woke me up." Her words trailed off.

"I hate this guy. But it's going to be okay. I'll stay here with you while you sleep."

"Thank you."

She let her eyes close. She couldn't stay awake any longer. No one would hurt her in her dreams because that's all they were. Dreams. The dolly would be fine. She would be fine.

"Hello, little dolly. Welcome back," the man said.

Jennifer smiled. She drifted away as the younger version of herself took the man's hand.

SIXTY-SIX

Sheridan, Wyoming
    Two days later

JENNIFER PATTED the bench and Kid took a seat, with Aaron on the other side of her. She was delighted, for once, to enjoy the proceedings from the gallery. Talk about a conflict of interest—the defendants had tried to kill her. She had promised Aaron's legal team a complete rundown afterwards, in the same group chat where she and Aaron had begged them to send invoices for their work on his case. They had flatly refused to take payment.

"We're friends," Emily had said.

"And in our tribe, that's family," Katie added.

Jennifer knew what private investigators and defense attorneys cost. She knew how valuable the time was that they'd given from their vacation, jobs, and kids. After a lot of cajoling by her and Aaron, they'd named charitable causes for contributions. She and Aaron had already transferred the money. Kid, she would take care of on her own, whether he liked it or not.

One of the updates she'd shared in the chat was the information from Delaney Pace, starting in a voicemail while Jennifer was in the hospital, and continuing in a long conversation after she was out of it. The most surprising tea was that Jerry Farinolo's private investigator, a guy named Skeeter Rawlins, was also the part-time nanny for Delaney's daughters. He'd taken the photos of Veronica with Victor. The real dirt was that Deputy Travis admitted Ollie was holding a secret over his head. He'd sworn all he'd done was cooperate with the arrest, and that he'd planned to come directly to Jennifer if Ollie demanded anything more. Delaney refused to tell Jennifer exactly what information Ollie had on Travis, calling it personal and irrelevant. Jennifer understood. She would need time to forgive Travis's role, but she appreciated Delaney's help and felt like she might have made another Wyoming friend.

Jack, in return, told the others that he'd heard from Joaquim, who'd told him that Victor had given Joaquim the picture of himself with Veronica, like he was proud of it. The revelation had caused quite a buzz in the group chat. As had Joaquim's bombshell that Benjy Mahones had been arrested by the FBI for money laundering. He and the other Half Circle Ranch employees were worried about their futures.

Judge Peters rapped her gavel. Her cheeks were a high pink. She looked feminine, pretty. Although Jennifer had a rocky start with the judge, she'd come to admire her unapologetic quirkiness and fearless strength in what was still mostly a stodgy men's club. "This is a novel situation. I have two defendants in related cases appearing before me today to respond to charges against them. I believe our first contestant is Greg Friedman. Is the defendant present and his attorney ready?"

"Yes, your Honor. Paul Edwards for the defense." Greg was being represented by a public defender. A decent one, in Jennifer's opinion, if a little long in the tooth. When he wasn't arguing cases, he was known for napping in the gallery.

"Mr. Singletary—the State?"

Ollie stood. "Yes, your Honor."

Jennifer squeezed Aaron's forearm. Her fingers didn't meet. "Sarah isn't here."

His breath tickled her ear. "She's staying far away pending a divorce petition."

"He's loser number three, according to the Connells."

"I hope she recalibrates how she picks husbands."

The judge read the charges, which included murder in the first degree, conspiracy murder, and conspiracy to commit theft of controlled substances. Larry Wyles's investigation into the inventory discrepancies at his clinic showed the opioids and bronchodilators as truly missing without explanation, and Aaron had confirmed that drugs had been stolen from his home clinic after he'd been released from jail. As part of his plea deal, Buster told law enforcement he'd done it all at the behest of Greg.

Greg agreed that he understood the charges brought against him.

"And how do you plead?" she asked.

The PD jumped to his feet. "Mr. Friedman pleads guilty as to all counts, your Honor."

Jennifer predicted an uphill battle for the PD. Her testimony alone was extremely damning.

Judge Peters replied, "We're done here, Mr. Friedman. Does everyone know the drill on how to get his bail set?" Bail was set in a different court, before a different judge.

Both attorneys agreed they did. The bailiff led Greg out.

"Moving right along, we have Veronica Farinolo. Are—"

"Defense for Mrs. Farinolo is present your Honor. I'm Charlie Sosa." A dark-haired, olive-complected attorney with an accent straight out of Jersey Shores burst through the bat wing door and parked himself at the defense table, interrupting the judge.

Judge Peters was frowning. She crossed her arms over her chest.

A young, nervous-looking public defender joined him. "I'm Mrs. Farinolo's in-state representation."

"Your name?"

"Becky Wills."

"And there's my client," Charlie pointed at Veronica.

The bailiff escorted her to the table. She had her head held high and jaw set.

From the back of the gallery, Jennifer and everyone else within earshot heard a woman's voice say, "Bitch."

Jennifer glanced back. No surprise—it was Celeste, who didn't seem to appreciate her mother sleeping with her fiancée. Just like Veronica hadn't appreciated Casey sleeping with her young lover. Jennifer wondered if Celeste would have killed Victor if Veronica hadn't gotten to him first. Or maybe Celeste would have gone for her mother instead. Jennifer felt like jail was probably going to save Veronica's life.

Judge Peters rapped her gavel and said sharply, "No more of that."

Kid groaned. "Remind me to tell you about the pickle I'm in with her."

"She's upset with you?"

"The opposite. She thinks we're dating."

The judge continued in a milder tone. "Mr. New Jersey, I'd ask that you please defer to your co-counsel, unless you're licensed in the state of Wyoming?"

"You got a separate bar association in this backwater?" He chortled.

"We do."

"And my licenses in New York and New Jersey aren't good enough for you?"

"They are not." Judge Peters rolled her eyes with a fluttering of lashes that could be seen all the way into the gallery.

Ollie cleared his throat. "The Prosecution is ready, your Honor."

The judge read the list of charges. It was a long one.

Ollie stood. "We reserve the right to amend the charges later as evidence develops."

"Mrs. Farinolo," Judge Peters intoned, "Do you understand the charges against you?"

Veronica looked around like someone was going to answer for her. Becky the PD nudged her. Veronica stood. "Yes."

"And how do you plead?"

"Not guilty, your Honor." Two voices rang out. Becky didn't spare a glance for her out-of-state co-counsel. Veronica looked around, uncertain what to do, and Becky tugged at her wrist. Veronica returned to her seat.

"Of course." The judge rapped her gavel. "Number two finished. And our esteemed local counsel, I assume you're up to explaining the next steps in our process to Mr. New Jersey?"

"Yes, your Honor," Becky said.

"I don't envy you. Move along."

The bailiff led Veronica out of the courtroom.

The judge mopped her brow. "As there are no other arraignments this morning, the court is in recess."

"All rise," the bailiff said quickly.

The spectators rose and the judge slipped out her private exit.

"I'll meet you outside," Jennifer said to Aaron.

Before he replied, she wove through the other spectators toward Celeste. She wanted a word with the girl before she returned to New York or Colorado or wherever she planned to go next.

"Ms. Farinolo," she called.

Celeste turned, again looking blank for a moment when she saw Jennifer, but then her face cleared. "You're the attorney who came to meet with my mom last week."

"Yes. I'm also the one she tried to kill Sunday."

Celeste's eyebrows rose. "So, I have you to thank."

"What?"

"If not for you, my mom might have lived the rest of her life a free woman."

"Depends on how good a job the prosecution does and how crafty her defense attorneys are."

Celeste's eyes were cold. "Well, I'll be doing everything I can to help the prosecution."

"Are you going to stay in Wyoming?"

"I think I will." Jennifer thought about Kid's earlier comment, that Celeste thought they were dating. *Poor Kid!* "Once she's convicted, I plan to guilt my father out of every last cent he has. He didn't treat me much better than she did. I want to be sure that when my mother gets out, they have nothing left."

"Best wishes to you."

Celeste nodded and sashayed out of the courtroom.

"Jennifer, a word?" Jennifer knew that voice. It was Ollie. She turned to him. "Out in the hall?"

She caught Aaron's eye, pointed at Ollie then at the hall and flashed five fingers. He nodded. From the looks of it, he was deep in conversation with Kid.

"Fine," she said, her voice clipped. After how Ollie had treated her and Aaron, she'd rather roll in fire ants than talk to him, but she was going to have to do it sooner or later. He was her opponent in most of her cases and would be in the upcoming election as well.

She walked into the hallway. The traffic near the door was congested, so she moved to an alcove at the end of the hall. Ollie followed her.

"What is it, Ollie? Have you come to apologize for single mind-edly ignoring exculpatory evidence in your zeal to prosecute my husband?"

He narrowed his eyes and leaned into her personal space. "Are you going to challenge me for the nomination or not?"

Jennifer stood in silence, gathering her thoughts. She had Aaron's blessing. Kid wasn't thrilled about it, but he'd survive. "So, the nomination—that's what all this was about? You cutting me out of the case, then going after Aaron. The photographer who came after me." She'd told Aaron about the photographer the night before, and he'd been livid.

"Look at us. The pot and the kettle."

"Excuse me? I have no idea what you mean."

Ollie bared his teeth. "I'd be worried about getting disbarred if I sought the nomination, if I were you."

Bile rose in her throat. He was threatening her with information that could have only come from one source. It put Jennifer in the same straits as Travis, which made it far easier to forgive him. Ollie, it seemed, was a serial black mailer. Unfortunately, he had a witness in Casey. She could prove prosecutorial misconduct if she involved Travis. But if she went that route, it was at best mutually assured destruction. If she took him out, he'd take her out. *Live to fight another day.*

She mustered her bravado and pretended for all she was worth. "For your information, my husband and I had already decided now is not the time for me to pursue your job. With my book coming out and the practice so busy, Aaron and I just both want space to enjoy life. The nomination is all yours—if you don't have another contender to beat you out of it."

He looked surprised. More than that, he looked disappointed.

She lowered her voice to a loud whisper. "Aaron isn't going to pursue a case for malicious prosecution against you. He wanted me to be sure to tell you that. We were a prosecution household for many years, and he understands that mistakes are made. We're just happy I was able to identify the killers for you and that justice prevailed." She gave him a sickeningly sweet smile. She wanted to run as far and fast as she could away from him, only she wasn't going to give him that satisfaction.

"The outcome is no different than it would have been once we'd finished gathering all the evidence."

She saw Aaron and Kid waving to her and took a step toward them, then stopped. "Of course. Of course. Have a nice day, and I'll see you in court." She put a hand on his arm. "Oh, and I'll be sending my invoice for my mentoring time by the end of next week."

She left him in the corner. She was halfway down the hall when she began to laugh. She suddenly felt lighter. A certainty came over her. This was the way it should be. For now, this is the life she should be living. Let Ollie keep his precious job.

"What's so funny?" Kid asked.

She locked eyes with Aaron, smiling. "Oh, I was just telling Ollie how much you and I look forward to kicking his ass for another four years."

"Does that mean..." Kid's wide eyes and half grin made her feel guilty for even thinking of deserting him.

She turned to him. "It means that you and the defendants in the great state of Wyoming are stuck with me. And to celebrate that fact and thank you for going above and beyond for Aaron, I have a gift for you."

"What is it?"

"A new chair."

Kid whooped. Aaron threw an arm around her shoulders and pulled her in tight.

SIXTY-SEVEN

New York, New York
   That weekend

THAT SATURDAY, Aaron placed his hand in the small of Jenn's back, basking in her shine. The standing room only audience in New York's hottest bookstore had hung on her every word as she told them the real story of the case behind BIG HORN, then lined up for her to sign their books. These people were here because of her talent and hard work and her absolute banger of a book. Joe had confided in him before Jenn's talk that early sales and reviews were stellar. He and her editor and publicist were beaming. Aaron had been cheered by screaming crowds many times in his life. He couldn't deny it had been great. This was better.

After the last book had been signed, the store owner came to thank Jenn. She was an imposing woman with kinked black hair and a unicorn pendant hanging from her neck. "I'm almost sold out already. I'm reordering in the morning."

Joe thumped Jenn on the back. "Way to go, kid."

Jenn's smile was megawatts. "That's fantastic."

The owner was nodding. "One of our book club mavens and her acolytes were here tonight. They run chapters all over the city and in the five boroughs. They've asked me to see if you'd be willing to do some Zoom talks? They understand you have a busy law practice in Wyoming, but they'd be so honored if you could find the time."

Jenn's smile grew even brighter. "I'd love to."

The publicist stepped forward. "I'll be happy to get those set up for you."

The owner said, "Splendid. Let's go talk to them right now. Congratulations again, Mrs. Herrington."

Joe did a happy jig when the owner walked away with the publicist and editor. He leaned in between Aaron and Jenn. "Your publisher has accepted the *Walker Prairie* manuscript as your second and final book under your first contract. They believe it's even better than *Big Horn*.

Aaron pulled Jenn into a side hug by her waist. "I told you so."

"Before long it will be time to start negotiating your next contract!"

Jenn said, "Shouldn't we hurry in case the books flop?"

"Nah. I'm waiting a week for Big Horn to blow up! A flop is impossible. The publisher has singled you out for mega publicity dollars. They're going all in on you. You better have a helluva idea for book three."

"We've been living it. A few days ago, our life was in absolute shambles." Jenn and Aaron had told Joe the story of his arrest and the attacks on her life earlier that evening. "Now, Aaron has been cleared and you're giving me this great news. I feel like I should pinch myself."

Joe's phone rang and he held up a finger, then walked out to the sidewalk to take his call.

Aaron turned to Jenn. "You leave all the pinching up to me. Very, very gentle pinching."

She laughed. She looked so beautiful when she laughed. "That will have to wait until we're back at our fancy hotel room."

"If you say so." He whispered in her ear, "Have I told you how sorry I am for the dumb decisions I made in my youth?"

She smiled. "You've mentioned it."

Overwhelming emotion flooded his senses. "I need you to believe in me."

She threw herself into his arms and nodded against his chest. "I believe in you. And I need you to believe in me."

"I do. I really do."

Her body tensed. "I'm still so sorry about the DNA thing—"

"You don't have to be sorry about that. I'm thankful to be married to a fierce woman who looks out for me." He stepped back and held her by the shoulders. "I'm going to put some healthy distance between Casey and us when we get back. She had a second chance, and she blew it. It's time for her to find a place of her own. It's also time for her to find another job. I'll give her a great reference. Dr. Wyles seems to need help."

"Thank you. I think it will be the right thing for all of us." She sighed. "I'll never be able to run for public office now, not with what she told Ollie."

"I wish I'd never asked you to do any of it."

She waved a finger in front of her lips. "Shh. That's past. Let's only look forward now."

"There's so much great stuff ahead of us. I know it with every fiber of my being."

She stole a glance at Joe, and Aaron looked out the window, too. Joe was still pacing the sidewalk with his phone to his ear. He saw them watching him and mouthed, "Just a minute."

Aaron had already learned that one minute meant five to ten, and that they'd be late for their dinner reservation. The editor and publicist looked to be deep into their phones as well. Everyone in this city seemed surgically attached to their devices. Texting, talking, scrolling. As much fun as this weekend had been, he couldn't wait to return to the peace and pace of Wyoming.

Jenn licked her lips. "About that."

"About what?"

"Looking forward to great things. I have something to ask you. Something big."

He tilted his head and searched her eyes for a hint of what was coming. "Okay. What is it?"

"I've been doing a lot of thinking after the hypnotherapist. I may never figure out the identity of the shooter on the playground." She took a deep breath. "But I can't let him steal any more of my life. I want us to have a baby. I want it soon. I want it right now."

He picked her up and swung her in a circle as she laughed. "I didn't want to push you. With the miscarriage, the mourning, the grief."

When he'd set her down, she shook her head. "I don't want to get pregnant. Now that I can separate my fears about the world and how my past has shaped them from the apprehension I have about pregnancy at my age and after a miscarriage, I know what I want."

Aaron tried not to frown. "What are you saying?"

"Emily called me. Did you know she and Jack fostered their daughter, then adopted her?"

"I had no idea."

"Let's find a baby to foster. Then we can adopt. We've talked about that option before. I know we've both had reservations, but I think it's the fastest way to bring a child into our home. And the best way we can make a difference in a child's life."

"You're not worried about losing a baby back to birth parents?"

"I am. I know it's possible. I also know that there are other risks. But isn't there always? We could spend five years on me trying to carry a baby only to fail or end up with harmful impacts on me or the baby because of my maternal age. I really believe I can handle the risks of fostering."

He surprised himself with how quickly his own reservations

vanished like a puff of smoke. This felt good. It felt right. "Then I say let's do it."

She bounced up and down on her toes. "Really?"

"Really."

"I'm so excited! Thank you."

"Thank *you*. It was your idea."

"We can even pursue adoption as a parallel path. By the time we're even close to adoption through fostering, we might be adding a second child. Creating a whole little family."

He grinned at her. "Look at all the great things happening already. Your next book is going to be published, and we're going to foster a baby."

Joe appeared, putting his phone in his pocket. "I hope I'm not interrupting anything. Because it's time to eat."

The publicist reached them at the same time. "We have a table at the absolute best restaurant for you to be seen at, and I have a friendly journalist who promises a photo and mention in the entertainment section this weekend."

The editor said, "It's time for us to go celebrate your baby!"

Aaron and Jenn looked at each other. He raised his brows at her. *How do they already know when we don't even have a baby yet?*

"Your book baby!" Joe said. "The very best kind."

Jenn said, "Oh, I don't know about that." She winked at Aaron.

They linked fingers and strolled out onto the busy New York sidewalk hand-in-hand.

***

Looking for more books set in rugged Wyoming until Jenn Herrington #4 comes out, with protagonists and relationships you'll love, within the world of characters created by Pamela Fagan Hutchins?

Try the **Detective Delaney Pace** series of six crime thrillers with characters from Jenn's world *plus* the unforgettable Leo Palmer. First up is **Her Silent Bones**.

Follow **Maggie Killian** from her love-hate friendship with Jenn into her mystery trilogy and early-days relationship with bullrider Hank Sibley, starting with **Live Wire**.

Or, dive into **Switchback** and the eight-and-counting **Patrick Flint** 1970s adventure mysteries with beloved characters from Jenn's books, in their younger years.

*For the husband who gave me France, where this book was written,
and who calls Wyoming home, with me.*

ACKNOWLEDGMENTS

Agent Joe Durepos pitched me a story. "A Houston attorney and her husband—he could be an executive in the oil industry, or you could make it something more interesting, like a veterinarian—move to Wyoming and run a mountain B&B, where they have a menagerie of pets and she solves and writes mysteries."

I said, "Joe, that's Eric and me."

He laughed.

I said, "Joe, that's narcissistic."

He said, "It's the type of escape other people dream of. Can you write it?"

Well, duh, of course, I could. It's my life, after all. Only, after I sat down to write it, it strayed some from the original blueprint. In a good way, I hope.

The murder idea came from the actual log splitter in our actual "Snowheresville" (aka Big Horn Hideaway Lodge) barn. I may or may not have based characters on real people I know ;-) And the setting is a little bit Snowheresville and a little bit make-believe.

Thanks for the idea, Joe. I was able to age up the Patrick Flint characters and draw them into the story and pull across What Doesn't Kill You characters as well. There are already five more books planned for this series if it turns out people like them and want me to keep going.

And yet there are more thanks to give . . .

Thanks to my dad for advice on all things medical. Love and hugs to my favorite kissin' cousin (who is not really my cousin), Dr. Kristine "Rockey" Millikin for helping Aaron sound like a real vet. Thanks to Stu Healy and Ryan Healy for keeping me from screwing up Wyoming law. If I did, that's on me, not you guys.

Thanks to my husband, Eric, for brainstorming with and encouraging me and beta reading BIG HORN, WALKER PRAIRIE, and RED GRADE with me despite your busy work, travel, and workout schedule. And for taking a chance on Wyoming and me.

Thanks to our five offspring. I love you guys more than anything, and each time I write a parent/child (birth, adopted, foster, or step), I channel you. I am so touched by your support for Poppy, Gigi, Eric, and me.

Editing credits go to Karen Goodwin. You rock. A big thank you as well to my proofreading and advance review team.

The biggest thanks, though, goes to my readers. It never ceases to amaze me that you read my novels, that your support has resulted in this mid-life career change that gives me so much joy. From the bottom of my heart, I offer you my gratitude.

BOOKS BY THE AUTHOR

Fiction from SkipJack Publishing

THE *PATRICK FLINT* SERIES OF WYOMING MYSTERIES:

Switchback (Patrick Flint #1)

Snake Oil (Patrick Flint #2)

Sawbones (Patrick Flint #3)

Scapegoat (Patrick Flint #4)

Snaggle Tooth (Patrick Flint #5)

Stag Party (Patrick Flint #6)

Sitting Duck (Patrick Flint #7)

Skin & Bones (Patrick Flint #8)

Snow Ghost (Patrick Flint #9)

Spark (Patrick Flint 1.5): Exclusive to subscribers

THE *JENN HERRINGTON* WYOMING MYSTERIES:

BIG HORN (Jenn Herrington #1)

WALKER PRAIRIE (Jenn Herrington #2)

RED GRADE (Jenn Herrington #3)

THE *WHAT DOESN'T KILL YOU* SUPER SERIES:

Wasted in Waco (WDKY Ensemble Prequel Novella)

The Essential Guide to the What Doesn't Kill You Series

Katie Connell Caribbean Mysteries:

Saving Grace (Katie Connell #1)

HER Silent BONES (*Detective Delaney Pace Series Book 1*)

HER Hidden GRAVE (*Detective Delaney Pace Series Book 2*)

HER Last CRY (*Detective Delaney Pace Series Book 3*)

HER Forgotten SHADOW (*Detective Delaney Pace Book 4*)

HER Burning LIES (*Detective Delaney Pace Book 5*)

HER Cold HEART (*Detective Delaney Pace Book 6*)

Juvenile from SkipJack Publishing

Poppy Needs a Puppy

George Finds a Friend

Nonfiction from SkipJack Publishing

The Clark Kent Chronicles

Hot Flashes and Half Ironmans

How to Screw Up Your Kids

How to Screw Up Your Marriage

Puppalicious and Beyond

What Kind of Loser Indie Publishes,

and How Can I Be One, Too?

**Audio, e-book, large print, hardcover, and paperback
versions of most titles available.**

ABOUT THE AUTHOR

Pamela Fagan Hutchins is a *USA Today* best selling author. She writes award-winning mystery/thriller/suspense from way up in the frozen north of Snowheresville, Wyoming, where she lives with her husband in an off-the-grid cabin on the face of the Bighorn Mountains, and Mooselookville, Maine, in a rustic lake cabin, when they aren't traveling the world for his work assignments. She is passionate about their large brood of kids, step kids, inherited kids, and grandkids, riding their gigantic horses, and about hiking/snow shoeing/cross country skiing/ski-joring/bike-joring/dog sledding with their Alaskan Malamutes.

If you'd like Pamela to speak to your book club, women's club, class, or writers group by streaming video or in person, shoot her an email. She's very likely to say yes.

You can connect with Pamela via her website
(http://pamelafaganhutchins.com)
or email (pamela@pamelafaganhutchins.com).

PRAISE FOR PAMELA FAGAN HUTCHINS

2018 USA Today Best Seller
2017 Silver Falchion Award, Best Mystery
2016 USA Best Book Award, Cross-Genre Fiction
2015 USA Best Book Award, Cross-Genre Fiction
2014 Amazon Breakthrough Novel Award Quarter-finalist,
Romance

The Patrick Flint Mysteries

"Best book I've read in a long time!" — Kiersten Marquet, author of
Reluctant Promises
"*Switchback* transports the reader deep into the mountains of
Wyoming for a thriller that has it all--wild animals, criminals, and one
family willing to do whatever is necessary to protect its own. Pamela
Fagan Hutchins writes with the authority of a woman who knows
this world. She weaves the story with both nail-biting suspense and a
healthy dose of humor. You won't want to miss *Switchback*." --
Danielle Girard, *Wall Street Journal*-bestselling author of
White Out.
"*Switchback* by Pamela Fagan Hutchins has as many twists and turns
as a high-country trail. Every parent's nightmare is the loss or injury
of a child, and this powerful novel taps into that primal fear." -- Reavis
Z. Wortham, two time winner of The Spur and author of *Hawke's
Prey*
"*Switchback* starts at a gallop and had me holding on with both hands
until the riveting finish. This book is highly atmospheric and nearly
crackling with suspense. Highly recommend!" -- Libby Kirsch, Emmy
awardwinning reporter and author of the *Janet Black Mystery Series*

"A Bob Ross painting with Alfred Hitchcock hidden among the trees."
"Edge-of-your seat nail biter."
"Unexpected twists!"
"Wow! Wow! Highly entertaining!"
"A very exciting book (um... actually a nail-biter), soooo beautifully descriptive, with an underlying story of human connection and family. It's full of action. I was so scared and so mad and so relieved... sometimes all at once!"
"Well drawn characters, great scenery, and a kept-me-on-the-edge-of-my-seat story!"
"Absolutely unputdownable wonder of a story."
"Must read!"
"Gripping story. Looking for book two!"
"Intense!"
"Amazing and well-written read."
"Read it in one fell swoop. I could not put it down."

What Doesn't Kill You: Katie Connell Romantic Mysteries

"An exciting tale . . . twisting investigative and legal subplots . . . a character seeking redemption . . . an exhilarating mystery with a touch of voodoo." — *Midwest Book Review Bookwatch*

"A lively romantic mystery." — *Kirkus Reviews*

"A riveting drama . . . exciting read, highly recommended." — *Small Press Bookwatch*

"Katie is the first character I have absolutely fallen in love with since Stephanie Plum!" — *Stephanie Swindell, Bookstore Owner*

"Engaging storyline . . . taut suspense." — *MBR Bookwatch*

What Doesn't Kill You: Emily Bernal Romantic Mysteries

"Fair warning: clear your calendar before you pick it up because you won't be able to put it down." — *Ken Oder, author of* Old Wounds to the Heart

"Full of heart, humor, vivid characters, and suspense. Hutchins has done it again!" — *Gay Yellen, author of* The Body Business

"Hutchins is a master of tension." — *R.L. Nolen, author of* Deadly Thyme

"Intriguing mystery . . . captivating romance." — *Patricia Flaherty Pagan, author of* Trail Ways Pilgrims

"Everything about it shines: the plot, the characters and the writing. Readers are in for a real treat with this story." — *Marcy McKay, author of* Pennies from Burger Heaven

What Doesn't Kill You: Michele Lopez Hanson Romantic Mysteries

"Immediately hooked." — *Terry Sykes-Bradshaw, author of* Sibling Revelry

"Spellbinding." — *Jo Bryan, Dry Creek Book Club*

"Fast-paced mystery." — *Deb Krenzer, Book Reviewer*

"Can't put it down." — *Cathy Bader, Reader*

What Doesn't Kill You: Ava Butler Romantic Mysteries

"Just when I think I couldn't love another Pamela Fagan Hutchins novel more, along comes Ava." — *Marcy McKay, author of* Stars Among the Dead

"Ava personifies bombshell in every sense of word. — *Tara Scheyer, Grammy-nominated musician, Long-Distance Sisters Book Club*

"Entertaining, complex, and thought-provoking." — *Ginger Copeland, power reader*

What Doesn't Kill You: Maggie Killian Romantic Mysteries

"Maggie's gonna break your heart–one way or another." *Tara Scheyer, Grammy-nominated musician, Long-Distance Sisters Book Club*

"Pamela Fagan Hutchins nails that Wyoming scenery and captures the atmosphere of the people there." — *Ken Oder, author of* Old Wounds to the Heart

"I thought I had it all figured out a time or two, but she kept me wondering right to the end." — *Ginger Copeland, power reader*

BOOKS FROM SKIPJACK PUBLISHING

FICTION:
Marcy McKay

Pennies from Burger Heaven, by Marcy McKay

Stars Among the Dead, by Marcy McKay

The Moon Rises at Dawn, by Marcy McKay

Bones and Lies Between Us, by Marcy McKay

When Life Feels Like a House Fire, by Marcy McKay

R.L. Nolen

Deadly Thyme, by R. L. Nolen

The Dry, by Rebecca Nolen

Ken Oder

The Closing, by Ken Oder

Old Wounds to the Heart, by Ken Oder

The Judas Murders, by Ken Oder

The Princess of Sugar Valley, by Ken Oder

Gay Yellen

The Body Business, by Gay Yellen

The Body Next Door, by Gay Yellen

Pamela Fagan Hutchins

THE JENN HERRINGTON SERIES OF WYOMING MYSTERIES:

BIG HORN (*Jenn Herrington #1*), by Pamela Fagan Hutchins

WALKER PRAIRIE (*Jenn Herrington #2*), by Pamela Fagan Hutchins

RED GRADE (*Jenn Herrington #3*), by Pamela Fagan Hutchins

THE PATRICK FLINT SERIES OF WYOMING MYSTERIES:

Switchback (*Patrick Flint #1*), by Pamela Fagan Hutchins

Snake Oil (*Patrick Flint #2*), by Pamela Fagan Hutchins

Sawbones (*Patrick Flint #3*), by Pamela Fagan Hutchins

Scapegoat (*Patrick Flint #4*), by Pamela Fagan Hutchins

Snaggle Tooth (*Patrick Flint #5*), by Pamela Fagan Hutchins

Stag Party (*Patrick Flint #6*), by Pamela Fagan Hutchins

Sitting Duck (*Patrick Flint #7*), by Pamela Fagan Hutchins

Skin & Bones (*Patrick Flint #8*), by Pamela Fagan Hutchins

Snow Ghost (*Patrick Flint *9*), *by Pamela Fagan Hutchins*

Spark (*Patrick Flint 1.5*): Exclusive to subscribers, by Pamela Fagan Hutchins

THE *WHAT DOESN'T KILL YOU* SUPER SERIES:

Wasted in Waco (*WDKY Ensemble Prequel Novella*): Exclusive to Subscribers, by Pamela Fagan Hutchins

The Essential Guide to the What Doesn't Kill You Series, by Pamela Fagan Hutchins

Katie Connell Caribbean Mysteries:

Saving Grace (*Katie #1*), by Pamela Fagan Hutchins

Leaving Annalise (*Katie #2*), by Pamela Fagan Hutchins

Finding Harmony (*Katie #3*), by Pamela Fagan Hutchins

Seeking Felicity (*Katie #4*), by Pamela Fagan Hutchins

Emily Bernal Texas-to-New Mexico Mysteries:

Heaven to Betsy (Emily #1), by Pamela Fagan Hutchins

Earth to Emily (Emily #2), by Pamela Fagan Hutchins

Hell to Pay (Emily #3), by Pamela Fagan Hutchins

Michele Lopez Hanson Texas Mysteries:

Going for Kona (Michele #1), by Pamela Fagan Hutchins

Fighting for Anna (Michele #2), by Pamela Fagan Hutchins

Searching for Dime Box (Michele #3), by Pamela Fagan Hutchins

Maggie Killian Texas-to-Wyoming Mysteries:

Buckle Bunny (Maggie Prequel Novella), by Pamela Fagan Hutchins

Shock Jock (Maggie Prequel Short Story), by Pamela Fagan Hutchins

Live Wire (Maggie #1), by Pamela Fagan Hutchins

Sick Puppy (Maggie #2), by Pamela Fagan Hutchins

Dead Pile (Maggie #3), by Pamela Fagan Hutchins

The Ava Butler Caribbean Mysteries Trilogy*: A Sexy Spin-off From *What Doesn't Kill You

Bombshell (Ava #1), by Pamela Fagan Hutchins

Stunner (Ava #2), by Pamela Fagan Hutchins

Knockout (Ava #3), by Pamela Fagan Hutchins

MULTI-AUTHOR:

Murder, They Wrote: Four SkipJack Mysteries,
by Ken Oder, R.L. Nolen, Marcy McKay, and Gay Yellen

Tides of Possibility, edited by K.J. Russell

Tides of Impossibility, edited by K.J. Russell and C. Stuart Hardwick

JUVENILE:

Poppy Needs a Puppy, by Pamela Fagan Hutchins

George Finds a Friend, by Pamela Fagan Hutchins

NONFICTION:

Helen Colin

<u>*My Dream of Freedom: From Holocaust to My Beloved America*</u>,
by Helen Colin

Pamela Fagan Hutchins

<u>*The Clark Kent Chronicles*</u>, by Pamela Fagan Hutchins

<u>*Hot Flashes and Half Ironmans*</u>, by Pamela Fagan Hutchins

<u>*How to Screw Up Your Kids*</u>, by Pamela Fagan Hutchins

<u>*How to Screw Up Your Marriage*</u>, by Pamela Fagan Hutchins

<u>*Puppalicious and Beyond*</u>, by Pamela Fagan Hutchins

<u>*What Kind of Loser Indie Publishes*</u>,
<u>*and How Can I Be One, Too?*</u>, by Pamela Fagan Hutchins

Ken Oder

<u>*Keeping the Promise*</u>, by Ken Oder

www.ingramcontent.com/pod-product-compliance
Lightning Source LLC
Chambersburg PA
CBHW072023020726
47501CB00006B/1929